One Degree South

a novel by
Stephen L. Snook

Rocket Science Press

Shipwreckt Books Publishing Company

Lanesboro, Minnesota

Cover drawing by Jessica Snook.
Cover design by Shipwreckt Books.
Map by Nick Thomas.

For Miriam, Jessica, Gabriella,
and especially Rosine, who never let me stop believing.

Table of Contents
One Degree South

The best hearts are ever the bravest.
- Laurence Sterne

1. The Lucky Ones

Lastoursville

T he Air Gabon Fokker slipped beneath a gray ceiling of clouds, and there was the African rain forest. Cramped in a window seat too small for his bulk, Charlie Sinclair hunched lower to see out across the dappled green wilderness, rolling to a hazy horizon. Scattered plumes of mist leaked upward like smoke. A fat river the color of tea glided by, a disorderly town along its bank. "That must be Lastoursville," he said.

Dabrian Lott leaned over to look past Charlie's deep chest. "Then that would be the Ogooué River."

The overhead warning lights lit up with a chime, and the Gabonese stewardess picked up the handset. "The captain has turned on the fasten seatbelt sign," she announced in French. "We have begun our final descent."

She flipped down the jump seat by the cabin door and buckled herself in. The right wing suddenly dipped and the Fokker banked sharply. Out the window, Charlie caught sight of a red gash floating into view. "Man, check it out."

Dabrian craned his neck again, until he saw the hilltop airstrip, drifting away as the pilots aligned on it. "We're going to land on that?"

"Looks like," said Charlie.

The wings leveled off, and they began to descend. The aircraft rattled and bounced through a pocket of turbulence. Charlie's ears popped. They were going in fast. At a hundred feet, the canopy racing past in a blur, the captain cut back the engines, and for an instant, the passengers hung weightless. Then they dropped down in among the trees.

"Never fails to amaze me," said Buck Buford at the sight of the Fokker coming in, its nose up and its landing gear down.

"Something to see all right," said Eric Slidell. He and Buck were former volunteers, contracted to teach the trainees onboard how to build a school.

The tires touched down flicking red spray. The nose settled and the thrust reversers deployed. The Fokker's twin engines rose to a racketing roar as the plane decelerated rapidly down the muddy runway toward where Buck and Eric stood.

The ground marshal in a bright yellow vest crossed orange wands above his head, bringing the weather-stained aircraft to a halt. The young French captain slid open the cockpit side window and looked out as the ground crewmen wedged wooden chocks tight against the tires. The marshal signaled to the captain, and the exit door dropped like a gangplank, unfolding a stairway to the ground.

It wasn't hard to spot the first of eight Americans. Buck raised his arm and waved. One by one, the trainees filed over to the trainers. All but two of them were white. There was only one woman. Rebecca Martin wore eyeglasses, like Buck. Dabrian Lott, the African American, fairly beamed. He stood nearly as tall but ninety pounds lighter than Charlie Sinclair, the only one not smiling.

"Welcome to *stage technique*," said Buck so softly the whistling jet engines nearly drowned out his voice.

"You the one teaching the technique?" demanded Hector Alvarado. Dark, short and fidgety, fired up to be out of those French classes, he was raring to get to the real work. He looked Buck up and down, taking in the lack of muscle tone, the beginnings of a beer gut. He turned to the other trainer, Eric, with an aquiline nose and a pageboy haircut. "What do you do?"

"I'm in charge of the logistics," said Eric, hired to keep the building site supplied, and to see to the laundry and meals.

Ground crewmen in blue jumpsuits dragged a handcart of baggage away from the plane, and the departing passengers began to embark. When the last was aboard, the ground marshal signaled to the captain all was clear. Inside the doorway, the stewardess yanked a lever, folding up the stairway. The door closed, and the captain slid shut the side window. He increased thrust to one of the rear-mounted engines, and the plane with a parrot logo on its tail turned in a tight circle until it faced the other way. The wing flaps moved up and down. Then the captain throttled both engines into a shrieking roar, and the Fokker began to roll. It went splashing past the Americans, gathering speed down the runway, to the far end where with a great leap the Fokker lifted over the trees. The wheels tucked up into its belly as it climbed. Streams of vapor trailed briefly from its wingtips, until a moment later the plane disappeared into the clouds.

A week earlier in Zaire, at a lakeside campus in Bukavu, the eight young Americans had completed six weeks of language training. There, they'd learned the French word for trainee is stagiaire. They'd arrived in Lastoursville as Peace Corps *stagiaires* headed for school construction training, a *stage* in a nearby village called Boundji.

The stagiaires walked to a shed to claim their duffle bags and lugged them to two mud-spattered pickup trucks. Dabrian settled in the back of the second truck by the tailgate opposite Charlie. As they sorted out where their long legs should go, Dabrian studied the wads of muscle filling out Charlie's shirt, his thick arms stretched out like anacondas.

Downhill in the small town of Lastoursville, it was market day. Double-parked trucks clogged the main street, their cargos swarmed over by gangs of boys. Throngs of pedestrians barred the way, mainly women, many with babies wrapped to their backs. As the two Land Cruisers inched along, Charlie got a good look at the things the market women carried in tin ware basins balanced on their heads, chunks of fur-covered meat, bundles of green leaves, heaps of pale mushrooms. One woman carried a basin of snails, and another a dead monkey that Charlie could have reached out and touched. The trucks crept past nondescript cinderblock stores, a gas station, the préfecture, the post office, the gendarmerie and then turned west on the road out of town.

The road narrowed. The tangled jungle closed in, a riot of greens, dense and impenetrable to the eye. Trees reached up a hundred feet and more, their branches closing off the sky. The stagiaires passed two men with machetes in their hands and shotguns on their shoulders striding along like militiamen on their way to a muster. Several yards behind the men trudged three women bent under the weight of baskets on their backs crammed with roots, a water jug and firewood. They passed through a village of low mud huts, rusted metal roofs hunkered among shaggy banana trees. A woman seated on a stool pounded a wooden pestle into a mortar clasped between her knees. Three half-naked children ran to the edge of the road to wave as the Americans swept by.

Boundji

At the third village, the trucks pulled off the road and stopped near three mud and wattle huts. The stagiaires pulled their gear from the trucks and marched to whichever building Buck and Eric assigned them. Each hut had thin concrete floors. Individual rooms contained a crudely carpentered double bed with a new foam rubber mattress shrouded by a gauzy white mosquito net.

Boundji lay on the banks of the Ogooué River. As soon as the stagiaires unpacked their belongings, they headed there to clean up. Rebecca Martin walked last in line wearing a towel wrapped around her one-piece swimsuit. Since their orientation in Philadelphia, she had demonstrated she could hold her own among the seven young men. She knew how to make herself heard. From the very first role-playing exercise, and all through language training in Bukavu, she had fought with Hector Alvarado about the nature of their assignment, once they got to Gabon. Best value for money, was Hector's view, build the schools as fast as you can, like in America. Rebecca maintained that Hector's view was wrong. They weren't going to be working in America. The people in charge of the Philadelphia orientation sided with Rebecca. They said she was right, the principles of sustainable development required aligning projects with local customs and values.

Hector scorned theories. He stuck to his guns. "Man earns his bread from the sweat of his brow," he said. "That's a fact of life the world over."

Hector was the only one in the group without a college degree, but he held his own too. What passed for conversation among the stagiaires at meals and at night was for the most part bluster and braggadocio, arguments about sports teams, brands of beer, rock bands and centerfolds. Dabrian was the only stagiaire interested in the international issues that Rebecca cared about, the only one who took her seriously. Generally, big Charlie Sinclair just listened, whatever the talk was about. He seldom had anything to say.

Village boys trooped alongside Rebecca down the muddy footpath to the water, asking her which stagiaire was her husband and where had she left her children. When they came in view of the river, the boys raced ahead, whooping across the sandy beach, and plunged headlong into the water.

Out in the middle of the Ogooué, a fisherman stood effortlessly in a drifting pirogue, casting a net and pulling it in. Rebecca watched the fisherman for a while as some of the boys waded back to shore. When she went into the water, the boys clambered up a tree, sidled out a branch that hung over the river and took turns leaping in. Charlie followed them, and when it was his turn to jump, the boys shrieked at the geyser he raised.

The next morning, the stagiaires ate at a picnic table Buck and Eric had hammered together in the front room of the cookhouse. There were baguettes from the bakery in Lastoursville, cans of Quaker oatmeal and instant coffee. "Hector is going to be assisting me," announced Buck.

"What!" Rebecca immediately protested. "Where did this come from?"

"We talked it over last night."

"Who did? Who talked it over? Nobody asked my opinion."

"I talked it over with Hector," said Buck uneasily.

"Hector!" Rebecca had plenty more to say, but when she saw from the set of Buck's jaw that he would not back down, she let it drop. Buck and Eric would be grading her, grading them all. Still, it made her angry. With Hector's new stature would come scope for him to put his wrongheaded ideas into action.

Hector handed Eric a list. "I'll need you to go to Lastoursville and buy some things," he said, glancing Charlie's way, trying not to look too pleased, a pugnacious expression on his face, the color of an old penny.

Eric looked at the list. He didn't know what to make of taking orders from a stagiaire who had just showed up yesterday. But when Hector and Buck led the stagiaires out to the site for their first day of training, Eric put Hector's list in his pocket and drove into town.

The sun peeped above the treetops when they straggled onto the worksite, chantier in French. It was muggy and there was no breeze. Buck introduced the stagiaires to the workers, all of them old papas who spoke French about as badly as the young Americans. Clouds of biting insects began swirling around them as they shook hands. When Charlie brushed his arm, there was blood.

"They're called fourou," said Buck. "You'll need repellant." One of the workers arrived with a bucket of blue diesel fuel. Buck slathered it on his arms, face and neck. The stagiaires did the same. When they were all shiny and reeking of gasoil, as diesel fuel was called, Hector led them to a jumble of cinderblocks stacked beside a concrete slab under a swayback roof.

"I know none of you's ever laid any block before," said Hector as the trainees gathered around. He unrolled a blueprint on a stack of new blocks the old papas had been casting, and pointed out twenty spots marked with an X. "These are the load bearing columns," he said. "They're the bones of the school. Today we're going to lay out the site. We're going to build the batter boards to mark where the footings will go and where the load bearing columns will sit on the foundation."

Nate Jenkins was the most experienced carpenter. He had traveled the shortest distance from his home in Harrisburg to Philadelphia. There, he told the other recruits about the summer he worked with Mennonites building barns in Alabama.

"Oh," said Rebecca, "so you've already lived in a foreign country."

Dabrian was the first to get it and laugh. He came from a community in Atlanta where Dr. Martin Luther King once preached, where people had a particular view about Alabama.

Hector put Nate in charge of sawing boards. Everybody else began digging holes where the posts for the batter boards would go. When she saw the trainers expected her to take up a pickaxe like the others, Rebecca became uneasy. She harbored the vague notion she would be a supervisor. She had never held a pickaxe before; she had never dug a hole in her life. Rebecca raised the pickaxe over her head, swung it down and it bounced off the red clay, wrenching her wrists. She raised it above her head a second time and brought it

6

down even harder, and it made an inconsequential mark on the earth. When she raised it for a third time, an old papa took the pickaxe from her.

With so many stagiaires digging postholes, even without Rebecca contributing, the job didn't take long. Into each hole, workers lowered a four-by-four Nate had sawed to length. When each hole held a four-by-four leaning way one or another, Buck waved the stagiaires over to the cement mixer and a convoy of empty wheelbarrows.

Buck lifted the mixer engine cover and showed them the dipstick, how to check the oil level. He showed them how to start the motor when it was cold using the choke. He told Toad to pull the cord and the motor fired in a burst of smoke.

Papas carried water buckets filled from a line of fifty-five gallon barrels. Hector cut open a sack of cement with a shovel and emptied it into the revolving drum. Toad and Dabrian shoveled in the correct proportions of sand and gravel while Hector added water. When the first mix was ready, Toad grabbed the wheel and flipped off the lock.

"The great state of Minnesota!" he hollered, summoning Charlie to come forward with a wheelbarrow.

As soon as Charlie pushed off with his load, Toad yelled, "The great state of New York!"

Phil Holmes gestured at Rebecca, his fellow New Yorker, with a malevolent grin "Ladies first," he said.

Rebecca pushed her empty wheelbarrow under the sloshing drum and set it down. Toad turned the wheel. Concrete slid into the barrow. He tipped the drum back up, the motor roaring, everyone watching Rebecca.

Intending to show she was up to the task, Rebecca drew a deep breath, gripped the handles and lifted. She pushed hard, took a step, then another. But the heavy load began to tip. Unable to right it, Rebecca let the wheelbarrow fall onto its side, spilling wet concrete across the red clay.

The sun blazed down when Hector led the stagiaires back to the chantier after lunch, his black hair gleaming plum highlights. The stagiaires carried with them the items that Eric had brought from town. At the worksite, Tommy Cleburne lifted an empty fifty-five gallon barrel over his head and carried it to where Hector stood fitting the new bit in the brace. Dabrian wrapped Teflon tape around the threaded end of the faucet while Charlie used a hacksaw to cut the brass fittings off the ends of the coiled hose. The others resumed helping Nate saw lengths of planks.

Hector tipped the barrel over and swung a leg astraddle it and sat on it like a horse, and drilled a hole six inches above the bottom. When the bit broke through, he took the faucet from Dabrian and slipped it into the hole, and then he pulled the barrel upright and reached down inside with an adjustable wrench and tightened the nut. He sent Dabrian to fetch cinderblocks and had Tommy carry the barrel to the middle of the site and set it on the cinderblocks. He called Charlie to him with the garden hose and shoved one end of it onto the faucet.

"Remplissez le fût," he instructed the workers.

As the papas began bringing water in buckets, Hector stretched the hose out to what he judged to be the lowest spot of the site. When the barrel was a quarter full, he opened the faucet and walked back to the end of the hose, and called everyone over to where the water began running out.

"You use this technique for when you don't have a laser level," said Hector. He felt his grandfather looking down on him as the water flowed. The old man did all he could to get his grandson started in business, and died proud of the boy before the business failed.

Hector told Tommy to go turn off the tap, and then he lifted the end of the hose and twisted the clear plastic funnel into it. He raised and lowered the funnel until he found the spot where the water was visible, bobbing up and down.

"Once the water in this funnel is steady," he said, "no matter where I go with the hose, it'll be the same level as in that barrel. We'll use it to mark where to nail on our batter boards. Pretty cool, huh?"

None of them understood.

Hector handed the funnel to Charlie, and Charlie followed him, dragging the hose to the first corner, where he knelt and held the funnel up against the post. When the water stopped moving up and down in the funnel, Hector marked the spot. Then he gave the carpenter's pencil and square to Dabrian. After two pairs of posts were marked, Hector told everyone else to go grab hammers, and they began nailing lengths of planks to the marks that Charlie and Dabrian made.

Rebecca stood off to the side talking with the papas, joking about men and their hoses. Her bawdiness shocked the old men, and made them roar with laughter. When the stagiaires had nailed the last plank, Rebecca yelled out, "Does anyone know the history of barter boards?"

"Batter boards," corrected Hector.

A wind came up. Suddenly they stood in the shadow of thunderheads.

"In the olden days," continued Rebecca, "the Arabs hauled salt in caravans across the Sahara Desert to trade with the Africans for gold. When the Arabs came into a village and opened for business, they put up barter boards like this one, and made their trades across them." She patted it.

"Batter boards," said Hector as thunder grumbled.

Everyone was drawn to Charlie Sinclair, with his square-jawed good looks and quiet ways. Six foot five, two hundred-sixty pounds, his size alone awed the Peace Corps recruits back in Philadelphia. They saw a guy who didn't talk much, just did whatever needed done. He was watchful and reserved, silent until something made him laugh, then his bonny young face came sparkling alive.

Hector liked having Charlie on his side, his moral force in Boundji. Digging the trenches, Charlie was a marvel to behold. He brought a pickaxe down with such power the blade knifed deep into the clay. The webs of muscle in his back jumped about as he pried loose chunks of earth the size of basketballs.

Rebecca objected to Hector's work pace. "This isn't the Peace Corps way," she complained. "The appropriate way – the Peace Corps way – is to work at the pace of the villagers, to bring the villagers along through every phase of the project, so they can feel ownership of the schools and will maintain them after we're gone."

But her objections were in vain. The other stagiaires sided with Hector. They wanted to see how far they could get, push as far as they could in their six weeks of technical training.

Hector and Charlie were first to arrive at the site every morning. While everyone else dug footings, Hector found less demanding work for Rebecca. One morning, Hector asked her to come over to the workbench with three papas he'd handpicked, near the mud hut that served as a storehouse. He asked her nicely, deliberately, knowing she might resist.

"I want you four to assemble the rebar cages that will go into the load bearing columns," he said. "You can use this tool here, called a hickey bar."

Rebecca laughed at the name.

"Men who do this job are called ferailleurs," he said. "In the States they're called rod busters." Rebecca laughed at that name too. "You four are going to be my rod busting crew."

After Hector showed them what to do, he watched for a while as the three papas cut the rebar with bolt cutters while Rebecca used the hickey bar to make spurs. They wired the cages together using baling wire from a spool, nipping it off with a wire cutter. They got faster at it through repetition, like an assembly line, and Hector went back to help with digging the trenches. Rebecca ran her mouth the whole time, making the old papas laugh.

With the trenches dug, Hector showed the stagiaires how to set grade stakes for the footings while the rod busters cut and bent rebar in the shape of croquet hoops with the hickey bar.

"These are called chairs," Hector explained. The stagiaires pounded chairs into the dirt along the bottom of the trenches, then wired full lengths of twelve-millimeter rebar to the chairs, so the rebar hung in the air. They placed the bases of the steel cages that the rod busters manufactured upright at the prescribed three-meter intervals. All the while, Hector clambered in and out of the trenches, checking their work with a spirit level and a measuring tape.

Village children found the Americans enormously interesting. Everything the stagiaires possessed was an object of great curiosity, their cameras, watches, and cassette players. When the stagiaires were in their houses, the windows filled with the faces of little boys. Everything the stagiaires did was fascinating, even just reading a novel. The older kids would whisper whenever a stagiaire turned a page, reporting this to the younger ones too short to see inside.

The biggest of the three houses served as the cookhouse, with the picnic table in the salon. Near the door to a side room, a kitchen where the *stage* cook worked at a stove hooked to a canister of gas, sat a kerosene refrigerator.

One night at supper, Nate asked about building the teachers' houses. The faces of village boys filled the windows, watching the stagiaires eat, and crickets shrilled outside.

Eric swept up his sweaty bangs. "That'll be about the hardest thing you'll do, getting your villagers to build the teachers' houses for free."

"Why are we building a three room schoolhouse when there's only one teacher here?" asked Toad, sandy-haired and burly like Charlie, but three-quarters his size. They'd all been wondering.

"One teacher is typical," said Eric. "Buck, can you think of a village with more than one teacher? Most villages are lucky if even one teacher shows up."

Buck nodded. "They don't like working in the rural areas. I don't blame them. They get stuck living in crummy houses; there's nothing to do; the schools don't have any facilities."

"The bums draw their pay whether they show up to work or not. Listen to the radio." Eric loved listening to La Voie de la Rénovation, when they read out all the names of absentee teachers, and ordered them back to their posts. He found it hilarious.

"As for building the schools," said Buck, "these days you can only hire ten men. In the past, guys used to hire practically their whole villages."

"It'll take you two years to build your school," said Eric.

"Bullshit!" Hector challenged with his mouth full. "You could build two of these schools in two years, they're so simple; maybe three."

Eric smiled a superior smile at all the reasons why this was impossible, and had started to explain this to Hector when Rebecca interrupted.

"This isn't supposed to be a race. Peace Corps expects us to learn about the culture here, do our job, and when we get back home, educate Americans about what we've seen."

Hector shook his head to disagree, but he had learned not to argue with Rebecca. She could twist his words into things he never said. He repeated what he'd been saying since the very first day. "We're going to set a record no one will beat."

Then he came down with a plague of boils. Hard and hot painful lumps erupted all over Hector's body, like mushrooms after a rain, becoming more hard and painful by the day, until they burst. Each boil that ran dry left a hole in Hector's skin like a bullet wound. No sooner would two boils start clearing up than three new ones came in. His lymph nodes swelled until it hurt just to move, and Eric had to go into town to buy him more bandages. But driven by his vow to set an unbreakable *stage*-school construction record, Hector never missed a day of work.

Meanwhile, parasites infested everyone's toes. The word in French was chiques, tiny swift sand fleas that burrowed into folds of their flesh. All the stagiaires were quietly wondering about the itching in their toes, when Phil Holmes showed his feet to a boy. He was shocked to learn that the tiny lumps lining his toenails were living fleas, swollen with eggs, like little peas in a pod. The stagiaires broke open their sewing kits, got out their needles and began pricking away in horror, piercing the little black dots to squeeze out the runny stuff, ignoring the shrill protests of the kids. They were doing it all wrong.

The kids were right. Within days, the holes the stagiaires had made in their toes were infected, creating a new routine. Every evening after work, before the sun went down, the stagiaires took a chair, pulled off their socks stained from the weeping wounds they had made, and placed one bare foot, then the other between the knees of a keen-eyed kid on a stool. The boys jimmied with sharp-tipped porcupine quills to widen each chique hole, pinched with their forefingers and thumbs, and rolled the swollen fleas out, glistening little white pellets.

At lunch one day, Rebecca asked, "Did you hear what's happening in Hungary?" No one said anything, their heads down, shoveling in lumpy rice and gristly beef they ate every day for lunch and dinner. "Hungary has scheduled elections for next year." Still, no one answered, forks clinking, kids whispering at the windows.

"This is the second Warsaw Pact country that's going to hold elections. This is really something."

"Yeah, it is," said Dabrian. He respected Rebecca for trying to get discussions going about the world events she followed on the BBC.

"Poland held elections last June," she reminded, "the same month the Chinese crushed the protesters in Tiananmen Square. Why isn't the Soviet Union doing that? It's what they did in Hungary in '56 and Czechoslovakia in '68. Why not now?" A few of the stagiaires looked at Rebecca, working their jaws, waiting for her to supply the answer. "This is significant," she said. "This could mean the end of the Cold War."

That remark provoked hoots of derision. The stagiaires knew the Soviet Union was America's indestructible and permanent foe. The Cold War would go on forever, or end in a nuclear holocaust. They'd all known this since childhood.

Dabrian admired Rebecca. She read important books, read them for fun, and read them more carefully than Dabrian ever had. She knew of Kwame Nkrumah's theory of consciencism for decolonization, for example, a claim few white people could make.

At Morehouse College in Atlanta, Dabrian had studied the heroes who fought back against enslavement. Reading their biographies had excited his pride. Toussaint Louverture in Haiti. Samory Touré of the Mandingos. Queen Yaa Asantewaa of the Ashanti. Shaka, king of the Zulus. Dabrian joined Peace Corps and went to Gabon expecting to form a mystical bond with a proud and noble people through some kind of deep racial memory. But he had been naïve. He saw that now. Gabonese villagers did not view him as a long lost brother. Nor were they particularly proud.

Back home at least there was struggle. There was pride, even when it was just the sagging, bling-draped, backward-cap mimicry of the gangster rap stars. In Gabon, if someone talked out against the government, the villagers cringed and looked around to see if anyone was listening. They accepted the fact that their own authorities kept them down.

Rebecca had a word for the system: Françafrique. The system only benefitted the elites. It enraged Dabrian to think African leaders of an African country blessed with an abundance of resources were oppressing their own people. Dabrian was confused, and Rebecca was the only stagiaire who seemed to understand why.

The others were more interested in the cook. Her name was Germaine. She was a terrible cook, but the stagiaires didn't mind as much as they might have, because Germaine was a voluptuous doxy. Each night, after they finished supper, the Americans waited at the picnic table in the lamp-lit cookhouse for Germaine to appear. She always took her time, crickets shrilling outside, the gleaming faces of a dozen kids looking in the windows. The Americans inspected sores, pinched pus, picked their teeth and swatted mosquitoes until Germaine sailed out from the kitchen to clear the dishes wearing just a sarong and a smile.

The gawping of her male counterparts disgusted Rebecca. Their blatant objectification of the uneducated village girl offended her. They ogled Germaine wiping down the table with a sponge, their eyes bugged out at the jiggling. Each night, Germaine paused for a moment to adjust her slipping pagne, a placid expression on her childlike face, a little smile. She knew very well the effect she had on the young men as she reached under one arm to tuck the fabric tight, her forearm pushing up the soft mass of her breasts. Eric, who had hired her, smirked at the nightly show, like Pander wiping his brow with a cold bottle of beer.

"It's free love over here," Buck liked to say. "Asking a girl to have sex is about the same as asking her if she'd like a stick of gum."

Some topics were too fatiguing for Rebecca. This was one of them, fueled as it was by male hormones and official government policy. High rates of fatal disease and low fecundity made Gabon a sparsely settled land. President Omar Bongo wanted his people to be fruitful and multiply. Promiscuous sex was officially encouraged and birth control was illegal in the country.

Gabonese commenced making babies at a very young age, and couples didn't stay together very long. This made relationships complicated. A young boy might introduce his little brother and specify whether he was a same-mother brother, or a same-father brother, or rarest of all, a same-mother-same-father brother. The closest siblings had the same parents and grew up sharing a bed under the same mosquito net: même-mère, même-père, mêmemoustiquaire.

In Gabon's kinship system, a mother's sisters were not aunts; they were mothers. A father's brothers were not uncles; they were fathers. In both cases, their children were not cousins; they were brothers and sisters. Thus, a person could have a dozen mothers and fathers and a score or more brothers and sisters.

Dabrian had much on his mind their first Sunday in the village, walking about taking pictures of things that caught his eye. He came upon a young girl with her head shaved from a case of lice, dandling a naked baby on her knee. Her gleaming scalp was oddly beautiful. As Dabrian approached, the baby on the girl's lap squirmed, prepared to burst into tears if he got any nearer.

"Photo?" he asked, and when the little girl smiled, he aimed the camera. "C'est ton frère?"

The little girl laughed as he snapped the shot, a flash of teeth and dancing eyes he hoped he'd caught on film. "Non, monsieur," she said, "c'est mon père."

How could a ten-year-old girl claim a baby is her father? Dabrian was trying to reason it out when he walked into the cookhouse and found Rebecca sitting at the picnic table. The others were all down at the beach, she said. Dabrian took a seat across from her. He didn't care for the beach, nor did Rebecca. She was reading a book.

Rebecca's first sight of Dabrian had been at the Double Tree Hotel in downtown Philadelphia, coming across the lobby in his loose-jointed gait, like Malcolm X without glasses. When he smiled, he reminded her of the teaching assistant she'd had in college, the smiling man from Africa who'd knocked her whole life right off kilter, Mukaz Muteb.

Mukaz was the first Zairian she had ever met. She remembered every detail of the warm, sunny spring afternoon when she went to ask Mukaz for ideas for her term paper. Mukaz suggested they sit outside, because he didn't want to remain in his stuffy little office on such a nice day. On a bench in front of the Bartle Library, with flocks of students streaming by, he told her the story of his uncle, by way of explaining the travails of his long-suffering land. The very idea of Africa swept Rebecca away, listening to Mukaz recount how the secession of Katanga province at independence in 1960 transformed his uncle from a gendarme into a foot soldier in the cause of a global mining company.

The following year, when General Mobutu sent the deposed Prime Minister Patrice Lumumba to be shot, chopped-up and dissolved in acid – a graphic detail Rebecca had needed a moment to absorb – Mukaz's uncle first saw combat battling U.N. troops, Irish soldiers who surrendered at Jadotville. The secessionists' victory was fleeting. When their leader fled into exile in 1963, the small army retreated into Portuguese Angola, embroiled in a vast guerilla war. The Portuguese formed the ex-Katangese gendarmes into a counterinsurgency unit they used for a year, until General Mobutu called them back in 1964 to confront his own Marxist insurrection. They marched a thousand miles to battle wild men draped in fetishes that made them bulletproof.

Mobutu did not disband the ex-Katangese gendarmes after the defeat of the Simba Rebellion, and for some reason neglected to pay them. Disgruntled and under arms, they mutinied in 1967, marching east, robbing banks along the way. They took the border town of Bukavu, of all places – the very same city where many years later the Peace Corps sent Rebecca for language training – until a negotiated settlement allowed them to cross into Rwanda.

Mukaz's uncle was among the fighters who found their way back to Angola, where once more the Portuguese took them in. Once more, the Portuguese put them to work bushwhacking the armed factions battling for independence. It was by then a losing cause. The freedom fighters were gaining the upper hand. When finally Portugal was forced to abandon its colonies, the Soviet-backed insurgents Mukaz's uncle had been fighting took power. The new rulers of Angola indoctrinated the ex-gendarmes, and sent them to invade Katanga. Twice they crossed the border, in 1977 and 1978, and twice they were defeated, before Mobutu offered them amnesty and called on them all to come home.

"Seventeen years of fighting," said Mukaz, "for Belgian capitalists, for the dictator Mobutu, for Portuguese colonialists, and finally for Angolan communists, and all for what, exactly?"

Wheels were spinning in Rebecca's mind. That was when it started for her, just a sophomore at the time, who until then had never really talked with a black man before, much less slept with one. She titled her paper, 'Switching Sides: The Ex-Katangese Gendarmes and the Cold War in Africa.' The essay impressed her professor so much he gave her an A-plus. He was the first of several professors to encourage her to consider graduate school.

"What's that you're reading?" Dabrian asked, bringing Rebecca back to the cookhouse. She wondered how Dabrian might respond if she reached across the table and touched his arm.

"It's about the resource curse," she said, and she saw the term spark his interest. "How extractive industries create an environment for corruption. Mines and oil wells are essentially chokepoints, you see, and easy to control. When dictators seize power, they gain control over the chokepoints, go into cahoots with the multinational corporations, and live like lords. What does it matter if the ordinary people remain exactly as before? Peasants don't know any better. That's the real reason why Bongo pays the schoolteachers, even though they don't work. Why the roads in this country are so crummy. Why the hospitals aren't as good as they should be. Bongo wants the people to be sick, ignorant and isolated. It makes them easier to dominate."

Dabrian nibbled at a thumbnail and muttered to himself. He hated hearing this.

"The core of the problem is the deficit of patriotism," Rebecca pronounced.

That was an opinion Dabrian didn't share. "The white man crushed the ones who stood up and fought," he said. Rebecca saw the world like a sister. He could talk freely with her, though he couldn't express his thoughts as clearly as she did. "Lumumba, Nkrumah. All the ones who challenged the white man, they were all overthrown."

"Maybe so." There were beads of sweat at Rebecca's hairline, long straight brown hair hooked behind her ears, pale blue eyes looking out through her big round glasses. "The best of the first generation of African leaders certainly tried to find a middle way, using the strategy of import-substituting industrialization, mainly."

Dabrian recalled hearing the term in a class on international political economy he'd taken his junior year. Suddenly, he wished he had paid closer attention.

"But today they're being beaten down by structural adjustment.

The African governments have to lower their tariffs, let their currencies float, and sell off their state-owned corporations, that is, if they want to keep on getting foreign aid."

Foreign aid. Dabrian could just see them in their meetings, as in the plantation days, smirking white folks tossing coins to the darkies who danced the best. Foreign aid.

Dabrian needed a beer. He went to the fridge, added two marks to his tally and returned with two green bottles of Régab.

"Thanks," said Rebecca. Gabon's popular beer, Régab, came in bottles so big Rebecca almost felt like she needed two hands to hold one. She took a swig and studied Dabrian. She liked him because he listened. She got so excited talking about ideas. She wondered what he thought of her. She didn't like the way she looked. She was too gangly. Her hips were too wide. She hardly had any boobs to speak of. He truly listened, even when she was talking on automatic pilot. Motor mouth her sisters used to call her, know-it-all.

"What's bothering you, Dabrian?" she asked.

Dabrian scratched his goatee and said nothing.

"Seriously. You okay?"

Dabrian did not reply at once. The political experiments of the early African leaders intrigued him. He believed they could have succeeded, could still succeed, wholly African systems that worked. He looked at Rebecca, cheerful when she was joking, fierce when she was debating. Her smile showed small teeth and a lot of pink gum. "The people in these villages," he began. He hesitated, seeking the words. "They're …"

"Yeah?"

Dabrian's whole family came with him to the airport, looking about with improvised sophistication, as if they'd been to the airport before. They took one of the electric carts because of their father Leander's condition, thin and worn from the chronic pain in his hip crushed in a loading accident at the Port of Savannah. He feared the operation to have it replaced. They moved to Atlanta, to the brick house on Ezzard Street, to be nearer their mother Ulandie's people, who helped her find the job at the Atlanta Life Insurance Company with the health benefits that paid for her blood pressure medication. They sat in the hard plastic chairs at the gate where Dabrian promised his momma a hundred times he would take care of himself, until they called out the flight was boarding. With a last round of hugs and a final wave to his family, Dabrian went down the jet way to the airplane and flew away Janus-faced, looking forward and backward in time.

"Really," coaxed Rebecca. "What is it?"

"I never thought I'd hear myself say this."

"Say what?"

"What Muhammad Ali said in 1974, when he got back to the States from Kinshasa after his fight with George Foreman, the Rumble in the Jungle he called it. A reporter asked him, 'Champ, what did you think of Africa?' " Dabrian took another swig of beer, as if to cleanse his mouth.

"What did Ali say?"

"He said, 'Thank God my granddaddy got on that boat.'" Dabrian peeled the paper label from the bottle, and looked at Rebecca and said, "Man, we're the motherfucking lucky ones."

2. Show's Over

T he elderly man exited his back door coughing. Ntchaga Justine called out in greeting through her open window. Her neighbor waved in reply, opened his sling chair and settled in to take the morning air.

Justine wore a printed cloth pagne wrapped around her nurse's uniform at the stove, reheating last night's leftovers. This would be her first day back at work. The pain had been far worse than menstrual cramps. At the first sharp contraction, she knew what it was. Concealing her distress, hoping she was wrong, she walked home from the hospital. The bleeding began as she undressed hastily in her bathroom. Blood ran down her leg, and in the shower ran pink down the drain. Later that night there were more contractions, successively worse, until shortly after midnight with a violent wrench, she passed the clotted tissue from her body, and it was done.

She lied to her younger brothers. Just a stomach flu, she said. They were identical twins, mirror images of each other, reviewing their homework at the table in the salon. They attended the collège in Akièni, slender, bookish and serious about their studies. They thanked their sister when she brought their plates to the table and sat opposite them, virtually the same voice, virtually the same person, fifteen years old with high foreheads and the appetite of jackals. They finished their food in minutes and pushed their plates away, pulled their books closer and went back to the algebra problems. In a second, their minds had fused. The Batéké gave the name Mbou to every firstborn twin, according to custom, and the name Mpiga to the second born. Mbou Blaise reached over and pointed to what Mpiga Gérard had just written. Mpiga Gérard nodded and erased his mistake. Neither spoke a word. Communication between them verged on the telepathic. It was

21

uncanny to see. One would open his mouth, and the other would know what he was about to say. They didn't have to finish their sentences. The effect was a shared secret language. They understood each other perfectly.

Justine took their plates to the kitchen and called, "Are you watching the time?"

"Oui," they chimed, and looked at their inexpensive wristwatches. It was time to go. They put their books in their book bags and came to the kitchen door, dressed alike in their school uniforms, white shirts and blue trousers. "Au revoir," they said.

Justine imagined them walking to school as she rinsed the dishes in the sink. Their futures were so bright with potential. Most young people did not have the opportunity her younger brothers enjoyed. There were not enough schools out on the Batéké Plateau. Would there ever be? Count your blessings, people said, but that was cold comfort for Justine, and did not dislodge the grief she felt for her lost baby, nor give her any inkling what the future held for her, a hundred-twenty kilometers due east in the village of Boundji.

Boundji

Hector set the two strongest stagiaires to work loading the mixer. Charlie and Toad wielded shovels as fast as they could, flinging sand and gravel into the revolving drum. The four oldest of the papas replenished the buckets with water from the barrels and wheeled fresh cement sacks out from the storehouse. Rebecca had been the last American to arrive that Wednesday morning, when they started pouring the footing. She lay prone in the line of six papas on the spoil, while Nate, Phil, Dabrian and Tommy wheeled the concrete to the edge of the trenches. When they tipped the wheelbarrows up, the concrete slid into the trenches with a slopping thud. Rebecca and the old papas, lying on their bellies, reached down with wooden floats and pushed the heavy gray mix flat in the trenches, leveling it to the grade stakes.

They finished the footing Thursday morning, about the time three beat up old Land Cruisers arrived, one right after the other. On the outside, the trucks were dented and rusty. On the inside, the vinyl seats were torn, and the interiors smelled bad. Buck had summoned them to Boundji, each with a name skillfully hand-

22

lettered on its doors by the smooth-cheeked young man driving the first. Skip Lomax had worked as a sign painter before joining the Peace Corps. He drove a truck named Air Afrique. P¢¢r B¢y arrived second, Joe Terravecchia at the wheel. The third Land Cruiser, Twisted Sister, was the ugliest of the three, having been rolled in an accident and repaired. Johnny Brasseaux drove it.

Dabrian had heard of Johnny at their medical orientation in Libreville. The Peace Corps nurse told Dabrian to keep an eye out for him, a fellow African American. She was a tiny woman with a sun-browned face and curly hair turned prematurely white. Her dire views had earned her the nickname Heavy Evy. "My word," she said when Dabrian told her where he was from, "it's nice to meet someone from home."

Johnny was glad to meet Dabrian too. A light-skinned brother the color of ginger ale, what people called bright where he came from, Johnny had a six-inch Afro and a patchy beard. Dabrian's arrival meant he was no longer the only African American in the Peace Corps school construction program.

After lunch, the stagiaires learned the basics of Land Cruiser maintenance. Buck assigned each a truck. Two had to double up, Rebecca with Dabrian, and Tommy with Nate. Buck circulated with Johnny, Eric, Skip and Joe, showing the stagiaires how to change the oil and filters, and grease the front ends and the drive trains. They finished in the middle of the afternoon, and went down to the river to clean up.

When the others filed back up to the cookhouse, Johnny and Dabrian stayed behind. They sat side by side on the branch that hung out over the river as the sun went down. They talked of home for a time, and Johnny described trail rides on horseback, gumbo and jambalaya, ice chests of beer, cowboy hats and line dancing to zydeco, the lyrics in French, accordions and fiddles and metal washboards called frottoirs. For Dabrian, Johnny's tales came from another country.

"My great granny lived in a cabin," said Johnny, "in Little Bayou des Ourses. She got her drinking water from a well and her heat from the same stove she cooked on. She lived all alone out there. She was what they call a two-head woman. A lot of people were afraid of her. My daddy said the skills Great Granny knew came from Africa. Folks traveled for miles to bring her their problems,

23

from Lafayette, Opelousas, Baton Rouge. What she did was part curing and part making contact with the spirit world, to ease people who were troubled. She could send hoodoo back on the sender, uncrossing, jinx-breaking, turning the trick. She was the one who inspired me to find a way to come to Africa, although she didn't know it. You got a chance to go deep here, Dabrian."

"Uh-huh, I know."

"You got a chance to see it all from the inside."

"What do you mean by that?"

The fading light brought out the planes of Johnny's face. "Have you heard of Bwiti?"

"No, what's that?"

"The ten dollar word for it is syncretism."

"What's syncretism mean?"

"The integration of different realities. Bwiti has many branches. Disumba is the mother, the most ancient. The Apinzi, the first people, the ones the white man calls the Pygmies, they introduced it to the Mitsogo, who founded Disumba. Bwiti's a way to unlock your atura afou."

"Unlock your what?"

"Your inner power."

Inner power. That was what Dabrian quested for. Ever since he was a little boy, he had thirsted to know the ways of his people from the time long before, the pure and uncontaminated ways from the Motherland of his imagination. He had grown up feeling compelled to find a way to Africa someday, and Johnny had too. "Say it again."

"Atura afou. You see, folks here are caught between two worlds. One part of them's trying to be in the Twentieth Century, and the other part's rooted in tradition. They don't see things like they teach us back home. Back home, the atheists, they think when you pass, your light goes out, bang! Church people are different." For an instant, listening to Johnny, Dabrian saw his mother Ulandie flailing one of the paper fans they kept in the pew, waving one fat arm over her head in praise. "Church people believe those that have passed are in heaven, or hell," said Johnny. "They can't reach us; we can't reach them, until we pass, and go off and join them. Here, the ones that have passed, they're still with us. The afterlife is close by. I've learned that, Dabrian. What you're going to find here in Gabon is that we're connected to everything."

On Friday, Hector announced, "It's time to start laying block."
Patches of ground fog lay in the hollows, and the rising sun wasn't
yet above the treetops. The mason's line strung from the batter
boards wet from the night's rain looked like yellow cat's cradle in
the early morning light. "I'll build the first lead to show you."

Hector had his workstation ready, a mortarboard, a trowel, a
spirit level, and carpenter's square, a bucket of water and a
wheelbarrow nearby, full of mortar. He climbed down into the
trench. The old papas pushed wheelbarrows loaded with
cinderblocks and stood the blocks upright in lines along the spoil.
Hector carried a plumb bob, a chalk line and a pencil in his tool
pouch. He lowered the plumb bob from the mason's line to the
footing and made marks at intervals with the pencil. He snapped
parallel blue chalk lines in both directions along the footing to
connect the marks, talking all the while. He chopped lines of mix
on his mortarboard and bent down to draw out twin beads of
mortar along the blue lines. He straightened up to butter head joints
on two upright blocks and slid the first block to the base of the
rebar cage, then the second at a right angle to it. He buttered the
head joints on two more blocks, lifted, turned and set them deftly in
place. He checked with the level, tapped with the butt of his trowel,
and checked with the square. He made it look easy, laying a second
course, then a third. It took him all of about twenty minutes to
build the lead.

It took the rest of them considerably longer. Rebecca couldn't
manage the job at all. Her fingertips were too tender, the
cinderblocks too heavy. She needed a papa to help. She couldn't get
the knack of buttering head joints. The mortar slipped off the ends
before she could get the block into place.

That night at supper Eric told them about a species of
nematode worms called filaria. "It's spread by black flies and
mosquitoes," he said. "The parasites migrate to the lymphatic ducts,
and form nodular masses. The condition's called lymphatic filariasis,
and if it's left untreated, it turns into elephantiasis."

The complicated words rolled easily off his tongue, and the
stagiaires were impressed. Eric knew all about lymphatic filariasis,

25

he said, because he'd been cured of the disease.

"The cysts can get into your nut sack. Your balls can swell up big as watermelons."

The stagiaires protested. That couldn't be true.

Eric chortled at their expressions. He'd seen pictures in a medical book, he said, before and after photos of a man who pushed his genitals around in a wheelbarrow, and afterward ended up smiling.

"Do you have to talk about this while we're eating?" Rebecca complained.

"The procedure is called a scrotectomy."

The stem walls were three courses high by Tuesday. They grouted the cores, caved in the trenches and started pouring the floors. It was the height of the autumnal rainy season, and the stagiaires were rising to meet Hector's challenge. The plan was to pour the floors in twelve slabs. They wanted to set a record no other *stage* group could beat, and each day they raced the rain.

Hector put Charlie and Toad to work at the mixer with a squad of papas to help, and they kept the concrete coming. Tommy, Dabrian, Phil and Nate wheeled the mix to the forms. Hector asked Buck to help with a two-by-four screed to level the concrete flat. When they'd filled the form of each slab, Hector directed the stagiaires out onto the kneeling boards. He showed them how to work the concrete with wooden floats to smooth it, and how to use steel trowels to give it a finished seal.

They poured four slabs a day, hurrying to finish the last as rain clouds rose over the jungle, dark as slate, often flickering with lightning. They covered the curing concrete with lengths of six-meter roofing sheets in the chill of the wind coming off the river, and many evenings they bathed outside their houses in twilight, in the rainwater streaming from the eaves.

Their six-week stage was halfway over when the floors were complete. Hector used the expanse of new concrete to lay out templates for the roof trusses. He measured and made marks in pencil on the slabs, and they helped him snap blue chalk lines. The stagiaires and the papas worked in teams. They lay planks to the lines and marked them, while over at the sawhorses Nate cut the boards with a bucksaw as fast as they brought him new ones. No one was as skilled with a saw as Nate. When others tried, the blade bound and bowed in the uncured lumber called okoumé. Even Eric pitched in with the hammering. They carried the finished trusses off to one side where the oldest papa painted them with a noxious chemical against termites.

When the ten trusses were done, with only two and a half weeks before the end of *stage*, it was time to start laying up the walls. Hundreds of cured cinderblocks sat waiting in stacks, and the old papas resumed casting more. Hector said master masons in the States could lay fifteen hundred block in a day, with someone to spread the mud and do all the jointing. But he didn't expect any of them to be able to do that, he said, which made the stagiaires want to see how many block they could lay. Charlie could lay a hundred by noon, which Hector allowed wasn't too bad, but they would need to do more if they wanted to meet the goal.

Rebecca no longer put up any resistance. She did her part, driving the pickup truck with old papas to dig more sand and to haul in water from a nearby stream when they ran low. Pushed by Hector at a pace that filled up their days, the stagiaires slept like logs at night. They worked through the weekend, the papas happy to be earning overtime pay, casting cinderblocks the young Americans lay up as fast as they cured. With two weeks to go, they worked up on scaffolds, the planks bowing under their weight, the walls coming up rapidly, square, flat, level and plumb.

Tommy grew increasingly enraged by any slight that set him off. Somebody took his trowel. No, you left it over there in the wheelbarrow. Somebody ate the orange he'd been saving. No, I saw you eating it at breakfast. Somebody was putting extra marks by his name on the beer tally sheet. That accusation in particular got everyone mad. It was the honor system. They weren't cheats. No one would fail to own up to the beers he drank. The tally sheet was sacrosanct.

They all knew the cause of Tommy's outbursts. At the medical orientation before leaving for Boundji, Heavy Evy, the Peace Corps nurse, sat on her metal desk wearing shorts, her tanned legs strong, worn white running shoes dangling in the air, her ankles crossed. She told the stagiaires about blood flukes, and every kind of worm there was, thumping her heel against her metal desk, boom, boom, boom, roundworm, pinworm, hookworm, whipworm, and tapeworm. "That one's the worst of them all," she said. "Tapeworms can get into in your brain. They produce cysts look like bunches of grapes when they do the autopsy."

She told them about malaria, how it could kill them unless they took their mefloquine, and even then, they could still come down with it.

"We have a new treatment called artemisinin," she said, "which comes from the Chinese, God bless their godless communist souls. Back in the 1960s they extracted artemisinin from the sweet wormwood bush they'd known about in their traditional pharmacology since before the time of our Lord and Savior Jesus Christ," she said, "and if any of you is Jewish or Moslem or atheist and I just offended you, I apologize."

That's when she asked which one of them was Tommy Cleburne.

Tommy raised his hand, to show he wasn't afraid.

"I have an uncle named Tommy likes to hunt white tail deer. You hunt any, Tommy? Go out in the woods much? Where're you from?"

"Boston." It sounded like Bah-stin.

"Oh, well, I don't expect you do much hunting there in Boston. They tell me you're ornery, Tommy. That true?"

"He's a frigging hothead," said Toad.

"That right, Tommy? You a hothead? Cleburne's Irish, isn't it? My sister married an Irishman name of Brown from Nacogdoches. You got any Browns for relatives? No? Well those Browns out of Nacogdoches, they got some tempers on them. You anything like those Browns, Tommy? Got a temper on you, like they say?"

They clamored that Tommy had a temper on him all right. At language training in Bukavu they'd all been eyewitnesses to his overreactions, to all slights, real or imagined.

"Boys, I've read all your files," said Heavy Evy, "from the PCMO in Zaire. Now with some people, mefloquine makes them edgy, and that's why we got Tommy taking the daily dose, instead of those big horse pills the rest of y'all are taking once a week."

With a week and a half to go, Tommy was even getting into it with the old papas, yelling at them when they didn't do what he wanted, or did something wrong, or did it too slow. One afternoon he began shouting so loud his voice cracked. Everyone looked over at him, beet red in the face, looking like he was going to haul back and hit the old man who was backing away from him in fear and bewilderment.

Charlie went striding over. He grabbed Tommy from behind and lifted him off his feet like he was made of feathers. Tommy twisted and kicked and tried to wrench free, his arms pinned to his side, spitting out vile invective, but Charlie's legs were planted like tree trunks. He locked Tommy to his chest, then hurled him to the ground with a thud, fell on him, and held him down in the mud.

"You done?" shouted Charlie. Tommy's chest heaved. He bucked and tried to kick Charlie off, as Hector trotted over. "You want to fight, fight me, asshole!"

Hector put his hand on Charlie's shoulder. "Let him up, big guy." Charlie looked up at Hector, something in his eyes none of them had ever seen. "Let him up, Charlie."

Charlie took a moment, before he rose to his feet. He stepped back, and Tommy got up from the mud, clenching and unclenching his fists, sucking air, his cheeks and his jug ears flushed red. Charlie had six inches and eighty pounds on Tommy, and was ready for anything he might try, but Hector stepped between them.

"Show's over, hombres," he said.

3. End of the Line

Boundji

T he stagiaires watched their blond-bearded APCD, Harry
Bowman, tack a map of Gabon to the mud wall. Blackened
by the sun, leaned down skinny as lizards, they had achieved
something no previous *stage* group had come close to
accomplishing. They had actually put a part of the roof on their
school. They had dug the trenches and built the foundation, poured
all the floors, laid up the cinderblock walls save the openings in the
windows where the breeze-blocks would come later, built all ten
trusses and mounted them cinched down with rebar anchored in
concrete and cross-braced to keep them plumb. They had nailed all
the purlins to the truss rafters, and just one day before Harry
arrived, they had put on a few roofing sheets, all in the standard six
weeks' time. They were proud to think their group would become
the stuff of legend. The following day, they would drive down to
the provincial capital of Koulamoutou where the Peace Corps
director, Stu Eaton would fly out from Libreville and swear them
in. One of them would return to Boundji to finish the school. The
rest were slated to leave Ogooué-Lolo province and head east to the
Haut-Ogooué. Some were bound for the legendary Batéké Plateau,
grasslands where no volunteer had ever served. A place of mythical
repute, people said the plateau was unlike anywhere else in Gabon.
They were all keen to know who would be the lucky ones posted
there.

The metal roof of the cookhouse crackled as the morning grew
hot. The trainers, Buck and Eric, were gone. They had flown back
to Libreville, their contracts completed. Just seven stagiaires
remained. None of them had actually seen what happened, when
Tommy went off for the final time. He flung a claw hammer that

31

hit one of the workers in the shin. Eric had to drive the bleeding old papa to town to get stitches, and pay him enough out of petty cash to keep him from filing charges. Harry came out on the next flight, and took Tommy back with him to Libreville. When Harry returned driving a Peace Corps SUV, Tommy wasn't with him. Everyone wanted to know what happened.

"Tommy was medically separated," said Harry.

"Like Siamese twins?" asked Rebecca, prompting little laughter.

"Poor tolerance for mefloquine," Harry explained, which the stagiaires understood to be the official reason, but maybe not the truth.

The volunteer leader of the school construction program sat in a sling chair near the open door. Jim Bonaventure had a mop of brown curls. The program's transport truck driver, Timo, a dark chocolate chatterbox with a movie star smile, who spoke a goulash of Pidgin English and French, had squeezed in with the stagiaires at the picnic table. The program was currently without a dump truck, because Timo had slid off the side of a mountain behind the wheel of the old one. He bore a marked limp as a souvenir. A new one was on order, and in the meantime, Timo had driven one of two brand new pickup trucks out from Libreville. Jim had driven the other. That made seven Land Cruisers parked outside. Harry's SUV made eight.

"I know all of you want to get one of the new pickup trucks," said Harry, "but that's not possible, so here's the deal. Three of you are going to be near a big town where there are garages and mechanics. Those three of you will get the old trucks. Is that clear?"

There were mutterings of apprehension. No one wanted to be one of those three.

"All right then, Toad, you're staying here in Boundji to finish the *stage* school."

Toad's broad mouth split wide in a grin and he raised his fist in triumph. Thickset, laid-back and good-natured, he was inclined to turn adversity into a joke. Staying here in a village with a beach on the Ogooué River, where everything was already set up, this would not be a hardship at all.

"Since you're getting a fully stocked chantier and you'll be close to Lastoursville," said Harry, "you're getting Twisted Sister."

Everyone howled that Toad was getting the ugliest truck.

32

"Nate and Phil, you're going to the southern end of the Haut-Ogooué," said Harry, and he put his finger on the map. "Here's the capital, Franceville." He moved his finger an inch east to a junction in the road, then swept it all the way to the edge of the map, from the green part showing the forest onto the beige of the Batéké Plateau. "Here's the préfecture of Lékoni. This is where the good road ends." He turned his finger north and ran it a short distance along a dotted line parallel to the Congo border. "This is an unimproved road. This here is Édjangoulou. Nate, this is where you're going, with the truck Buck's been using."

Nate clasped his hands above his balding brown head, and smiled.

"Phil, I'm posting you here in Djoko, the next village out. You're getting the new truck Eric's been driving."

Phil Holmes made a curt nod. He had darting eyes that didn't fit his baby face. Back in Philadelphia, he'd told them he worked summers in the Long Island concrete trade, trying to impress everybody with hints about Mafia ties. No one believed him. No one liked Phil. He'd spent his free time in Boundji trooping about with a pack of boys. He was reconciled to his unpopularity, and more than ready to take leave of them all.

"Charlie, Rebecca, Hector and Dabrian," said Harry, and he looked at a piece of paper in his hand, "you're going to Ondili, Obia, Otou and Okouya." He turned to the map, put his finger back on the provincial capital of Franceville and pushed it slightly east. "Here is Ondili." He pushed it four inches north, within the green. "Obia is here just south of Akièni, which is also a préfecture." His finger passed through Akièni and turned northeast from the green part of the map into the beige. "Otou is here," Harry said, "on the edge of the plateau." His finger continued up a dotted line to the next village. "Okouya," he said, "is the second."

He turned to face them. "Dabrian," he said to the only one among them who claimed to have come home to Africa. "Your French skills are the worst in the group."

The stagiaires whooped to hear this.

"I want you near a place with a phone where you can get help if you need it. I'm putting you in Ondili, here close to Franceville."

"All right!" exclaimed Dabrian.

"You're getting Air Afrique, and you're expected to stay in your village," said Harry, "not in Franceville. And Toad, you will live here in Boundji, not in Lastoursville. You're both expected to live in your assigned villages, not hang around in town. Is that clear?"

Dabrian's face remained neutral, though Toad grinned at Dabrian.

"Now Hector," Harry said, "you got the highest score in technical training."

Hector looked down under shouts of derision. Raised speaking Spanish and working construction, he'd had an advantage in Boundji, and at Bukavu too, where he had nearly edged out Rebecca for the highest score in French, little Hector Alvarado, who had never been to college.

"I'm assigning you to Obia," said Harry, "here, near Akièni, where there's a phone at the post office, so you're getting Poor Boy."

The oldest truck of them all, with P¢¢r B¢y painted on its doors, the jeering rose again.

"Shut up, guys. There's an announcement I want to make about Hector."

They fell quiet, curious, looking at Hector, to see if he knew what this was about. It seemed he did.

"Last year, as you know, President Bongo asked Peace Corps to triple the size of the school construction program."

The stagiaires had learned of this at the briefing they'd received, shortly after their arrival in Gabon.

"Even though the government pays for the cost of the schools, Peace Corps covers the cost of the volunteers, and you guys don't come cheap. We weren't sure we could agree to the request, because of the budget implications. Then word came down from the White House: do it. It seems Bongo was the first African head of state to call President Bush and congratulate him on his victory. The White House wanted to say thanks, and so they found the money to triple the number of construction volunteers in a single year. Now, suddenly, this program has become very political. People in high places are watching what's going on with you guys. You're the first of two supplemental groups. The other is already forming. There will be a third group coming in the normal cycle, in the cohort of volunteers that'll come next summer. Recruiting volunteers is not an easy process. We had to ask Paul D. Coverdell himself to spur on the recruiting drive with an Action Cable."

They all knew Coverdell was the Peace Corps administrator. A few, those whose recruiters had shown them the Action Cable, nodded their heads.

"Our operating budget isn't big enough to afford guys like Buck and Eric, not two more times in one fiscal year. So we have to economize, which is why we've decided Hector is going to be running the next two *stage* sites."

"I don't believe this," said Rebecca.

Hector tried to keep his face humble. But the smile beneath his wispy mustache gave him away. They all could see he had known about this ahead of time.

"Hector," said Harry, "you've got to make this work."

"Count on it," said Hector.

Charlie now knew he was getting one of the last two coveted new trucks, one of the two that had just come out from Libreville, and that he was going to the Batéké Plateau.

"Rebecca," said Harry, "you have the strongest French in the group. You've also got the weakest construction skills."

There were no catcalls this time, as everyone digested the news about Hector. Charlie watched Rebecca, looking to see her reaction. She didn't seem to care that she was getting one of the new trucks, or that she was going to the plateau. She looked angry.

"Rebecca, you're going to Otou with the third new truck. I'm putting you in between Hector and Charlie, so they can help you whenever you need it. And Charlie, I guess you've figured out where you're going. You're getting the fourth new truck. You're going to Okouya, the end of the line."

Akièni

A full-fledged Peace Corps volunteer at last, Dabrian had arrived. He was jubilant. Five muddy trucks were parked off to one side. Dabrian sat where Harry had placed him, in the center of the row of Americans lining one side of two tables placed end to end, facing an assembly of villagers. Hector, Charlie and Jim sat to his left. Harry, Rebecca and the chief of Ondili sat to his right. Print pagnes covered the tables. Several old whiskey bottles full of milky palm wine stood before them in welcome, with sturdy glasses and pink kola nuts.

Harry grumbled to Dabrian that the Ministry of Education had not sent out the announcement ahead of time, as they should have. This was why the chief of Ondili was astonished when Americans showed up in his village.

Harry rose to his feet. The assembly fell silent as he explained in French that an American volunteer had been sent to build them a school. He waited for the translation into Téké. The chief listened attentively. The American was to be lodged free of charge, said Harry. The villagers were to build three teachers' houses. They were to do this with free labor. The only paying jobs would be for building the school.

The chief nodded.

Then Harry had Dabrian stand up. "This is Dabrian Lott," he said, "the American who will build your school."

The chief looked confused to see the American was black.

Dabrian's smile faded only slightly. He shook hands with the other Americans when they left, happy to be on his own, in his own village, Ondili.

Rain fell hard on the way north to Obia. Water flowed across the road like a shoal of fish. The four Land Cruisers splashed past one and then another village where volunteers were building schools, the cement walls dark gray in the pouring rain. The volunteers were buttoned up in their mud huts, incongruous pickup trucks parked out front. Harry didn't stop. He was in a hurry to finish the installations.

The rain had blown over by the time they reached Obia. Harry, Jim, Hector, Rebecca and Charlie got out of the trucks. Villagers approached them curiously. Dripping green trees glistened under fluffy white clouds. Rays of sunlight shot into a brilliant sky. The air was filled with the songs of birds, as the elderly chief of Obia came picking his way to them through the mud. He did not understand what this was about. He did not speak French. A young man handled the translations, while the villagers brought out tables, chairs and bottles of warm beer for the visitors.

Hector's installation went quickly. Harry, Jim, Rebecca and Charlie were back on the road an hour before dark. Near dusk, Harry turned splashing into the Catholic mission in Akièni. Rebecca and Charlie turned in after him. They parked the three Land Cruisers behind the church near a cluster of buildings. An African came out of the priest's house to receive them. Harry asked if they could spend the night. There were rooms available in the guesthouse, the man said. He went to get the keys. When he came back, he said they were invited to dine with the priest.

Père Dominique wore a carved wooden crucifix. He had small black eyes, but no eyelashes. Webs of blood vessels covered his cheeks. "I've lived in Gabon since 1959," he said, tossing down the red wine that his houseboy served with the soup course. The old French priest swallowed so many of his words that Charlie couldn't follow half what he said.

He asked where they were going, and snorted when he learned they were bound for Otou and Okouya.

"There was a time, years ago," the priest said, "when that part of the plateau was rife with witchcraft. You may not believe me, but you will learn. What I am telling you is true. I put a stop to it. Ask the land chief when you meet him, the nkani-ntsie, the old man Oyamba Paul it if isn't so. I brought them the Word, and ended the practice of witchcraft on the western plateau."

Charlie looked across the table at Rebecca to see her reaction to what the old priest had just said. She smirked. Harry beside her, eating pasta, listened without expression. Jim, seated next to Charlie, said quietly under his breath in English, "Typical old Africa hand. Don't believe it, Charlie. He's having us on."

With an old man's impatience at the unfounded optimism of youth, the priest told them, "Your project will make no difference. What good are schools without teachers?"

There was no moon that night across town when brakes squeaked in front of Ntchaga Justine's bungalow. She was in her kitchen making chicken stew, home from a long day at the hospital. One of her brothers came in to tell her Milla was at the door, the bush taxi driver who plied the route between Akièni and the Congo border. Everyone called him Milla, after the Cameroonian soccer star. He had a lean face and a sparse mustache, and when Justine asked what he wanted, he smiled, tired from a long day on the road.

"Something smells good," he said. He had a note in his hand, and wanted to come in.

Justine barred the way. She took the note from him and read it. It was from her mother, written by someone else, because her mother had forgotten how to read. The note said that Papa Osandji had died.

Justine let out a wail, and Milla averted his eyes and looked down to have brought tragic news.

The twins Mbou and Mpiga came to their sister and read the note, and began to wail too.

Milla looked concerned for the three of them. He was returning to Onga tomorrow, he said. He could come by in the morning and get them, if Justine wanted.

She nodded and dried her eyes. "Thank you. Yes, that would be very kind."

"Then I'll pick you up first thing in the morning."

Justine thanked him again, closed the door and told her brothers to go clean up. She went back to the kitchen thinking about the arrangements she would have to make. Her brothers were about to begin their end-of-term exams, and would have to be left on their own for two nights, unless Milla could be persuaded to adjust his schedule to hers. That was an idea. She could ask him nicely. Would he bring her back with her brothers as soon as Papa Osandji was buried?

A pipe clunked through the wall and began to wail as the shower turned on. Stirring the stew, Justine thought of what she would pack, she thought of Papa Osandji, and then she thought of the tall, broad-shouldered Zairian at the hospital with the striking eyes, Emanuel Muengo.

Dr. Muengo.

"You were early in your pregnancy," he said when she told him, the brilliant man she had wished to love. "The earlier it happens the better."

She had been stunned to hear him say that. Better?

"The body is more likely to expel all the fetal tissue by itself if the miscarriage happens early in the first trimester. That's probably the case with you, but we should be sure."

She was nothing to him. Justine understood it with cold clarity, lying on her back with her feet in the stirrups while he performed the dilation and curettage. She was just another patient to him at that moment, just another copine before then, and the realization

38

had enraged her. He truly felt nothing! It had been his child too!

When he put his hand on her shoulder, his touch revolted her.

"I understand how you feel," he said. "Your feelings are normal."

"You don't understand at all."

Justine lifted plates down from the cupboard with a violent clatter. How could he know how she felt? How could she ever — with such a —

Justine suddenly became aware of Mpiga Gérard, the second born twin, standing in the doorway.

"Set the table," she said, untucking her pagne at the waist to dry her eyes.

Mpiga came forward and touched his sister's arm. He thought he knew why she was crying.

Okouya

Harry led the way to the Akièni préfecture in the morning, to introduce Rebecca and Charlie to the local authority. They parked the three Land Cruisers and went inside, then waited for someone to run and inform the Préfet. Almost twenty minutes later, a muddy Renault pulled up. A short man with a shiny shaved head wearing a short-sleeve brown tropical suit entered. There had been a mix up, he said in a voice that resonated like a foghorn. This was the first he had heard of the ceremony. "But no matter," said the Préfet, "I want to come along for the installations."

The Peace Corps convoy followed the Préfet to his house so he could pack a bag. The Préfet got into Harry's SUV, and they set off for the plateau, three Land Cruisers in a file, knobby tires spattering mud. Jim rode with Rebecca. Charlie brought up the rear, music cranked up on the boom box he'd wedged under the dashboard, direct wired to the truck battery.

Harry led the way, curving back and forth on a road like a winding corridor through towering trees. Charlie was on Rebecca's tail when they crested a last wooded ridgeline, and he got his first look at the Batéké Plateau, a green-gold escarpment rising out of the forest, clumps of sage-colored brush clinging to its grassy flanks like patches of fur. Then the road dropped away like a roller coaster ride, and Charlie rode the brake going down. At the bottom, he downshifted to second, and his engine roared following the others up a steep grade, passing through a cut that had exposed not red laterite but tawny sand, carved by wind and water as if on a lathe, crenulated towers, minarets, and rock-topped campaniles.

It was foggy on top of the plateau. The other two trucks had stopped, their brake lights lit up like red beacons. Before them, the laterite road gave way to crisscrossing troughs of wheel-churned sand, like the strands of an unbraided rope disappearing into the mist. It seemed impossible a vehicle could traverse this terrain, but there went Harry and the Préfet waddling off in the hardtop, followed by Rebecca and Jim in her pickup truck. Charlie pulled the transfer box lever back to four high, slipped the clutch and plunged his truck into the sand. It rolled like a boat in a chop and went on. Charlie looked at himself in the rearview mirror, grinning at the novel sensation, driving a brand new brute diesel pickup off road. A tarp covered the load in the bed, his duffel bag and tools and jerry cans of fuel and his foam rubber mattress rolled up and tied with rope, and his bed frame he'd knocked apart in Boundji, and the things he'd bought in Franceville, his kitchenware and food supplies.

It seemed arbitrary choosing which track to follow; they all led north, diverging and converging through the grass, entwining around the hummocks of stunted trees. There were conical termite hills, some a living ochre, others a dead-looking gray. They loomed in the fog like the heads of Easter Island. Some rose to a height of twenty feet, and some had trees sprouting out of them.

As the sun continued to climb, the mist began to burn off, and more of the countryside became visible, sandy tracks rolling across empty hills.

Presently, they came to a steep descent. Charlie followed the others down a switchback trail into a narrow valley where all the trails converged. The valley floor looked like a beach. Tires churning through year after year had stripped away the protective mat of grass. The brown sand lay in crested heaps.

Charlie noticed the metallic flash of aluminum roofs atop the hill ahead. That was Otou, a half mile on.

They clawed their way up a steep slope into the village, where they shut off their engines and got out in the first plateau village

Charlie and Rebecca had seen. It looked no different from Boundji, or any other Gabonese village they had been through before, except that it was built on sand. It seemed deserted, save for chickens and goats, a few dogs and a small number of timid children.

A man emerged from between two houses with surprise on his face. He hurried forward to greet the Préfet, and shook hands with Harry and the three volunteers. There were four white people suddenly in the village. This was big news. He snapped his fingers and sent a child running to call the chief, and the boy dashed off showing a pair of flashing heels.

A few minutes later a man reeled out from behind a house wearing a pale blue Arab caftan, drunk as a lord at eleven o'clock in the morning. This was the chief, named Petie, the Préfet said.

Chief Petie shook their hands and welcomed them to Otou. Then he hollered imperiously, and men began to appear, bearing two tables they placed in the shade of palm trees with chairs on which the chief regally bade them to sit. Women brought bottles of palm wine and placed them on the table. Chief Petie himself tipsily served, first ceremoniously pouring a small amount into a glass and casting it onto the ground for the ancestors. Then he filled the glasses by rank, beginning with the Préfet. More villagers began to straggle in from whatever chores they'd been doing, and they stood scrutinizing the white strangers, whispering to each other as they watched them nibble their kola nuts and sip from their glasses of palm wine.

The Préfet stood and said in his foghorn voice, "Je vous présent le directeur adjoint du Corps de la Paix et ses volontaires américains. Ils sont envoyés par Son Excellence El Hadj Président Omar Bongo pour vous construire une école en dure," and then he switched into Téké to explain that the Americans they saw before them had been sent by the President to build them a school. The villagers burst into applause at the news.

"Notice," said Rebecca in Charlie's ear, "how Bongo takes credit for everything."

"In exchange," said the Préfet, "you people must build three houses for the teachers. This will be voluntary labor. Then, after the three houses are completed, the Americans will hire ten men to build the school. These men alone will receive the government wages. C'est comme ça, n'est-ce pas, Monsieur Air-EE?"

41

Harry nodded, the crowd smiling and whispering to each other at the prospect of getting a job.

The Préfet sat down. Harry stood up and formally introduced Rebecca, gesturing for her to stand. She got to her feet, bright blue eyes behind glinting glasses. She smiled and waved. The crowd applauded. Harry explained that Rebecca had come from very far away, from beyond France, from the other side of the sea, to build a school for them. He admonished them to take good care of her. Chief Petie, standing unsteadily, translated into Téké. The villagers nodded, protesting that of course they would take good care of Madame Rebecca.

Then Harry sat. Still standing, the village chief acknowledged Harry and the Préfet, before launching into a drunken speech in French about the honor they had brought to Otou. "Americans have nothing to fear in this village," he avowed. "Their every need will be attended to! They will not suffer from want of anything!" he concluded with a sweeping gesture, and nearly lost his balance. The chief did not understand that Rebecca and Charlie were not husband and wife, and that only she would be staying. The chief plopped into his chair and helped finish the palm wine. Charlie thought it was an odd thing to do, drinking palm wine with a crowd of people watching.

"So what do you think of the plateau, Rebecca?" asked Jim.

"I think it's as beautiful as people say," she replied.

Presently they heard the sound of a vehicle climbing the hill, coming from the direction of Akièni. It stopped at the far end of the village. After a few minutes, the engine started up again, and a battered old Land Cruiser overloaded with passengers churned through the sand toward them, the faces of the people onboard agog at the fact that white people sat in the middle of the village.

After the taxi passed, Charlie noticed the chief speaking urgently to the Préfet, who became annoyed and assured him dismissively, "Il n'y a pas de problème." Then the Préfet turned back to talk with Harry. Rebecca remarked to Charlie, "See how the traditional authority defers to the political authority? Bongo has eviscerated the chieftaincies of this country."

Charlie thought about that word as a white and tan Basenji dog with upright bat ears and a corkscrew tail ventured forward, and one of the villagers delivered it a thumping kick in the ribs. That broke things up. They went to look at a house for Rebecca. It was a dilapidated four-room mud house with a zinc roof and a sand floor. She said it would be okay, and Harry struck a deal with the owner. Rebecca would fix the place up in exchange for living there rent-free. Then, while a dozen men began unloading her things into the house, the three remaining Americans and the Préfet said good-bye to her, and drove off in two Land Cruisers, heading north out of Otou.

This time, Jim rode with Charlie, who put on Tom Petty and the Heartbreakers. When the song 'Refugee' came on, Jim asked, "Do you feel like a refugee?" Charlie just smiled, and shrugged. "Kind of hard on your group," said Jim, "swearing in so close to Christmas."

Charlie shrugged again. Holidays meant little to him.

"Rebecca's really got some kind of beef against Hector, doesn't she? What's the issue? What do you think about it?"

"Hector's a good guy," said Charlie. "So's Rebecca."

Jim lit a cigarette and changed the subject a third time. "The Préfet wants us to take him out to Onga. He says it's about three hours on. He says it's quite the locale touristique. He wants us to meet his colleague, the Sous-préfet. My guess is he's got a woman out there." Jim blew smoke out the window. "Harry's up for it, to help with you guys' relations with the Préfet, he says, though between you and me Harry's always up for a road trip. That means we're going to keep on after we get you installed and spend the night out there."

Charlie tried to remember where Onga was located on the map. The names of the villages in these parts all seemed to start with the letter O.

Jim was dozing when they entered a rough, hand-cleared trail through a tendril of rain forest that had crept up onto the plateau. It was cool and shady under the trees, and ahead there was light, looming brighter until suddenly they burst into the village of Okouya.

The sand was loose and deep. Charlie had to gear down to low range. With his tires churning and his engine howling, he crept after Harry through the village at an absurdly slow speed. They proceeded to a flagpole and a big mango tree that marked the middle of the village, where they didn't need their brakes to stop.

Charlie switched off the engine. There was no one around. Okouya was as deserted as Otou had been. They got out. The only sound was the ticking of the engines. Charlie peeled his shirt loose from his back and stretched. A rooster crowed. Ragged laundry hung drying on some lines. There were chickens pecking, goats wandering about, and a couple of children peeking cautiously around the corners of the mud and wattle houses, but no adults in sight. A Basenji dog trotted daintily up, sniffed Charlie's tire, and lifted its leg and peed. Harry opened the door to the SUV and honked the horn just as two old men came around the corner of a house, the older one walking with a staff.

"That is the nkani-ntsie, the land chief of the westernmost Louzou," the Préfet told them, "in charge of all the villages in this area. His name is Oyamba Paul."

Père Dominique had told them at dinner about Oyamba. The nkani-ntsie, the chef de terre, did not look the part of a powerful chieftain. His clothes were ragged. He was barefoot and his hair was white. As he drew near, Charlie could see his eyes were milky from cataracts.

Two women trailed behind him bringing chairs, hollering out for others to bring more. Charlie shook hands with the land chief and his companion, an old man who was not introduced. No table materialized, and no refreshments were served, and the small crowd that began to gather was made up of old people and a dozen or so children. In Ondili, Obia and Otou, villagers turned out in large numbers to welcome the new volunteers, and the chiefs ordered welcoming drink and made speeches. Charlie felt embarrassed for the sake of his village that his installation would be the worst by far.

Chief Oyamba sat with his staff between his knees and listened to the Préfet's explanation of their purpose here, and the conditions that would have to be met before the school was built, a speech the Préfet made more concise now that there was no prospect of something to drink. The land chief was able to say but one thing in French, it seemed, and that ungrammatically. "C'est comme la d'accord," he kept repeating to Charlie, reaching out his bony old hand to shake.

The chief's bare feet were cruelly swollen, mottled skin the color of liver, the toes splayed and the nails rotted off, the consequence, Charlie decided, of a lifetime of chiques and nematode worms.

A house was available for Charlie, and they went to look at it, but the door was locked. Chief Oyamba sent for the landlord, Obongi Louis. The Gabonese put the less esteemed name, the prénom last, Charlie had learned. It was les grand types, mostly the political big shots like Omar Bongo, who followed the Western convention.

The sun had moved past two o'clock when they returned to the shade of the mango tree. The Préfet was anxious to keep going, so Harry and Jim wished Charlie good luck and said they'd see him on their way back, and they drove east toward the Congo border.

Charlie sat in the shade with Oyamba and the other old men, who sat in sling chairs in a half circle staring at Charlie. The old women stood behind the men. The men spoke to each other aloud. The women spoke in whispers. They were all discussing Charlie. When he smiled, they all smiled back. Children collected on the fringe of the small gathering, and Charlie motioned to them to come closer. A few approached, led by a brave little boy with a herniated navel sticking out like a pickle.

Charlie dug into his pocket for a five hundred franc coin to do his magic trick. He had discovered in Boundji the trick astonished children, raised as they were in a culture that considered witchcraft real. He showed the coin to everyone. Then he closed both his fists and moved them back and forth, and when he opened the one, the coin had disappeared. The onlookers exclaimed to see it gone. Then he reached forward and plucked the coin out of the brave little boy's ear.

There was a gasp and the children shrank away, holding onto each other's arms, ready to stampede. The old men began jabbering, the women buzzing behind their hands.

Charlie rose hugely to his feet, and all the children backed away. He went out into the fierce sunlight to his truck, and got the bag of candy. The villagers watched him return. He got down on one knee and coaxed the brave little boy forward again, this time with a sweet.

The boy came forward cautiously, eyeing what Charlie held in his hand. When he saw what it was, the boy snatched the candy, popped it into his mouth, and backed away. Seeing that, the other children swarmed forward, clamoring for a piece of candy too.

45

Onga

A log snapped sending a flurry of sparks into the air. Night had fallen. The mourners were gathered. The men sat in sling chairs, the women on mats in the sand. Justine's mother was pleased to have her children with her. Justine and the twins, Mbou and Mpiga had traveled six hours in Milla's taxi. They picked up the oldest brother Jonas along the way, and reached Onga in the late afternoon.

Justine wept upon arriving like a loving daughter, although Papa Osandji was not her father. She wept for something other than him. Her mother Mama Angélique wept from more than grief too, although she wouldn't say so. Mama Angélique was terrified at the prospects before her, the lowly third wife of Papa Osandji, and a widow now for the second time. Papa Osandji had taken her as his wife when his older brother, Mama Angélique's first husband died. There were no more surviving brothers. What would become of her now? Who would want her? She would spend a year in mourning living in the house Papa Osandji had provided her, and then they would tear down the house and shave her head, and what would become of her then?

Justine wanted to distract her mother, and spoke of what they had seen on the drive, the four white people in Otou, with the Préfet of Akièni. One of the etangani was a woman. Two of them and the Préfet had reached Onga behind them, right after sundown. They were all at the house of the Sous-préfet.

"Who are they?" Justine asked.

Mama Angélique didn't know.

"Do you remember, Mama," said Justine, after a while, "when Mpiga Gérard was little, and he couldn't stop wetting the bed?"

A gleam of remembrance came into her mother's eyes. Mama Angélique knew what tale would follow. She smiled at her twin sons seated on the mat by her side, and they both smiled back, their identical smiles.

"Papa Osandji started scolding Mpiga that he was too old to be wetting the bed. Do you remember, Mama, how he kept after Mpiga, day after day? How old was Mpiga? Maybe four? Or five?"

"Four," said Mama Angélique.

"This went on and on, for months, was it?"

"For weeks."

"Until one day Mpiga looked at Papa Osandji and said, 'You will see.' Was that how it was, Mama?"

"Yes, that's how it was."

"Do you remember this, Mpiga?"

Mpiga Gérard shook his head. He had heard the story told many times, but he did not remember this happening.

"And the following morning, was it? Papa Osandji woke up, and he had wet his own bed."

The twins giggled.

"Yes."

"And he couldn't get up."

"That's right."

"And he couldn't hold his urine."

Mama Angélique made an affirming sound, smiling, looking into the fire.

"So Papa Osandji called for you, and told you to call little Mpiga to him. 'I need to apologize, so he'll stop this,' he said. Was that how it was?"

"Yes, that's how it was."

"And when you came, Mpiga, Papa Osandji gave you two fifty franc coins. He placed one coin in each of your hands, and he said to you, 'I'm sorry. Now I know what you are going through.'"

Mpiga smiled to hear the story told again.

"And you said, 'I forgive you.' And that was when Papa Osandji stopped peeing. And after that, he could walk again."

They were all smiling now, at the story oft told, even by Papa Osandji himself, for it was a confirmation of the power of twins.

But Mama Angélique had something else on her mind, something she had sensed as soon as her daughter arrived. "You lost another baby, didn't you?" she said quietly.

Grief whelmed up in Justine at her mother's words, tears that surprised her. No one who saw this thought anything of it, besides her mother. Everyone thought she was mourning Papa Osandji. But her sorrow was for her lost baby. A great weight of silence hung over the subject among the Batéké, and this was the second time Justine had miscarried. It was a subject of shame, and Justine knew from her textbooks that such silence intensified the psychological trauma. It was important to mourn openly, but among the Batéké this wasn't done. Where in her mind would she place this loss, in

47

order to make room for a new child? Could she? Would she ever feel interested in a man again in that way? If she did, it would take a very long time. Of that much, she was sure. Did she have some defect in her, that she could not carry a pregnancy to term?

The Batéké called a barren woman kakouma. Justine worried people called her kakouma behind her back. Kakouma women were branded as unmarriageable.

Watching the shifting coals in the fire, Justine wondered, would it be so bad to live as a single woman. Did she really want a husband? These days it was not as before. Things were changing. She had a profession, her own income. Her bothers depended on her for their schooling, and when her mother came out of mourning, she would need her daughter as never before. What did Justine need a man for? Two times this had happened to her now, and her mother was sure there must be some unnatural cause. Her mother wanted to take her to see someone who could help her stop losing her babies, an ngaa-bwa, a shaman. But Justine did not want to follow that path.

The other nurses knew what had happened. Everyone at the hospital knew about the affair. The affair was not the secret Justine had supposed. You can always get pregnant again, the nurses told her. It's probably better that you miscarried, anyway. Something must have been wrong with the baby. God must have done it for a reason.

Well, if that was so, then God had some explaining to do.

4. A Place to Get Water

Okouya

C harlie awoke to a rooster crowing and did not know where he was. He knew what to do when he woke up lost, because of all the times he'd had to move. Breathe, look about, and remember.

Early morning light shone under the eave, sufficient to see that the walls of the house were made of mud. This was Africa. Beads of condensation hung on the underside of the metal roof. He lay in bed in a room even more orange than the bedroom in the other house, the cocoa brown house, in Boundji. This was the house provided him by the land chief, Chief Oyamba. This was the house in his new village, Okouya. Outside, a nanny goat bleated.

A kerosene lantern sat balanced on an upright cinderblock. Charlie remembered turning it down the night before, when he went to bed. A yellow flame guttered in the smudged glass globe. Half a dozen villagers had helped him unload the Land Cruiser, packed with supplies, when the landlord, Obongi Louis, turned up in the late afternoon and unlocked the house. They carried in the planks and the mattress, and Charlie hammered together the bed, unpacked his duffle bag, and arranged his clothes over there on that rough sawn plank, spanning two more cinderblocks that he'd brought with him from Boundji.

The rooster crowed again, and Charlie got moving. He flung off the covers and blew out the lamp. In the front room wearing only a pair of shorts and flip-flops he opened the plywood windows and the front door facing east. He had an unobstructed view of a low, grassy hill, the sky a luminous gray. It was noticeably cooler at fifteen hundred feet above sea level, much cooler than down in the jungle. Charlie rubbed his bare arms against the chill, and set off across the sandy way.

Villagers left off what they were doing to watch the spectacle of the enormous otangani emerge from the house. He was the first of his kind ever to spend a night in Okouya. They watched him go into the tall grass. Moments later they watched him return and go back inside. They watched him come out again with a towel and toilet kit and a plastic bucket, and perform his morning ablutions.

Charlie was aware of all the eyes in the village watching his every move. He went back into his house, put his toilet kit and towel away in the bedroom and slipped on a shirt. A small table and four chairs stood in the dry loose sand of the salon, the only furnishings that came with the place. On the table was a small yellow pineapple an old woman had given him yesterday. The room to the right was going to be his kitchen.

On the brand new white hotplate he'd bought, set on another plank on two more cinderblocks, he placed a shiny new aluminum saucepan full of water for coffee and opened the gas canister valve. He lit a cheery flame and set the table in the salon. He brought out a blue box of sugar cubes, a yellow can of powdered milk, and instant coffee in a brown tin.

When the water boiled, he carried the steaming saucepan to the table. In the straight back chair facing the window, he spooned dark coffee crystals and a heap of white powder into his cup, dropped in two sugar cubes, and stirred his morning coffee. The spoon clinked the side of the cup, and at that moment, the sun shot through the window, dazzling his eyes, lighting the mud wall behind him. The warm sun on his face was surely a sign, and Charlie's heart filled with gratitude.

He began to carve the pineapple. Tart juice dripped across his fingers, and he licked them. The three long months of training were behind him. The three long months of living cheek by jowl with other stagiaires were over. "Here I am," he said. "This is my village." It felt good to be able to say that. He smiled, and cut a wedge from a slice of pineapple. Just as he lifted the fork to his mouth and squinted into the sun, a troll popped into his window and gave off a violent snort.

Charlie gasped and recoiled from the horrible face, sinking the back legs of his chair in the sand. Suddenly he couldn't breathe. The pineapple was lodged in his throat! He huffed, fighting off panic. He huffed again, in danger of actually choking. What a way to die!

He huffed a third time and managed to clear his windpipe. He spat the pineapple across the room, drew in a ragged lungful of air, coughed, and immediately grew enraged at the intruder, the ugly little dwarf in his window.

"What do you want?" Charlie rasped.

Lalish nickered. He was daft. He stood scarcely four feet tall, his black face as winkled as a prune, his chin just inches above the windowsill.

At that moment Chief Oyamba rounded the corner of the house, walking with his staff and an avocado in his hand, and at the sight of Lalish peeping in Charlie's window, he barked out an order, and Lalish shrank away.

The old chief appeared in the open door, and Charlie rose and helped him step over the threshold. Charlie saw Akoa Édouard approaching, and called out a greeting to him. Édouard was Oyamba's oldest son, in line to succeed his father as chief. He came inside and shook Charlie's hand, narrow hips and a high waist, a thin mustache and wide-set eyes. One front tooth was chipped, and he was not yet thirty years old.

Charlie served the two men coffee and pineapple. Chief Oyamba scrabbled with his gnarled fingers for sugar cubes in the blue box, while Édouard examined the otangani across the table. Hair covered his face and his arms. The day before, bathing at Kampini Creek, he had seen the otangani's chest and his legs, covered with black hair too. The otangani had come out of his house that morning without a shirt, wearing only shorts, and people said he looked like a huge chimpanzee. When he arrived in the village the previous afternoon, in broad daylight, and in front of many witnesses, he had made a coin disappear, and then retrieved it from a child's ear.

He was obviously a white wizard, and when the sun went down, Chief Oyamba convened the village council of elders to consider what to do. To have such a person come live among them was an ominous prospect, and the palaver lasted nearly two hours. It ended when Édouard offered to keep an eye on the otangani and report any suspicious behavior. The elders agreed this was all that could be done for the time being, while they gave the matter more study.

"Are you well?" Édouard asked. "How did you sleep? Is this

house satisfactory? Is there anything you need?"

"Everything is fine," said Charlie, "but I'm going to need a place to get water."

Charlie meant water for the construction project. He knew where to go for his drinking water. Late the previous afternoon, after he had moved his things into his new home, Édouard and several teenage boys led him down off the plateau into the woods. Charlie carried two plastic jerry cans down the steep hill through trees to a rivulet that burbled from a leafy fissure into a creek, clear and cold. Charlie refused the offers of help coming back. He carried both jerry cans up the hill, forty liters of water weighing eighty-eight pounds.

"Would you like to see the schoolyard this morning?" Édouard asked.

"Yes, I would."

They finished their coffee. Oyamba declined to come with them, and returned to his house. Charlie walked beside Édouard through the deep sand of the main thoroughfare. Édouard was among the tallest men in Okouya, but his head did not reach Charlie's shoulders. Édouard greeted everyone they saw, and introduced everyone to Charlie.

They came to a woman named Clementine leading her blind husband Hilaire outside to sit in a sling chair beneath a shady palm tree. The man's face hung slack. He was unable to speak. He was the victim of a stroke, Charlie surmised.

At the schoolyard, Édouard was proud to point out the preparations the men of Okouya had made for this moment, years before, when with great foresight they had planted hardwood étogo trees in a rectangle to enclose the grounds. The rickety three-room schoolhouse at one end of the schoolyard resembled a goat stable, thought Charlie, though politely he didn't say so. The men of Okouya had planted more étogo trees in a second, smaller rectangle that enclosed the ramshackle hovel.

"This is where the schoolteacher lives," said Édouard. "He is away right now, due to a death in the family."

"Uh-huh," said Charlie, and he began to pace off distances. The new school would not take any space away from the soccer field, he calculated. There was plenty of room for three teachers' houses.

While he was considering the spatial relations, an engine became audible, coming from the east. Soon, a battered old Land Cruiser HJ-47 pickup truck overloaded with passengers hove into view, grinding through the sand until it stopped at the schoolyard. A man climbed over the tailgate.

"That is the schoolteacher," said Édouard. "His name is Ngaleka Jonas."

Charlie watched Jonas retrieve his shotgun and a small handbag from one of the passengers. Curious about the otangani, Jonas approached Charlie, the largest man he'd ever seen.

Jonas and Charlie shook hands as the bush taxi pulled away south toward Akièni. Jonas was as slender as Édouard, and sported a neat goatee.

"I'm the schoolteacher here," Jonas said.

"So Édouard told me. I'm an American Peace Corps volunteer," said Charlie. "I've come here to build a school."

"Ah, c'est bien ça! Corps de la Paix! Soyez la bienvenue au Gabon!"

"How was the funeral?" Édouard asked Jonas in Téké.

"It was very well-attended. Papa Osandji lived a full life."

The schoolteacher had a deep voice, Charlie observed, and he wondered what he was saying.

Jonas turned back to him. "I would be interested to see the plan for the school."

"Sure," said Charlie. "How about now? The blueprint is up at my house."

Jonas put his bag and his gun in the shack and the three of them walked through the village. They passed a strip of metal roofing bent in an arc and nailed to a board on top of a pole leaning over in the sand like a derelict mailbox. Charlie reached to open the partially closed door and bent down, but before he could peek inside, Édouard slapped Charlie's hand away. "Don't look in there!"

The sudden roughness angered Charlie. "Why?"

"You'll go blind like Hilaire!" cried Édouard, alarmed at what Charlie had nearly done.

"What's in there?"

"The bones of a twin."

"What? Bones?"

"Yes, the bones of a twin."

Charlie looked at the mailbox again. "What is this thing?"

"It's an ndjo okira. The bones of all twins must be kept in an ndjo okira, even bones sent home to us from the cities."

Charlie looked about and counted another half dozen or so rickety little mailboxes here and there, some of them very much older than others. So these were shrines containing human bones, he thought in wonderment. "Why do you keep the bones of twins in these things?"

"Because twins are a special gift from God," said the schoolteacher. "They have very strong powers. They can sense things we can't see. That's why a twin can't be buried like an ordinary person. We put the body out in the forest until the flesh has rotted away, then we put the bones in an ndjo okira."

A lesson floated in from Charlie's school days. The Lakota Sioux once wrapped their dead in hides and placed them on a scaffold on the open prairie.

"Don't the wild animals eat the bodies?"

"It doesn't matter. The bones will always remain."

"And if I looked inside this thing, I would go blind?"

"Il ne faut jamais jouer avec les os d'un jumeau!" said Édouard. The bones of twins were never to be trifled with! "That's why Hilaire is blind. And not only Hilaire. Lenkongi Francis was once sent the bones of his twin baby nephew, but he threw them away in the woods. The next morning he woke up blind. Okorogo René restored his sight."

"Who's Okorogo René?"

They had resumed walking.

"He's an ngaa-bwa. He has gone off to the Congo. You'll meet him when he returns. He had the courage to retrieve the bones from the place Francis threw them."

"What's an ngaa-bwa?"

"A healer."

"And Hilaire? What happened to him?"

"The same thing. Hilaire has a sister in Libreville who gave birth to twins. One was stillborn. She sent the bones to her brother

Hilaire, but he threw them away, and you have seen what happened to him. No one can help him though, not even Okorogo René, because Hilaire can't talk. He can't tell us where he threw the bones."

This is ridiculous, thought Charlie. He recalled what the old priest, Père Dominique had said about sorcery on this part of the plateau.

They reached his house and went inside. His visitors sat at the table in the front room while he put on water for coffee. He had much to learn about the people he would be living with for the next two years.

"Are you the only teacher?" Charlie asked Jonas.

"Yes. I'm responsible for all six grades, a total of forty-seven children."

"Are you from around here?"

"I'm from a village to the east named Onga. Do you know where that is?"

"I've heard of it."

"My mother lives there with several of my brothers and sisters. I have a sister who lives in Akièni. Our twin brothers live with her."

"You have twin brothers! Do they have supernatural powers?" Charlie grinned.

"Of course," said Jonas.

"What sorts of things can they do?"

Jonas recognized it as a snide remark, and took a moment to consider the otangani coolly, before he replied. "What can twins do?" he said. "Why, twins can make things happen you would never believe."

Otou

The village women seemed so concerned for Rebecca that it tickled her. They all asked the same questions. Where was her husband? Where were her children? They found it strange Rebecca insisted she didn't want a husband, or babies. She was obviously a silly sort of woman, they said among themselves, but then, who knew what white women were like? Every evening, they took turns bringing meals to the white woman, who had come, she claimed, to do a man's job building a school in their village. That was hard to believe as well. The women brought her every type of food the Batéké ate, and it greatly amused them to see Rebecca eat their provender.

Every meal included manioc in one form or another. Rebecca had brought with her a big fat book entitled, *Flora of Central African Forests*. From it, she learned manioc's scientific name: manihot esculenta. It was a woody shrub of the spurge family, domesticated by tribes in the Amazon, and brought to Africa by the Portuguese, where its cultivation rapidly spread. Manioc was resistant to disease and drought. The name for it in English was cassava, mandioca in Spanish, and macaxeira in Portuguese.

Each day except Sundays and Thursdays, women left Otou for their fields. They carried hoes and machetes, empty baskets on their backs that they brought back full of roots, leaves and firewood. On her third day in the village, Rebecca accompanied a group of giggling women. They were amused that the silly, helpless white woman wanted to join them. She said she wanted to see their fields and learn more about their daily routine.

The fields the women cultivated lay in the forest at the foot of the escarpment. The heavy rain and intense sun depleted the soil, and the people were obliged to clear new fields every other year. Manioc grew swiftly and produced edible dark leaves and starchy tuberous roots that unfortunately contained cyanogenic glucosides. These converted to cyanide when exposed to air, and the roots had to be soaked for several days to leech out the poison. Near the fields were small pools of water for this. The small lithe Batéké women were able to carry nearly their own weight in dripping manioc roots up the hill.

In the village, they dried the roots on the low metal roofs, and then grated them into flour as dense as cornstarch. The women prepared manioc in two forms: onguélé, a heavy loaf, and fou-fou, a sticky paste eaten balled up in the fingers when it cooled. Fou-fou had to be eaten at once or it spoiled, but onguélé could keep for a week. To prepare manioc as onguélé, the women kneaded the flour into dough and wrapped the dough in huge leaves called phrynium, making loaves they boiled in water.

The principal green the Batéké ate came from a wild vine called gnetum africanum, nkoumou in Téké. It proliferated in the woodlots of the plateau. The girls of the village went out several times a week to gather the youngest of the vine's dark leaves. The women rolled them into fat cigars and shaved the ends with knives, making fine cuttings they boiled with mushrooms, if any were available, and served alongside meat, if any could be had. The people relied on the wild game the men hunted. Villagers ate the goats and chickens only on special occasions. Protein deficiency was why the Batéké were so small, Rebecca decided, and insects were an important source. The women gathered insects in their various seasons: black and green caterpillars called etchitcheri that looked like inchworms, termites called antchama, locusts called ngoudji, and big white grubs the size of a man's thumb that thrived in the palm trees, called mbouo.

Akièni

Rebecca was in the fields with a group of women when Charlie passed through Otou en route to meet Hector in Akièni. Hector was just coming out of the Préfet's office when Charlie pulled in, on time for their rendezvous to see about renting trucks. The new Peace Corps dump truck on order for the rural primary school program still hadn't arrived. Until it did, the construction volunteers had to find their own ways of hauling supplies.

Hector trotted over and shook Charlie's hand. Their hope was to rent three trucks, two to go to Franceville for a load of cement and a load of gravel, and a third to go to the manganese mine in the city of Moanda to bring back as many empty 55 gallon metal drums as possible. Hector had come earlier in the week, and now he showed Charlie the signed letter the Préfet's secretary had just given him. It instructed the Directeur de Travaux Publique and the Chef de Collectivité to render the Americans full cooperation and assistance.

"This should work," said Charlie. He had shaved this morning, which he hadn't done for some time. The lower half of his face looked pale.

Hector led the way to a door marked Collectivité. Inside, an

57

attractive young woman carefully painted her fingernails. The odor of the nail polish was strong.

"Bonjour," said Hector. "Le chef est là?"

The secretary gave them both a look of disdain. "Il n'est pas encore arrivé," she said, and returned to her nails, the polish very red, the nails very long. There was an old manual typewriter on her desk, and nothing else.

"Il viendra bientôt?"

"Peut-être." She blew on her nails and began the other hand.

"Where is he? I have a letter here for him from the Préfet."

That got her to look at him again. She didn't take the letter when Hector extended it. "Il est encore chez lui," she said.

They drove their two trucks to the government bungalows near the hospital where she said he lived. Hector was in the lead. He stopped on the street to ask a boy which one. The boy pointed out the house.

They pulled into the bare dirt yard. Hector led the way to the front door. There was music coming from inside, and Hector had to knock a second time, louder, before a woman opened the door. Her eyes widened at seeing the two etangani on her porch, one of them small and dark and the other a veritable giant.

The chef de collectivité sat in a brown vinyl chair working his way through a bottle of palm wine at nine-thirty in the morning. The two strangers startled him because the music was so loud he hadn't heard their trucks arrive. The chef pointed a remote at the stereo, lowered the volume and indicated for them to sit. First Hector and then Charlie reached across a table to shake the chef's hand. Hector explained, "We're Peace Corps volunteers."

The chef de collectivité had sparse chin whiskers grown long. His eyes were deep set. He sent his wife to fetch more glasses, and when she returned, he served the two Americans.

Hector showed him the letter from the Préfet while Charlie sipped the tangy palm wine.

"Il n'y a pas de problème," the chef said, handing the letter back. His smile revealed a missing incisor. "J'ai certains camions disponibles."

"Quand est-ce?" Hector said. When were the trucks available?

"N'importe quand," said the chef.

58

"Today?" Hector said. "Right now, this morning?"

"Oui, c'est possible."

"How much do you charge?" Hector asked.

And the man's smile grew wider.

At that very moment, in an examination room at the nearby hospital, Ntchaga Justine examined the swollen wrist of a little girl who had fallen from a tree. "Why were you climbing a tree?"

"I was picking nkoumou," said the little girl.

"She did not leave the machete behind," her mother boasted. "She brought it back to the village. She is a very strong girl."

With no money to pay for a bush taxi, the mother and daughter wearing her best dress for town, faded blue with a white bow tied in back, had walked thirty kilometers to the hospital. The stoicism of the rural people never failed to amaze Justine. She gave the girl an injection of xylocaine. The x-ray machine was out of film. Dr. Muengo had gone to Libreville for supplies. Justine would have to make the diagnosis by palpation.

The textbook said people involuntarily put out a hand to break their fall. This was why and how people usually broke their wrist. The radius, the larger bone in the forearm, was the most commonly broken bone in the arm. The girl's injured wrist should be getting numb by now.

"I'm going to look at your arm," said Justine. "Is that all right?" She pressed the swollen area with her thumb. The girl did not react. The wrist looked slightly bent. Generally, the fracture would be two or three centimeters from the end of the bone. Justine pressed until she located the fracture. She readied herself. This would be the third time she had set a broken bone. She got a firm grip, pulled and twisted. The girl sucked in her breath. Justine felt the bone slide into place. It was over.

"There. You're very brave. That didn't hurt at all, did it?"

"A little," the girl said, tears in her eyes.

"Now you'll have to have a cast to protect your arm, so the bone can heal correctly. Do you know what a cast is?"

The little girl nodded. "Félix had one at school last year."

"Well now you'll have one too, like Félix. I'm going to lay your arm out on the table here, like this. I want you to hold very still. Can you do that for me?"

The girl's eyes were big, her knees knobby, one of them freshly skinned from the fall.

Justine took the soft cotton roller bandage from the tray and wrapped it around the arm from just below the elbow to the middle of the palm. Then she opened the first roll of plaster and dipped it in the bowl of warm water. Starting from the elbow and working toward the hand, Justine began to apply the plaster, wrapping it around the forearm, around the fracture, around the base of the thumb, smoothing it with the palm of her hand. She opened a second plaster roll and wrapped it around the first, working swiftly. She folded the edges of the roller bandage into the plaster to guard against the cast breaking or cracking, and then she dipped her hands in the water and smoothed the cast, applying pressure to make the plaster conform to the arm.

"There," she said, "how's that?"

"It's warm," said the little girl.

Otou

Rebecca watched the shiny black scarabs as she squatted in the grass, screened from view of the men. The scarabs swarmed over a pile of human excrement like miniature earth moving equipment. Their outsized claws pulled manageable portions loose from the pile, and then they spun and lifted their rear legs and formed the portions into balls, and rolled the balls backwards away. Where did they go? What did they do with the balls of shit? Bury them? Eat them? Lay eggs in them? Rebecca didn't know. The scarab had been sacred to the ancient Egyptians. A scarab rolled the sun across the sky.

She rose and pulled up her panties and smoothed her skirt. Men had such an advantage when it came to peeing. So did the Batéké women. Going to the field with them, she'd been amazed to see women step off the trail, hike up their pagnes, pull the crotch of their panties aside and shoot their urine straight into the ground. She hadn't yet attempted this herself.

The small circle of men was just as she'd left them, sitting under the avocado tree where Chef Petie could be found every day holding court, drinking beer or palm wine or, now that the fruit was in season, pineapple wine. Among them, a man named Ongongi Faustin had appointed himself Rebecca's helper. He ran the crew of men pouring the floors in her house with the cement and gravel she hauled out to Otou from the stockpile at Hector's village. No one was working. The village was in the midst of preparations for New Year's Day, the biggest party of the year. Younger men felled palm trees and drained the sap into demijohns to ferment. Older men pressed the juice of the little pineapples their women raised into old bottles. Hunters smoked meat from their kills over fires in little huts.

Rebecca settled back in her new sling chair. The discussion was where she had left it: the university student strike. The opinion leaders of Otou were discussing whether anyone would listen to the college students. They spoke in veiled terms and never used the name of President Bongo, except to praise him, because Bongo had ways of knowing who was talking about him. There were machines called satellites that circled the earth that enabled him to listen to what people were saying.

One of the men said he had heard through a passing relative, who had a cousin who worked at the Presidential Palace, that the cabinet ministers were discussing multiparty elections.

This, Rebecca thought with a smile as she raised her glass to her lips, is why I'm here.

5. L'Homme de l'Ombre

T he chancery of the United States embassy had once been home to a French merchant family, stucco-sided with a deep two-story porch and square wooden pillars under broad eaves. In her second floor corner office, Ambassador Darlene Jones was surprised to hear a rumble of thunder in the middle of the winter dry season. She turned to look out the window behind her, and saw a curtain of rain had veiled the sea.

She opened the small cream-colored envelope with embossed gold letters in the upper left corner. The envelope came from l'Ambassade de France, and was addressed to Son Excellence l'Ambassadeur des États-Unis. Inside, she found a note printed in flowery cursive requesting the pleasure of the company of Madame l'Ambassadrice Darlene Jones for dinner au Restaurant la Bonne Auberge, lundi, le 11 décembre 1989 à 19h30; signed by the French Ambassador, Philippe Berrier. A diplomatic invitation of this sort should have specified the occasion, but there was none.

The omission would normally have puzzled Darlene, but she was distracted by rising tensions in the capital city. Today, at a noonday press conference, the labor unions had announced their plans for a general strike, should the government fail to accede to the demands of the university students and schedule multiparty elections. Darlene was in the middle of reviewing a draft reporting cable on the situation that her political officer had composed, when a senior FSN was stricken with chest pains, and they'd had to phone for an ambulance. Just an hour before the envelope arrived, the DCM radioed that the embassy car he was riding in had been in a minor collision. So Darlene did not remark on the omission in what appeared to be a routine diplomatic invitation. Mary, her secretary, did not notice it either when she consulted the calendar and said there was no commitment for the evening of December 11. Darlene told Mary to RSVP that she would attend and Mary sent the reply back by driver that same day.

The dark Chevrolet with an American flag fluttering above the fender slid to the curb at the appointed hour, and a uniformed African doorman came forward to open the door. The restaurant owner stepped outside. He was plump, pallid and surprised to see the American ambassador was a very attractive woman. She wore a royal blue skirt suit with a lacy white blouse, her short hair styled in waves.

"Marcel Chambon," he said with a bow, making a fuss as he ushered Darlene inside and into a dark paneled room.

It was a private room draped with heavy curtains, icily air conditioned, and Darlene was glad for her jacket. Ambassador Berrier stood smiling in a gray silk suit that nearly matched the color of his silver hair. His blue tie matched the color of his eyes. Darlene had met him many times at diplomatic functions, and he held both her hands and bussed her on both cheeks. His mustache prickled. Then he extended his arm to the table behind him, set for two.

The private room was reserved for just the two of them, and Darlene's suspicions were aroused.

The restaurateur pulled out a chair for her, and Ambassador Berrier took his seat opposite Darlene. Marcel recited for Darlene the fixed menu that Monsieur l'Ambassadeur had personally selected, and trusting this was satisfactory, he withdrew.

"Where in France does the name Berrier come from?" Darlene asked lightly, to seize the initiative. Her high school basketball coach had taught her how to juke and feint before she drove in for the shot. Seize the initiative was the core tenet of U.S. Navy doctrine. Her question pleased the French ambassador, as she knew it would, asking a European about his ancestry, and one end of his mustache lifted in a half smile. She had hit the mark.

"It is believed," he said, "we are named for the Berri tribe of the Celts. The Berrier name can be dated to the fifteenth century in Autun, a city founded by the Romans in 20 BC. There is a very beautiful ruin there, a temple to Janus."

A waiter arrived with a tray bearing small plates of nuts, olives

64

and crackers for the aperitif, and tulip glasses filled with a pale amber drink. Darlene took a sparing sip. It was chilled sherry.

"Is Autun where you were raised, Monsieur Berrier?"

Philippe smiled again. "Yes," he said, and told her of summertime family bicycle trips, cycling into the Morvan forest, the rivers and lakes and the many species of birds, the vineyards of Vosne-Romanée and Gevrey-Chambertin and the villages with their twelfth-century churches. He spoke of the Route des Grands Crus, a sixty-kilometer wine lover's meander. In fact, the wines he had selected for tonight came from there.

The French Ambassador was still talking when Marcel came in with the waiter who brought the entrée: crudités – cauliflower, broccoli, asparagus, radishes, sliced cucumber, cherry tomatoes, yellow zucchini and red bell peppers on a bed of endives and rose cabbage. "All flown in just this morning," Marcel said proudly as he uncorked a Matrot Meursault, 1986, a Bourgogne blanc.

Philippe tasted the wine. "Superb. Pour for Ambassador Jones. Tell me of you, Madame," he said, as the restaurateur and the waiter withdrew. "What is your family background?"

"African American and Choctaw," said Darlene. People said the Choctaw blood accounted for her high cheekbones and what her husband called her regal nose.

"Choctaw?"

"Yes. It's the name of a Native American tribe from the lower Mississippi."

"I see. Is that where you grew up?"

"My mother and father did, in Tupelo, Mississippi."

Philippe loved the sound of the name, and asked Darlene to repeat it, and he sounded out the seven syllables.

"After they married, my parents moved to New York. I was born and raised in Brooklyn," said Darlene. In a flash, she was across the street in Tompkins Park, skipping Double Dutch with her sister Eunice in the late afternoon as her father came home tired carrying his lunch pail. He called to them, and in the next instant, she was back in the here and now, the Ambassador of the United States of America, dining with the Ambassador of France.

"Forgive me for saying, but you seem very young," said Philippe.

Darlene smiled. She had risen nimbly in her career; she had to admit, after a book she'd written as an associate professor caused a small buzz in policy circles, a comparison of political transitions called *Reverse Dominoes*. It came out the year Ferdinand Marcos fell. The timing was fortuitous. General Colin Powell read it, and when President Reagan named him national security advisor, she was among the people the General called to come work for him. She was the NSC member of the U.S. government team that participated in the negotiations, which led to the withdrawal of the South African and Cuban troops from Angola in 1988 and paved the way for the independence of Namibia scheduled for 1990. It was a foreign policy triumph.

"I must have performed my duties with some distinction," said Darlene, "because they made me Ambassador to Gabon."

Philippe was impressed. "My advancement was not as dramatic as yours," he said, and he was in the midst of recounting one of the more amusing indignities he had endured as a young second secretary in Chad when for the plat de résistance Marcel Chambon led in a waiter bearing plates of bœuf bourguignon with bacon, carrots and mushrooms. He uncorked a Grands-Echézeaux, a dark vin rouge from the Domaine de la Romanée-Conti.

Philippe swirled the wine, held the glass to his nose, breathed in deeply, then tasted. His expression said it all.

The waiter removed Darlene's nearly untouched glass of white and Marcel filled the second glass set for her with red.

"May I have more water please?" she asked.

"Bien sûr, Madame." Marcel snapped his fingers at the waiter.

Darlene couldn't remember the last time she'd had dinner alone with a man, and she thought for an instant of her husband Calvin, and started to wonder how often – but then she drove that poisonous thought from her mind.

Ambassador Berrier was already in country when Darlene presented her credentials. She knew from the Embassy briefing book awaiting her own arrival that President Bongo made the French change their ambassadors as often as he changed his socks. She asked herself, "How much longer will Philippe last?" He looked to be in his sixties, expensively dressed, attractive for a white man.

Philippe liked Darlene looking at him, and took his eyes off her only to cut dainty morsels of beef, selecting a slice of baguette and buttering it with manicured fingers, a slim gourmand, necktie perfectly knotted, discreet gold cufflinks and a thin gold watch.

"It is good to taste different dishes," he said with a look that Darlene didn't like. "À l'amitié," he said, and raised his glass.

The stemware was crystal, the silverware heavy.

She steered into safer waters. "What is your view of events in Eastern Europe?"

"Ah, incroyable," said Philippe. "To see such things on the télé, they bring tears to my eyes. Do you know the people in Berlin have started calling themselves *mauerspechte*? It means wall peckers." He smiled. "It's ironic, don't you think? The whole thing was set in motion quite by accident. The spokesman for the ruling party, what is his name? Günter Schabowski, yes? He read a note they handed him at a press conference. Literally, he read it aloud, with the international media there filming. 'East Germans will be allowed to cross the border with proper permission'. He was completely unbriefed. Incroyable."

Darlene shared his amazement. A worldwide reporting cable from Washington had come bearing the same information. Within hours, there were thousands of East Berliners massing at the checkpoints, and no one had given any instructions to the long-feared East German border guards, known for shooting down anyone trying to cross. To everyone's astonishment, they had simply stepped aside. Now the TV cameras of the international media were broadcasting images of the people of Germany tearing down the Berlin Wall.

"I know what it feels like to be liberated," said Ambassador Berrier. The emotion he displayed was genuine. He had entered lycée during the last year of the occupation. "I knew life under Nazi rule."

"Five whole years, wasn't it?" said Darlene, thinking of two hundred-fifty years of slavery, and a hundred years of Jim Crow.

"Yes, five long years." Then Philippe brightened. "Ah, but let us speak of more pleasant things. In life, one must faire l'effort à passer partout. Perhaps one Saturday we could boat across the estuary to Pointe-Denis? My Embassy has a very comfortable beach house there. The view of the city at night is magnificent."

"Monsieur Berrier, what is the purpose of your invitation tonight?"

Philippe put his hand to his breast. "Is it wrong for a man to ask a colleague to dine? Of course, the pleasure is that much greater if the colleague happens also to be a beautiful woman."

Darlene gave him a look to desist, flattered all the same. She cut into a slice of meat. "Please remind yourself of my position."

"Eh bien. Then let us speak of cooperation. Perhaps from time to time I will have information of interest to you." He cocked his head, one side of his silver mustache rising toward one of his blue eyes. "And perhaps from time to time you will have information of interest to me."

"That is normal."

"Good. Then I shall begin. I'm sure you are familiar with the term Françafrique."

Darlene was surprised that he mentioned it. "Some joke it means 'France à fric. How would you translate that, Monsieur Berrier? France on the take, perhaps?"

"An amusing play on words, certainly. What do you understand Françafrique to mean?"

"I would prefer that you tell me."

"It is a half-hidden system of unbalanced exchanges that operates off the resources of our former colonies, and freely uses corruption and force. How is that?"

"That is very frank language."

Philippe Berrier made a shrug. "One must admit these things. You know of the Foccart system, of course."

Indeed Darlene knew of the legendary l'Homme de l'Ombre, the man in the shadows who once ran de Gaulle's secret network of hard men. In the best known of the few official photographs he had permitted, Foccart was posed with a parrot on his shoulder, an African gray appropriately, and that black and white photograph was very like Ambassador Berrier tonight, with his gray suit, silver hair and mustache.

"Officially, Jacques Foccart was the President's adviser for African affairs. I suppose you know he also had many other functions. He supervised the intelligence community, for example, and brought Elf very close to our intelligence services."

Elf was the acronym of the French oil company, Essence et Lubrifiants de France.

"You no doubt know that the first president of Elf was a Gaullist militant. The profits Elf reaped from African oil were a major source of finance for the Gaullist political movement. That must be understood. Foccart made certain Elf was closely associated with our intelligence services. Many intelligence officers took early retirement to join Elf's department of security, which has its own intelligence branch. The same position for much higher pay. Very nice, eh?"

"Such things are true in my country as well, as I'm sure you know. It's the way of the wicked world, it seems."

"I should imagine you know of the SAC, the Service d'Action Civique?"

Darlene knew of it, the one-time Gaullist party militia; a hodgepodge of right wing nationalists, intelligence agents, and Corsican gangsters.

"Foccart founded the SAC. It had close ties to Omar Bongo's Presidential Guard. For Elf, Gabon has always been of extreme importance. As for Bongo, his number one priority has always been to protect his privileged relations with Paris. This dates back to the cooperation accords that Foccart put in place, the guarantee to intervene in the event of a military coup, especially. That was the strongest of the many bonds the Foccart system created. When Foccart was forced to retire, many thought it was the end of his system. But Françafrique has endured. It is very stable, actually. It has the enormous resources of Elf."

The door swung open and a waiter came in to clear their dinner plates. Another waiter followed with dessert, and behind him came Marcel, plump as a pigeon and doting as he told Darlene this was mille-feuille, thin layers of unleavened flour dough with crème pâtissière filling, whipped cream on the inside and a thin layer of lemon icing on top, dusted with powdered sugar.

Darlene tasted her pastry. She would have to do penitence at the gym.

Seeing her expression, Marcel bowed, and satisfied, withdrew once more, leaving the two ambassadors alone again.

"Do you see what I am telling you?"

"I want to be sure that I do."

"I am describing for you a web of political, financial and espionage relations all connected through a variety of organizations into a single network, with almost limitless money from oil. The network includes social organizations, the freemasons most particularly. Do you know about them?"

Freemasons. Shriners. White men wearing red fezzes. A parade of miniature cars. What was she expected to make of this?

Berrier saw her puzzlement. "To do business on a large scale in French-speaking Africa, you must be a member of a lodge. Do you know that Bongo is a Grand Master? He founded the lodge in Gabon called the Grande Rite Symbolique. The introduction of freemasonry in our former colonies is another legacy of Foccart. He forced the lodges to accept African members. They had been reserved for Europeans, previously. All the Francophone African independence leaders became freemasons. In the lodges, they formed associations with French businessmen. Since that time, all Francophone African presidents have been freemasons. This is perhaps the most essential of the reasons why President Bongo trusts me."

"Because you are a freemason?"

Philippe smiled rather than reply. "There are no real boundaries to the Foccart system. You might say it is a nebula of networks, the Gaullists and the SAC during its time, the intelligence service, the freemasons, the oil company Elf, it is all a single system. It draws on the money from the oil in Africa as its source of power."

Philippe paused to give Ambassador Jones time to absorb the vastness of what he was describing. She did not finish her pastry, dabbed her mouth with her napkin and saw the lipstick she left behind.

"As I said, it has been very stable, this system. For years, there were never any major surprises. So of course, the African presidents were unsettled when suddenly the Socialists sent Foccart into retirement. His system provided for every contingency. The cooperation accords guided all. They were worried what his retirement would mean for their security. The Africans have not wanted to lose the certainty the system provides."

"The African presidents have not wanted change, you mean.

70

The African people might feel otherwise. The system has done very little for the ordinary Africans, some might say."

"Yes, the Socialists."

"Not only the Socialists."

Berrier ignored that. "The Françafrique system has survived the departure of Foccart; that is my point. It is still intact today. But today, here in Gabon, there is now a distorting factor, because of what is happening in Eastern Europe."

"And what is the distorting factor?"

"It is a problem that I happen to know President Bongo is very unhappy about."

"May I know what the problem is?"

A waiter wheeled in a cart with cheeses, a basket of baguette slices covered by a linen napkin, clinking bottles of liqueurs, brandy and port, and a silver pot of coffee. Philippe Berrier dabbed his mustache and pointed to the cheeses he wanted. He asked for a glass of port, and coffee.

Darlene Jones wanted just more water.

The waiter wheeled the cart away.

"There is a man, Commandant Gilles Clermidy, who has been meeting with your chief of security, n'est-ce pas? You should know that Commandant Clermidy is acting under my orders."

"We have assumed that is the case. But what is this problem, this distorting factor, Ambassador?"

"You know of Jean-Jacques Mitterrand?"

President François Mitterrand's corpulent curly-haired son; special advisor to his father for African affairs, the job that had once been Foccart's.

Philippe lifted his glass of port and sipped. "For the past two years Jean-Jacques Mitterrand has been trying to – how do you say? – strong-arm better terms for the Socialists." His pale blue eyes were on his glass of dark red port for a moment, and then back on her again. "You see, President Mitterrand wants for the Socialist Party what the Gaullists got from the oil concessions when they were in power. Mitterrand has had only limited success. The mission of his son since his reelection last year has been to – what is it you Americans say, turn up the heat?"

71

"Yes, that is the expression."

"Jean-Jacques hasn't had any success either; rather the opposite. His pressuring has upset President Bongo. This is why President Bongo ordered the full-scale review of the oil concessions. This was before you arrived, but I'm sure you know of it. While the review was underway, he invited a number of your top oil company executives to high-level meetings in Libreville, all in order to – what is the expression? – rattle our cage. But now, with the events in Eastern Europe, and here in Gabon, university students demanding democracy and now labor unions expressing support for the students, threatening to call a general strike, the situation has become very uncertain." Ambassador Berrier sipped his coffee. "Of course," he said, his eyes twinkling, "perhaps it is all an elaborate ruse by the students to get out of taking their exams."

Darlene indulged him with a laugh.

Philippe grew serious again. "I invited you here to tell you, Madame l'Ambassadrice, that President Bongo believes he must soon agree to a democratic opening."

"You are certain of this?"

"He himself has told me, personally."

"Then I must say, this a major new piece of information for me. I trust you understand that I will report this to Washington."

Philippe inclined his head. "When President Bongo does finally agree to a democratic opening, it will give Jean-Jacques Mitterrand a new angle to try. What is it called, tit for tat?" he asked, arching an eyebrow.

"Yes, tit for tat. What precisely are you referring to?"

"I'm certain I don't need to tell you that President Bongo twice tried to prevent the Socialists' victory at the polls. He first made campaign contributions to the Gaullists in 1981, knowing François Mitterrand would learn about the contributions if he was elected, and might retaliate."

The Embassy briefing book recorded hints Bongo made to the American Ambassador at the time, about the possibility of new oil concessions, a quid pro quo for something he never clearly defined. Post recorded they saw the overture for what it was: an attempt to move closer to the Americans after the Socialists' surprise victory.

"This indeed happened. When he assumed office, Mitterrand

learned of the contributions. He dissolved the SAC, and this touched one of Bongo's most sensitive nerves. Bongo feared what Mitterrand might do next, specifically with the Deuxième Régiment Étranger de Parachutistes. As you know, they are permanently garrisoned at the airport. Another legacy of the Foccart accords, I might add."

"Are you saying Bongo was worried Mitterrand would unseat him by military force?"

Ambassador Berrier shrugged. "Such things have happened before. That was almost ten years ago. Some things have changed a great deal. Other things have not. Bongo contributed again to the Gaullists last year, in the 1988 general elections. The Socialists knew about this. They've just been biding their time. They know that Bongo must yield on the question of multiparty elections, or face civil unrest. That would be a great blow to President Bongo. He prides himself on the fact that Gabon has been a peaceful country, ever since he came to power."

"Yes, that is well known."

"So you asked me what I mean by the distorting factor. Here is what I mean, Ambassador Jones. President Mitterrand's son, Jean-Jacques, is grooming a candidate to field against President Bongo. The man's name is Antoine Badinga."

"I don't know the name."

"You will soon know. Frankly, Antoine Badinga is little better than a hoodlum. Is that the correct word? He made a fortune brokering arms for African diamonds. It was in this connection that young Mitterrand learned of him. Top political consultants have now been hired. Image-makers are preparing Badinga for a return to Gabon. He will come here cast as a successful businessman who has made his mark in the world, and who now for the good of his country is ready to challenge President Bongo at the polls."

"So that is the distorting factor? And why is it so important you tell me?"

"Madame l'Ambassadrice," said Philippe, "President Bongo would like you to know, in the event that something should happen to change the current dynamic, he would be most appreciative if the United States were to take no position. Do you understand what I am saying?"

"I'm not sure I do."

"In plain terms, Madame l'Ambassadrice, President Bongo wants Jean-Jacques Mitterrand stopped, and he is requesting no interference from the United States."

Okouya

When Charlie returned from Franceville, Édouard helped the otangani unload seven empty barrels outside his house. Into the small house they carried four sheets of plywood, two corrugated aluminum roofing sheets, four lengths of two-by-fours, shovels, sacks of assorted nails, heavy-duty plastic buckets, a fifty-meter coil of nylon rope, a single bright blue plastic funnel, a cardboard carton containing a handsaw, a wood float, a plane, a tape measure, a three-pound mall and a cold chisel.

Édouard was learning more about the American. Unfailingly polite, before he did anything, Charlie always asked Édouard first. "Is this all right?"

Charlie was a large and powerful man, but something about his face did not fit. There was a feminine quality to his eyes and long lashes. The shape of his mouth held a suggestion of cruelty.

Charlie stripped off his shirt and with the chisel and the three-pound mall he hammered the tops off the metal drums, making the village reverberate with a great and hollow booming. He began streaming sweat as he pounded, and the hair of his chest became matted to his leaping pectorals. Édouard wondered what it would be like to be as big as the white man. He stood half again taller than most village men and weighed twice as much, far stronger than any man Édouard had ever seen, muscles rippling with each hammer blow.

During a breather, Charlie asked, "Why don't the rural Batéké use latrines?"

Édouard explained, "Holes dug in the sand collapse in no time. Besides, there are dung beetles to clean up the mess."

Villagers squatted in tall grass to do their business. A sharp handclap meant come no closer. Charlie had been doing the same, but he did not intend to crap in the weeds for two years. There was plenty of space available, immediately across from his house and

Chief Oyamba had given him permission to build a latrine there.

Charlie flipped the seventh barrel over and cold-chiseled the bottom off it too, and then Édouard helped him dig the hole. They lowered in the barrel and tamped sand around it. The hole would not cave in until the metal drum corroded away.

Charlie sawed up one of the planks and one of the two-by-fours and built a floor with a hole for the latrine. With more two-by-fours, he built a frame. Édouard wove palm fronds to close in three of the walls. The two of them tacked on a single sheet of tôle as a roof, and it was done, the first latrine ever built in the village.

"Thanks for your help," said Charlie. "So, now I have to ferry my share of the cement and gravel from Obia. Can you arrange a place to store the cement?"

"Of course," said Édouard.

The place Édouard found was a termite-riddled abandoned house that threatened to fall over in a hard wind. Charlie affixed an impressive padlock to the door, and took Édouard with him on the runs. Often they stopped in Otou. Édouard was surprised the Americans had sent a woman to live there alone. She had freakish blue eyes, and had to wear glasses as a result. Perhaps that was why she had no husband.

The American in Obia was very dark for a white man, Édouard observed.

"More Americans are on the way," said Hector. "They're coming here to learn how to build a school. I'm going to put this school under roof in six weeks' time."

There was a bulldozer pushing aside trees and brush and a grader leveling the torn red dirt. The Americans were in a great hurry, it seemed, but Édouard didn't voice his opinion. He didn't know them sufficiently well. He enjoyed riding in the truck with Charlie, back and forth to Obia, his right arm crooked out the window, looking at the scenery rolling by.

As for the question of a source of water for the construction, Édouard told Charlie about a place they could get to with the truck. One day, Charlie put one of the two intact oil drums in the Land Cruiser. Édouard rounded up a half dozen men, and directed Charlie over rough open country three miles east to a stream called Aliga Creek. There the men used machetes and axes to reopen a trail through the trees down to where an old rotten log bridge crossed the stream. They filled the barrel using the buckets and the blue plastic funnel.

Back in the village, Charlie rolled the sealed barrel onto the ground with a thud. Now they had water to go with the gravel and cement, and Édouard helped Charlie pour concrete floors in his house. They mixed the concrete with shovels on a sheet of plywood, using sand they took from each room. Charlie agreed with Édouard's idea to let the concrete follow the terrain, except for the step up into his bedroom, which necessitated sawing two inches off the bottom of the door. Charlie found the look that resulted quite in keeping with the wavy mud walls.

Édouard helped Charlie fashion a concrete channel along the base of the front wall of the house. Together they poured a square concrete slab by the corner. This, Charlie said, was for his drinking water. "You'll see when I'm back from Franceville," he said, and he left carrying the second of the barrels he'd left intact.

Charlie returned a day later with the barrel full of diesel fuel. He rolled it off the truck and into the rickety storehouse where he stood it upright. He opened the bung and stuck in a hand pump. This was how he would refuel.

He had brought back more two-by-fours and plywood. He also had an aluminum sink, and plumbing fixtures for the counter he was going to build under the eastern window in his kitchen, that was full of the morning sun.

Édouard helped him cut a hole in a sheet of plywood and build a frame. As they worked, down at the other end of the village a vehicle stopped at the schoolyard. There was a commotion of passengers. Charlie and Édouard carried the plywood inside. They were tacking it to the frame under the window when Milla's overloaded bush taxi roared by in low gear. He and his passengers all had their eyes on Charlie's house, trying to see what was going on inside. Jonas, the village schoolteacher, sat among the passengers in back.

Jonas' sister, Ntchaga Justine, sat in the cab, in the middle seat, which Milla always gave her so he could flirt, though Justine always ignored his advances. Along with Jonas, her twin brothers, Mbou and Mpiga, also rode in back. They were all on their way to celebrate New Year's in Onga. A sour-smelling woman on her way to the Congo sat next to the passenger door, embarrassed at having been carsick two times. Passing Charlie's house, a pickup parked outside, Justine caught a glimpse through the window of a white face and the signs of improvements going on inside.

Milla said, "That's one of the new Americans."

The new American drove the last nail into the counter as Lalish looked on through the window, updating the records he kept in his well-thumbed blank tablet that contained everything he had ever written down. He noted with his dry Bic pen that the otangani was now down on his hands and knees poking holes in the mud walls beneath the counter, while outside Édouard was cutting a perfectly good sheet of new aluminum roofing lengthwise in three, using a machete. The white man came outside and with Édouard fashioned the three lengths of aluminum into a gutter they hung under the eave. Lalish wrote how they were nailing together a wooden stand on the concrete slab. When the otangani boosted a rain barrel onto it, Lalish asked Édouard, "What's he saying?" to get it on record.

"He says the bottom of the barrel is two inches higher than the sink."

Lalish scrawled as Charlie took the barrel off the stand. He sat astride it and drilled a half-inch hole in the barrel. Lalish clucked his tongue at the waste. The otangani had just ruined the barrel. He and Édouard watched Charlie stick a half-inch length of threaded bronze pipe wrapped with a generous amount of Teflon tape into the hole. Charlie had Édouard hold the pipe steady while he stuck his arm down in and tightened the nut. Then Charlie lifted the barrel onto the stand and covered it with plastic mesh. When the rains started next month, had there not been a hole drilled in the barrel, it would collect water off the roof, and the mesh would keep out leaf litter and prevent mosquitoes from breeding. But the barrel had a hole in it, a length of pipe sticking out. It would not hold water.

Back in the kitchen, Charlie lay on his back and screwed the drainpipe to the sink. He twisted the elbow joint to run the pipe out the bigger of the two holes he had poked in the wall, to drain into the concrete channel. He clamped one end of the plastic hose to the gooseneck faucet, and he slid the other end out through the second hole. Édouard followed the American outside and watched him clamp the end of the hose to the pipe in the barrel. Now Édouard understood. He told Lalish water would flow through the hose to the sink, and Lalish wrote that down.

When Charlie was done, he threw the second of the intact barrels into the truck with the buckets and funnel. Édouard hopped in the cab, and with a squad of singing boys in the back, Charlie drove to Aliga Creek. By nightfall, he had running water in his house.

Charlie liked having Lalish around, a kind of mascot bleating at the goats, shooing the chickens away, a regular spectator to his projects, offering advice in gibberish and recording everything he saw in his blank tablet with his dry Bic pen. Lalish was forever imitating goats in rut, as on the first morning, when he popped up in Charlie's front window and blew out a snort like a cross between a Bronx cheer and a sneeze. He was always asking Charlie for whatever struck his fancy. "Mpa mi funke," he'd said that first day: Give me your hair.

Lalish crafted bamboo thumb pianos. He coveted socks and watches, and especially shoes, which on the plateau lasted practically forever in the sand. His favorite pair, black patent leather platform shoes, dated from the 1970s. He wore four or five pairs of socks at a time, each so ratty and worn that when he lifted a pant leg to show them off, the holes exposed the inner-next unmatched pair. When school was in session, he'd often stand by the door listening. Then later, clumping through the sand on his village rounds, wearing his platform shoes, broken watches clattering like bracelets on his wrists, a blank notebook in his back pocket, thunking tunelessly on his thumb piano, Lalish would recite the lessons he'd heard: "Eight minus four equals nine hundred. A-B-C-W-Q-R-T. I am, you are, he is. That says, that says, understood?"

Whenever he came stumping up to Charlie's house and gave off a snort, the first thing Charlie did was ask Lalish the time.

Lalish consulted his many watches. "Quatre heures moins dique. Ça dit que, ça dit que, pardon monsieur, ça dit que, donnes la cigarette."

Lalish liked to smoke, and would smoke as many cigarettes as he was given, one right after the other, so he had to be rationed. Whenever he asked, Charlie shook out one of the short little unfiltered Gabonese Fortes he'd begun keeping around to hand out to smokers, gave Lalish a light through the window, and then oftentimes asked him, how is your love life these days?

Each time Charlie asked, a sly look came over Lalish's face, and he puffed white smoke and turned his face in profile, crooked his skinny arm up on the windowsill, stuck out his lips and said, "Slip à côté, cassé!" by which he meant, just over there, he'd torn off some girl's underwear.

Libreville

The day after Christmas 1989, Harry Bowman ate a bachelor's breakfast at the coffee table in his living room, watching TV. He lived alone in a three-bedroom bungalow in Charbonnage, a neighborhood near Léon Mba Airport. He was putting his stamp on the Peace Corps program, especially on the school builders, who once had been out of control. Animals with trucks they'd come to be called, until he put an end to their hell raising. Hector Alvarado was a gift from heaven. He showed up already believing in what Harry was trying to achieve.

As a perquisite of his job, Harry had the decoder box that enabled him to receive U.S. Armed Forces Radio and Television Service – A-Farts everyone called it – which carried American news and sports. This morning he was watching ESPN. The NFL playoffs would soon be getting underway. The Rams and the Eagles and the Steelers and the Oilers were slotted for the two wild card games.

Harry switched to CNN in time to see the anchor warn viewers they might find the following images disturbing. A handheld camera moved toward unrecognizable lumps. As it drew closer, Harry could see it was crumpled bodies, a man and a woman in winter coats. It closed in on the first, the woman, leaking a stream of blood in the snow. Then the camera panned to the man, dead on his back with his legs bent under him. Two soldiers stepped into the frame to lift up the shoulders and the head so the camera could show the face of Nicholae Ceausescu, the President of Romania, machine-gunned by firing squad on Christmas Day.

Ondili

Dabrian's mother, Ulandie, would not have hesitated to point out to her son that the villagers in Ondili were all pagans. Christmas passed without any of them noticing. New Year's Day was fast approaching, and Dabrian looked forward to the experience. The men were taking to the woods to haul in as much nyama as they were able to kill. The word nyama meant both animal and meat. The Téké language made no distinction between the two. The men of Ondili preferred to hunt with nets and dogs because that was the cheaper way. Shotgun shells were expensive, while nets lasted indefinitely. The breed of dog the Batéké raised, Basenjis, were intelligent dogs, known for their hunting skills, and for the fact that they didn't bark or bay. The men kept their dogs chronically hungry, feeding them just enough to keep them from starving while keeping their hunting skills keen.

Dabrian's main man in Ondili, Dabanyini Paul, had big splay-toed feet. His deal was if Dabrian found him shoes that fit, he would see to it the three teachers' houses got built. Dabrian took that deal, and soon construction of the teachers' houses got underway. 'Grand Paul', everyone called Dabanyini, Big Paul. Two days after Christmas, he and a few other men came by Dabrian's place to ask him to take them hunting.

Big Paul rode in the cab with a machete in his hand and a shotgun between his knees. He directed Dabrian to the junction of the Talking Tree, where a protective spirit resided. When Dabrian first heard the story, he took a picture of the massive iroko tree. People said the tree broke every chainsaw blade the road crew used, trying to cut it down. The tree spoke to the Gabonese workers and warned them if they didn't stop, they would die. They promptly threw down their tools, and the French engineer walked over to see what the commotion was about. He didn't believe what the workers said, but when he picked up the chainsaw and tried to cut the tree down himself, the tree threatened him in French.

They built the road around the talking iroko tree at the junction. A dirt road bent north toward Akièni. A tarred road led east toward

Lékoni. Big Paul directed Dabrian east onto the pavement. A short distance up onto the plateau, he directed Dabrian off the highway and straight across country, bumping and wallowing over trackless grassland toward a woodlot that Big Paul said no one had hunted in some time. A dozen men were crammed in the back with coiled nylon nets slung over their shoulders, waving their machetes and clubs and singing Téké hunting songs, dogs vomiting at their feet and trying to jump overboard.

When they reached the woodlot, the men and dogs jumped down, and while a smaller group of men took the dogs off to the other side of the woods, the remainder got busy with machetes cutting branches to prop up the nets. They strung the nets end to end in a continuous line, encompassing several hundred meters of the forest perimeter. Anything that came running out of the woods in their direction would run into the nets.

The sun was past mid-morning on a cloudless day when the men finished stringing the last nets and positioned themselves along the perimeter, twenty yards between each man. Dabrian took a few pictures of the hunters in the sun, each holding a club or a machete. There came a whistling signal that all was in readiness, and the men began to look at each other, gesturing that something was afoot. Listening hard with his city boy ears, Dabrian was the last to hear the rustling of the drivers and the dogs coming toward them through the trees. Then out from the undergrowth waddled a gleaming little animal. It scurried straight into the net at Dabrian's feet.

"Kill it! Kill it!" Big Paul shouted.

Armed only with a camera, Dabrian snapped a picture of the porcupine struggling in the blue nylon mesh as Big Paul ran over to slay it with two hard whacks of his machete.

A cry broke out from the drivers off to the left, "Bimba! Bimba! Bimba!" A loud crashing came from the woods. Something big was coming, and suddenly an antelope with long straight black horns burst from the trees with two dogs on its heels. It veered instantly toward the gap in the line left by Big Paul. He dropped his machete and shouldered the shotgun just as the bimba leaped over the net. Big Paul fired a shot that hit the bimba square in the flank, and the antelope catapulted onto its side and began to thrash in the grass, its black hooves flailing in the air. Dabrian rushed over with his camera to take a picture of the antelope as it quivered in the long grass and died.

The first day of 1990 dawned cool and overcast, and the carousing began in Ondili. This was the day, once every year, when the old people shined. By eight in the morning a singing circle had formed, old men on sling chairs in the middle drumming and shaking rattles, old women waving fly whisks and swaying their rears as they sidled around the men, hollering old chants in Téké, and taking swigs from the bottles being handed around. The old people were celebrating yet another year of life together.

In the afternoon, the women brought tables outdoors and loaded them with comestibles. There were hearty male shouts at all the food to eat, and all the alcohol still to be had. The quantity of bones thrown away was sufficient for the dogs to eat their fill, snarling and snapping to maintain their status in the pack.

As dusk fell, the old people retired and the young people took over, led by the Ondili dance troupe called Group Choc Ntchoulakou. In mixed French and Téké, the name meant the Despite Death Storm Troopers. They were locally renowned for having once won a prize from the former First Lady, Madame Josephine Bongo.

Two boys in the center named Boniface and Honoré pounded out a galloping beat on a pair of conga drums. Four girls chanted in singsong calls to which, on cue, all the dancers responded as one, moving in a ring around four kerosene lanterns set in the dirt. Unmarried girls and young mothers with babies on their backs swayed slowly on one side. The boys and young men capered on the other, taking turns showing off. A young man with a withered arm named Anatôle pranced about, exhorting everyone to dance harder, sing louder.

Zizi, the lead singer, wore a whistle around her neck, and when she blew it, everyone broke into the chorus, sidling around the drummers in the yellow circle of light. Zizi blew the whistle. The children dropped to all fours and made a bucking motion with their backbones. Zizi's whistle shrilled again and the children leaped to their feet. The boys clapped their hands. The drummers beat harder and quicker, their drumming like hooves on a bridge. At another whistle signal, the whole group sang out. Anatôle shook his good arm overhead, high stepping it around the circle. There was a woman's trilling ululation, the young men bouncing, the drummers' heads bobbing, their hands a blur over the drumheads, the beat strong and wild and flowing, and then at a whistle the dancers all clapped as one, a feral sound, loose motion, and then another whistle, and the drums boomed louder still. The smallest children jiggled in place. The older ones rolled their eyes, their hands limp, their mouths hanging open. One poor little girl stood stock-still crying as all around her the heated bodies moved to the thunderous drums.

Dabrian sought out a place among the young men. They made room for him and shouted, "C'est bien! C'est bien!" Zizi yelled out even louder. The dancers responded, drums, voices of children, boys and young men, young women and girls, hips bumping, hands clapping, a happy loose serpentine motion. Zizi blew her whistle rhythmically. Motion, darkness, smiling faces in lamplight, hearts and bodies, souls and minds, voices singing, singing, singing a glad song rising to heaven.

At that instant, Dabrian saw himself back under the Friday night lights with an alto sax in his hands. His high school boasted just about the hottest damn marching band in the city. They wore white and royal blue flattop shakos with shields, chin straps, visors and white plumes, white spats over black shoes and white capes over blue tunics. Fifty strong, maneuvering in tight formation, they performed the pinwheel, the crisscross, a dozen variations of the high-step called the chair. They blasted out *Funkytown*, *Love Train*, *Super Freak*, the pompom girls leggy eye candy in satin white short-shorts and white boots shaking silver-blue pompoms and shimmying to the snippety-snack click-clack of the drum corps, and right there in Ondili, Dabrian broke into the step-and-slide, the foot drag, and when Group Choc Ntchoulakou saw him, they shrieked in approval.

6. One Degree South

Otou

A large map of Gabon hung on the wall of Rebecca's front room, a small circle drawn around her village and another around Charlie's. Otou and Okouya lay fifteen kilometers apart on the western edge of the plateau, at nearly the same latitude, one degree south of the equator. Along the foot of the western face of the escarpment flowed Kampini Creek, which wasn't featured on the map. Both villages used it as their source of water.

A well-trod footpath led out of Otou to a steep grassy slope. When the schoolteacher dismissed them, girls and boys rushed in a flock down the flank of the plateau strung out by age, the older ones whooping and scampering ahead, younger children toddling uncertainly behind, pausing at the steeper spots to sit on their bottoms and slide. Downhill they'd go to a stream hidden in the forest below. The oldest and fastest children disappeared into the woods first.

Kampini Creek was wider and deeper at Otou than at Okouya, which was closer to the source. All around, the restless forest rustled and rang with the shouts of children. Rebecca loved to sit on a knife-scarred stump on the bank, her feet in the flowing water and take it all in, watching the women washing clothes on a log that Ongongi Faustin had placed on top of a small dam he had built, thinking to be constructing a fish-breeding pond. When he hauled the last thin log out of the forest on his head, Faustin spotted a passing column of army ants, voracious nomads moving through the undergrowth in their thousands. He set the log down, waved Rebecca over and caught a grasshopper that he gave to the ants. The ants cut the grasshopper to pieces in a matter of minutes. Rebecca poked at their column with a stick. The soldiers formed a protective tunnel of scissoring mandibles through which the bustling torrent of workers hurried on.

The sun shone bright through the trees when Faustin stacked the last loose log across the creek, expecting the water to back up into a pool. But it didn't. The clear water swept through the chinks in the logs, and over the course of several weeks sand accumulated upstream while the flowing water eroded out a hollow downstream. Now the women were able to stand on the downstream side in water up to their waist and use the top of the dam as a surface to wash clothes, working without bending over. Thus, the dam was an accidental success.

With yellow cakes of soap and stiff brushes, the women scrubbed their laundry clean, their breasts bobbling in time with their arms. They plunged the clothes to rinse them and then wrung them out and waded over to toss them into woven baskets on the bank.

Upstream, other women, bent over, straight-backed and lock-kneed, washed plates, glasses, silverware, crockery and sooty cookware using wads of grass and sand to scour. Girls waded further upstream to fill green glass demijohns with water they would later carry up to the village.

The boys at the creek did nothing but engage in horseplay, slapping each other and racing off into the woods in high-spirited games of tag. The youngest children plashed by the creek banks, some hugging themselves, their teeth chattering.

Sitting on a stump with her feet in the chill stream, the shimmering green forest all around, boys splashing and shouting, women and girls working with repetitive motions, for Rebecca going to the creek was a glimpse of what the world would have been like had there been no apples in Eden. A woman paused in her labors to adjust her slipping pagne, opening it without quite opening it, tugging it tighter and then tucking it fast. Another woman stacked pots and plates with a clatter and clank. Two little boys squatted to inspect skating water bugs. A girl waded downstream towing a submerged demijohn full of water by its neck. A woman washing told a story that made all the other women lean back cackling with laughter, their faces glowing, teeth and eyes flashing, clapping their soapy hands. A naked little boy with big eyes and a fat belly came sloshing over to Rebecca, his skin aglitter with droplets of water, and he placed his small iced chocolate hand on Rebecca's knee, and with the other solemnly held up for her to see a bright red feather dripping wet.

Okouya

Next to the shiny white gas stove in Charlie's kitchen sat a shiny green kerosene refrigerator, just arrived all the way from Libreville. His new appliances had come with a cement mixer, a metal locker full of tools, and a dozen boxed wheelbarrows that Charlie had to assemble. All of the new sites got the same delivery, for Timo was back on the road, back in his glory, back behind the wheel of a ten-ton four-wheel-drive yellow behemoth of a dump truck, supplying all the Peace Corps schools in two provinces as fast as he could.

Charlie had carpentered a double bed for visitors in the spare bedroom, shelves in his own bedroom for clothes, bookshelves in the salon for his paperback novels, and a cupboard in the kitchen for his dishes. With a counter and sink, running water and concrete floors, the new kerosene refrigerator and gas stove gave Charlie all the creature comforts he could ask for, and he was ready to start building the teachers' houses.

First, he planned to ask the chief to hold a palaver. This was Rebecca's idea. "A palaver," she explained, "is the appropriate way to discuss and agree on important rules. I held one in Otou, Charlie," she said, "and you should do the same."

Charlie asked Édouard to come with him and translate the request to Chief Oyamba, who lived in the biggest house in the village, as befit the nkani-ntsie, the great land chief of the westernmost Louzou. Oyamba only used one room anymore, eating, sleeping and receiving visitors in what had once been the salon, where he kept a perpetual fire burning. He sat in a sling chair next to the fire flanked by several stools for visitors, a filthy, unmade bed pushed against the back wall.

Édouard and Charlie entered, shook hands with the old man and took seats. Édouard told his father the otangani had a request. Charlie asked Chief Oyamba to convene a palaver and explained why it was necessary.

The old land chief nodded when he understood the request. He and his son conferred in Téké. After some time, Chief Oyamba agreed. That night, he walked through the village crying out that every man should come to the palaver the following day.

The men came in the late afternoon carrying sling chairs they unfolded facing the towering mango tree. Butts of green beer bottles buried upside down ringed the base of the village flagpole nearby. Charlie was given a place under the tree next to Chief Oyamba and the chief's son, Édouard, facing the men, who kept an attentive eye on Charlie. Charlie could feel their anticipation.

When everyone had gathered, Édouard stood up and said, "Monsieur Charlie called you here to make an important announcement." He gestured for Charlie stand.

Charlie hated public speaking. With Édouard translating into Téké, he explained that before starting construction on the school, the villagers would have to build three teachers' houses. "You will not be paid for work on the teachers' houses. I want to see who puts in the most time and works hardest. I will hire and pay those ten men to build the school."

The announcement set off a lot of excited chatter. The next morning, plenty of volunteers gathered in front of Charlie's house at first light. They came with machetes and axes and clambered into the back of his truck.

Charlie followed directions to a nearby bosquet, one of many small stands of timber scattered about the plateau. He walked with the men single file down a narrow trail into the woods, and the men fanned out into the dense growth and began cutting down small straight hardwood trees they selected, whacking and hacking and making loud yodeling sounds as they felled the saplings and lopped off the branches. They dragged the surprisingly heavy thin trunks out to the trail, and Charlie helped lug the poteaux to the truck, making mental notes about the men.

Édouard was there, Charlie's first friend in the village, son of Chief Oyamba and heir apparent, a reliable helper all along. It was Édouard who found a man to do Charlie's laundry. Eloumba Jean-Paul was there, the village carpenter, furniture maker and scrivener with a goatee and high cheekbones. There was Oloumba Bruno, a quiet family man with a brilliant smile, and Oyali Albert, a loud mouth with bad teeth who always offered opinions nobody listened to. Albert had worked as a rod buster building the hospital in Akièni. There was Oyamba Benjamin, named, as were both his two older brothers, Jacques and Hilaire, after the land chief of the westernmost Louzou. Benjamin, a bachelor, was the village drunk, enabled by the fact that the middle brother Jacques owned Okouya's only bar. Hilaire, the oldest, was blind, mute and partially paralyzed from a stroke, although people said it was because he once threw away the bones of a twin. Benjamin spoke with a permanent slur and his sweat smelled of alcohol, but somehow he showed up every day, and said he had papers showing he'd worked five years as a mason, as had Assélé Laurent, who showed up regularly too. But Laurent had an attitude, always bellyaching, griping and grousing about this and that in Téké, so Charlie wouldn't understand. Charlie noticed the other men tried to avoid Laurent. The few teenage boys who had stayed on in Okouya after finishing primary school turned out. They liked to hang around Charlie, happy to try out their French, happy to ride in the truck, helping load and unload the poteaux.

One afternoon, heading out empty for another load, Charlie felt a sharp twinge in his gut. The boys were singing in the back, but abruptly, he needed the privacy of a latrine. Spotting a bosquet to the left, he steered urgently toward it. The boys yelled, "No, this is the wrong way!" but Charlie stopped, grabbed a roll of toilet paper from the glove box, leaped out and hurried toward the trees. The boys understood.

Charlie hastened into the woods, pushing aside branches, far enough to be screened from the truck. He turned and dropped his drawers just in time to avoid soiling himself. Some guys go the whole two years with the Hershey squirts, their volunteer leader Jim Bonaventure had joked, a few days after Charlie arrived in Libreville. You're going to miss farting with confidence.

The chirping and twittering of birds filled the woods. Charlie could hear the voices of the adolescent boys, and as he let nature run its course, he didn't notice at first when the birds suddenly fell silent. Squatting vulnerable in the muted green light, he sensed something far back behind him, deeper in the woods. His most primitive senses grew aroused. The hair on the back of his neck stood erect, and his nostrils flared. Was it an animal? The leaves of the trees and the brush seemed to be quivering, making a sound like whispering voices. He couldn't hear anything except the rustling of leaves, and then the trees began to sway, began lashing their branches violently about, for a thing long dormant had been disturbed, an ancient thing with many names, coming for Charlie like a wraith through the leaves.

Scudding clouds blew across the faded blue sky in the gusting wind that had blown up from nowhere when Charlie came racing out of the woods. The boys were pointing at something lifting out of the grass, an eagle rising into the air with a writhing snake gripped in its talons. They exclaimed as the eagle flapped its powerful wings and flew away, and they didn't see Charlie running toward the truck with consternation all over his face.

Akièni

The weekly Air Gabon flight brought the mail to Akièni every Thursday at two o'clock. Every Thursday at noon, Charlie piled a dozen or so villagers chosen on a rotating basis in his truck and drove them to town to do some shopping. Édouard with his chipped front tooth always got a spot if he wanted, as did Eloumba Jean-Paul, the village scrivener, the person responsible for Okouya's mail. Jean-Paul was shy. His pointed goatee accentuated his hollow cheeks. He laughed at almost everything Charlie said, in order to avoid making a reply. The deep-voiced schoolteacher Ngaleka Jonas always got a spot too, whenever he wanted to come.

Each week Charlie stopped in Otou, where normally Rebecca climbed aboard for the trip into town. She received ten times the mail Charlie did, a lot of it books and journal articles her former professors sent. She never failed to remind others that she had her sights set on graduate school, deferred at three universities to complete Peace Corps service.

One Thursday, Charlie had three pretty girls dressed up for town crammed in the cab with him. When he wallowed through the bad spots, the girls were tossed from side to side. They whooped and wrapped their arms around each other, laughing like it was a carnival ride, their slender thighs straining the light fabric of their dresses, a tangle of young female flesh he wished he could somehow insinuate himself into.

Whenever he was in town, no matter who he was with, Charlie always drank at a little hole-in-the-wall tavern called the Bouchon. The owner Papa Clément was a diminutive man with a grandiose mustache. He had nailed green and orange bottle caps in a wavering line around the interiors of the warped plywood walls, believing his establishment to be named the Bottle Cap Bar. Rebecca once pointed out to him in amusement that the word bouchon meant cork. The word for bottle cap was capsule, but Papa Clément didn't care. It was too late to change anyway. The walls were painted brown, white and blue in an ugly checkerboard pattern that Rebecca considered quite cheerful. Dusty record jackets, their contents long ago ruined, were displayed on the walls as posters. The phonograph no longer worked. The cement floor was chipped and cracked. A plywood counter served as the bar. A tired electric refrigerator powered by the state-owned diesel generators on the Lékoni River under the bridge on the highway south out of town chilled beer and soft drinks.

Sometimes Hector came across the bridge to join them, and whenever he did, he talked incessantly about all he was doing setting up for *stage*, and he interrogated Charlie and Rebecca about the progress they were making. Rebecca hated that, and always changed the subject to the topics she preferred, the entertaining things she was observing in Gabon; the best things back in America; her favorite foods; the good books she'd read; the best music and movies. And politics, always politics.

While Charlie enjoyed cold beers in the Bottle Cap Bar, the villagers he brought to town shopped for victuals. Malians and Senegalese owned all the boutiques in Akièni, la petite commerce being a livelihood the Gabonese considered beneath them. Owning a bar was the exception. Lots of Gabonese owned bars, and the bars were always full of Gabonese, they being a nation of ambianceurs, a term they liked, meaning party animals.

Papa Clément's daughter, Isabelle, a young single mother, did most of the work running the Bouchon. "She isn't paid," said Rebecca. "It's a typical arrangement." It was a Thursday, and Hector wasn't at the bar. "The attitude of Gabonese men toward work is completely the opposite of Americans," Rebecca pronounced, "the Japanese too, for that matter."

Outside, the afternoon sun was blinding. Inside, the metal roof cracked and popped from the heat. Jonas at the bar with Charlie's money, buying a second round, was talking with Isabelle, and Rebecca was speaking to Charlie in English. "Think about small town Middle America. Think of the equivalent of Akièni, the little bank on Main Street, the feed store, hardware store, volunteer fire department, a school named after a president, three or four churches, a diner or two, maybe a movie theater, gas stations on either end of town, a Little League baseball park with the Kiwanis and Rotary signs."

Charlie could see exactly what she was describing: the farming towns of Minnesota. Édouard had not come along that day, and when Jonas rejoined them, Rebecca began speaking in French, so Jonas could follow.

"Our government didn't build small town America," she said. "The people did. That's the difference with Gabon. Here, the government builds everything. Bongo and his people do it with a portion of the wealth they don't extract for themselves. The elites all unite around Bongo and maintain him in power to protect the process of pumping out the oil, in order to maintain their share of the money. This suits the French just fine. They get preferential access to Gabon's resources. The ordinary people get screwed, but they don't do anything about it, because they fear the state. They've all heard what happens to anybody who dares talk back. The law is terrifying to ordinary people. The law protects only the powerful. The best that ordinary people can hope for is someday to have a government job. That's why they don't revolt. You see what I'm saying, Jonas? Tell me if you disagree. Bongo doesn't want what you find in small town America, problem-solving self-reliant people who question authority and demand their rights. He wants his people to depend on the government, which is the opposite of what we're taught to be like in America. In Gabon, the political leaders want the people to be passive, want them to fear authority, don't you agree?"

The schoolteacher in Otou, Ondinga Gustave, liked talking politics with Rebecca. The topic of politics made Jonas profoundly uncomfortable, and he looked relieved when a massive red rooster strutted in the front door, looked about, and began pecking at the cracked floor. Jonas hissed at the rooster, and it strutted back out.

"Have you ever wondered how it is the people in the villages always seem to have ready cash? Do you know where they get it from?"

Charlie refilled his glass, thinking of the shoppers he'd brought to town. Where indeed did they get their money?

"Those who have an income are expected to share with their kin who don't. One scholar has called it the economy of affection. The obligations of kinship and tribe require Africans to help their relatives. It's one of the reasons a middle class hasn't formed. Everyone is constantly being bled by their relatives. It impedes the accumulation of capital."

The big red rooster came strutting back in. Jonas hissed at it again, and waved his arm, and this time it fluttered back out the door.

Rebecca loved applying the theories she read in books to the customs and practices she observed in Gabon. "In a patronage system, Jonas, in a country like Gabon, it's actually possible to maximize leisure and minimize work, at least if you're a man. This doesn't extend to women, of course. They're expected to work, and work hard. It's their lot in life. While the men, don't you agree, Jonas, spend their time waiting for things to come to them, whether it's their meals brought to them by their women, or money from their kinfolk in the cities, or something from the government. Of course, this isn't the case for all men. You, Jonas, for example, are a teacher and you work for a living. The bar owners like Papa Clément actually have a bit of entrepreneurial spirit, although the real work usually is done by their unpaid female relatives, as you can see here."

Rebecca's glasses caught the light, her blue eyes happy, and she nodded in the direction of Isabelle, sitting on a stool beside the bar cutting nkoumou. Isabelle smiled back at Rebecca.

"Money for nothing," Charlie said, "and the chicks for free."

"But now, the students have gone on strike at the university," said Rebecca, "and the execution of Ceausescu has sent a shock wave through the continent. That's why Bongo summoned the

93

Central Committee of the PDG into session. Do you know about this, Jonas? Are you following world events? Is democratic change coming to Gabon? You have to ask, is multiparty democracy even possible in Africa? What do you think?"

Jonas mumbled something.

Rebecca hardly stopped for breath. She kept on as she always did, and began examining all sides of the question. "Democracy requires an active and informed citizenry. So you have to ask, is democracy even possible in the developing world, where people value socializing more than they value material goods, and governments have to contend with a backward-bending labor supply curve?"

Charlie tuned Rebecca out, watching Isabelle cut nkoumou, sipping his cold beer on a hot day while the villagers from Okouya shopped, until the roar of the Fokker went by low overhead, coming in for a landing. That was the signal for Charlie's passengers to come straggling back lugging demijohns of kerosene and baskets laden with salt, sugar, onions, matches, canned sardines, tomato paste, packets of razor blades, bundles of salted codfish, bolts of cloth, some of the men with sacks of rice on their shoulders.

When they had loaded their purchases and climbed aboard the Land Cruiser, Charlie drove down to the post office. Eloumba Jean-Paul came in with Charlie and Rebecca. On the other side of the wall into which the mailboxes were built the clerks were sorting the mail. Rebecca called to them through the open door of the mailbox she shared with Charlie, joking with them, yelling that she knew they were holding back on her. There had to be more.

Okouya

That evening, a motherly woman named Bernadette brought Charlie dinner. This happened frequently, usually around sunset, always a different woman, sometimes two, delivering food in lacquered tin ware bowls, a bit of bush meat if someone's husband had luck, nkoumou with mushrooms, manioc leaves with salted fish, black and green caterpillars or termites, onguélé or fou-fou, usually with hot pepper sauce on the side. The women of the village pitied Charlie, separated from his family, far from home, and they

94

never asked him for money.

Charlie knew what they were doing. They wanted him to hire their husbands.

The young boys were always begging him to drive them to Aliga Creek and wash the truck, or out to the old village to pick from the abundant fruit trees there. Charlie always got a clean truck out of the deal, or a bucket of avocados, or limes, or mangos.

The girls of the village brought him things as well. It began one Sunday afternoon when Charlie was sitting outside his house reading a novel, enjoying a late afternoon breeze, when a slap of water hit the sand. A girl named Chantalle approached with a bucket on her head, one arm up, her hand steadying the bucket, water splashing down her wet sarong. She wore no bra. Her nipples were puckered and her wet round buttocks shifted as she walked by, turning her eyes to give Charlie a smoldering sidelong look that made him forget what he was reading.

That night there was a knock and there she was at his door, short legs hurrying in so as not to be seen, a long waist and small breasts that disappeared when she lay on her back and let Charlie shuck her out of her panties. When they were done, Chantalle said she wanted two sheets of plywood for her uncle and a new dress for herself and a job for her father.

Chantalle was the first of many. A few nights later, Pétronie, a young woman with wide hips and thick ankles brought him supper. She liked it on top, and wanted six meters of wax cloth, a soccer ball for her brothers, and a job for her dad. She was followed by Josephine, tall by Batéké standards with big eyes, skinny calves, and an alarming gouge from her navel to her pubic bone, the first mother Charlie had ever slept with, hot-bodied and rubbery, demanding that he drive her, batter her, cleave her in two. When she left his house before first light he was so drained he could barely open one eye. She wanted clothes for her daughter, which Charlie felt odd buying. She also wanted a job for her brother.

The girlfriends seemed to have a rotation worked out. They didn't want exclusive rights. They just wanted the stuff they asked for, that and a promise of jobs for their male relatives. As far as Charlie was concerned, the cost of the gifts he bought them when he was in town was more than offset by the free food and sex he was getting in the village.

But the question of jobs was worrisome.

Every evening, Édouard paid a call on his father, Oyamba Paul, the nkani-ntsie, the great land chief of the westernmost Louzou, and recounted the events of the day. Increasingly the discussions were about the things the otangani was doing.

"He has prodigious appetites," said Édouard. "He is bedding all the girls in the village. They say he uses something on his bangala, a balloon."

That puzzled old Chief Oyamba. "Why would he do that?"

"Who knows? We don't know how things are where he comes from."

"That is true."

"He buys the girls gifts when he goes to town."

The old chief reflected on this. "That is well, but the men who are cutting the poteaux, it takes up their whole day."

"Yes, he is in a hurry with the work, this otangani. He is making things happen at a pace never seen before."

"That is the way with them," said Oyamba, and he told of the Frenchman long ago, before independence, who came in a truck every year, making the rounds of the villages, buying the harvests of tobacco and coffee. Oyamba wondered where he had gone. Perhaps he had gone back to France. Perhaps he was dead.

"I suppose we must do as the otangani wants," the old chief said, "because Bongo has sent him here."

Once Eloumba Jean-Paul judged they had hauled in sufficient poteaux, he sent one group of men into the forest to cut vines they brought back looped in coils, and he put the remainder of them to work with axes and machetes, sharpening one end of each poteau. As this was going on, Jean-Paul began to lay out the three teachers' houses. Charlie asked him if he knew the principle of the 3-4-5 triangle.

"Of course," said Jean-Paul. "A-squared plus B-squared equals C-squared. I learned it in school. All the houses will be nine meters by twelve," he said, "and we will measure the diagonals to ensure they are fifteen meters, so the houses will be square."

Charlie helped Jean-Paul use stakes and mason's line to lay out the three houses, and held the end of the thirty-meter tape measure. He and Jean-Paul double-checked all the diagonals and then Jean-Paul organized a third team of men to set the studs. These men used machetes to dig narrow, meter-deep holes at half-meter intervals along the lines, and then they rammed the sharpened end of the poteaux like pile drivers into the holes, until the poteaux stood upright on their own.

While the men were setting the studs, Charlie drove to Obia where Timo had recently delivered a shipment of lumber, and Hector let Charlie take all he could haul. When Charlie returned, the studs for the walls of the first house were set, and Jean-Paul was sawing the last of the tops to length. Charlie unloaded the lumber and joined in with the men who began nailing two-by-four plates to the tops of the poteaux, to align the walls. Then they began framing the roof. They used planks as the ridge board, and two-by-fours for the rafters and purlins, and when the roof was nearing completion, Charlie went to get another load of lumber.

The following afternoon Charlie stood on a ladder in the racket of hammers framing the roof of the second house. As he fished for a nail in his tool pouch, he happened to glance into the trees on the other side of the road. There was a woman half hidden in the foliage looking at him intently. The expression on her face was odd, as if she knew him, and had something vital she needed to tell him. As soon as she caught his eye, she began speaking urgently, but she did not approach, or raise her voice enough to be heard.

"Who's that?" Charlie asked Jean-Paul. "What's she want?"

Jean-Paul took hold of the two-by-four Benjamin had brought him and turned to look. "Who?"

"That woman over there," said Charlie, and pointed, but the woman was gone. "Did you see her, Édouard?"

Édouard on the ground had to take a few steps to one side to see where Charlie was pointing. He shook his head.

"There was a woman over there, trying to say something to me, a woman I never saw before."

Others began asking what this was about, looking where Charlie was pointing. There were exclamations in Téké. Charlie couldn't follow what the men were saying, and he asked someone to explain.

"It's nothing," said Édouard.

"You shouldn't worry," said Jean-Paul.

"What do you mean don't worry, it's nothing?"

Some of the men grew agitated, and two actually walked off the job, gesticulating and shaking their heads. Édouard calmed all who remained. He was the heir apparent to Oyamba Paul, their future land chief, and he commanded respect. They listened to his reassurances, and gradually resumed working, but they kept talking among themselves.

"What are they saying?"

Édouard shook his head. He would not say. No one would. Charlie concluded that they thought he had seen a ghost. He chuckled at their superstitions, their strange beliefs, like the way they put the bones of dead twins in boxes, and resumed nailing. But then Charlie remembered what the priest, Père Dominique had told them about sorcery on this part of the plateau, and he remembered that day in the bosquet, when the trees began beating their branches at something coming from deep in the woods, and the boys saw an eagle catch a snake. Once again, the hair on the back of his neck felt crawly to think a strange woman had just appeared to him, and then vanished.

It was only the wind in the trees, Charlie told himself, hammering with his twenty ounce Stanley, just an ordinary woman. They'll eventually clear this up. They'll find out who she was and what she wanted. Everyone will have a good laugh.

That evening sitting with his father in the salon where the nkani-ntsie kept a fire perpetually burning, Édouard told the old man what had happened. "The otangani saw a woman who spoke to him, and then disappeared."

"Was it an ofou?" asked Oyamba Paul. Was it a ghost?

"The men argued about that," said Édouard. "Some of them became upset, and two of them left. They said the otangani's project is cursed."

"Ah, if the people start believing that, it will be serious," said Chief Oyamba. "What did the woman say to the otangani?"

"He said he couldn't hear her."

"H-m-m-m. So, most likely it was an ofou. Is this a sinye babi, do you think?"

"I don't know if it's an evil sign. Perhaps the otangani was just seeing things."

Oyamba shook his head. "No, we shouldn't assume he was mistaken. He must have seen something, or he wouldn't have spoken up. What would you counsel me to do, my son?"

Édouard pulled the end of a stick from the fire and poked with it at some coals. "For now, Father, perhaps we should do nothing."

"H-m-m-m-m, yes, I can see why you say that. So I shall wait, and we shall see what comes of it."

Charlie got jittery lighting the lanterns as the sun went down. What if he had seen a ghost? What if the woman who had vanished, reappeared in his house at night with something to tell him? He recalled the urgent expression on her face. What if she appeared in the bedroom and woke him up? He imagined a vaporous shape, icy cold, and he didn't have an appetite for supper. He forced himself to eat some manioc and nkoumou. He washed the dishes then tried to resume the novel he been reading, a story set in Florida, it opened with a girl being thrown off a bridge. But he couldn't concentrate.

A soft tap on his front door made him leap from his sling chair. For several seconds, his heart racing, he was afraid to go to the door. He was relieved when he opened it to see Pétronie.

She slipped in. She had already heard the story, but she made him tell it to her. They sat at the table, and she asked him questions. She had a way of looking at him he liked, one side of her mouth tipped up in a knowing half-smile. But she wasn't smiling. She told him pointblank, "You saw a ghost."

Later, in bed, he complained, "I don't feel like it, not tonight. I just want to sleep."

Pétronie flipped his limp bangala dismissively. "You see. It's tired. Why is that?"

"Sometimes I'm not in the mood."

"Huh! Something has already started. You saw a ghost. You must consult a féticheur!"

Charlie forced a laugh. "My people don't believe in

99

witchdoctors."

"You see, that's your problem," said Pétronie. "You're not with your people anymore, Charlie. You're here with us."

Around eight the next morning, Charlie tossed an overnight bag in the truck and headed to Franceville to cash two postal money orders he had received in the mail, his monthly stipend and his petty cash reimbursement. He would be doing a lot of shopping. He was low on coffee and out of beer and he needed to buy the corrugated aluminum roofing sheets for the teachers' houses and more nails, and that month's gifts for the girlfriends. Jean-Paul, Édouard and about a dozen men had begun the job of weaving in the walls of the teachers' houses with vines when Charlie rolled past in his Land Cruiser. He waved and honked the horn on his way out of Okouya.

An overcast day, Charlie drove alone across the plateau, his boom box wedged up under the dash. He put on Guns N' Roses. When the song *Welcome to the Jungle* came on, he smiled at the congruence, and cranked up the volume.

But he couldn't shake the willies, even here driving across the beautiful Batéké Plateau in broad daylight listening to loud rock and roll. Talking about it with his countrymen would help. He stopped at Rebecca's house in Otou.

They sat in her salon drinking coffee. He asked her what she thought about witchcraft.

Rebecca immediately elevated the question into abstraction, and related it to what they'd learned about cultural immersion back in Philadelphia. "The villagers," she said, "often see a perfectly ordinary thing as something that isn't at all ordinary. Do you know what I mean?"

"Not really," he replied.

"As Americans, we grow up knowing immigrants, at least if we live in cities. Immigrants are everywhere. There are always people around speaking English with accents. Outsiders can never completely assimilate. It's no different in Gabon. The best we can do is try to immerse ourselves in the culture, but there's no way for us to integrate fully. Not in two years. The amount of understanding we share with the villagers is always going to be very limited."

"I don't know," said Charlie, wanting to discuss the subject in more practical terms. "The way all the men reacted when I said I saw a woman who disappeared. And before that, the feeling I got out there in the woods, when I had the runs. I'm not sure these things were just my imagination."

Rebecca scoffed and hooked her hair behind her ears. She took off her glasses and polished them on the hem of a pagne she wore like a village woman. "Don't fool yourself, Charlie. Of course it was just your imagination playing tricks on you. It was just the wind, like you said, when you went into the woods. And when you were framing the roof, you were the only one who thought a woman was there. It was probably just a trick of light in the trees. I mean really, get a grip. Come on."

In Obia, Hector climbed up out of the trench where he was building a lead. His shirt off, speckled with cement, Hector was pleased as always to see Charlie. He showed Charlie around the site, proudly explaining the progress he was making. "The footings are poured. I've got a crew laying the stem walls of the foundation." Hector pointed to a covered shed some distance away. "Laborers are busy with molds casting cinderblock. There's another crew roofing the teachers' houses."

"Impressive," said Charlie.

"I refuse to be bound by the ten-man rule," said Hector. "Not for *stage*. I've hired every man in the village who wants a job, and I've asked the chief to call in more, from Akièni or Franceville or wherever. Any reasonably fit man who presents himself, I'll hire him. I'm going to break the record again."

Walking together back toward Hector's workstation, Charlie told him things were going good in Okouya. "The teachers' houses are coming along. You should drive out sometime and visit."

Hector sensed something in Charlie's voice, something amiss. "Anything bothering you, buddy?"

"Well," said Charlie, "since you mention it, weird things have been happening lately."

"Yeah, like what?"

Charlie told Hector about the wind in the bosquet, and the woman who vanished.

"That's spooky," said Hector, looking deep into Charlie's eyes.

"One of the villagers says I need to see a féticheur."

"Yeah?"

Charlie nodded. He didn't mention it was a girlfriend, Pétronie.

"A curandero," said Hector.

"What?"

"A kind of faith healer. My grandfather used to tell me about them. They practice traditional ways of healing, folk remedies. Their abilities are a gift from God, people say. The curandero is much respected in the community. He is different from the brujo. The curandero heals. The brujo uses evil spells. People ask the curandero to release a person from the spells of the brujo."

"Huh. So what you're saying is you think I should see a féticheur too?"

"I don't know. Hey, I got to get back to work. Good luck with all that, Charlie."

"Yeah, well, I got to get going too," said Charlie, laughing despite his unease. "Maybe," he said, shaking Hector's hand, "now I got a ghost story to tell."

Charlie returned to Obia a few days later to meet Timo, the little fireplug of a man with a radiant smile who put his arms out and hugged him, then grabbed his hand and shook it. Talking a mile a minute, Timo shook hands with the half dozen men Charlie had brought with him, along with shovels and planks to the rendezvous.

"This is Catta-peel-AHR," said Timo, pointing to the brutish Nissan model UD TZA dump truck with a long boxy snout, Caterpillar, because it was yellow, like an earth-moving machine. It was the first time Charlie had actually seen the truck. All the deliveries he had received from Timo to this point had been unloaded at Obia, Hector's village. Timo led Charlie around Caterpillar, loaded with two hundred sacks of cement, and proudly pointed out the features of the four-wheel-drive dump truck. They were going to drive the load right through to Okouya.

"You know, my brudder," said Timo, as he spread his arms out joyously to encompass Hector coming over to say hello, "we get all de nex' t'ings we need. Yah, now we must go flog it down!"

Ntchaga Justine sat next to Milla with her twin brothers in the back. They had dropped off Jonas in Okouya. Their two-week New Year's holiday was over, and they were on the way back to Akièni. She was thinking about what she would find at the hospital when she got there. Dr. Muengo, the Zairian, would still be in Kinshasa with his family.

Milla slowed. There was a situation ahead. A shiny yellow truck had sunk to its axles in the sand, blocking the way. Milla yelled out his window to the people in back, "Hang on!" He cranked the wheel, gunned the engine and turned the taxi, cracking through bracken. Branches clawed the truck's sides until it jounced down onto an alternate route. They passed the yellow truck at some distance. Sweating men with shovels shouted and dug sand from around its wheels. The enormous otangani who lived in Okouya was there. He watched them pass, and raised a hand in greeting.

The whole village turned out to gawk when Timo pulled into the village with two hundred sacks of cement. All puffed out with pride at making it through the deep plateau sand, his new truck the center of attention, Timo blatted the horn once to thrill the kids. While Charlie and his workers unloaded the cargo like a trail of ants, Timo walked around chatting with the onlookers. The small sized village men fairly tottered under the weight of the hundred pound sacks when they tried to carry one on their shoulders as Charlie did. After one or two tries, they paired up to carry the sacks between them at waist level.

When they finished, there was still enough daylight for Charlie to take Timo down to Kampini Creek for a bath. Men had cleared a route through the brushy timber behind the village so that Charlie could drive part way there. The pickup truck lurched and wallowed over roots and stumps on the big knobby Michelin tires, branches lashing the windshield, the tailgate chains slapping behind.

Charlie told Timo about the experience in the bosquet, how he had sensed something, like an evil spirit. Or was it just the wind blowing? He told Timo about the woman who appeared, half concealed in the forest, needing to talk to him, a woman he had never seen before, trying to tell him something he couldn't hear. She had vanished, and since then hadn't reappeared. Was she a ghost? Or had he just been seeing things? What did Timo think of all this?

Timo frowned. "What you say is very serious," he said, speaking French. "You know, there are things here in Africa that are very different from how things are in America. The things you describe should be taken seriously." He switched to his broken English. "You know, my brudder, de ones dat come to tell you about t'ings, dey telling you dese people sometimes try to kill you out, tout de suite. You mus' leave dem like you find dem, you know."

Charlie was about to ask a question when suddenly a powerful force flipped the front of the truck into the air, whipped the steering wheel out of his hands and banged Timo's head against the door pillar.

"Jesus!" exclaimed Charlie as he hit the brakes, "what was that?" He looked at Timo. "You okay?" Had they run over a stump?

"Yah," said Timo, rubbing his head.

They got out to have a look. It was a stump, sure enough. They checked to make sure there was no damage to the tire, or the truck, and then got back in and resumed their way.

With his mournful eyes and a sly smile beneath his pencil mustache, Timo asked, "Est-ce qu'on va bien dormir ce soir?" wanting to know if they would sleep well tonight. He wasn't talking about ghosts. He wanted to know if there would be girls.

Charlie laughed as they came out of the timber and headed down the escarpment.

"You know," said Timo, taking no notice of the magnificent view of the rain forest below, sweeping away to the horizon, "de African ladies not like de ladies you get in de States. De African ladies is de ol' school, you know."

Three young women bent under heavy baskets on their backs were coming up the steep hill. Charlie recognized them. It was two of the girlfriends, Chantalle and Josephine, and another girl named Alphonsine.

"Tell dem we give dem a ride," Timo said.

Charlie angled his truck over and eased to a stop alongside the young women. They were leaning forward almost parallel to the hillside under the cruel weight of the baskets on their backs, leaking sour-smelling water from the lumps of raw soaked manioc root.

Timo limped swiftly around the front of the truck. "Bonjour!" he cried to the girls with a dazzling smile, "Here," he fawned, "let me help you with those."

Standing on the steep hillside the girls glanced at Charlie for a sign as Timo relieved them of their burdens. His biceps bulged from the strain of each basket as he lugged it under a tree.

"We're going down for a bath," he told them, leaning the third basket upright against the others. "You three wait right here and rest. When we come back, we'll haul your manioc for you."

The girls exchanged glances, and looked at Charlie again.

"Now, don't any of you move!" Timo commanded, and then he clambered back in the cab and grinned at Charlie like a satyr. "Let's go!" he shouted as he slammed the door, and cawed in approval like a raven.

Charlie took his foot from the brake.

"Hee hee HEE!" cackled Timo, grabbing onto the handhold above the glove box as the truck went bouncing downward. "Yah! Dat's de ol' school, you know!"

At the forest verge, Charlie swung the Land Cruiser around and gunned it to face back uphill. He got out with his towel and his toilet kit and looked up at the girls sitting on the hillside. He waved, and they waved back.

"Il faut attendre là!" Timo called to them, telling them to wait.

Then Timo followed Charlie hurrying into the woods along the steep footpath downhill to the stream. Timo chortled and chattered away. There were no voices ringing through the forest, so Charlie knew they would have the creek to themselves, a luxury he seldom enjoyed. They were able to strip to wash, flopping onto their bellies to get wet, a white man and a black man naked in the great green outdoors standing shin deep in the clear clean cold water lathering. They hurried because the girls were waiting, dried hastily and dressed on the creek bank, and then hustled back up the trail. Even with his limp Timo made good time.

From the looks they'd been exchanging, Charlie half expected the girls to make a break for it. But when he and Timo came huffing up out of the trees in the dying light, there they were, lazing halfway up the hill right where they had left them, chewing grass stems and chatting when Charlie steered the bouncing truck back up alongside.

"I want de black one," Timo announced, swinging open his door.

They needed sand, and Édouard knew where there was a choice deposit. "It's not far," he said, "in a valley a half kilometer from the village, just to the east."

Charlie began blazing a trail there with whichever men and boys came along to help on a given day. They chipped away the grass and began to open up what would become an ever-deepening hole in the valley floor. They filled the Land Cruiser with as much sand as it could hold, and coming back the frame bounced off the rear differential. The diesel engine growled and shrieked by turns, and the men and the boys sat atop the sugar-white mound with their shovel handles sticking out like porcupine quills.

When they had enough sand stockpiled, Charlie went to get more 55-gallon drums from the manganese mining company in the city of Moanda. Moanda lay between two mountains, one of which was being shaved flat. Back in the village, Charlie hammered off the barrel tops and set them under gutters slung beneath the eaves of two of the teachers' houses in anticipation of the rainy season.

But the rains wouldn't begin for another month. Charlie took two intact drums and a handful of men to Aliga Creek. He backed the truck down the trail using his mirrors. On clear days when sunlight filtered down through the canopy, clouds of yellow and white butterflies fluttered by the stream. Each man filled two buckets at a time and handed them up to Charlie in the truck, who poured the water through the blue funnel into the barrels. When the two drums were filled, he screwed the caps back in the bungholes. By this method, every drop of water taken out of the creek made it back to the site.

They told Charlie it would take a long time to weave the walls in with vines to make the wattle. He asked where the mud to fill in the wattle would come from, out here on the sandy plateau. The answer was termite nests. Only nests at a certain stage of development were wanted, nests the color of ripe pumpkins. Charlie had by this time wired several layers of plastic mesh to the grill of his truck, to prevent grass seeds from clogging the radiator. The men took him crisscrossing the plain on the prowl for suitable termite mounds. Whenever they found one, Charlie, and whichever men had come along that day, broke through the outer crust with pickaxes to get at the core. The plateau teemed with flies no bigger than gnats, and little bees with no sting that were drawn to human sweat. As they dug into the moist and heavy inner soil, the termite soldiers came swarming out biting. The flies and the bees got into their noses and mouths and covered their glistening torsos as they shoveled, pausing to sweep the flying bugs from their faces and to slap the biting termites from their legs.

Finally, when the workers had finished the wattle walls and Charlie had stocked enough water and termite dirt, the time came for the women to shine. The men wheeled the orange dirt into the houses using the brand new wheelbarrows. When all was to their liking, the women poured buckets of water and stepped barefoot onto the orange piles of dirt, churning it into mud with their feet, grinning when Charlie took pictures. They added water until the mud was the consistency of cake batter. Then the women scooped mud up in handfuls and shoved it in between the vines, packing the walls solid, laughing the whole time, singing, whooping and shouting, careless for a change about the presence of men.

Lalish was seemingly everywhere at once, clomping around in his platform shoes, taking careful notes, waving his pen like a sword, barking out orders like a general, emitting an occasional bleat and a snort, checking the time on his many watches, pausing in his tireless labors only to bend down and pull up his many socks.

While the women were mudding in the walls, Charlie made several trips to Obia for gravel. It was a pleasant job, loading the truck, driving back and forth across the scenic plateau. For the first time in his life, Charlie felt he was somewhere he belonged.

When he had a pile of gray gravel on one side of the new blue cement mixer, and a mound of white sand on the other, with the walls of the teachers' houses mudded in, and plenty of cement, it was time to plaster the walls and pour the floors. A retired mason named Atcholo Jean-Luc supervised the plastering. The men mixed sand and cement in the cement mixer, wheeled the mix across planks in the new green wheelbarrows, and slung the plaster against

107

the walls with shiny new trowels, using wood floats to smooth it flat. While one group was plastering, Charlie worked with a second group pouring the floors. Oloumba Bruno displayed the most interest in pouring concrete, and Charlie let him take charge. They dumped concrete in the far bedroom of each teacher's house and worked their way to the front door. They used a length of two-by-four as a screed to scrape the concrete flat, letting it swoop and flow with the lay of the land, and then they got out on kneeling boards to float and trowel it off.

Jean-Paul manufactured all the plywood windows and doors, crafting the frames from two-by-fours laboriously sawn lengthwise by hand. After hanging each window, Jean-Paul made sure the bolts shot home. After hanging the front doors, he made certain that the chrome handles all locked with a key.

When the walls of the houses were plastered, the floors poured and all the doors and windows hung, the crew whitewashed the walls and painted the windows and doors in Gabon's national colors, one house green, the second blue, the third house canary yellow. By the end of February, Okouya's first housing development was finished, three snug little patriotic cottages at the entrance to the village, like a Dr. Seuss drawing, hardly a straight line about them.

7. A Murder in the Village

Ambassador Jones couldn't concentrate on the neat stack of cables on her desk. She'd awakened from a dream that morning half expecting to find her husband Calvin downstairs, filling the residence with his big personality, his big voice, his big booming laugh, talking to the staff in English, and laughing as if they understood. Darlene had spoken with him on the phone the night before, and with their eight-year-old son, and somehow time telescoped. Six weeks had already passed since they opened presents under the festooned plastic tree, Christmas Day on the equator.

Darlene had planned their three-week stay around her busy schedule. Calvin Junior was fine doing cannonballs and back flips into the pool while she was at work, shooting hoops with his dad, but her husband needed something more to do. The U.S. Ambassador to Gabon was also the Ambassador to the island country of São Tomé y Príncipe, so she scheduled a tour of the projects supported from the Ambassador's Self-Help Fund. They flew in a small plane over the open ocean to tour a women's sewing cooperative, a bee farming club, a community piggery. On weekends, there were day trips up the coast to Coco Beach in a chauffeured embassy car, or across the estuary to Pointe Denis in the embassy boat.

But it wasn't enough. Openly bored, the boy's father made little effort even to seem to care how things were going for Darlene. His questions were perfunctory, and eventually he bent every conversation back to himself: his restaurant, how well it was doing; his investments, oh his investments, they were going to start paying off big time, any day now. He predicted that soon, people would be walking around with cellular telephones small enough to fit in a purse, or even in a shirt pocket. Darlene wasn't sure about that. The devices she'd seen were the size of a man's shoe; but Calvin said the new ones would be small, and cheap enough that everyone could afford one. People would someday be calling each other from anywhere, all the time, all over the world. It was hard to imagine, but there was more.

For years, it had been possible for the military and research institutions and the government to send information from computer to computer through something called the internet. Calvin reminded Darlene this was currently the domain of the gnomes in federal government communications who spoke in a language only they understood, but the internet was on the verge of becoming accessible to the general public. The number of households with a home computer was growing, and there was now a commercial device called a modem that was easy to install and made it possible to link your home computer to the internet through your telephone line. People were already talking about something called the worldwide web, an information superhighway. Soon ordinary people would be using their computers to browse for merchandise and send each other messages without ever leaving the comfort of their homes.

All this sounded like science fiction to Darlene, but what her husband Calvin was saying in so many words was that when her tour was up, he expected her to come live with him in New Orleans, like a proper wife. Darlene wanted to ask him, Don't you see this is my career, what I'm called to do, what I'm meant for? Somehow, she lacked the strength, though it was roaring in her ears. It was all about his mid-life crisis, the half share in the restaurant that his uncle Web had talked him into buying, two years ago when one day Calvin came home from the office and said he was tired of taking orders. He wanted to try his hand at building a business. The restaurant Uncle Web had his eye on was in the most fabulous part of New Orleans, the French Quarter, and Calvin described strolling along herringbone brick sidewalks, the smell of magnolia in the evening air, the sound of jazz flowing from the clubs.

The words hit Darlene like body blows. Her husband wanted to be his own boss, but her position at the NSC was very senior, and the work energized her. She was the NSC member on the State Department team charged with the Reagan administration's top priority for Africa, resolving the linked problems of Namibia, apartheid and the civil war in Angola. Was she supposed to drop everything and follow him? Was Calvin really forcing her to choose?

Over the course of several difficult weeks of trying to talk it out, they finally made a partial decision. They would try living in different cities a thousand miles apart. It would be temporary, they promised Calvin Junior, who could not be consoled. Daddy had promised his son that after he left the Navy, he would never go away again. Just for a time they told him, while they decided if this could work.

In a Top Secret briefing at the Eisenhower Executive Office Building, Darlene first learned of the true gravity of the situation in southwest Africa, the Africa watchers' highest priority. The Soviets had upgraded the Angolan national army with fighter jets, tanks and attack helicopters. The Cubans had sent 15,000 troops. On the other side, to support the UNITA rebels, the South Africans had introduced a self-propelled howitzer with a range of 25 miles, and had called up 140,000 reserves. All this was public knowledge, widely reported in the media, but very few people knew that the stakes were about to rise dramatically. South Africa was preparing an underground nuclear weapon test in the Kalahari Desert.

This would bring on a catastrophic escalation of hostilities. Preventing it was essential, and the engrossing, urgent geopolitical challenge made it hard for Darlene to untangle herself from work in time to go pick up her son at the afterschool program. Most days he was the last child there, crying sometimes, or nodding off. She needed a nanny, but at the moment, funds were tight. Against her wishes, Calvin had taken out a third mortgage and bought a partially restored Dolliole cottage in Faubourg Marigny.

Darlene managed to find time to get away from work, and took her son to New Orleans. Calvin Junior was over the moon at the prospect of seeing Daddy, the adventure of flying, and insisted on packing his own suitcase. He hugged his father fiercely, refusing to let go. Darlene had to agree, the neighborhood was charming. It was the birthplace of Jelly Roll Morton. French-speaking free people of color once lived there, before the Louisiana Purchase. But she did not approve of being saddled with three mortgages.

The time she had available to spend in New Orleans was short, and soon over. Darlene urgently needed to get overseas. Negotiations had reached a critical point, and the Soviets were cooperating, working with the Americans to force the Cubans and South Africans into direct talks. It was like pushing two scorpions into a bottle. This was a chance to secure in one fell swoop the withdrawal of all foreign belligerents from Angola and independence for Namibia. Darlene was expected to play a critical role. She needed Calvin to take care of their son while she traveled.

During the spring, her husband shuttled grudgingly over from New Orleans whenever she crossed the ocean with the U.S. government team, to London in March, and then Cairo in May. School was out when Darlene traveled to New York in June, and Calvin took their son with him back to New Orleans to spend the summer. In August, Darlene went to Geneva, and when she returned, she flew to New Orleans to bring Calvin Junior back to Fairfax for the start of school.

The Dolliole cottage was nearly finished, and the painted brick, the slate roof and fireplace duly charmed Darlene. Inside it had the cozy feel of a two-story apartment, with floor to ceiling shuttered windows facing the street, and a tiny lush backyard where Calvin barbecued. He wore an apron that said 'Real Men Don't Use Recipes'. Uncle Web came with a pretty, new girlfriend half his age.

After the guests left and their son went to bed, Calvin told Darlene he had some news. "Calvin Junior will be staying here with me," he announced, his eyes locked on hers. "I've enrolled him in the Stuart Hall School for Boys. We visited the campus and the boy likes the place. I haven't told him yet. I wanted to tell you first."

"What about the tuition! On top of three mortgage payments?"

"Darlene, I got this." Calvin's voice was calm. "There will be no discussion." He spoke as if on deck, issuing a routine command. "I don't want any more tears. The Frenchman Street Bistro is doing a roaring business, and not just with tourists, with residents. It's a steadier trade. I can show you the books, the figures to prove it."

It was a relief for Darlene, actually, to relent, which only added to her feelings of guilt, going back to Washington alone. That autumn she visited eleven countries on three separate trips, submerging her emotions in work. She played her part in the tripartite peace accord signed on December 22, a final diplomatic triumph for the lame duck Reagan administration, and she was at the United Nations for the ceremony, presided over by Secretary of State George Schultz. Darlene watched the Angolan, Cuban and South African foreign ministers sign the accords. The South African and Cuban delegations were sullen, and their foreign ministers traded barbs in their remarks for the press. Then, two days later Darlene was in New Orleans for the holidays with her husband and son, when a call came from the transition team of the president-elect. Chase Untermeyer was on the line, in charge of personnel. They were working out every detail, he said, right down to the lower-level appointments. Would Dr. Jones be interested in the post of Ambassador to Gabon?

Calvin was shocked. His anger almost spoiled their son's first Christmas in the cottage. With Darlene's stint at the NSC winding down, he had assumed she was preparing to leave public service, and now this? An overseas assignment was out of the question. He had absolutely no interest in becoming a trailing spouse. He would not for one moment consider accompanying her to post. What about their son's education? Was there even an American School in Libreville?

"This is my turn now," said Darlene, getting angry too. "My turn to be in charge, my chance to apply all my skills. I'm being recognized, and this is an opportunity I will not pass up."

Her husband went quiet, so she softened, and assured him it would only be for two years. She would understand if he didn't come with her, but he had to let her do this. He and Calvin Junior could visit her next Christmas. And the following summer she would have thirty days home leave.

Calvin never quite said no.

A week after the inauguration, President Bush sent a list of 104 names for confirmation to the Senate Foreign Relations Committee, and Darlene Jones's name was among them. She was eminently qualified, with her Ph.D. from Princeton, her five years of previous service in Naval Intelligence, her two years teaching at Howard University, currently serving with distinction as Special Assistant to the President and Senior Director for Africa under the outgoing national security advisor General Colin Powell.

They put the house in Fairfax on the market right after she

swore in, and it sold in just two weeks. They were pleasantly surprised how much their home had appreciated in value, and the question of finding a tax shelter for the capital gains mitigated Calvin's hard feelings about Darlene's mobilization to Libreville.

Was Calvin being faithful? In her darkest moments, Darlene imagined he wasn't. Could she blame him, really? They were past the cash flow crunch; the restaurant was making money hand over fist, and there were plenty more pretty girls wherever Uncle Web's pretty young girlfriend had come from, she had to suppose. Might Calvin be considering a divorce?

Her son's voice on the phone always brought a lump to her throat. She had to coax complete sentences out of him. He liked his new school, even though they had to wear uniforms. He was playing on the basketball team. They were learning the pick and roll. Daddy was helping him make a volcano for the science fair. Her husband on the extension prompted their son to say what they were using: papier-mâché, and did Mom know what that was? It's really messy. They were smearing it around a plastic bottle, and tomorrow when it was dry, they would smear on more. It was going to look like a mountain, and they would paint it, and then at the science fair they would put baking soda and red food coloring inside, and pour in vinegar to make the eruption.

I wish I could be there to see it. I'm glad you and Daddy could come be with me for Christmas. It was a good Christmas, together, wasn't it? Did you like Coco Beach or Pointe Denis better? Or flying over to São Tomé? Are you excited about me coming to be with you this summer?

Yeah, said her son, but it didn't seem so.

Darlene dabbed her eyes, blew her nose and forced herself to focus on the top page before her, a worldwide reporting cable on events in the Soviet Union. The Central Committee had endorsed Mikhail Gorbachev's recommendation that the Communist Party give up its monopoly on political power. A paragraph classified Secret ordered missions to issue no written pronouncements on the subject. Any communications with the Soviet embassy on the subject were to be strictly verbal, and to congratulate President Mikhail Gorbachev and the Central Committee.

Darlene wondered when she might next encounter the Soviet

ambassador. She could picture his dour face but couldn't recall his name. There was a tap on her open office door. It was the regional security officer and the political officer looking in.

"Good morning, gentlemen, come in." How long had they been there?

Ray Sims and young Tom Hughes took the chairs opposite her desk.

"Whatchya got?"

"I went to meet Gilles Clermidy last night," said Ray.

Tom said, "Here's the bio we requested this past November. It came in a week ago, but somehow got buried in the reading file." He handed a sheet of paper to Darlene.

Gilles Clermidy held the rank of Commandant in the National Police in Paris, it said, with the Directorate of Territorial Surveillance. In Libreville, he served as an advisor to the Center for Documentation.

"CEDOC," said Darlene.

"Yep," said Tom, "he's with the secret police."

"He wanted me to meet him at The Cedars," said Ray. As the RSO, Ray was an agent of the Bureau of Diplomatic Security. That made him the Ambassador's security advisor. It was his job to locate trouble before it arose. He had a staff of Gabonese investigators and contacts with the Gabonese National Police, both handed down from his predecessors. Ray depended on his FSNs to interpret for him. They all spoke English. He suspected some of them reported both ways, and so he never shared any truly sensitive information with any of them, not that they handled that much here in Libreville. The Cedars was a Lebanese restaurant, a favorite of the diplomatic community.

"Let me get this straight," said Darlene. "A French advisor to CEDOC meets you at a place everyone knows is watched by CEDOC agents?"

Ray didn't laugh. He never made jokes, and never managed to laugh at anyone else's. Darlene liked him, a former District of Columbia police detective, freshly barbered alternate Mondays, dark hair graying at the temples. She saw him in the gym if she went in the evening, running on the treadmills.

"He had a man with him, the cultural attaché, to translate. I don't believe that man is any kind of cultural attaché." Ray consulted his notes. "He said the labor unions are definitely not backing down from their threat of a general strike in support of the university students, if the Special Commission on Democracy doesn't act. He said this could be like Paris in '68. If there's not political change, there could be violence."

"Should we be going over this in the Bubble?" asked Tom.

Darlene shrugged. Sometimes they overdid it with the security concerns. "I don't think that's necessary. What's your read on this, Tom?"

Tom had unruly black hair and wore small glasses and a perpetual frown. "Well, as I see it," he said, "Bongo has two options. He can crush the democracy movement like Deng Xiaoping did last June in China, or he can try to steer it like Mikhail Gorbachev is trying to do in the Soviet Union. It seems to me, Bongo is taking the latter course. Either way, Ambassador, your model is playing out here in Gabon."

Darlene did not react to her youthful political officer letting on he'd read her book, with its small contribution to political theory. Transitions spread because activists learned from other activists' successes. This in fact had begun happening here in Gabon, late last autumn when the Gabonese college student leaders were inspired by televised images of white people in Eastern Europe rising for their rights, and called a strike that shut down the university. Then the video images of the execution of Ceausescu on Christmas Day unnerved Bongo completely. Darlene wrote a cable on the reports they got about Bongo's meltdown at the Palace. In January, Bongo did what Gorbachev had done; he summoned the Central Committee of his party into session. They were in session when the Gabonese labor unions threatened to join the students in a general strike, and it wasn't too many days afterwards that the Central Committee announced the formation of a Special Commission on Democracy.

"Where are we, Tom, on scheduling meetings with the members?"

"Not much luck, so far."

Darlene's small country team got no further with ranking Gabonese authorities than the teams of previous ambassadors had managed. Just a month earlier, Darlene completed her round of calls on the cabinet ministers. There were almost fifty ministries. Each was a channel for patronage. It had taken nearly a year after first presenting her credentials to meet with them all. The amount of time required provided Darlene an indication of the low status the Gabonese government accorded the American mission.

Okouya

The vernal rainy season had finally arrived. Overnight, the grass of the plateau turned a brilliant green, the sky a scrubbed cerulean blue. Early one morning, Charlie had all the half dozen teenage boys still living in Okouya helping him with the truck maintenance. He thought of them as his bolt warmers. They held the bolts patiently in their fists until he needed them back. He had his boom box playing loud, and they were all around him, wherever he was, standing on the front bumper and bent over under the hood, crawling under the truck. They had changed the oil and the filters and tightened all the bolts when the tape popped off.

Their ringleader, Makokomba Alphonse, asked, "Monsieur Charlie, would you like to hear a tape I have?"

"Sure," said Charlie, and the boys cackled in anticipation as Alphonse slipped a cassette from his pocket. There were no markings on the jacket, Charlie saw. He thought nothing of it. Rural Gabonese listened to pirated tapes. The first song was one he had never heard. It made the teenage boys snicker.

"What are they singing?" asked Charlie, lying on a sheet of oil-stained plywood pumping grease into a tie rod end. "It sounds like they're saying 'Bongo'."

"Yes," said Alphonse, on his knees watching Charlie, "it's about President Bongo," and suddenly he looked up.

"Bema lessa!"

Charlie's landlord, Obongi Louis strode over wearing a blue beret. Normally a jovial man, Louis was furious. He berated the boys in Téké. Charlie caught the word for dangerous, and Alphonse got up and punched off the tape and ejected it and sheepishly handed it over.

"What's the matter?" Charlie asked Louis.

"No," said Louis, "this is something no one must hear," and he sent the chastened boys away, and walked off with Alphonse's cassette.

Later that day, after a bath and lunch, Charlie sat in his sling chair in the shade by the side of his house, taking time off to kick back with a paperback novel. He wasn't ready to start work on the school, not yet, and had escaped into a legal thriller.

"Bonjour, Monsieur Charlie."

He hadn't seen the man approach, the man Édouard had found to do his laundry. It had to be a man, Édouard said, because it was taboo for a woman to wash the underwear of any man she wasn't related to. His name was Ongari Ambroise. When Édouard introduced him, Ambroise showed Charlie a letter of recommendation from a French mining engineer he once worked for in Moanda. It didn't occur to Charlie to ask why Ambroise had returned to the village. He was thirty or so and had a neat mustache. He spoke very good French and absolutely loved the subjunctive.

"Bonjour, Ambroise."

"Bonjour, Monsieur Charlie. You are reading a book?"

"Yes, I am reading a book."

"That is good. It is good to read."

"Yes it is. Hey Ambroise, have you heard a song that goes something like this?" Charlie hummed a bit of the tune from the cassette that Louis had confiscated from Alphonse a few hours earlier.

"Ah yes," said Ambroise, and lowered his voice and looked around to see who might be in earshot. "That song is by a Gabonese musician who lives in Canada. The song is called *Bongo Ye Kwa*. It's forbidden. The gendarmes arrest anyone they find with it."

"Huh!" said Charlie. "What does that mean, Bongo ye kwa?"

"S-s-s-s-h!" said Ambroise, and he looked around again. "It means Bongo get out of here."

"Wow!"

"Yes," said Ambroise, "so it is forbidden." He nodded. "Actually, Monsieur Charlie, I've come for a reason."

118

"Yes?"

"I've come to ask you for an advance on my salary."

"How much?" said Charlie, and then he went inside and got the minor amount Ambroise requested. He had Ambroise sign for it, then resettled in his sling chair and went back to reading his novel. Later he took a nap. When he awoke, he resumed reading. He still had about fifty pages to go when he stopped and went over to Oyali Albert's house, where he'd been invited for supper.

Albert's two wives were busy in the cook hut out back when Charlie arrived. Albert served him a warm Régab in his salon. He and Charlie sat in two straight-backed chairs made by Jean-Paul at the dinner table that Jean-Paul had made as well. Night was falling and the table was lit by a kerosene lamp, and was set for two. They would be eating alone. This was typical. Women weren't supposed to eat with men.

Charlie asked, "So how is it, having two wives?"

Albert's face reminded Charlie of a mule, with long yellow teeth. He was no catch, but neither were his wives, work-worn women who had never been to school. Albert thought it was a rhetorical question.

"Tell me," Charlie insisted.

Surprised that the otangani was serious, Albert began explaining as one would explain something to a child. "If you have two wives, you must have two of everything. You must never buy just one of them a dress. Oh, that will provoke a fight! You must buy both of them a dress, or neither. You see?"

"Do you all sleep here in this house?"

"No, each wife must have her own."

"Her own house? So you have two houses?"

"No, three."

"Why three?"

"Monday, Wednesday and Friday I am with Juliet at her house, Tuesday, Thursday and Saturday I am with Marie-Claire chez elle. Sunday I sleep alone, in this house, to rest."

"Tu es fort-o!" said Charlie.

Albert was flattered, and had leaned forward to refill Charlie's glass, when outside someone screamed. Albert frowned and got up and went to the door and opened it on a babble of voices, and more screaming from further away. He stepped outside, closing the door behind him.

Charlie sipped his beer, content to wait to learn what the uproar was about.

The door suddenly swung open and Albert came in, looking stunned. "Monsieur," he cried, "there's been a murder!" He stood there waiting for Charlie to act, the American sent here by the government who was supposed to know what to do about everything. Charlie didn't know what to do about a murder in the village, so he followed Albert outside, where a dozen men were gathered. Albert ordered them aside and they fell in behind Charlie, who followed Albert to an agitated crowd by the door of a little cook hut. Albert shouldered his way through. Charlie had to stoop to enter. It was dark inside, and the hut was low.

"There," said Albert, holding up a lantern.

The corpse was slumped on a stool in the corner. It was an old man. His shirtfront was drenched in blood. There was a visible gash on his forehead.

Suddenly the corpse spoke, and it gave Charlie a terrible start. The bloody face speaking was ghastly.

"He's not dead!" said Charlie.

"He says Ambroise almost killed him," said Albert.

Ambroise, Charlie thought. My laundryman did this. "Where is Ambroise?"

Albert asked the crowd in the door.

"No one knows," he said.

"Okay," said Charlie, bent at the waist, with his hands on his knees like the quarterback in the huddle, thinking dress the wound. "Okay," he said, "I'm going to get my medical kit."

Charlie cracked his head on the lintel of the low doorway going out and emerged cursing and rubbing his head. The people backed away. When he returned from his house with the medical kit, the crowd parted, and he made certain to stoop low enough going back inside. Albert held up the lantern and Charlie got down on one knee. He took out the cotton balls and the bottle of iodine and told Albert to have someone bring him some hot water. Albert shouted the order to the faces in the doorway, but no one did anything.

Albert held the lantern closer. Charlie leaned in to examine the wound, a deep gash about two inches long in the middle of the forehead. It appeared to Charlie to be the result of a hard whack with the business edge of a machete. White glistened deep in the wound. He wondered, is that the skull? The wound had bled a lot, as the book said head wounds do, but it had stopped.

Charlie soaked a cotton ball in iodine and cleaned sticky blood from the face. It took dozens of cotton balls, a waste, but this was important. Charlie wiped the blood from around the wound, and began to clean the lips. He expected the old man to hiss at the sting, but he made no sound.

Finally, Charlie splashed iodine on a square of gauze and taped it onto the old man's forehead.

"Comment s'appelle-t-il?"

Albert said he was called Lengori.

"He needs to have that wound stitched up."

Charlie returned to his house and got in the truck to take the old man to the hospital. When he pulled up, there was a weird shifting light from all the lanterns swinging about. Instantly the truck began rocking from the weight of people clambering aboard. Villagers jumped at a chance for a free car ride, even if it was for no particular reason in the middle of the night to a place they hadn't planned on going. Tonight on an empty stomach, Charlie didn't have the energy to argue.

Four men came hurrying like litter bearers out of the hut carrying the wounded old man by his arms and his legs. They heaved Lengori into the cab like a sack of potatoes and scrambled in back.

"The land chief wishes to go with you." It was Édouard at the window, with old Oyamba at his side. "He wants to report this to the authorities."

"Bonsoir, Chef."

Oyamba shook his head, leaning on his staff. "C'est comme la mauvais."

"I'll come with you," said Édouard. He helped old Oyamba into the cab next to Lengori, slammed the door, and somehow managed to squeeze on board.

It was only about twenty-five miles from Okouya to Akièni, but it took an hour to drive there. Neither Lengori nor Chief Oyamba spoke much French, and Charlie didn't speak very much Téké, so he yelled out the window to Albert sitting behind him on the wall of the bed to find out what had happened.

Ambroise had spent the day drinking with the money Charlie gave him, and got so drunk his sister refused to serve him supper. He picked up a machete and threatened her, and the old man Lengori intervened, so Ambroise turned on him, chased him into the cook hut, chopped him on the head, and then ran off into the woods. No one had seen him since.

Charlie drove as fast as he could. The truck swayed from the fluid weight of all the people in back. He passed through Otou without stopping on a night lit by a half moon and drove straight to the Akièni hospital. The pack of men descended chattering, cold and stiff from the wind. A number of them helped old Oyamba get out, helped old Lengori climb out, and then helped Oyamba climb back into the cab to wait where it was warm.

The brightly lit emergency room was open but unattended. Woozy in his blood-soaked shirt, Lengori was glad to sit on a stool. Charlie walked around the campus of one-story buildings hallooing for someone to come. There was no one on duty. Angry at the annoyance of having to go find a nurse, he went back to the emergency room. Albert met him on the way.

"I know where we can find him," he said.

"Who?"

"The nurse who's on duty tonight."

They returned to the truck. Albert got in the cab next to Oyamba and the men from Okouya scrambled back in, leaving Lengori alone in the emergency room.

Albert directed Charlie where to go. They stopped in front of a bar. The men of Okouya jumped down and trooped inside. Albert followed them, and while Charlie waited with the engine idling, Oyamba kept shaking his head. "C'est comme la mauvais."

Albert came back to Charlie's open window. "He's in there, and he wants to see you."

"Quoi?"

"Il t'attend."

Tired and hungry, swearing in English, Charlie switched off the engine, got out and followed Albert inside. It was a small bar, built of plywood. The men of Okouya had filled it, and they were sitting at tables with their eyes on Charlie, hopeful as he came in.

"Here he is," said Albert, leading a grinning man holding a glass of red wine. He had bloodshot eyes and a mustache like two black fangs. "This is the nurse who's on duty tonight at the hospital."

The nurse nodded happily, his features concentrated in the middle of his face, his eyes not well focused.

"What are you doing here?" Charlie demanded. "We have brought in a man with a serious head wound. Let's go."

"Pas sans boire," the duty nurse said.

"What!"

The nurse tipped back his head, drained the contents of his glass and momentarily lost his balance.

Charlie dragged him outside by the arm, yanked open the truck door, lifted the nurse by the back of his shirt and shoved him nearly onto Chief Oyamba's lap. The men of Okouya came trailing out disappointed, but not wanting to be left behind.

At the hospital, they found Lengori just as they'd left him, sitting on a stool in the emergency room. The nurse, still sullen at having been manhandled out of the bar, tore the red-stained bandage off Lengori's forehead. He inspected the wound, clucked, went to a drawer and removed a curved needle and a spool of catgut. He dragged over a stool and with his unwashed bare fingers tried to thread the unsterilized needle, taking a lot of stabs at it, squinting and closing one eye. Then, without administering any anesthetic or cleansing the wound, he pinched the lips of the gash together and punched the needle right through. Blood began to stream down Lengori's wrinkled forehead, and the nurse wiped it away with a filthy sponge. The stitches were coming out crooked. The old man made no noise. From his expression, Lengori looked mildly annoyed, like he was waiting for a bus that was late, but his toes were curled on the floor.

Akièni

Justine emptied the garbage pail into the pit in her side yard. On her way inside, she paused to watch the hullabaloo next door in

Commandant Lentchidja's front yard. The outsized American from Okouya, the one she had seen by the yellow truck stuck on the plateau, talked loudly with three Gabonese, one of them an old man leaning on a staff. If she was not mistaken, he was the nkani-ntsie, the great land chief of the westernmost Louzou. The white man knocked on the front door. When the door opened, Justine went back inside. She would enquire about it in the morning.

The Commandant's wife answered. Her eyes widened at seeing an otangani on her porch. She showed them in, frail barefoot Oyamba going in first, followed by Charlie, Albert and Édouard.

The Commandant slept soundly in a vinyl wing chair in front of a game of European soccer on TV, his under lip sagging open. There was an empty bottle of Coke in front of him and a bottle of Johnny Walker half gone. His wife shook him awake. Startled to see people in the living room, surprised to see a white man, the Commandant indicated chairs, and the four of them sat. His wife turned off the TV.

Chief Oyamba looked seedy and out of place on the vinyl chair. The Commandant sent his wife to bring more Coca Cola and glasses. Édouard asked for water. The chief wanted hot coffee to warm up.

Charlie told the Commandant what had happened in the village.

The Commandant was a burly man afflicted with a wandering eye, and he fixed Charlie with an approving look. "You did well," he said. "And now you must bring him to justice."

"Who?"

"The perpetrator." The Commandant read Charlie's question in his face. "Our vehicle has a technical problem, you see. You Americans have Land Cruisers, correct? They belong to the government, n'est-ce pas?"

Okouya

In a foul mood, Charlie spooned down sweetened plums from a can, thinking about what he had to do. Édouard rapped on the open door and stepped in to deliver the news. Ambroise had barricaded himself in his house.

Sunlight streamed flat across the land when Charlie followed

124

Édouard outside on their way to make the arrest. It was so early there were still only a few people about. They threaded their way between houses, and Charlie gave the low jagged edges of the sharp metal eaves a wide berth. When Édouard pointed out the door, Charlie stepped up and pounded on it.

"Come out of there, Ambroise!" he yelled. "You're under arrest!"

A window swung open in the house next door. "Bonjour, Monsieur Charlie," said a small boy.

Charlie pounded on the door again. This time there was a muffled reply.

"He says he's going to kill himself."

Charlie pounded harder. He was ready to boot the flimsy door in if he had to. "Come on out of there, Ambroise! I'm here to arrest you!"

People were coming outside to see what the noise was about when the door opened and there stood Charlie's laundryman in bright red bikini briefs looking like he would rather be dead.

"I'm here to take you in," said Charlie, "so get some pants on and let's go."

"Ça va," said Ambroise, "but first you must give me a beer."

They left the village early on a sparkling clear morning, the shadows still long. Édouard rode with his arm out the window. Ambroise sat between Édouard and Charlie, burping up the aroma of beer. He'd chugalugged a bottle at Charlie's house before they set out.

They came to the site of the old village where mature fruit trees and palms marked the place where once there had been homes, and Ambroise yelled, "Stop!"

Charlie braked, fearing Ambroise was about to throw up. Édouard got out so Ambroise could get by him, and then Ambroise took off at a trot toward the trees.

"Goddamn!" Charlie yelled, shoving the truck in gear. "Get in, Édouard! He's making a break for it!" He cranked the wheel to head him off.

But Édouard just stood there lighting a cigarette. "He's only going to get his palm wine."

125

And indeed, that was where Ambroise headed. He knelt before a felled palm, reached his arm down under the trunk and dragged a demijohn out of the hole. He tipped it up and guzzled down the night's contents. Then he wiped his lips, replaced the demijohn, got to his feet, swatted the sand from his knees and started back to the truck.

"I may be gone for a while," he told Édouard as Charlie set off once more, "so make sure the rest of that wine doesn't go to waste."

Otou

Rebecca stood in front of her house brushing her teeth when Charlie rolled up. "Your laundryman, huh?" she laughed. "Is this him?" She reached across Charlie to shake Ambroise's hand. "Bonjour," she said. "Ça va?" She wouldn't miss this for the world. Édouard climbed up in back, leaving Ambroise the prisoner in the middle, and Rebecca made small talk with him on the way, asking him about his career as a domestic servant, what it had been like working for a French family. She could talk to anybody about anything.

It was mid-morning when they reached Akièni. Goats wandered the streets. Charlie scattered a flock of chickens when he turned in at the gendarmerie, locked up tight, like the night before. Rebecca laughed at the hours the Akièni constabulary kept.

"I know where they are," said Ambroise, "Gaboprix."

Gaboprix was Gabon's answer to America's convenience stores, with the difference that Gaboprix sold alcohol that customers could drink on the premises. Rebecca got out of the truck and went to the entrance to see if they were in there. "Bonjour tout le monde!" she cried, and went inside.

The entire Akièni gendarmerie was lined up in full uniform at the bar, working their way through a gallon jug of red wine when Charlie walked in. Rebecca was pumping the Commandant's hand in high good humor.

"Bonjour, Madame Rebecca," said the Commandant. "Comment vont les américains ce matin?"

"Très bien, merci, Commandant," Rebecca replied.

"Commandant," Charlie said, "I have brought you the prisoner."

"Prisoner?" Wall-eyed Commandant Lentchidja looked in puzzlement at Rebecca and at Charlie simultaneously.

"The one who attacked a man with a machete last night in Okouya," Charlie prompted. "Remember, you sent me to arrest him?"

"Where is he?"

"He's out in the –" but Charlie stopped short. There was Ambroise sidled up at the bar, hoisting a glass with the cops.

"That's him there," said Charlie.

The Commandant realized what this looked like. He hitched up his pants, strode over and clapped his hand on Ambroise's thin shoulder. "You're under arrest!" he declared.

"I know," said Ambroise. He toasted the Commandant, emptied his glass, and came along peaceably.

Charlie drove the whole fragrant crew over to the gendarmerie. "Well, Commandant," he said as Lentchidja swung open the door, "I guess we'll be going now."

"Oh no!" said Commandant Lentchidja, heaving his girth out the truck. "First you must give us your statement."

Rebecca slid out after him, and the gendarmes in back jumped down. One of them with a bunch of keys trotted ahead of the Commandant to unlock the police station.

Charlie and Édouard followed the two gendarmes who frog-marched Ambroise inside. The Commandant was unlocking his office door. He went in and the two cops picked up truncheons as they pushed Ambroise along after. A third gendarme told Rebecca and Charlie to follow, and told Édouard to wait outside.

The two gendarmes with the nightsticks stood behind Ambroise in front of a bare desk. Commandant Lentchidja settled his bulk in a chair behind it, and gestured to Rebecca and Charlie to take the chairs in front of him. A third gendarme went about opening the room's wooden shutters. A fourth gendarme came in carrying a heavy manual typewriter. He sat at a rickety table, loaded the typewriter with forms and carbon paper then began hesitantly pecking away.

"Name," the Commandant said.

Ambroise gave it.

"Strip him," the Commandant growled.

The two gendarmes ordered Ambroise out of his clothes.

Ambroise undressed unsteadily, almost falling over, hopping on one foot, and then he stood there skinny in his bikini briefs.

The gendarme at the typewriter sat with his index fingers aimed like pistols at the keys.

"Do you admit to having attacked a man with a machete in Otou last night?" the Commandant demanded.

"Okouya, Commandant," Rebecca corrected. "It happened in Charlie's village. I live in Otou."

"Non, chef," said Ambroise, "ce n'était pas moi."

With that, one of the gendarmes reared back and cracked Ambroise on the head with a tock. He fell unresisting, like a toppled tree, and his face hit the floor with a splat.

"Jesus Christ!" shouted Rebecca.

"Put him in the cell!" the Commandant snarled.

The two gendarmes holstered their truncheons and grabbed Charlie's laundryman under his arms, his head hanging and his nose streaming blood as they dragged him from the room, the yellow soles of his feet going out last of all. The fourth gendarme picked up his clothes and went out, and then came back with a mop and swabbed up the blood. He closed the door gently behind him.

Rebecca looked physically ill.

The Commandant leaned forward and interlocked his blunt fingers, one eye on Charlie, the other on Rebecca.

"Right," he said. "Now let's have your statement."

Akièni

The gendarme at the typewriter hunted out letters and stabbed them with a peck. A gentle rain swept across town while they were at it, but it didn't cool the air. It was hot in the office and the gendarme was irritated, telling Charlie to go slower. He didn't want to make any mistakes, or he'd have to start over again. It was nearing noon when at last he pulled the pages from the typewriter. The Commandant told Charlie to sign all five copies.

When Charlie was done, he and Rebecca headed for the door.

"We're not finished," said the Commandant. He told the gendarme to take the typewriter away, and waited for him to close the door. "The question," he said, "is who is to pay for the crime?"

"You have Ambroise," said Charlie, a split second before he understood.

So hungry he was almost dizzy, Charlie climbed into the broiling truck. Édouard slid into the middle seat, and Rebecca closed the door.

"Lengori is still at the hospital," said Édouard.

Charlie erupted into fuming hot Anglo Saxon.

"Calm down," said Rebecca. "I talked him out of the bribe."

Charlie steered the truck violently toward the hospital, trying to get some wind blowing through the cab. There was a great blundering flock of idiot goats in the way, and he laid on the horn. When he pulled into the hospital yard he stomped on the brakes, and the truck slid to a halt in the mud. "Go get the old man," he ordered Édouard.

It was hot in the cab, and Charlie got out and walked to the shade of the veranda, crowded with sick people on benches and mats. They watched him approach. Rebecca came and stood next to him, and began talking about human rights. Charlie was in no mood for her high-minded blather.

Édouard appeared. There was a problem, he said. Lengori would not be released until someone paid five hundred francs.

Charlie's blood boiled over. He headed into the admissions room to sort this out, and Rebecca hurried after him.

Outside, a sudden uproar scattered patients off the veranda and startled Justine. It sounded like some kind of wild beast. A massive white man filled the door. He let out another roar and rushed the desk, and the new girl screamed, and then he stopped in his tracks and his hairy jaw snapped shut at the sight of Justine.

This was the white man from Okouya Justine had seen at the Commandant's house the night before. Behind him came a white woman wearing large eyeglasses hurrying forward to shake hands and say hello and apologize for all this, and ask about the patient with the machete wound.

Wide-set up-tilted almond-shaped eyes, high cheekbones and lips pursed in severe disapproval, the beautiful nurse had short-circuited something in Charlie, and he could not take his eyes off her. Rebecca was talking to her now, but she kept glancing at him, to hold him right where he was.

"Yep," said Rebecca, "five hundred francs to discharge the man."

Charlie reached into his pocket and handed a red note to the girl at the desk. Without another word, the beautiful nurse gestured to Édouard and with him departed through a side door.

After a while the patients began to edge toward the admissions desk again, keeping a nervous eye on Charlie, and he moved out of their midst. The new girl looked worried that he might still pose a threat. He didn't want to listen to whatever Rebecca was saying.

Édouard appeared, leading old, barefooted Lengori, a fresh bandage on his forehead, the bloodstains on his shirt turned brown.

"It's time to go," said Rebecca.

But the beautiful nurse hadn't come back, and Charlie did not know her name.

8. Justine

Okouya

"Her name is Ntchaga Justine," said Édouard on the drive back to the village, amused that Charlie had asked. Afterward, in the days and nights that followed, at odd random moments the image of that face with the almond-shaped eyes came flickering into Charlie's head, Justine, like lightning, interrupting Pétronie with her wide hips and peasant ankles, Josephine with her caesarian scar, short-legged Chantalle. There were others now too, Pascaline, plump with shapely arms, Lisa with fake Rasta braids, Charmaine with a gap between her front teeth, coming in the night to slip in, slipping out before first light.

Charlie had trouble keeping them straight. It was gluttonous, almost sickening, like eating a whole bag of marshmallows at once. Here he was, nearly twenty-three, juggling girlfriends, young women with new textures and smells. The black girls came in all different shades, sienna and mahogany, cocoa and burnt umber.

Back in Minnesota, growing up, Charlie had never felt much of anything for girls, beyond the physical pleasure they could provide. The high school girls who looked at him in class, in the hallway, in the cafeteria, who didn't look away when he looked back, who sent him notes through their friends, those girls came mostly from the blue-collar neighborhoods; their fathers worked at the stockyard or at the meatpacking plant. After he moved into Coach Dawber's house, with a bedroom of his own for the first time in his life, and wearing clothes that fit right, girls with wealthier fathers started looking at Charlie too, the big quiet boy with the story people said was so sad that he never talked about it.

In Okouya, Charlie's girlfriends were accumulating expectations, a growing worry and another reason he didn't feel ready to start building the school. Could they really believe he would give all their fathers, uncles and brothers a job? He avoided the question, sleeping late in the mornings, loafing during the day, reading his way through a pile of disintegrating paperback novels left behind by departed volunteers.

He couldn't stop thinking about the beautiful nurse, Justine. In the briefest of instants, she'd made him feel something he'd never felt before, like an electric shock. She'd become fixed in his head. How could that be? It was too much. When Thursday rolled around, Charlie decided to go meet her properly, see where it might lead. He drove to Akièni with a plan.

The weekly rotation of shoppers was in back. The scrivener Jean-Paul was in the cab. Charlie picked up the schoolteacher Jonas at the blue teacher's house he'd selected to live in. The yellow house was the new magasin, full of cement, and the green house stood empty, awaiting a second teacher, should one ever be assigned. Several of the men had helped Jonas move his things into the blue house, while others helped Charlie move the tools and materials out of the derelict ruin they'd been using as the storehouse. They stripped the roofing sheets off the hovel where Jonas had lived, while Charlie studied how to demolish it. He decided to pull it down with the truck. He looped a stout rope around the walls, tied it to his truck's front bumper, and then got in behind the wheel. A crowd turned out to watch. They cheered Charlie backing up hopping in four low, like a tractor with the engine roaring, and they applauded as the groaning walls came crashing down in a great cloud of red dust and cockroaches.

Otou

Rebecca shuffled out of her house wrapped in a pagne, her hair mussed. Without her glasses, she resembled a blinking, blue-eyed owl.

"Looks like you're not coming," said Charlie.

Rebecca handed him some stamped letters to mail and turned back inside to her new boyfriend, Philbert.

At the hospital, two men painted over graffiti, some of the letters still visible. It said, "Bongo = Ceausescu." Charlie needed a moment to recall the second name, then it came to him, the

Romanian dictator who'd been executed on Christmas Day. Rebecca will be interested to know about that, he thought.

In the admissions room at the hospital, a cranky man at the desk said nurse Ntchaga had the day off. Charlie didn't think it wise to ask where she lived, so he drove to the Bottle Cap Bar and sat sipping beer, considering what to do next. He was refilling his glass when there were two thumps in the back of his truck, and Jonas and Jean-Paul came in. They went to the bar and Jonas came to the table with a bottle of beer and then Jean-Paul with a bottle of orangeade.

Jonas said, "I have a problem. My sister wants to come visit me for a few days."

"That's not a problem," said Charlie. "I'll give her a ride." Then he asked if they knew a nurse at the hospital named Justine.

"She's my sister," said Jonas.

Akièni

Jonas directed Charlie to the government bungalows where his sister lived. Charlie knew he would have to proceed with caution. What would the schoolteacher make of a show of interest in his sister? Her house happened to be next door to the commandant of the gendarmerie. As Charlie pulled to a stop, Justine came out the door wearing a burgundy and white striped strapless dress and carrying a small overnight bag.

"Bonsoir," she said, glancing at Charlie, climbing into the cab, a narrow waist and a round backside scooting over to make room for her brother. The gold bangles on her slim wrist jingled when she slipped her slender hand into his, and Jonas climbed in beside her and chunked shut the door.

"Are you feeling better now?" Her eyes were teasing. "You were quite deranged the other day."

"Well," said Charlie, starting the engine, "yes I was, and I'll tell you why."

Justine clucked to learn what Charlie's laundryman had done.

"No one was on duty at the hospital. I had to go drag a nurse out of a bar."

Justine said she knew the nurse he was referring to.

"And then the Commandant sent me to arrest Ambroise."

Justine laughed at imagining Charlie arresting his laundryman in his underwear.

"The gendarmerie was closed when I got there first thing in the morning. They were all down at the Gaboprix drinking wine, so I had to haul them up to the gendarmerie. The Commandant made me come inside. He told Ambroise to confess to what he'd done. When he didn't, one of the gendarmes hit him over the head with a nightstick. Knocked him out! They dragged him off to jail, and then the Commandant demanded a bribe from me!"

Justine knew how this looked to a foreigner, the way such things were handled, and she began talking with her brother in Téké. Night fell, and Charlie snapped on the headlights as they climbed the steep escarpment to the end of the laterite road and headed out into the sand. The truck practically drove itself on the plateau, running in second gear, four-wheel high, hardly needing to be steered, the front wheels guided by the ruts. It was chilly now and they rolled up the windows, and Charlie became even more aware of Justine sitting next to him, the scent of her lotions and soap. Once when he reached down to shift the transfer lever, he brushed her leg, and she swung her knee away to give him room.

Okouya

Charlie awoke with his head full of images of Justine sliding into his truck, sliding toward him, her round knees swinging closer as she made room for her brother, the gold bangles on her wrist jingling when she put her hand in his. Cooking his breakfast his head was full of her, and he decided as he ate, he would make a show of taking a promenade through the village, and then he would go see her, down at the schoolyard.

He began at Chief Oyamba's house with a rap on the door. He stepped inside to greet the old man in his smoky den. Then he went to Albert's house, where he learned from the hunter Ndebe Marc that Albert had gone with one of his wives to the old village to gather fruit. He strolled on to Édouard's and paused on the way to chat with gangly Alphonse, who'd had his forbidden cassette confiscated. Alphonse agreed things were very fine indeed.

Édouard's senior wife Nadine was outside her house sitting on a stool using a wooden pestle to pound manioc leaves into a green mash in a mortar between her knees. She paused when she saw Charlie, and told him her husband was up visiting Bruno. Charlie patted the head of the infant sleeping on her back. He had driven Nadine into Akièni to give birth to this little boy. He tried to remember if this was Édouard's fifth child or sixth. He tried to remember the name.

Charlie saw the cool amusement in Nadine's eyes, the unspoken question, and went on to Jean-Paul's house where, at his workbench out back the village scrivener, carpenter and furniture maker was putting the finishing touches on a dining room chair. Charlie admired the handiwork, and was pleased to be able correctly to identify the red wood as padouk.

But his mind was focused on his destination as he strolled toward Oyamba Jacques' bar. He saw Assélé Laurent across the way, waved and popped into the bouvette to greet the fixture inside, Benjamin, nearly finished with his first bottle of the day. Benjamin's face lit up at the sight of Charlie coming in, but Charlie declined his invitation to come join him and buy him another beer.

Charlie went back out into the sunlight and crossed the open space to the schoolyard, and he was puzzled as he approached to see there were no children in the school, and disappointed to see the blue teacher's house shut up tight. It was Friday morning. Jonas had clearly gone somewhere. Justine must have gone with her brother. Certainly, they would be back this afternoon.

When the brilliant green and yellow weaverbirds began shrilling in the ongoumou tree, Charlie stepped outside and headed straight for the schoolyard. Jonas was outside his front door in a sling chair cleaning his twelve-gauge shotgun when Charlie walked up.

"Bonsoir," Charlie said, shaking his hand. "I didn't see you today."

"I dismissed the pupils and went hunting."

"Ah. And your sister?"

"She went too."

"Really! She hunts?"

"No. She went out to explore." Jonas broke open his gun,

135

pointed it at the evening sky and peered through the barrel.

"Did you have any luck?"

"Only one gazelle." Jonas snapped the barrel shut.

"Only one! Half the men of the village would be bragging."

Jonas shrugged modestly.

"Where is your sister? I would like to greet her."

"In there." Jonas jerked his head toward the little cook hut. Smoke rose through the thatched roof.

"Koh-koh-koh," said Charlie, stooping through the doorway. In the dim light, he could barely make out Justine. Despite the smoke, the aroma was wonderful. "Bonsoir," he said. His eyes adjusted until he could see her sitting on a wooden stool tending a blackened pot on a three stone fire. "I understand you went into the forest with your brother today."

"Yes. He shot this gazelle that I'm cooking."

"It smells delicious."

"Would you like to eat with us?"

It was dark by the time the three of them headed for Charlie's house after he insisted they eat there. "There are more comforts at my place," he said.

A crescent moon lay low in the sky. Charlie walked through the deep sand shining Jonas's flashlight. Jonas on his left carried a two-handled pot of stew and Justine on the other side of her brother a hamper. Charlie carried nothing, being an otangani and not permitted.

As they neared his house, Charlie saw a girl slip away from where she had been waiting in the shadows, one of his girlfriends, but he couldn't tell which one. He opened the door and Jonas and Justine stepped inside and set the things on his table. Charlie lit two lamps and asked them what they'd like to drink. Jonas smacked his lips at the mention of a cold beer. Justine wanted orange soda pop and wanted to set the table. She went into the kitchen and Charlie followed her with a lamp. She looked at the shelves, the countertop, the stove and the refrigerator. She saw the sink and stepped over to open the tap. Water really ran out of it, like in a city.

"You built this?" she asked. He moved close to her, two meters tall, one hundred-ten kilos of muscle. Adult Gabonese women were not half his size. What sort of person was he? Justine liked the gentle humorous expression in his eyes. In the light of the lantern, she could see his lashes were long, curved like a bird's wings. But the curve of his lips hinted of cruelty, lips the color of tounou, the little red fruit so sour it had to be sucked. He was too close, and she took a step away.

He helped her set the table, and Justine served them, ladling the stew and the nkoumou onto Charlie's plate, setting four slices of onguélé and a dollop of red pepper on the side. The warmth of her gaze was like heat on his face; those up-tilted eyes saw clear into him, down into his scary spaces. Charlie watched her break off a chunk of onguélé to swab up a clump of dark green nkoumou and slip it all into her mouth.

"Do you like nursing?"

Justine nodded, her jaws working, a ravenous beauty, slim fingers glistening with oil. She bared white teeth to strip gristle from a bone.

Jonas was talking with his mouth full about signs of chimpanzees he'd seen. "Those beasts are very bad," he said. "If they get habituated to coming around, they'll eat up everything in the fields. We'll need to go out and kill one, to chase them away."

Charlie looked at Justine, at her brother across the table, and he wondered where and how he could ask her to spend some time with him, alone, so they could get to know each other. In Minnesota, he would have invited her out to a fancy restaurant. She clearly liked to eat. He imagined asking her out to do something unusual, like go-cart racing. How would she like that?

"What did you do while your brother was hunting?"

"I passed through the fields greeting the women I saw," she said. "I'm interested in traditional healing, in tropical pharmacology, and I wanted to see the plants they use for their remedies." She drained her glass, and the ice cubes clinked against her upper lip.

"I'd like to see that," said Charlie.

The next morning, a boy delivered a message from the chief summoning Justine's brother Jonas, the schoolteacher, to attend a meeting of the council of the elders. The council meeting would last the whole morning. Her brother's absence left Justine free to invite Charlie on a walk in the woods. This was fate at work, she knew, but she resisted even so. The thought of intimacy with a man both allured and repelled her.

On an impulse, she decided, why not. Nothing need come of a walk in the woods. As she approached Charlie's house, she could see him through his open front door. He was sitting at his table, writing. Drawing nearer she wondered if he would come with her. Maybe he would say no. Maybe he was too busy. She knew about all his girlfriends. Her brother had told her about them. She didn't care. Did she? She wondered. What was she doing? If he came along with her, what might happen then? She became less sure the closer she drew. Was this wise? He hadn't seen her yet; she could turn around and go back if she wanted. But fate drew her on.

Zigzagging behind Justine between houses, Charlie took care, as always, to avoid the sharp edges of the low corrugated roofs. It charmed him to see that Justine was slightly pigeon-toed. Angling toward one of the several footpaths that led to the edge of the plateau, Charlie nodded to the people they passed. Some of them were grinning like they knew something he didn't. He saw two of the girlfriends talking to each other, and they turned their faces away when he raised his hand in greeting. Lalish fell in behind noodling on his thumb piano. He followed Charlie and Justine as far as the edge of the village where he stopped.

"Pardon, monsieur, pardon," he called after them, "pardon, mais, ça dit que, ça dit que, ça c'est ma femme!"

Justine made a face over her bare shoulder at Charlie, at the crazy little man's ridiculous claim she was his girl.

The path took them through Chief Oyamba's coffee plantation. Charlie admired the clench of Justine's calves, how her in-turned toes made her sweet bottom sway. He said, "So, you've come to visit your brother."

Justine frowned at him over her shoulder. That was a stupid thing to say.

"And you come from Onga?"

"Hasn't my brother told you that already?"

"You and he, are you même-mère même-père?"

"Même-père. I'm the first-born. He was born one month after me. Growing up, we were always close."

"How many siblings do you have?"

"Thirteen."

"Wow!"

"My father had three wives."

"So you have twelve brothers and sisters, même-père."

"That's right. Most of them live in Libreville. How many brothers and sisters do you have?" she asked, and opened the door onto Charlie's terrible things.

He slammed it shut by answering a different question. "I'm from Minnesota," he said. "Do you know where that is?"

"Where?"

"Minnesota."

"I've never heard of it."

"No one has. It's in the north, next to Canada, where it gets very cold. It gets so cold the lakes freeze over. You can walk across them in the winter. Can you imagine that, walking on water?"

"It must be awful."

They were nearing the edge of the plateau.

"How are you getting back to Akièni?"

"In Milla's bush taxi."

"I could take you."

Justine stopped and turned so suddenly Charlie bumped into her. This time she didn't back away. "That wouldn't put you out?" she asked, looking up into his face.

"No! I'd be happy to!"

This was the biggest man Justine had ever seen close up, a white man no less, so physically powerful, and in a moment of dizzy vertigo she wanted to lean into him. There was something familiar about him, as if their souls had recognized each other. But how could that be, with a man from so far away?

Charlie sensed what she was feeling, and started to put his arms around her, but she recovered and said thank you and turned away.

She had almost let herself go. This meant she was recovering from her psychological trauma, from the trauma of miscarriage, from the trauma of Dr. Emanuel Muengo, with his gentle hands.

"So I can give you a ride?" he asked.

Walking behind her, he couldn't see her face, and she was glad for that. She felt a frisson of fear. In normal times, she trusted her ability to keep atop situations. But she hadn't felt normal for months.

"Yes," she said without turning around. Wherever this was going to lead, it would go no further than she allowed. If something started, and it had to end, she would be the one who ended it, at a time and on terms she decided.

Charlie was smiling at new prospects coming out of the trees to the rim of the plateau, and looking out over the rolling blue-green rain forest he moved up to walk by her side, their flip-flops snapping in unison as they started downhill.

Justine looked up at him. "How do you find Africa?"

Unbidden words poured out of Charlie in a way words never had before. He described the training center in Zaire, the Ogooué River at Boundji, seeing the plateau for the first time, Lalish popping into his window with a snort that made him choke on his pineapple, not knowing where this itchy feeling was coming from. Something deep in him was saying, Hurry to where your heart is leading, a feeling he'd never experienced before. He wanted to woo this woman from Africa, but he had no clear idea how to do it, especially with nothing in the village to invite her to do. Back home in the Twin Cities, he might suggest, some night when she was free, that they go listen to live music, or grab a bite to eat, or take in a movie. Instead, he was gabbling about having kids dig new chiques out of his old chique holes. Jesus Christ, he thought, shut up!

Suddenly, Justine grabbed his arm and made him stop. "Let me see," she said. "Sit down." Sure enough a nurse, she knelt in the sand to examine his feet.

Oh Lord, Charlie groaned, sitting on the side of the steep slope as she examined his toes. Her fingers tugged back the skin from beside each nail and brushed the grains of sand from the weepy chigger holes. Her probing was a tender sensation. She noticed the angry red sores that climbed up his lower legs. She clucked, and parted the black hair to look at them more closely. "Tu es trop poilu."

"I guess I must come from a line of hairy men," said Charlie.

He didn't actually know. Looking at her lowered eyes, he wanted to touch her cheek, stroke the smooth gloss of her shoulder.

Justine got to her feet, clapped her hands, put them on her hips and looked down at him. "Why do you go around in sandals?"

He rose to tower over her.

"You should wear shoes and socks. And start using an antiseptic soap."

Her face looking up at him was like a stern bronze moon. If she had demanded anything of him right then, he would have obeyed without hesitation.

"You know, I've seen you at the hospital before," she said, as they resumed their way down the hill, looking up at him sideways now, but this time with a little smile. "A different time."

"Really?" How could I not remember that? he wondered.

"You brought in the small boy who'd been scalded."

"O-o-oh," said Charlie. His smile dimmed at the memory, the horrible day flying at top speed over the plateau with a screaming two-year-old boy, wrapped in a pagne in his sobbing mother's arms, passing out, waking up, screaming again the whole way to the hospital. The little boy had tipped over a pot of boiling water. Later, Charlie learned, the boy died.

"I didn't notice you. I should have."

"I've seen you other times too."

"Really?"

"Three times I was in Milla's taxi and saw you. The first, you were sitting at a table outside in Otou with other white people and the Préfet. The second time you were in your house, building something. I saw you through the window. The third time there was a big yellow truck stuck in the sand. You were there with men digging it out, and you waved. And the fourth time it was the night you were knocking on Commandant Lentchidja's front door."

They were approaching the edge of the woods, halfway down the hill, and Charlie marveled at all those times he had somehow not seen her.

He let her go first into the canopied gloaming, down the narrow steep trail. She answered his questions about her nursing job as they negotiated the broken path to the stream. It was early enough in the morning that there were only two women washing clothes to say hello to when they sloshed across Kampini Creek and climbed up the opposite bank.

Charlie had not yet ventured across the stream before. He'd grown up in a city. For him the jungle was a menacing place. He'd first felt it in the bosquet, an ancient evil stirring, when he came hurrying out into the wind.

Charlie pushed aside a branch and followed Justine up a crooked trail. The forest for her was a familiar place, a grocery store and a pharmacy. She led the way to a fork and chose the path to the left, ducking beneath two tree trunks that leaned upon each other. Charlie had to get down nearly on all fours to fit through. Ahead, Justine leaped over a fallen limb as neat as a deer. Coming behind, Charlie stubbed his bare toe painfully. Thorns snagged him, and he had to pick them loose from his shirt. After he swung one leg over the fallen branch, Justine was gone from view. He crashed on uphill in her wake, a clumsy barge in a race with a little canoe.

Justine could hear Charlie coming. She waited for him to round a turn in the trail and appear again, sweating, altogether too big for this place. She smiled, plucked a twig from his beard and began showing him the flora of her world.

"That's lantana," she said, indicating a small bush, its yellow flowers like cups in a violet spray. "The leaves are boiled in water and used to cure diarrhea."

Justine led Charlie to a larger bush several yards on. "This is douga," she said. The plant had thorny stems and light green leaves shaped like serrated garden trowels. "Batéké women use it to hasten the healing of their newborns' navels." She led him off the path to point out adjayi, long leaves and red flowers that produced black seeds used to make ceremonial rattles. Just beyond, a bed of mint-colored okourou carpeted a clearing created when one of the giant trees of the forest fell.

"We call it the shy plant," said Justine. "It's a species of mimosa. Touch the leaves."

Charlie bent down to press with his finger, and marveled to see the small dark lozenge-shaped leaves curl up like the fists of sleeping babes.

Justine led him to a plant with yellow flowers shaped like miniature daisies. "This is called ngari. We use it to treat rashes.

This over here is entchégé, lemon grass." She picked a spiky blade and put it to his lips to taste. "It can be brewed into an herbal tea. The roots are used to treat coughs."

They walked further from the path. "This is an olou tree," said Justine. It had smooth bark, slender branches and pale green leaves. "The leaves are edible," she said. "They're a great favorite of the Batéké to the south."

Charlie noticed an improbable tree nearby, looking like a five-foot knobby carrot stabbed into the ground, narrower at its base than at the top of its trunk. "What's that called?"

"That? It's called a bandjiami tree. Midwives use its bark to induce contractions."

Not far away grew a patch of kaya, the same name for tobacco, which its large soft dark leaves somewhat resembled. "Batéké mothers administer this to their babies, to help them learn how to walk," said Justine, and then she pushed a short distance further into the underbrush and holding back a branch, she beckoned Charlie to come see. With a sly smile, she pointed to akata-kata, a plant used by women to make their men love them so much they would overlook all their indiscretions.

9. Something No One Knew

Akièni

T hey shaved the pubescent boy before wheeling him into the operating theater. The boy cried out in pain when they lifted him off the gurney and lay him on the operating table. Tears leaked from the corners of his eyes as he squinted against the brilliance of the surgical lamp. Nurses covered him with green surgical sheets, leaving his lower abdomen bare. The nurse anesthetist placed a breathing mask on his face and adjusted the strap behind his head. The scrub nurse swathed his abdomen with red benzalkonium chloride. The circulating nurse fitted a blood pressure cuff on his arm.

"Nurse Ntchaga," Dr. Emanuel Muengo said to Justine, his warm eyes above his surgical mask drawing her to him, even now after their relationship had ended. "Please review." When he focused his full attention on her, he still had the power to make her feel childish. For several breathless and dizzy seconds, Justine had trouble framing what to say.

Just days after first arriving in Akièni, he'd come after her, the handsome doctor from Zaire. "I am protected," he told her, "by the Minister of Health." A niece of the former First Lady, the Minister of Health somehow managed to hold onto her post after Bongo divorced his wife and purged of all Louzou clan members from government. "I can take care of you," Emanuel promised Justine; but he wasn't talking about marriage.

Justine admired his skills as a surgeon. That would not change. She was grateful for everything he had taught her, and was teaching her still.

"The patient reported pain around his navel," she began. An elevated place in her mind opened up, and words began to flow. "He was experiencing nausea and vomiting. Yesterday the pain

145

relocated to his lower right abdomen."

"Diagnosis?"

"Suspected appendicitis."

"And what was done to confirm this?"

"The lab work revealed elevated white blood cells. This morning the lower right side of the abdomen remained tender and tight. This confirms an enlarged appendix."

"And what have we done to prepare the patient for surgery?"

"We have given him a single dose of ampicillin-sulbactam as a prophylactic antibiotic. Now, Nurse Kawari will induce general anesthesia."

Dr. Muengo nodded at the nurse anesthetist.

"Count backward from one hundred," Nurse Kawari said to the boy, and he twisted open the knobs on the oxygen and the nitrous oxide tanks. He squeezed the reservoir bag, and watched the ball in the flow meter rise. In seconds, the boy was limp.

"Let's start," said Dr. Emanuel Muengo to the circulating nurse, who stood ready by the instrument table. She placed a scalpel handle-first in his right palm. Dr. Muengo pressed the gloved fingers of his left hand around the two dots he had made with a marker on the boy's abdomen. "The classic incision," he said, "is perpendicular to a line here between the umbilicus and the anterior superior spine of the ilium."

He drew the blade across the skin, and there was no blood. He spread the incision with one, then a second locking retractor. With the scalpel, he divided the thin layer of underlying yellow fat. He repositioned the retractors to open the incision deeper, and expose the underlying internal oblique muscle. It was a deep red, in contrast to the silver surgical instruments, and the patient's dark skin. He used a scissors to split the muscle in line with the fibers, and drew it open with two hooked retractors. Beneath was the transversus abdominis muscle, and with the scissors he spread it open along its fibers as well. Then he repositioned the self-retaining retractors a third time, exposing the peritoneum, a pale membrane.

"Nurse Ntchaga," he said, "observe how I use the forceps to make a fold in the peritoneum. I must ensure there is nothing below. Scalpel. Now, I make a nick in the fold, to incise the peritoneum, and I open it." Murky fluid emerged. "Swab," he said, and the scrub nurse blotted away the fluid. Dr. Muengo slid his gloved forefinger into the cavity. "I can feel the appendix. It's free from surrounding structures, so I can deliver it into the incision." He hooked out the thin wormlike appendix, shot through with blood vessels and sickly dark.

"Hemostat."

The circulating nurse handed the instrument to him, and with it he pinched the tip of the appendix, and tugged it all the way out into the light. "You see the appendiceal artery?" He tied two small ligatures in the thin artery. Justine trimmed off the surgical thread. He used the scalpel to cut the artery in two. "Now I will crush the base of the appendix with a clamp." He tied two ligatures on either side of the instrument, released the clamp, and with his finger and thumb stretched the appendix out. "Nurse Ntchaga, cut between the two ligatures, with the scalpel."

The circulating nurse handed Justine a scalpel, an expression in her eyes that Justine couldn't read. Justine placed it carefully between the ligatures, and sliced.

Dr. Muengo lifted the inflamed appendix free and dropped it in the wastebasket. The scrub nurse promptly irrigated the incision with saline solution.

"Now, Nurse Ntchaga, I want you to make a purse string suture. I will show you how."

The circulating nurse placed a toothed forceps in Justine's right hand, a curved needle and thread locked in its teeth. Justine reached with the forceps toward the open incision. Dr. Muengo looked at her, with knowing eyes. She knew he was smiling behind the mask.

Justine pressed the tip of the needle against the glistening cecum, concentrating on what her hand was doing, willing her fingers steady, and the scrub nurse dabbed perspiration from her forehead.

"Push it through."

She pressed, and when the point of the curved needle emerged, Dr. Muengo fastened a second forceps to its end.

"Release your forceps."

She did as he said, and he pulled the curved needle and drew the thread through.

"Another beside it," he said. "Three will do. Then we'll pull the purse strings closed, and we'll bury the stump."

Walking home, Justine reviewed all that Emanuel had showed her, and tried to commit it to memory. "You never know when it might be you," he said, making it sound easy. Would she be able to remove an appendix if she had to, if faced with that emergency? Would she be able to tie surgeon's knots as neatly as he could? Her movements had been slow, unpracticed, awkward; not at all like his hands, swift and sure.

Justine heard a scuffle of feet and a thump coming from the other side of her bungalow. Only then did she notice the white pickup truck in front of her house. She knew at once that Charlie was there.

A soccer ball bounced into view. Her second born twin brother, Mpiga Gérard, ran in pursuit. With a reaching stab of his foot, he stopped the ball, settled it, kicked it back the way it had come, then disappeared from view. When the ball came back, Mpiga's twin, Mbou Blaise dribbled it, with Charlie chasing after him. Justine felt a thrill she turned off at once. All three of them saw her at the same time and stopped. Mbou called out, "Charlie brought us this wonderful ball!"

Charlie jogged toward her, smiling and breathing hard, sweat shining on his forehead, his cheeks flushed above his coal black beard. "Bonjour," he said, offering his huge hand. He was big enough to blot out the sky. "I brought your brothers a soccer ball," he said, not realizing Mbou Blaise had already told her this. "And I brought you a leg of antelope. Your brother Jonas shot it with one of the shells I picked up for him the last time I was in Franceville. Your brothers put the meat in your fridge."

"Thank you." she managed. What else could she say to this sudden jumble of generosity?

"See here," said Mbou, showing her the soccer ball, "it's an Adidas!" The soccer ball, a high quality Starlancer, had red stripes.

"I thought I'd buy them one that would last," Charlie said.

"You're too kind."

"And I thought I'd ask you to dinner."

Three small boys appeared in the open window, and one had a

148

runny nose. Justine spoke to them in Téké, and they disappeared. An overhead fluorescent tube cast a blue-tinged glare in the private room Charlie had requested. Justine's yellow sundress was brilliant against her skin. They sat at a table for two. Charlie had made the arrangements with the owner of Akièni's lone restaurant ahead of time. It catered to truck drivers and taxi men. He was the first person ever to bring a date here.

Justine hadn't wanted to go out to dinner. Her brothers' wheedling wore her down. She was tired. After a quick shower, she wondered irritably about what to wear. She'd been a fool with Emanuel. Never again. Never again would she put herself in that position. Never. The American with all his girlfriends, smiling through his beard, what did he expect?

A woman came to take their order. There was fried chicken and rice. That was all. Charlie complained. The owner had assured him there would be a variety of dishes to choose from, and a candle to light their table.

"The owner isn't here," the server said.

Charlie became exasperated. Justine felt bad for him. He meant well. On that walk in the woods, she'd discoverer something both ponderous and endearing about him. Where had the feeling gone? She didn't want him to get wrong ideas. She had thanked him for the soccer ball. That was a generous gift. It secured him the twins' affection. Justine had thanked him for the meat. She could tell he hoped that whenever she cooked it, she would invite him to dinner.

"How are things with you?" he asked, trying to recover his good humor. "How was your day?"

"All right, I suppose. I assisted in an appendectomy."

"Oh?" Charlie wrinkled his nose. "I don't think I could be a surgeon. I'm kind of —" He didn't know the word for squeamish. "I don't think I'd be able to cut someone open."

Justine thought of the shining scalpel slitting open dark skin.

"Tell me a bit about you," he said, the tack he had planned, even though, in his experience, most girls didn't enjoy talking about themselves. Justine turned out to be one.

"Why?"

"I'm interested."

"Why are you interested?"

"I'd like to know a little about you."

"Huh! Well, I was born in Onga. I grew up and went to nursing school. Now I'm a nurse. There, you know a little about me."

Charlie was taken aback. "Where did this attitude come from?" The Gabonese often spoke brusquely, he had learned, so maybe it wasn't intentional rudeness. But it sounded rude. And what was that look? This is a woman of many layers, he thought to himself. Where was the Justine who took him on a walk in the forest, then turned away laughing from his kiss?

He persisted. "You and Jonas are même-père, as I recall. You're the first-born. Jonas was born one month after you, right? You have, what was it you told me, twelve brothers and sisters? Your father had three wives."

"Yes," she said, "I told you that."

She looked out the window into the night, and all he could do was watch her in profile, wondering where she was. Nothing he said seemed to come out right. Where was the other Justine?

The server brought their drinks, opened the bottles and filled their glasses. Justine sipped her orangeade, looking at Charlie, his dark eyes with their long lashes. When she was tired, she became peevish and irritable. She knew this about herself. She should make an effort. Charlie had brought them gifts. She should try. "Actually," she said, "Jonas and I aren't truly même-père. My natural father died when I was nine."

"Oh, wow. I'm sorry."

"It doesn't matter. I never knew him. Right after I was born, my mother was given to Jonas's father. He was already an old man, and when he died, my mother was given over to become the wife of his younger brother, who died this last December."

"Three fathers, all dead. Wow. I'm really sorry. What did your natural father die of?"

Justine hesitated.

She had changed her style of braids, Charlie noticed. She had on gold earrings tonight. There was a virtue about her. Shared intimacies would draw them together, he wanted to believe, and he planned to draw out of her intimate details of her life, so he could reciprocate, and tell her about himself, tell her something no one knew.

"His name was Mathias." The expression on Justine's face was strong and determined, softened by a childlike forehead. He saw she was going to tell him. "My mother was only thirteen when she gave birth to me. She grew breasts during the pregnancy."

Charlie scowled, ready to dislike the man named Mathias, who had gotten a schoolgirl pregnant.

"He was a schoolboy too. He came from a different village. During the long vacation, he came to visit a relative in Onga. He met my mother and went home without knowing he'd made her pregnant. She was forced to leave school. That's what they did in those days. He was too young to provide for her, so my mother was consigned into marriage as the second wife of Jonas's father, the man I grew up knowing as my father."

The server set two plates before them, and Justine said something to her. Charlie recognized the Téké word for hot pepper.

"What became of your natural father?"

"He went on to secondary school. He did very well. People say I take after him because I always did well in school."

They began to eat. Charlie had driven to Akièni that afternoon convinced he and Justine were kindred spirits even though they came from different worlds. He came intending to learn if she thought so too. Now he wondered, maybe they weren't. Maybe things wouldn't work out.

"My father won a government bursary to attend university in France," Justine continued. "They say he graduated with high distinctions. When he came back to Gabon, the government gave him a job in the Department of Foreign Affairs. They assigned him to the Embassy in Paris. He was very fortunate to get that assignment. He was rising fast, and people were jealous of his success. After two years in Paris, he came home on leave to see me, his firstborn child, for the first time."

Suddenly her nostrils flared, like she was taking Charlie's scent, her eyes fierce, not looking at him.

"I remember wearing a frilly dress and black patent leather shoes that were too small. I was so excited, waiting to meet my real father; a man I had never seen. I imagined him great and tall, a strong smiling man with kind eyes and a mustache. All day long, I was not allowed to play with the others, so I would stay clean. I had to stay indoors. He was coming to the village to see me, and I was so excited. But he never arrived. He spent the night here in Akièni, on his way to Onga."

"What happened? Why didn't he arrive?"

"An uncle brought him a plate of pineapple. After eating a piece, my father fell to the floor and died at age twenty-four."

Charlie was shocked. "Did he choke?"

"He was poisoned."

"Poisoned! You mean he was murdered?"

"Yes. That's what they say."

She said it so plainly, with those up-tilted eyes, lips the color of a bruise, parted slightly as she chewed another bite, her yellow dress setting off the rich brown of her skin. She was sitting so near him, across from him, but she was completely alone.

"So I never met him. I don't have even a photograph to know my real father by."

This was in so many ways far worse than what Charlie was planning to tell her. "It sounds like probably he choked, maybe. Why do they say he was murdered?"

"Because of his success."

"I don't understand. Why would someone murder him for being successful?"

"There is much about us you will not understand."

She had receded from him, cutting more chicken from the bone. What she said was true. The Gabonese had seemed quite uncomplicated to young Charlie Sinclair when he first arrived in the country. Now, he was learning, among them were people who used poison to kill.

But he didn't want to give up. "So you and Jonas don't have the same father, but Jonas's father is the man who raised you, and he had three wives."

"Can we talk about something else?" said Justine. "Why are you looking at me like that?"

Charlie didn't know how to say it. "I .... You're such ... you're a pure person, Justine. I've never met anyone like you."

"You've known lots of girls."

Ah, so she knew of the girlfriends. Her brother Jonas must have told her. For a moment, there was silence. Then Charlie said, "But I've never known anyone like you."

"Huh!" she said, setting down her fork.

"This food isn't very good, is it?" said Charlie. He pushed his plate away. "My chicken's pink in the middle. What do you say we get out of here? What do you say we go look at the stars?"

Plateau

"The thing I like about the rainy season," said Charlie, his voice raised over the roar of the engine, climbing the flank of the plateau, "is all the humidity gets rained out during the day. The night skies are so clear."

At the end of the laterite, he stopped and switched off the lights and the engine.

"And the thing I like about it up here on the plateau is there're hardly any mosquitoes. We can sit on the tailgate and look at the stars."

I need to be careful, Justine thought to herself as she stepped down from the cab into the cool sand. She walked warily to the rear of the truck as Charlie let the tailgate down. Suddenly his hands were under her arms and she was swinging up into the air. He set her down lightly on the tailgate, as if she weighed nothing at all.

Charlie raised himself on his hands, and the truck sagged under his weight as he settled his rump next to her. There was no moon, and not a single cloud. The stars were brilliant, like buckets of diamonds dashed out on black glass.

"Do you know the names of any of the stars? The constellations?"

Justine was astonished he lifted her into the air like that, like a three-year-old child. Her feet dangled in the air.

"I know a few. That one's Orion." Charlie leaned closer so she could sight along his arm, his finger pointing. "See the belt? That's the sword. Over there just above the horizon is the Southern Cross. See it? And there on the northern horizon, just to the side of those trees is the Big Dipper. Here on the equator, at the equinox in March, like now, and in September, you can see both at the same time."

She shivered.

"Are you cold?" He hopped off, and the truck lifted. He went to the cab and came back with a pagne he wrapped around her shoulders. "How's that?"

The truck sagged again from his weight.

He swept his hand across the sky. "All that is the Milky Way. The stars are so beautiful, don't you think?" He lay back, looking up. "I never noticed the stars, growing up in a city."

Justine turned so she could look down at him, and curled her legs under her.

"You know, I felt something," he said, "when you told me about your father. Ever since I first saw you, I've felt something, like maybe there's a reason we met. Do you ever believe things are meant to be? I felt that way when we went on the walk in the woods."

He is preparing to tell me something, she could hear in his voice, see in his face, pale in the starlight above his beard.

"My life is not like yours," he said. She was the first person he had ever wanted to tell. She was righteous, and he wanted her to know. "I was raised in what they call ..."

Justine could feel something strong surging inside him, wanting to come out.

Charlie groped for the word in French for foster home. He didn't know it. Growing up, he'd been passed from one household to another, like a parcel who brought an extra ten thousand dollars a year from the state. The first place he remembered, there were seven or eight and the grownups were always out. The oldest boy did those things. Charlie screamed and cried for help. The others just watched, except the littlest girl. He could see in her eyes she felt sorry for him, living in that place where the oldest boy choked him so he wouldn't tell. "Shut up! Shut up your screaming!"

Another foster home they yelled at him, "You're retarded!" the third or the fourth – they became blurred in his mind. His clothes were always too small. It was pointless to try to make friends at school because he'd soon be moving again. The next place, they hit him with a belt, and he tore a towel rack off the wall, because now he was getting big. They put him in a chair and bound him with straps, and a government van came. In the courtroom, the judge said criminal charges should be preferred because the case manager had failed to keep this child safe. They moved him again, but it didn't matter. By then, Charlie knew how to steel himself against the abuse. He had learned to shrink down inside where no one could touch him or hurt him anymore.

One day at school, Coach Dawber stepped in front of him in the hallway and said, "You're a gall darn big one. You should come out for the football team."

Charlie said nothing, his jaw clenched, his lips tight, and Coach Dawber saw immediately in the narrowed eyes the boy desperately needed someone to talk to. "Come with me to my office, son."

"I'll be late for biology."

"I'll write you a note."

In Coach's office off the gym, Charlie began to tell his story, in bits and pieces, for the first time. Shocked at how the foster system passed him around, shocked to hear of the physical abuse the boy had endured, Coach Dawber blurted out, "Son, would you like to come live at my house? My children are grown now. Me and the wife can talk to Human Services and see what we can do, if you like."

Everything began to change for Charlie after that, starting with new clothes, the first new clothes he ever had. Charlie began seeing Dr. Campbell, a therapist with twinkly eyes, like an elf. Every session drew another terrible story out of him and into the open where Charlie, sobbing, could see them for what they were, through his streaming tears, and lock them away in a place where they would never hurt him again.

Coach Dawber's brother, Uncle Vince, gave Charlie a summer job on his landscaping crew, working with college kids mainly, ten, eleven, sometimes twelve hours a day. It was physical work, wielding a shovel, pushing heavy wheelbarrows around shoveling, spreading and raking gravel, planting trees, bushes and shrubs, laying sod. The job demanded little more than brute animal strength from Charlie and scraped the hide from his hands. When August came, hot and humid, football camp started. A different kind of physical work, Charlie learned football meant stretching, running, calisthenics, and more running, sweating in helmets and pads, agility drills, and finally scrimmage.

The first time Charlie fired out of a three-point stance, he flung his blocker aside. Coach tried a double team against him, and Charlie bull rushed right through both linemen.

His chest rose and fell, breathing fast and shallow, and Justine could feel the injury deep within him, a heartache like her own.

Finally Charlie spoke. "Growing up," he said, struggling to keep his voice even, "I had to live with a lot of strangers."

"Why did you live with strangers?"

"Because they kept moving me around."

"Who kept moving you around?"

"Human Services."

"Who are they?"

"They oversee where kids without families live."

"What does that mean, kids without families? How can a child not have a family? That doesn't make any sense. Everyone is born to someone. Everyone has a family."

Charlie had no words.

He was struggling with a torment she could not comprehend, to have no family, to be alone, with no one in the world. Without thinking, she reclined and put her head on his chest.

Charlie stroked her shoulder. "When I started to get big, the football coach asked me to try out for the team. He took me in, to live with him. I guess you could say he and his wife were my family, sort of. Football saved me, I guess. Because of my size, I was good at football. Football was good to me. It gave me an excuse to hit people."

"Hit people?"

"I'm not talking about soccer. American football. You know about that? Where the players put on helmets and pads and smash into each other as hard as they can?"

"That sounds very strange."

"There are things about my people that you'll never understand."

He smiled at repeating what she had said to him in the restaurant, although with her head on his chest she couldn't see his smile.

She was smiling too, though Charlie couldn't see it. His fingers located hers; his hand swallowed hers. She felt the roughness of his palm, like a villager's hand, and she felt his strength. He wanted to be comforted, and to comfort her, and resting her head on his chest under the stars, she could hear the steady beating of his great heart.

10. Sunlight through Trees

Okouya

In the late afternoon, Eloumba Jean-Paul appeared at Édouard's house with the sling chair Charlie had ordered. The otangani came back late from Akièni the previous night, which surprised Édouard. He expected the otangani would spend the night with the schoolteacher's sister. His urges were well known.

But he was back, and so as planned, Édouard and Jean-Paul started over to the otangani's house. In his pocket, Jean-Paul carried the list of names he had written out for Chief Oyamba. As they walked, they discussed how odd it was that with all the girls he had here in the village, the otangani seemed to be pursuing Ntchaga Justine.

"Perhaps he doesn't know she is kakouma," said Jean-Paul. "If he finds out she is barren, he will certainly lose interest in her. Also, she is a great beauty. Beautiful women cannot be trusted."

"True," said Édouard, "everyone knows that."

Lalish watched Charlie through the window as he removed food for dinner from the refrigerator. When Édouard and Jean-Paul knocked and entered with the second sling chair, Charlie got five thousand francs from his bedroom. As he handed the blue note to Jean-Paul, Édouard nodded, and Jean-Paul presented him with a folded piece of paper.

Formally headed with a date – Sunday 18 March 1990 – the paper contained a list of names written out in the neat hand of the village scrivener.

"Those are the men Chief Oyamba wants you to hire," said Édouard.

Charlie frowned. The surprise put him in a delicate situation. He would have to handle this carefully. He gestured for the men to sit at the table and went to the kitchen to put away the food. He hadn't yet reached a decision on the ten men to hire. He had been paring down the names, winnowing out those who hadn't worked much building the teachers' houses, but he hadn't yet gotten himself into the right frame of mind to actually start building the school. But this list was something he could not ignore.

Charlie joined them at the table and told them, "Ça ne peut pas être comme ça."

Now Édouard frowned. Why couldn't it be as the chief had decided? He lit a Forte and waited for the American to explain himself. Lalish changed windows to bum a cigarette from him, and stood there in the window smoking too.

"I will decide who to hire."

Oyali Albert came to the door. With a single sharp rap, he stepped inside and joined Charlie, Édouard and Jean-Paul at the table. He took a cigarette from Édouard and lit it. Behind him came Oloumba Bruno. Bruno didn't smoke. He was obliged to stand. Oyamba Benjamin arrived with Assélé Laurent and Ngani Jean-Baptiste, Jean-Paul's father, who was bald and had not shown up to work on the teachers' houses much. Lenkongi Francis was right on their heels. Once blinded by the bones of a dead twin, this was a man who, the girlfriends had told Charlie, by virtue of having the biggest bangala in the village, had screwed most of their mothers in his day, and was still screwing some of them now. Francis had showed up to work not at all. These men weren't here just to wish Charlie good evening. Greeting each other, shaking hands, they were sniffing around in the cigarette smoke for advance information about who was going to get the jobs. They believed the decision was being made. Next came Oyamba Jacques, Benjamin's brother and owner of the village bar. He squeezed into the room with Ndjièmi Joseph. Crowding in behind them came a wizened old codger whose name Charlie didn't know.

This was not as Charlie had been planning. He had to nip this thing in the bud. He had to assert control. Thinking rapidly he decided the thing to do now would be what Rebecca had done in Otou. He would explain to the chief a second palaver was needed, to discuss how the school would be maintained, after it was built. He would use that as an opportunity to remind the gathering of the hiring rule. And then he would make them all understand that once he was gone, it would be their responsibility to take care of the school. Then he would lead them in brainstorming how this would be done. That was the word Rebecca had used: brainstorming. And he would start in on the school at once. The time of loafing was over.

Charlie rose from the table with his hastily made plan and shouldered his way through the men. He stepped outside and started for Chief Oyamba's house, and the men came after him talking loudly.

Édouard trotted up to his side. "What are you doing?"

"I'm going to tell your father how the decision will be made, and I'm going to ask him to call another palaver."

"What do you mean?" Édouard had trouble keeping up with Charlie.

Seeing the otangani leading a procession to the house of the land chief, other men realized the decision was in fact being made. Cries went up, and all over the village, men dropped what they were doing and came on the run.

Édouard pulled on the otangani's arm as they neared his father's house, to stop him from doing this thing, but Charlie would not be stopped. He knocked on the open door sharply.

Oyamba called out in welcome from his sling chair next to his filthy unmade bed. His best friend, Ngawanaga Bernard, the only Christian in Okouya was visiting. A grandson was at his feet shoving a log into the fire.

Charlie stepped inside and shook the two men's hands. "Wémindjuska, Nkani-Ntsie," he greeted the land chief.

"Eh, nawé," Oyamba replied. "Wé bounou li?"

"Mi ndi yemingyi," Charlie said. He was feeling fine. "Wé bari bounou ali?"

"Mi bari ali yemingyi." The people were all fine.

Charlie sat on a wooden stool, having run through most of the Téké phrases he knew. Édouard took a second stool as Oyamba leaned over to retrieve a kola nut from the store he kept buried fresh and handy in the sand. He gave it to Charlie and cocked his head at the sound of men yelling and arguing outside. The grandson poked at the flames with a stick, stirring up small plumes of ash.

Acrid smoke hung about the blackened rafters.

Charlie thanked Oyamba for the kola nut. To Édouard he said, "I want you to translate for me." Charlie picked his words carefully. He reminded the chief with all due respect that the purpose of having the men build the teachers' houses voluntarily was it gave him an opportunity to see which men worked the hardest. He took the list from his shirt pocket and handed it back.

"I will decide who to hire, Chief, if you please."

Édouard shook his head. "You can't say that."

"I must be the one to decide who to hire, and it has to be based on who worked the hardest on the teachers' houses. It's the only fair way. Tell him."

"The chief has selected those names."

"Tell him."

"There have been discussions."

"This is the rule I gave at the palaver. I can't change it now. I have to follow the rule. Tell him."

"He has given a great deal of thought to those names."

"Tell him, Édouard!"

"Do you know what this will do?"

"Tell him!"

Against his better judgment, Édouard did what the otangani wanted. He told his father, and Bernard's mouth fell open.

Oyamba's hazy eyes flashed at Charlie's audacity. The chief raised his whiskery chin and glared.

"I must do it the way we do these things in America, Chief. I must hire men based on their performance. It's called the merit system."

A look of bewilderment clouded Oyamba's face as his son translated these unfamiliar words. He looked into the fire with the folded slip of paper he couldn't read in his hand.

Charlie said, "Chief, you can hear the men are gathering. They want to know. So I think we should have a second palaver, right now."

Oyamba stared into the fire as Édouard translated. Bernard seemed unable to believe what he was hearing. The grandson sat in the sand by the fire watching, not really understanding, but aware this was terribly serious. Ashes fell from the smoldering log.

"Do you agree, Chief?"

Oyamba asked a question.

"The chief asks why. He asks what is wrong."

"Chief, nothing is wrong. We need to make sure that everybody understands how the selections will be made. Also, I want all your people to understand that since the school will be for them, they must take care of it once it is finished."

Bernard said something to Chief Oyamba, who thought for a while, his cloudy eyes back on the fire. He looked out the window, hearing the gathering crowd. He began to speak, and as he did, his whiskery chin rose, and his voice lost its quaver.

Édouard translated, grim-faced, speaking in a monotone. "The chief says your people have sent you to us from far away, to give us a great thing, a school for our village."

Charlie grunted.

"Soon the chief will die."

"No!" said Charlie, surprised at the catch in his throat.

"When he dies, you must write to your people and tell them that old Oyamba is dead."

Charlie laid his large hand on Oyamba's bony shoulder. "Chief, you'll be here to see the school finished!"

"S'il a mauvais," Oyamba said. Then he said something in Téké, and Charlie caught the words Gabon, etangani, school and government.

"The chief says in Gabon, the whites have always been welcome. He does not agree with what you are saying. It is not the right way. But the school project has been brought here by the government, and a school is a good thing for any village to have, so Chief Oyamba will not forbid this."

"Forbid what?"

Now Édouard looked angry. "What are you saying? You will not do as the chief has commanded, but you do not know what you will do in its place?"

"I know what I'm going to do."

Édouard foresaw terrible consequences, all because this otangani would not submit to his father, as he should.

Charlie waited to see if there was more. Then he said to Oyamba, "Chief, your people must start thinking about how to organize themselves to maintain the school after it's built and I'm gone."

Oyamba listened to his son translate. Then he looked at Charlie. "C'est comme la d'accord."

Édouard argued with his father, that he should not yield on this point. His father responded that they had no choice. They were not building the school. Omar Bongo had sent the otangani, and they must do what the otangani said.

Charlie heard, 'Bongo.' 'Otangani.'

"So it's all right with you, Chief? Can we shake on it?" Charlie asked. Oyamba accepted, and Charlie shook the Chief's leathery hand, his fingers like twigs. "You'll help me explain?"

"S'il a mauvais, pas comme la d'accord!" the old man said with sudden fierceness. "Tout ça, tout ça," he said, squeezing Charlie's hand with surprising strength and sweeping his left arm out to indicate everything, "c'est pour moi!"

Angry orange sunlight slashed through the trees when Chief Oyamba left his house for the palaver. He walked with a staff, Charlie at his side. Every man in the village sat in a sling chair in the fading light, joined by many women. The old grandmothers sat on mats they had spread in the sand, their legs straight out, the soles of their feet in a row. Behind them, all the grandfathers, the village elders, faced two sling chairs that had been readied under the giant mango tree. One chair was for Charlie and the other for Chief Oyamba. Younger women stood three-deep in a half circle behind the men, some with babies on their backs, some nursing babies. One of the old women smoked a pipe. Charlie could see the girlfriends here and there. A nervous energy ran through the crowd, and out on the fringes Lalish paused from taking notes to berate an imaginary person next to him.

As he and the chief took their seats, Charlie leaned over and asked Oyamba if he wanted to say anything first. Édouard translated. The old chief shook his head, No.

So Charlie did the thing he hated most and got to his feet, and all conversation instantly ceased. "I'm glad you all could come on such short notice," he began, a poor joke that fell flat. "I want to explain two things to you; actually, to remind you of the first one." He waited for the buzz of translating voices to die down. "The first is about the jobs to build the school."

At the mention of jobs, the men let out a low roar of approval.

"The second is I want to start everybody planning about how to get organized to keep the school up after it's done." He waited for the translators to finish.

"Now, as I've been telling you all along, everybody has had the same chance to get one of the ten jobs building the school. The candidates all took a test. You know the rule. The ten men who scored the highest on the test are the ones who are going to get the jobs. The test was working on the teachers' houses. The ten men who worked hardest building the teachers' houses are going to get the jobs."

As the translations were made, faces looked shocked, as if they were hearing this for the first time. Angry voices burst out, and arguments sprang up. Albert raised his hand with a question. Sitting next to him was Ndebi Marc, the best hunter in the village. Marc was scowling angrily.

"Monsieur Charlie," Albert said, "Monsieur Marc wants to know why the hunters are being passed over."

Charlie looked at the man. "Monsieur Marc, how many days did you work on the teachers' houses?"

Marc shook his head, and there was a mounting grumble of men talking among themselves, hiding their mouths behind their hands. "The otangani saw an ofou!" one of them shouted out. "The otangani said so himself, a woman who clearly must have been sent by the ancestors to tell him to be fair on this question!"

Again, the crowd roared.

The father of the village scrivener and carpenter held up his hands for quiet. "I did not work much on les maisons des maîtres, so that means I probably will not be chosen. No doubt, my son Jean-Paul will be chosen because he has worked very faithfully. Monsieur Charlie is correct. This is a fair way for selecting the men."

A man Charlie didn't know jumped to his feet and began yelling. More shouting broke out, and Charlie caught snippets:

Bongo sent the otangani, the school will be Bongo's, c'est pour l'état, the jobs should be for everyone!

Édouard stood up and addressed the angry ones. "How many villages will have such a school? It's a privilege for us to have been singled out by President Bongo, and we must do as Monsieur Charlie says!" He sat down to the applause of a few.

The dissenters began shouting even louder. Several of them got to their feet and gestured angrily at Édouard. "Who will pay us for the work we did on the teachers' houses?" one of them demanded.

Albert yelled at them to be quiet, to show some respect and listen to Monsieur Charlie.

More men rose up and turned on Albert. One of them shouted, "What are we going to get out of this?"

"Bongo is rich!" another man yelled. "Why should this otangani prevent everyone from having a share?"

All the men were standing now. Some were irately folding their chairs and stalking off. Most of the grandmothers were on their feet getting safely out of the way, but the old grandmother smoking a pipe sat resolutely on her mat. She watched Chief Oyamba, his expression wooden as he stared straight ahead.

Charlie knew then he had lost control.

In the watery predawn light, he awoke from his dream. He had been hanging on a rock face, trying to climb a rope ladder up out of a dark chasm. Each time he put his weight on a rung, the ladder descended another foot. As long as he remained still, the ladder remained steady, leaving him suspended above shadowy peril.

Outside, the village came to life, roosters crowing, goats bleating, babies crying, scattered coughing. The halest, earliest-rising women were shouting to each other about who was going to water; who was going to their fields? Charlie looked at his watch. Ten after six. He shrugged off his covers, rose into the chill and blew out his lamp. He pulled on a pair of shorts and wiggled his toes into his flip-flops. He went out of his bedroom, grabbed the roll of toilet paper, opened his front door, and there in the gray gloaming were men.

There were five of them, and they closed in and wished Charlie good morning and inquired how he had slept, shaking his hand and peering deeper into his eyes than was decent at this early hour. He crossed the sandy way with his flip-slops snapping, the end of the roll of toilet paper fluttering from his hand like a pennant. He brushed through wet grass to his latrine where he stepped out onto the plank floor.

The sun brimmed on the edge of the horizon like a molten bead. As it rose, the red light caught the top of the ground fog, and dew on the delicate tracery of spider webs in the grass grew visible. A lizard in the woven fronds stirred to life. As the sun came bulging up from the horizon, the great ongoumou tree suddenly exploded with the weaver birds welcoming a new day.

Back at his house more men were coming. They all wanted to shake Charlie's hand, which he would not do until he had washed. Inside he got his towel and his toilet kit from his bedroom, went to the kitchen, opened the window and ran water into his sink. He washed his hands and face. He could hear the men exclaiming at his drainpipe. He saw them looking in through his window.

He fixed a breakfast of fried eggs. Men gathered outside, their Basenji dogs nipping and scratching fleas while he ate. He washed the dishes, determined to hold firm, rinsing the plate and the mug and the frying pan and the silverware and setting them on a towel to dry. He had made his decision. And he would stick with it. He had set a performance standard for hiring the crew. He dried his hands, went back to the salon and sat down at the table to review his final list. There would be no turning back.

He would hire four manœuvres, laborers who would earn the equivalent of seventy-five dollars a month, and six skilled workers, ouvriers – one carpenter, one rod buster and four masons – who would earn one hundred a month. Choosing his carpenter was easy; no one was more qualified than Eloumba Jean-Paul, and Charlie ticked off his name boldly. Because he was literate, Charlie would also make him the magasinier, in charge of the inventory.

Oyali Albert would get the job for which he had lobbied long and hard. He would be Charlie's ferrailleur, his rod buster, a trade for which Albert had papers. In addition, Charlie intended to put him in charge of the cement mixer.

For his first mason Charlie selected the elfin retired master mason named Atcholo Jean-Luc who had directed the plastering of

167

the teachers' houses. The problems started with the second mason. There was a tie between Oyamba Benjamin and Assélé Laurent. Both had shown up regularly to work on the teachers' houses and both had papers showing experience. Benjamin was an alcoholic and Laurent was a chronic complainer. Laurent would be a divisive factor on the crew, Charlie decided, so he was out and Benjamin was in.

Picking Oloumba Bruno was going to be controversial too. He had no construction experience, but Bruno had shown the most interest in finishing concrete. Choosing Édouard as the fourth mason was natural. He'd been Charlie's helper from the very first day and was a faithful worker on the teachers' houses. But Édouard had no previous construction experience. Giving him a top-dollar job as a mason would be a reward, people would say. Perhaps the fact that he was in line to be the next land chief would make this okay.

Selecting the four laborers was the hardest decision of all. There were so many men to choose from. There were all the girlfriends' fathers, brothers and uncles to consider, and the husbands of all the women who had been bringing him food. And there was Jean-Paul's dad, who had spoken up for Charlie at the palaver.

Charlie picked Makokomba Alphonse, the leader of the teenage boys. He would be the youngest. Charlie would have to pass up men with children to support, but he was going to do it because Alphonse had always been there to help whenever it was time to work on the Land Cruiser. Another laborer Charlie decided on was the hunter Ndebi Marc. He had not worked at all on the teachers' houses, and that was going to cause dissention. But picking Marc would soften the hard feelings that other choices were going to make, because Marc had been brave enough to speak out against Charlie at the palaver. Also, Marc had provided him with so much meat, and always refused payment. Mamva Joseph and Kankourou Daniel completed the laborers.

Not one of the men Charlie picked was a girlfriend's relative. It was impossible to satisfy them all; better to disappoint them all equally. He knew, however, that it meant none of his girlfriends would come to his house ever again.

The list was complete. The moment of decision had arrived.

Charlie went to his open door and called in Édouard first.

Schoolchildren scampered by with their notebooks and pens when Édouard stepped inside. Charlie told him to close the door and indicated the chair across the table. A few moments later Édouard gave Charlie a small smile of thanks, shook his hand and went out.

Jean-Paul gave Charlie the two-handed handshake. Albert tried to kiss Charlie's hand. Mamva Joseph received his good news with dignity. Young Alphonse grinned, whooped and leapt out the door like a gazelle. Benjamin didn't smell of alcohol when he came in and shut the door behind him. Sitting there, he calmly said thank you. Jean-Luc made a slight smile and gave a quick bow of his head. Ndebi Marc had to be called for, and was genuinely surprised.

When it was over, sharp splintery cracks shot through the village like fault lines. Men who hadn't been chosen came to Charlie's door demanding to be heard. He wouldn't give way. The process was closed. Some just pursed their lips and left. Some stormed off yelling. Assélé Laurent came to the door and gave Charlie such a foul look that it chilled him to the bone.

11. A Chair of Bones

Otou

Moundounga Philbert bulled his way into Rebecca's life on the wild night they broke her bed. Things might not have happened that way.

"Do what?" he demanded when she pulled out the box of Tahitian Treats. "Put it where?" The condoms came in four colors; a U.S. Government-issue brand the Peace Corps nurse provided to all the volunteers. Philbert unrolled a green one and examined it. "What if it doesn't fit?" He laughed, and snapped it at Rebecca like a big rubber band. The next night he brought over a few of his things, and the third night he came expecting dinner.

Built like foam-covered steel, Philbert had broad shoulders, narrow hips, round buns and a V-shaped back, a navel poking out from his washboard abs like the tip of a tongue. He had only completed the sixth grade, but Rebecca wasn't interested in Philbert for deep discussions. He wasn't bitter about the advantages she grew up enjoying, compared to his childhood. He didn't complain about the unfairness of life, as she would have done, had their fates been reversed. He adjusted to using condoms. He already had three children running around in Otou, and half a dozen others scattered about in several villages on the plateau.

Rebecca liked Philbert's kids, and enjoyed it when they stopped by to visit, but she felt awkward around their three different moms. The oldest child, a solemn boy of ten, impressed her as the only schoolboy in Otou with ambition. He did not dream of playing soccer in Europe. He wanted to be a mining engineer. The middle child, a second son, was an imp, a willing accomplice for Rebecca's practical jokes, like sewing his older brother's pant legs shut or filling his dad's toothpaste tube with mustard. The third child had just turned six. She was one of the cutest little girls in the village.

Philbert wondered why Rebecca read books all the time. "What's that one you're reading now?" he asked one night.

"It's a book about the ideas of two men from long ago. The first man was named Hobbes. He wrote during a time of civil war. He believed people are selfish by nature."

"That's true," said Philbert. He took a sip of beer. He sometimes surprised Rebecca with sharp opinions. Every morning he did a hundred pushups, and then a hundred sit-ups. Three or four times a week, he went for long runs. Her food and beer bill had soared since Philbert moved in.

"So you're a Hobbesian," she said.

He looked at her, to have that explained.

"Hobbes said in man's original condition, there was nothing to protect ordinary people. There was nothing to stop the strong from oppressing the weak. So the people set up chiefs to band them together and rule over them and impose peace. In exchange, people had to give up the freedom to do whatever they wanted. Fifty years later, the other man, Locke, disagreed. He said it wasn't like that at all. He said everyone is born with natural rights, the right to life, liberty, property, and the right to follow your dreams."

Philbert laughed. "Only big shots can follow their dreams. Look at the rest of us."

Rebecca liked the way Philbert's small neat ears lay flat to his skull. "Karl Marx would have agreed with you."

"Who's that?"

"Another famous man. I'll tell you about him some other time. Locke said the reason we set up chiefs was so we could have impartial justice. He said the relationship between the chief and the people is one of equals. The people have the right to petition their chief if they have a grievance. If the chief deprives the people of their rights, then the people are entitled to overthrow him."

"You like politics."

"Yes, I do. Politics is very interesting. How could it not be, with all that's going on in the world?"

"You should be careful," said Philbert. "Here in Gabon, politics is a dangerous thing."

Libreville

Ambassador Jones looked around the conference room table at her Country Team members gathered for their Monday meeting. "Good morning, everyone. I hope you all had a good weekend. Stu Eaton won't be joining us. He's en tournée in the Franceville area, installing the new Peace Corps school construction volunteers."

The caustic Deputy Chief of Mission, Jerry Andrews, jumped in. "Are they going to build a school in Bongoville, finally? I'm holding out for Bongoville. Ever been to the Chinese Farm they got there? All these grumpy bachelor Chinese, living in a dorm, wearing matching blue jumpsuits like uniforms, driving little tractors look like toys. Can't any of them speak any French, hardly, but they sure can grow vegetables. Chinese grow the only fresh vegetables I've ever seen in this country that aren't imported from France."

"I'm not sure if they're going to be building a school in Bongoville, Jerry," said Darlene. The DCM was getting close to retirement. His career had come up short of an ambassadorship, and he didn't care anymore. "But I'll be sure to visit the Chinese Farm, the next time I'm in the Haut-Ogooué."

"Green peppers, lettuce, zucchini, eggplant, cucumbers, tomatoes. Makes you wonder why the Gabonese don't grow vegetables."

"Before we start in on this week's agenda," said Darlene, "I'd like to take a few minutes to discuss the Soviet Union." Digressions were Darlene's prerogative. She was the Ambassador. Her occasional impromptu seminars at Country Team meetings no longer surprised her senior staff. She was a former college professor, after all, and she kept the discussions short.

"Let me frame my question with three facts. Fact one: the Central Committee of the Union of Soviet Socialist Republics has voted to give up its monopoly on power. Fact two: three of the republics, Lithuania, Latvia and Estonia have now claimed their independence. Fact three: just last week, Boris Yeltsin, the president of Russia, announced he supports the Baltic republics. So, my question is, does this mean the Soviet Union has begun breaking apart?"

Her question set everyone off.

"No matter what happens," said Jerry, raising his voice to be heard above the others, and everyone stopped talking to listen, "count on the Russians to screw it up." He stroked his gray beard, straight-faced, as everyone laughed.

"For as long as most of us can remember," said Tom Hughes, the young the political officer with an earnest frown, "the Soviets have been America's greatest existential threat. But now, I wonder if the world could possibly be moving toward a single system of democracy and capitalism?"

"That seems a bit far-fetched," responded Pamela Rossow, the green-eyed USIS director, with a hint of disdain. "Human beings have an infinite capacity to solve human problems. Gorbachev will hold the Soviet Union together. Glasnost and perestroika are beginning to work. The Soviet Union will be transformed into something different."

Captain Caleb Rogers, the Defense Attaché in Libreville on temporary duty, raised his hand. Black as sable, his hair cut high and tight, he voiced a question from a military point of view. "If the Soviet Union splits up, who will be in charge of their nuclear weapons?"

The Consular Officer chimed in, a new arrival to the Embassy, a junior officer with a wife and infant daughter. "There will be a huge wave of emigration, if the Soviets open their borders."

Darlene sometimes wondered what her life would be like if she had remained in academia, leading graduate seminars on important topics like this. She would have tenure by now. Likely she would have moved on from Howard University. And of course she wouldn't be separated from her husband and son. She noticed that two members of her staff sat silently, listening to the debate. "Ray? Dick?" she said, "anything to add?"

Ray Sims, the morose ex-cop, the Regional Security Officer shook his head no. Dick Williams, the middle-aged TDY currently serving as GSO said he found it hard to believe the Soviet Union would somehow just disappear.

The discussion began to flag, and Darlene called the meeting to order. The RSO was first on the agenda. Ray reported that Gilles Clermidy, the French advisor to the Gabonese secret police, had phoned to set up a meeting. It seemed Gabon's law enforcement agencies had recently been ordered to increase vigilance. With the changing political situation, the police expected an increase in reports of witchcraft.

The word – witchcraft – caused a fresh eruption around the table, about sorcery in Gabon. Bizarre rumors circulated in Libreville, tales of black government Mercedes screeching to a stop to snatch urchins off street corners and bundle them away, never to be seen again. People said that body parts from children were essential to the most potent spells, spells commissioned to protect politicians and to enhance their power.

Okouya

Sunday night, several villagers spotted an owl perched on the roof of Chief Oyamba's house. Many heard it hoot once, before it spread its wings and flapped away. The powerful omen was just one in an accumulating number of signs that Oyamba Paul would soon die.

Monday morning, he did not come out of his house. People heard the old Chief inside talking in a strange voice, and they feared to come near. Only Ngawanaga Bernard dared go inside, and he began praying in a punctuated monotone.

Oyamba's two surviving wives, gray-haired women wrapped in dark pagnes, kept vigil outside the Chief's house on small stools under a raffia palm. Oyamba's eldest son, Édouard reported to the worksite with the rest of the crew. Everyone in the village expected he would succeed his father as the nkani-ntsie, and become the next land chief of the westernmost Louzou. As the prospect of an actual succession grew imminent, Édouard found the thought increasingly daunting. He had become less sure of what others considered to be his hereditary obligation to the people of the western portion of the Louzou clan's domain. Édouard was pleased to be learning masonry. This new and employable skill would open a way for him to leave the village of Okouya, should he decide to move to the city, and look for work.

The laborers wheeled cinderblocks out to the walls and lined them up on end. The masons prepared their workstations, setting up their mortarboards, laying out their tools, stringing line to the leads. Alphonse pushed a wheelbarrow with two sacks of cement along the planks through the sand from the yellow house to the cement mixer, where Albert filled the tank with gasoline.

At eight o'clock, Jonas, the schoolteacher, called out to the children to stop their clapping games and chasing around. He assembled them in a circle around the flagpole and handed a folded flag to the eldest girl. The work crew stopped as she ran up the flag. Then the children sang the national anthem, La Concorde.

As the children filed into the decrepit old schoolhouse, the hubbub at the worksite resumed. Presently they heard the buzz of a motor approaching from the direction of Otou. A shiny white SUV sped out of the woods and pulled to a stop. Harry Bowman was at the wheel and the country director Stu Eaton was in the passenger's seat. The Préfet of Akièni was in the back.

The Préfet, wearing a short-sleeved tropical suit, greeted Charlie in the abrasive voice Charlie had first heard the day of his installation. The workers stood back in deference, until the Préfet moved toward them and began shaking hands. Stu Eaton, wearing a khaki bush jacket, came forward to greet Charlie. Charlie told Stu not to worry about the little man a short distance off, scowling ferociously and writing things down. "That's Lalish. He's a little crazy is all."

Harry Bowman, the bearded assistant director, dressed in a colorful African shirt, said, "How's life au village, Charlie?"

"Same thing every day."

"Glad to see you again, Charlie," said Jim Bonaventure, the curly-haired construction program volunteer leader. Another motor could be heard, and a brand new white pickup truck shot out of the woods, veered, and came tearing dangerously around the building site, right onto the school grounds. Cleon Renfrew got out, a tattooed Texan sporting a no-shit straw cowboy hat. He walked up and grabbed Charlie's hand like they were old friends. Another shiny white pickup truck came out of the woods and pulled in behind the SUV. Jason Richards opened the door, a young man with blond dreadlocks and acne. A third pickup truck was right behind it. Kevin Pfeiffer came toward them with a plodding gait as another pickup truck pulled in behind his. Chris McDowell climbed out bare-chested, crooked teeth, shouting, "Bonjour!"

These guys weren't stagiaires anymore, Charlie reminded

himself. Technical training in Obia was over. They were full-fledged construction volunteers, cocky and strutting about. They had beaten the seemingly unbeatable construction record that Charlie's group had set just six months earlier in Boundji. Of course, the Obia *stage* had an unfair advantage, everyone said. Hector had built the foundation ahead of time with a massive crew of Gabonese. No wonder they'd put the roof on with a week to spare, enough time to help Rebecca dig trenches and pour footings in Otou.

The new volunteers chattered excitedly about their shiny new rides and the expansive view up on the plateau, their home for the next twenty-four months.

"Ronnie's going to finish Obia," said Harry, referring to the fifth stagiaire, who wasn't here with the others. Ronnie had a long beard, Charlie recalled.

"Toad's back in Boundji getting the teachers' houses finally built," said Jim. "He did such a good job handling the logistics in Obia, he's going to be doing it for Hector at the next *stage* site too. Victim of his own success."

"Next *stage* is going to be in Franceville," said Harry. "In Quartier Sable. After that, Toad's going to Onga."

Jim remarked, "Your site's looking good, Charlie."

Ten roof trusses leaned against the green teacher's house and the masonry walls of the school had been laid up waist high.

"Stretch your legs, guys!" Harry yelled. "We're going to have a quick word with Charlie." He put his hand on Charlie's back. "Is there a place where we could talk?"

Charlie gestured toward the yellow house he used as a magasin. "What's this about?"

"Just something we want to ask you," said Jim, letting Charlie go in first through the door. "We want to put a bug in your ear."

"We've been talking to Hector," said Stu. "Has he mentioned anything to you?"

"About what?"

Stu Eaton was plump, close-shaved and well barbered. The bush jacket didn't look right on him. He was enjoying his first visit to the plateau. He looked around the yellow teacher's house Charlie used as a depot. Sacks of cement in low stacks filled one bedroom. A second bedroom contained lumber. The third bedroom contained two barrels of diesel fuel and gasoline in blue plastic jerry cans. Toyota truck parts in red and white boxes were neatly arranged on handmade shelves. Wheelbarrows and hand tools were stored in the salon where in one corner sat a desk that Charlie shared with Jean-Paul, where they filled out paperwork and kept the inventory.

Charlie turned around the chair for Stu.

"I'd just as soon stand," he said.

"We'll be on our butts all day," said Harry, "driving and at the installations. You know how those things go."

"What's this about?"

"The thing is," said Harry, "Bongo wants a school in every village on the plateau."

"There are fifty-six volunteers coming in the next cohort," said Stu, "with twelve of them signed up for the construction program. They'll all be doing their language training at the lycée in Oyem."

"You out-of-cycle guys were lucky," said Jim. "You got to do your language training in Zaire."

"If all twelve make it through to swearing in," said Harry, "with the four guys outside, that will make sixteen new sites. Plus the new *stage* site in Franceville will make seventeen. Then there's Phil in Djoko, Nate in Édjangoulou, Rebecca in Otou and Ronnie finishing Obia. With Okouya, that makes twenty-two, plus the five guys finishing their second year, that'll make twenty-seven schools under construction in two provinces that will have to be supplied."

"The logistics are going to be insane," said Jim.

"It'll be a full time job," said Stu. "We're going to need someone to handle it. We asked Toad, but he wants to build a school on his own, from start to finish."

"He deserves it," said Harry. "We asked Hector, but he wants to kick back after this and finish the site in Quartier Sable. He's earned the right."

Charlie saw where this was going. "You're asking me to take the job."

"You'd be the regional logistics coordinator, based in Franceville," said Harry.

"You're our top choice," said Stu.

178

"After Toad and Hector turned you down. Who would finish here in Okouya?"

"We'll assign someone from the incoming group," said Harry. "That would give you two more months."

"We don't expect you to give us an answer right now," said Stu. "In fact, I don't want you to. Give yourself some time to think it over. Could we have your answer next week, say, when I'm back in Libreville? You could call in from the post office telephone in Akièni, right?"

"Where would I live?" Charlie asked, smiling, seeing possibilities with Justine unfold.

Stu nodded his head. "That will be one of the perks."

"Hector's fixing up a house near the *case de passage*," said Harry.

Jim was grinning. "The guy who takes this job is going to live in a house with electricity and hot running water."

Chief Oyamba lay in his bed surrounded by all the souls gone before him, the ancestors passed away. Their numbers were legion, yellow lights dancing, the spirits of the dead all around. Nearest to him, he recognized souls he had known in life. Some among the flickering lights were souls he had eaten to obtain their knowledge and to gain their power. He had long ago asked their understanding. The old chief knew he was dying, and would soon be one more light dancing among them.

Bernard prayed loudly, "Most merciful Jesus, lover of souls, I beseech you by the agony of your most sacred heart, and by the sorrows of your immaculate mother, to wash in your most precious blood this sinner Oyamba Paul."

Memories flooded Oyamba, ancient mysteries learned long before, at the sacred ancestral site, Amaya Mokini, memories of the powers he used to force chiefs from the surrounding villages to submit to him, or die.

"I was a leopard!" shouted the dying Chief. "I ate the souls of those who defied me! I ate the souls of those foolish enough to go into the forest at night!"

At the fiendish sound of the voice, Oyamba's old wives looked at each other in fear.

"I could rise into the air and fly like a bird!" the Chief roared.

"How wonderful it felt! And no one remembered! I made everyone forget!"

The old women's eyes grew wider at sudden delirious laughter.

"President Omar Bongo knew of me!" howled Oyamba, at the memory of the great shining machine that descended from the sky in a lashing roar and took him to Libreville flying fast over the forest below. It came to earth inside a walled compound in the capital city. Uniformed men led Oyamba into an enormous building that burned with cold inside. Doors slid open when he approached. They took him into a windowless room with red walls where three ngaa-mpiaru who ministered to the President waited. One sat on a chair constructed of bones. One sat on a leopard skin stool. One sat cross-legged on a mat between two massive elephant skulls. The ngaa-mpiaru on the chair of bones told Oyamba the President had learned of him, of the great powers he marshaled. The President had brought Oyamba to him, to pledge his loyalty. Was Oyamba willing? If he pledged his loyalty, he would have nothing to fear, ever again. There was a bowl of bitter broth to drink. They made small cuts on the backs of his hands, and rubbed herbs and powder into the wounds. These bind you to the President, they said, and will mark you forever, and suddenly President Bongo was there with them. He held an ornate box. He opened it, and removed a small sachet. You must never open this, said President Bongo. You must take it with you, and bury it under the house where you live. If you do, you will have my full protection. The President pinned a medal to Oyamba's chest. Before they returned him to the flying machine, the President's men gave Oyamba a fat envelop. With the money it contained, Oyamba built a big house and buried the sachet underneath that house, where now he lay dying.

The French priest came in a car soon after Oyamba returned from Libreville. He brought the black book white people called the Bible. It was written, strangely, in the Téké language. The priest demanded Oyamba stop practicing sorcery. The one called Jesus Christ commanded it, he said, the Son of God, the God who sent his son Jesus to live among men, to show men how they must live. It was written in the black book that Jesus sent seventy people to every village and town, and they returned joyful that even the demons were subject to them.

Father Dominique left the Téké Bible with Bernard, a catechist he brought with him, to live in Okouya. Over the next many years, Bernard taught Oyamba to recite the prayer of Our Father. He read Oyamba the great Bible stories. Slowly trust was established. Oyamba remembered the story first told by the white priest, his favorite, when Jesus saw Satan fall like lightning from heaven, and gave his apostles the power to tread upon serpents and scorpions, and over all the power of the enemy. Bernard called Oyamba's powers names in the language of the etangani: witchcraft, spiritism, sorcery and said he must abandon them. It was many years before Oyamba was persuaded to set his powers aside. Finally, grown older and tired, he relented, and with that, his powers began to dissipate, as moist soil dries up in the sun.

And that was what all the old souls were saying to him now, speaking to him over the steady praying of Bernard. Just as after the fire green shoots emerge from the ash, so there was another one coming, coming home from the Congo, the one they called Okorogo René.

Libreville

Tom Hughes watched the Embassy guards process the chauffer-driven Mercedes idling at the main gate. Joseph Rendjambé was right on time. Ambassador Jones wanted to meet the most credible figures being mooted as future opposition presidential candidates. She intended to meet them all, and Tom had scheduled Rendjambé first. He watched from inside the front door of the chancery as one guard looked under the hood while a second used a convex mirror to check the undercarriage for bombs. Then the gate slid open and the guards pointed to where the chauffeur should park.

Tom opened the chancery door and walked down the steps to greet Rendjambé as he got out of the car. He wore a double-breasted suit with a tie slightly askew. He had just one aide with him, a young man with hair that needed cutting.

Tom escorted them inside to the Marine in the blast resistant cage who took their ID cards, handed them badges, and buzzed them through. Making small talk Tom walked Rendjambé and his aide upstairs to the dark paneled conference room where the others were waiting. USIS director Pamela Rossow and DCM Jerry Andrews rose, came forward and shook hands. On the polished teak table were bottles of water and glasses on a silver tray. A few moments later Ambassador Jones entered through a side door wearing a scarlet pantsuit and asked everyone to be seated.

Rendjambé had an odd smile, as if thinking of something ironic. He thanked the ambassador for inviting him to the meeting. "I value the honor extended," he said. Since the agenda was his, Rendjambé proposed they get right down to business.

"That's fine," said Ambassador Jones, a bit surprised by the directness. This was not the Gabonese way.

"I am a believer in democracy," Rendjambé began. He had a high forehead and slippery eyes. "I know, and my people know, the transition to multiparty elections will not be easy. In fact, the process may fail. We know the character of Omar Bongo. We know he is preparing pitfalls. He has already taken a first step to sidetrack the process. Do you know what I am referring to, Ambassador?"

"I'm not sure I do."

"Last month he called Paul Mba Abbesole to a secret meeting at the Palace and offered him the post of Minister of Waters and Forests. Then he summoned Antoine Badinga and offered him the post of Minister of Mines and Energy."

Antoine Badinga, Darlene knew, enjoyed the support of the son of the President of France. She had learned of this initially from the French ambassador, but now it was widely known in diplomatic circles. Paul Mba Abbesole was a different case. He had spent almost a decade in exile. A former priest and founder of a group called the Mouvement de Redressement National, MORENA, now he was back in Gabon reclaiming the legacy.

Waters and Forests and Mines and Energy were ministries with enormous potential for personal enrichment.

"Might I ask, Monsieur Rendjambé," said Darlene," if these meetings were secret, how do you know of them?"

"A fair question," said Rendjambé. "I know because President Bongo himself told me when he called me to my secret meeting with him." He grinned.

"Is that so? What cabinet position did he offer you?"

"The post of Prime Minister. He believes I am the most formidable of all the people who might run against him. Or so he told me. Perhaps he said the same to the others as well. I told him I am not interested in being a member of his government."

Pamela brushed her blonde hair back from her face. "It may be obvious, but I want to make sure I understand. What does Bongo expect in return?"

"It's not so complicated. He does not want us to run against him." Suddenly Rendjambé's smile seemed weary. His aide, who was taking notes in a schoolboy cahier, had an air of suppressed rage.

"You have invited me here," said Rendjambé, looking at everyone in turn, at Ambassador Jones last of all, "and I have honored your invitation. I come with one question for you that I ask in all sincerity. How does the United States government plan to assist my country in this transition?"

Tom, Pamela and Jerry looked to Ambassador Jones to give the answer. None of them knew that within the week, Joseph Rendjambé would be dead.

12. The Unmanageable Ones

A sparkling sun shower fell as Charlie splashed into town. He attracted little notice on a Saturday morning. Peace Corps Land Cruisers had become a familiar sight.

The front door of Justine's bungalow was open. Mpiga Gérard the younger twin brother and Mbou Blaise the older sat at the table in the salon studying when Charlie came up on the porch. They rose to their feet.

"Hi," said Charlie, already in the house. "Can I come in? How're you boys doing? Studying hard?"

"Yes," they responded with the same bright smile.

"Where's your sister?"

"At work," said Blaise.

At least Charlie thought it was Blaise. He had trouble telling them apart. "It's a shame to have to be studying on a Saturday," he said. "Say, how old are you guys?"

"Sixteen," they chimed.

"In my country, you would be driving by now. Have you boys ever driven a car?"

They exchanged astonished glances. What an amazing question! "No," they said.

Charlie grinned. "How would you like to give it a try?"

Charlie's mud-spattered white pickup truck sat in front of Justine's house late that afternoon when she came home from the hospital. Her brothers rushed her at the door, interrupting each other in the telling of their great adventure, actually driving Charlie's truck! Charlie had taken them up onto the plateau, they told her breathlessly. The twins couldn't stop talking about the gearshift

185

lever, the steering wheel, the clutch and the gas pedal, how many times Mpiga had stalled the Land Cruiser and whether Mbou had stalled it more.

Justine gave Charlie an appalled look. He smiled guiltily. "It's not legal for them to drive," she scolded. "Why are you here? Why have you interrupted their studies?"

"I have something I want to tell you."

From the eager expressions on their faces, Justine could see her brothers were in on whatever this was.

"Tell me."

Charlie saw she was trying not to smile. Here as he'd thought was a key to getting closer to her, this girl who somehow made him feel complete, who could magically make everything in creation shine, and then withdraw down into a hole and make it rain. When she was beside him and happy there was more oxygen in his lungs; he was weightless, and could run a hundred miles if he had to. When she was diffident and rabbit, he wanted to move mountains to make her happy again. Because of her, he had come to realize how tired he was of being alone in the world.

"There's something I want to show you in Franceville. I want to take you and your brothers there to see it."

"What is it?"

"It's my secret until we get there. Do you know that your brothers have never eaten pizza? Do you know they have never been to a movie?"

Charlie glanced at Blaise and Gérard, and on cue, they began wheedling their sister to please, please, please say yes.

Otou

Sunday morning, Philbert left for Akièni in Milla's taxi. A half hour later, Ondinga Gustave knocked on Rebecca's door smelling of cologne and bearing a two-liter bottle of palm wine. Rebecca doubted Gustave coming by just after Philbert had left was an innocent coincidence. She invited the schoolteacher in because he knew a lot of history that she wanted to learn, and it wasn't long before she had her journal open on the table in the salon, taking notes in her personal shorthand.

Rebecca began by asking how President Bongo originally became involved in politics, and Gustave commenced the tale from the beginning. But whenever he hit a point of history she didn't know, he shifted the narrative further back in time.

"Do you know about Amaya Mokini?" he asked, his head freshly shaved and shining, his goatee meticulously trimmed.

"No, never heard of him."

"It's not a person. It's a place. And to know about Amaya Mokini, first you have to know about Onko ou Ma-Onko, commonly shortened as Makoko."

"That was the King of the Batéké, right, who signed the treaty with Savorgnan de Brazza?" said Rebecca, referring to the nineteenth century French explorer after whom the capital city of the Congo was named.

"No, not correct. Makoko, to use the shortened version, is the name of the line of Batéké kings. The royal court is called the Nkwe Mbali, in the village of Mbé, in the Congo. The court is guarded by lions, kept by the mother of twins."

"The mother of twins?" said Rebecca, writing furiously, "keeps lions?"

"Yes, on the falls of the Lefini River, where six anvils are fitted into a large rock. The first Makoko ruled over twelve domains. Do you know that?"

"No," said Rebecca, her pen flying.

"Yes, and then long ago the Louzou and the Assiami clans of the Batéké saw that the King, the Makoko was becoming too involved with affairs along the Congo River, and so the two supreme councils of elders met at the mountain which is the highest point on the watershed, at the sacred ancestral place called Amaya Mokini. There they decided to cease paying tribute to the Makoko, and they created the system we have today."

"Tell me about this system."

"At the very top is the Makoko. Under him are the twelve domain chieftains, but these do not really exist anymore. Within each domain there is the ntsie, or the land, and our land chief here, the nkani-ntsie is Oyamba, who lives in Okouya, where the giant American is. Then is the mpugu, which is the village, and for us that is Otou, which is ruled by our Chief Petie, who is a drunk. And at

187

the bottom, there is the ndjo, which is the household, which is ruled by the father of the family. That is the basis of our mpu, our power, and this is what was here when the French came."

"And made all the chiefs subservient to the colonial state."

"Yes, but in our case the subjugation was not immediate." Gustave looked pleased that Rebecca showed such interest, his eyes roaming all over her. She knew he had come with ulterior motives. Why else would he come bringing palm wine, wearing cologne on a Sunday morning?

"The sands of the plateau are not a good soil, you see. All the agricultural concessions the French tried here failed, for coffee and cacao, timber and rubber, the Société de Haut Ogooué, the Société d'Entreprise Africaine, the Concession d'Exploitation Forestière Africaines. By the 1930s, they all were out of business. Once they saw our land held little of economic value, the French left us essentially alone."

Gustave waited for Rebecca to finish writing.

"They called us the hardheads, the unmanageable ones. It is true we had very little interest in working for them, working for money. In the olden times, our people were completely self-reliant. We had blacksmiths who made our tools. Our women made cooking pots from clay. The French forced this modern way of working for money on us, working for money so you can buy things other people manufacture."

"They all did that," said Rebecca. "All the imperial governments imposed a cash economy on their African colonies. They had to. The colonies were not popular with their citizens. The citizens didn't want their taxes going to the colonies, so the colonies had to pay for themselves."

"Correct," said Gustave, and he nodded at Rebecca as he would at a promising pupil, "very good," and they both took a drink of palm wine. "So you must know about the corvée, then. Tell me what it was."

"The corvée was France's system of compulsory labor. All the imperial powers used forced labor."

"Correct again. And so you know how the corvée worked."

"Not precisely."

"It was quite simple. The French placed a tax on every

188

household. The head of any household who didn't pay his taxes was whipped. In most cases, the heads of household had no cash. In this case, to pay their taxes, to avoid being whipped, they had to send their sons to work. Around here, forced laborers were sent to work on the Congo-Ocean Railway. That was how the French built the railroad, by whipping people to make them contribute labor. They began the railroad in Pointe-Noire in 1924 and they finished it in Brazzaville in 1934. Seventeen thousand men died building that railroad, thirty men for every kilometer of track."

"Terrible. All the colonial projects used forced labor. They all took a terrible toll in human life."

"Did you know," said Gustave, and his prominent eyes bulged wide as if what he was about to say greatly surprised him, "during the time the railroad was being built our province the Haut-Ogooué was part of the Congo?"

"No, I didn't know that."

"Yes. In the earliest years of French colonization, in the 1890s, this region was known as the Haut-Ogooué. From time to time, the French redrew the boundaries of their colonial provinces, and sometimes they renamed them. In 1925, they renamed this province Niari-Ogooué and joined it to the Congo. Then in 1950, they transferred the province back to Gabon and restored the old name of Haut-Ogooué. Then in 1958, two years before independence, they found manganese in Moanda and uranium in Mounana."

"H-m-m-m," said Rebecca, as she finished this note. "That's interesting. Thank you. But where we started was, I asked you how Bongo first got involved in politics."

"Patience! I'm going to answer your question. Do you know why Bongo was sent to Brazzaville in the first place?"

"No. Why was Bongo sent to Brazzaville?"

"To pursue an education in the capital city."

"Hang on." Rebecca turned back a page. "When Bongo was in school, wouldn't that have been after 1950, after the province was given back to Gabon? If he was sent to the capital city to go to school, from a province in Gabon, why wasn't he sent to Libreville?"

"Exactly. That is what I'm trying to tell you. You see, both because it was part of the Batéké homeland and because for so many years the province was called Niari-Ogooué, and was joined to the Congo, the elders thought of Brazzaville as their capital, even after the province was given back to Gabon and renamed Haut-Ogooué. And Libreville was too far away. It takes over a month to walk there through the forest. Who would be brave enough to walk one month through the forest? Who would give you food along the way? You might be killed, and who would know? It was easier to walk to Brazzaville across the grasslands. It was closer, and all the way there people speak Téké, so in every village you could count on a place to eat and sleep. That's why, back then, when you went to the capital, you went to Brazzaville."

"Okay, so you're saying Bongo got involved in politics because he was sent to school in Brazzaville. But tell me exactly what happened."

"After he finished his studies Bongo worked for the colonial Post and Telegraph Service for a time, and then he joined the French colonial Air Force, which he left with the rank of captain."

"In Brazzaville."

"No, not in Brazzaville. In those days, Gabon and the Congo were part of French Equatorial Africa, which was a federation of territories consisting of Gabon, Congo, Chad, Cameroon and Oubangui-Chari, which today is the Central African Republic. The French Air Force moved him around. He was stationed in Brazzaville, and then Bangui, and then Fort Lamy, which today is Ndjamena. Are you beginning to see?"

"You're confusing me," said Rebecca, and refilled their glasses. Gustave was disconcerting. With his goggling eyes, his shiny head, and his pointy dark goatee, he looked like an upside down acorn, a pop-eyed upside down acorn. It made Rebecca giggle.

"Sorry," she said. "Can we get back to what I first asked you? How did Bongo get started in politics?"

"It was at the time of independence," Gustave began, "during the elections for the National Assembly, in 1961. Bongo left the Air Force with the rank of captain and returned to the Haut-Ogooué to campaign for a man named Marcel Sandoungout, who won the seat. In appreciation, Sandoungout took Bongo with him to Libreville. When Sandoungout became Minister of Health under our first president, he brought Bongo to the attention of President Mba and presented him as a man of talent. President Mba gave Bongo a position in the Ministry of Foreign Affairs, and then named him Assistant Director of the Cabinet, and then Minister of Information, and finally he made him Vice President, and in 1967 Mba died in office, and Bongo became President, and that's how he got started in politics."

Gustave drank while Rebecca finished recording the sequence.

"Tell me, Rebecca, why do you think President Mba elevated Bongo so swiftly?"

"I don't know. Why?"

Gustave raised his chin. With his goatee thrust forward, suddenly he looked like Vladimir Lenin, and Rebecca's laugh came out a snort.

"I'm sorry, please go on."

"The fact that we were part of Congo, and then we were part of Gabon, that doesn't give you a clue?"

"No, it doesn't."

Gustave folded his arms and began nodding his head, and now he looked like Mussolini.

"Politics," he said, "is not something women naturally understand. Let me explain it to you in simple terms."

"Yes, please do, in simple terms." Rebecca's sarcasm sailed right past him.

"Keep in mind, back then, many Batéké did not consider themselves to be Gabonese. You understand that now, n'est-ce pas? Next, you must understand the Fang people's role during this same period of time. Do you know about that tribe? You have to, in order to understand where our first politicians came from. And to understand that, you have to know about the conference in Brazzaville, in 1944, when the French promised to reward us for our loyalty in providing soldiers to fight for them in their war against Nazi Germany. You know about that?"

"Yes, I have heard of the Second World War."

"Good. What the French did, when the war ended and they established their Fourth Republic, they gave each African colony representation in the national government, in Paris, and limited self-government at home. We were permitted to elect one," and Gustave held up one finger, "deputy to the National Assembly in

Paris, and we were permitted to elect deputies to our own territorial assembly," and he waved his hand palm down across the table. "It was at this point," and Gustave slapped his palm on the table, "that a political class began to form." He leaned back in his chair. "You see?"

Rebecca was writing. "I'm beginning to."

"Good! The mayor of Libreville, Léon Mba, he formed the Bloc Démocratique Gabonais and the Deputy in the French National Assembly, Jean-Hilaire Aubame he formed the Union Démocratique et Sociale Gabonaise. The first post-independence election was held under a parliamentary system. Do you know what that is? Good! Mba and Aubame were the most important politicians. They were both Fang. The Fang dominated the political class. That's my point. Do you see? The Fang were collaborators."

Gustave nodded, as if affirming someone else's statement.

"The Fang worked closely with the French. They grew rich planting cocoa; their children went furthest in the French schools; they got the bulk of the civil service jobs. All of the leaders of our independence movement were privileged Fang, educated in Catholic schools. And we out here in the hinterlands, we were the hardheads. The unmanageable ones."

Gustave tipped back his head, his eyes wide, as if astounded.

"I'm not quite sure," said Rebecca, "how all this explains why President Mba elevated Bongo so rapidly."

"Of course it doesn't. We haven't come to that. First we have to consider Charles de Gaulle."

"We do?"

"Yes, and his vision of restoring France to glory. You must understand, after the defeat of the Second World War, de Gaulle was determined that France would never bend her knee again, so he created the Force de Frappe. You know of that?"

"Yes, I know of the French nuclear capability."

"Good! For nuclear weapons, de Gaulle needed uranium, and as it happened, the French had just discovered uranium here in Gabon. You know where they found it, of course."

"Mounana," said Rebecca, beginning to see.

"And in which province is Mounana?"

"In the Haut-Ogooué."

192

"Good!" Gustave nodded. "Correct! Here in the Haut-Ogooué, which, remember, not so many years earlier was called Niari-Ogooué and was part of the Congo. So in 1961, when Léon Mba, a Fang, became president, the French, who now had an interest in our land, and wanted access to our uranium for their nuclear weapons, they advised President Mba to pick someone from the Haut-Ogooué, the place where the uranium is, for a senior position, to shore up the loyalty here. And that's why Mba promoted Bongo so rapidly."

"Because of the uranium."

"Yes. And when Mba died, Bongo succeeded him. But before that came the coup."

Milla's taxi roared past Rebecca's house. She hadn't heard it enter the village. Philbert stepped into the salon. It was mid-afternoon. He looked at the nearly empty bottle of palm wine, the two glasses, and greeted the schoolteacher suspiciously.

"What's for dinner?"

Rebecca ignored him, "Gustave, you were saying, and then came the coup in '64."

"Is she talking politics again?" said Philbert from the kitchen. He came back with a glass, sat down and filled it. "She is always talking politics."

"We're talking about Gabonese politics," said Gustave.

"You should meet my brother," Philbert said to Rebecca, "when he comes back from school in Romania. He's interested in politics too."

"I'd be delighted," said Rebecca.

Gustave emptied the bottle into his glass, looking at Philbert. "Aren't you going to tell her the rest?"

Libreville

Tuesday morning, Ambassador Jones reread the profile of major opposition figures that Tom Hughes had acquired from a lecturer at Omar Bongo University, recently returned from a tour of American colleges, and since then giving every indication of being a new and eager friend of the Americans, which was what the International Visitors Program was intended to achieve. The profile was close to a hundred pages. The length and level of detail surpassed what an ordinary lecturer in African social systems could reasonably be expected to know. The lecturer, Darlene concluded, was not the author. Either he had received a leaked document, or it had been handed to him to pass on to the Americans. In either case, he was being steered. She wondered, Who is doing the steering?

The section on Antoine Badinga interested Darlene. Badinga was born to a teenage mother named Assélé Brigitte, in a village called Okouya, in the Haut-Ogooué, in the préfecture of Akièni. Darlene made a note in the margin to find Okouya on a map. Badinga's place of birth made him a member of the Louzou clan of the Batéké, the people of the former First Lady. His maternal grandmother raised him while his mother attended high school in Brazzaville, where she became a close friend of Josephine Bongo, the future First Lady. Through this connection, once Bongo was president, Badinga's mother wangled her husband, Epolo Calixte, who was not the father of Badinga, a position in the Department of Forests responsible for approving logging permits. There over the years Epolo Calixte grew wealthy from the illicit payments the French logging companies paid. Meanwhile young Antoine Badinga was sent to a private school in Paris, again through his mother's connection to the First Lady. He did not prove to be a good student, and dropped out to disappear into the immigrant underground in Europe. When he resurfaced, it was as an associate of a man who specialized in enlisting lost souls, a wealthy arms dealer named Sarkis Soghanalian.

Soghanalian had made a fortune arming the Argentine military during the Falklands war, and the Christian militias during the civil war in Lebanon. When Badinga was introduced to him, Soghanalian was setting up the biggest arms deal he had ever attempted, the sale to Iraq of a hundred million dollars of embargoed South African weapons, using Austria as a transit country. This was Soghanalian's first foray into Africa, and as Badinga was from Africa, Soghanalian enlisted him, initially, as a lowly courier. Badinga proved to be intelligent, discrete, and reliable, and soon he was one of Soghanalian's trusted envoys to the South Africans, who were also supplying weapons to the UNITA fighters in Angola, paid for with diamonds.

It was at this time that the First Lady of Gabon absconded with thirty million dollars from the Banque Nationale de Développement and ran off to Los Angeles with a guitar player. Bongo was humiliated and enraged and he purged all members of her clan, the Louzou clan from his government, including the husband of Badinga's mother. By this time Badinga was brokering his own arms deals, trading guns for African diamonds, which brought him to the attention of the son of the President of France, the man they called Papa m'a Dit. Daddy Told Me.

The telephone rang.

Ray Sims, the RSO, sounded concerned. "Ambassador, we're receiving reports of a disturbance at the Dowé Hotel. It sounds like it might be something pretty major. I've activated the emergency phone tree and I've put the MSG on alert. I'm heading over there to see what's going on. Gunny's got Post One."

Ray was responsible for the physical security of the Embassy, and as operational supervisor of the Marine Security Guard, he had just put the Marines on alert.

Darlene phoned her political officer who said he was just about to come to her office. A moment later, Tom Hughes sat across the desk from Darlene repeating something his FSN secretary heard in the taxi on the way to work. "They've found Joseph Rendjambé's dead body in a room at the Dowé Hotel."

Darlene pushed the button for the Peace Corps office. A receptionist put Darlene straight through to Director Eaton who reported that the DCM had already called him.

Glad to see the emergency phone tree was working, Darlene hung up and looked out her window in time to see two carloads of Marines coming in through the gate, the ones who'd been off-duty at their residence. She pushed the button for the American Cultural Center. Tom watched as the Ambassador listened to the telephone ringing. Darlene identified herself to the receptionist at the Cultural Center who answered, and when Pamela came on, Darlene told her what Ray had said, and then the walkie-talkie on her desk squawked.

Darlene hung up the phone and lifted the walkie-talkie from its cradle, and keyed the mike and said her code name. "Brooklyn."

"Columbia," Ray responded. "I'm in view of the hotel." Darlene could hear shouting in the background. "I can see smoke coming from two windows. There are, looks like hundreds of males already here and more arriving from both directions. Looks like some of them have got inside and are setting fire to the place. No sign of the police, but I hear sirens, over."

"Should you move out of there? Over."

"Roger. I'm walking back to the car now, returning to Post. Out."

Darlene set the walkie-talkie back in its cradle and now it began crackling with terse male voices, the Marines checking in with Gunny as they drew weapons and ammo and took up their positions around the Embassy compound. Darlene turned down the volume, lifted the telephone and dialed the number for the French Embassy. The line was busy. She hung up and pressed redial. Busy again. She called Mary Dobbins and told her to keep trying the French Embassy until she got through.

Finally, Darlene looked at her frowning political officer, the vertical lines between his brows deep with concern. "What do we have on our hands, Tom?"

"Ambassador, if Rendjambé is dead, we have to guess he didn't die from natural causes. And we'll be expected to find out who was behind it."

"I'm listening."

"I'm almost afraid to say what I'm thinking."

The phone rang. It was Mary calling to put Darlene through to the French Embassy. The Frenchwoman on the other end sounded harried. Darlene confirmed this was the Ambassador of the United States and asked to speak with Ambassador Berrier.

"He is on another line."

"Don't hang up! We had trouble getting through."

"There are many calls."

"Can you put me on hold until he's available?"

"Wait. His line just cleared. One moment."

Darlene nodded at Tom.

Berrier asked, "Darlene, you have heard about Rendjambé? How are you? Are you all right? And your people?"

"Yes. Our Gabonese nationals say Rendjambé was found dead this morning at the Dowé Hotel. My security officer just radioed from in front of the place. He says there's a mob forming there. He saw smoke coming from inside. He says it looks like it's been set on fire."

"It's much worse in Port-Gentil, Darlene! They've set our consulate on fire! I just got off a call from Paris! They are sending another regiment of the Foreign Legion!"

13. Vine Bridge

Franceville

"Just friends," Natalia said aloud, talking to herself as she sometimes did when she was alone, especially when thinking about Hector, who was late for lunch. "It is natural. We are the only two Spanish-speaking cúmbilas in Franceville." She lifted the ladle from the steaming pot of sancocho de gallina and tasted the stew a final time: chicken, green plantains, corn, potatoes and manioc. Yes, Natalia had said, when Hector asked her, the weekend before last, without giving it a second thought, yes, she had said, he could spend the weekend at her house. "So where is he?"

Hector swept into Franceville like a human whirlwind after *stage*. In just two weeks, he refurbished a house in the Cité de la Caisse. By the end of the month, he had a crew of three dozen men digging the foundations at his second *stage* school. The previous Sunday he drove Natalia in his battered pickup truck to see the site in Quartier Sable, a poor neighborhood with crooked little houses built of plywood and roofing sheets, not so unlike the neighborhood where Natalia grew up.

"Another of the school builders is coming to Franceville," Hector explained, as they walked alongside fresh mounds of dirt, "a volunteer, un hombre muy grande. He wishes the use of my house for the weekend. This is why I am looking for a place to spend the weekend."

"Why, because you are afraid of this very big man?"

"No, I am not!" Hector looked at Natalia in reproach. "That is not the reason. He is bringing a special girl with him, you see."

"O-o-o-o," said Natalia, still teasing.

With a click in the salon, the cassette player switched to a second tape. The soft salsa of David Pabón began flowing through the house, and the music set Natalia's hips to swaying. Shifting her feet front and back, back and forth, she looked about the kitchen, through the pass-through kitchen window into the salon, where the dining room table was set for two. Everything was in readiness, and she turned, and there was her housekeeper Paulette in the doorway, and Hector, smiling at the sight of Natalia dancing, with a travel-worn bag in his hand.

"Welcome," said Natalia. She hadn't heard his truck pull in. She hadn't heard him knocking at the front door. "Take his bag to the back bedroom," she said to Pauline in French, then to Hector in Spanish. "Would you like a beer?"

"Maybe with lunch," he said. "Sorry I'm late." He ran his hand across his shining black hair, trying to make it lie flat, but it had been cut too short. It sprang back like a shock of wheat. "Something smells good."

Hector went to wash his hands. When he returned, Natalia seated him at the head of the dining table and took a chair to his right. Pauline brought the tureen of stew and set it before them, then returned to the pass-through window.

"Have you ever had sancocho de gallina?" Natalia asked.

"You have a maid?" asked Hector.

"Just two days a week. I'm here alone, so I don't need her every day. I share her with a colleague."

Impressed, Hector said, "I've never known anyone with a maid before."

Pauline set a basket of sliced bread and a butter plate next to the tureen. She said, "Bon appétit," and left to resume her ironing.

Natalia served Hector, then herself.

"All those roadblocks they've set up!" Hector blew on a spoonful of stew. "I was stopped probably four times driving here!"

"They say no one has ever seen it like this," said Natalia. "The Gabonese say it takes three hours now, or longer, to drive to Moanda. Do you like it?"

"Delicioso," said Hector.

Normally, it took an hour to drive to Moanda from Franceville, but following the riots in Libreville and Port Gentil, the government had placed roadblocks at major intersections in all the cities, and along all the highways in the provinces. Gendarmes and soldiers carrying automatic rifles bullied everyone they waved over to the side of the road.

Natalia enjoyed watching Hector wolf down his stew. In minutes, his spoon clinked on the bottom of an empty bowl. "How long will it last, do you think?" he asked, and tore a slice of baguette to wipe the bowl clean.

"Have seconds. There's plenty." Natalia dipped the ladle into the tureen. The bungalow came with dishes. Her residence was furnished with everything, right down to sheets and towels.

"Thank you," said Hector. "So, we're going to see gorillas today?"

"Yes, one gorilla."

"I'm excited," he said, spooning a bite from his second bowl. "You know, Natalia, I've never asked you. What is it exactly you do at CIRMF?" His question referred to le Centre International de Recherches Médicales de Franceville where Natalia lived and worked.

For the first time since they'd met, she explained her job. "I have a grant to research the biology of viral and bacterial pathogenesis. My focus is on the interactions between transcription factors."

Hector stared at her, chewing chicken. Sometimes, when she met his eyes, as she did at that moment, his mind went blank and he couldn't hear what Natalia said. She was from Colombia. He liked the smooth glossy look of her skin.

"Ever since I can remember," she said, "I have wanted to do something about all the sickness that takes the lives of so many. Where I come from, in the town of Quibdó, on the Atrato River, in the Department of Chocó, it is like Gabon, one of the most densely forested and rainiest places on Earth. It is plagued by endemic disease."

Natalia was raised in a tight knit religious family of modest means. She was among the smartest and hardest working of her classmates, and no one was surprised when she overcame the double discrimination that black girls faced, and won a scholarship to the Universidad del Valle in Cali.

"In my third year studying bacteriología y laboratorio clínico, I

201

was awarded a Martin Luther King fellowship. They are reserved for Afro-Colombian students, to prepare them for graduate studies in the United States. That is how I learned English."

"¿Dónde estudiaste?"

"En Filadelfia, en la Universidad de Pennsylvania."

"I've been to Philadelphia. That's where Peace Corps sent us for orientation."

"Is that so? When I was writing my dissertation, I learned about post-doctoral grants offered by a medical research center in the heart of an African country I'd never heard of before, Gabon."

"I'd never heard of Gabon either," said Hector, "until I joined the Peace Corps." The failure of his small construction company still stung. He'd been forced to go back to working for wages. One night, sitting up late, despairing that he'd never get a second chance, an ad came on TV, the sound of a reed flute as a young woman walked along a dike passing water buffaloes in a rice paddy. White letters filled the screen: The Toughest Job You'll Ever Love.

Hector thought about it for a few days, then one morning he took off work and drove to the recruiting center in El Segundo. The recruiter said it was his lucky day, and handed him something called an Action Cable to read. It was all in capital letters, like an old-fashioned telegram. They were recruiting out of cycle for a construction program, building modern schools in remote villages in a country called Gabon. Did Hector know where that was? Qualifications included construction experience, ability to train and manage a work crew, and cross-cultural sensitivity. Skills in French and auto mechanics were highly desired. It was no wonder they were having trouble finding people, the recruiter said. Hector was just the kind of guy they were looking for.

Peace Corps was Hector's ticket out of situations like on the baking hot afternoon several weeks later, with several weeks still to go until he was scheduled to leave, when a profane Anglo named Red with biceps the size of small hams started yelling about what he thought of Hector's decision. "Gonna go live in a mud hut with spearchuckers!" Red shouted, "burr heads, jungle bunnies, jigaboos!"

"Shut the fuck up, Red!" Hector shouted back.

The cough and scrape of trowels instantly ceased. Every man within earshot looked over, to see if there was going to be a fight.

Hector balled his fists, glaring at Red. Seeing that little Hector was game, all five foot five, one hundred-fifty pounds of him, if he was lucky, Red grinned at Hector's nerve.

"Did you know CIRMF is funded by Elf, the French oil company?" Natalia asked. "I was the first South American ever to apply for one of their research grants."

"And now, here we are." Hector had finished his third bowl. He leaned back, liking how when Natalia smiled at him, dimples appeared.

They'd met at Franceville's lone nightclub, Le Dazzling, where Natalia roped her fellow CIRMF researchers into going as often as she could. Dancing was in her blood. Her father played a battered old guitar for extra money in a band that performed at weddings and neighborhood festivities. She liked African music, with its infusions of Cuban rumba, and she began bringing her tapes for the DJ to play. The clientele loved the new sounds, cumbia, vallenato, marimba and bachata colombiana, and Natalia enjoyed teaching dance steps from her homeland to the bar girls.

"The night I met you was my first time ever at Le Dazzling," said Hector. "Did I tell you that? I didn't know you're not supposed to show up until eleven or twelve. I don't know how I was able to stay up so late. I get up every day with the roosters."

Hector nursed an overpriced beer, alone at the bar, hoping to get lucky as he watched the nightclub fill up with girls. In twos and threes the girls in low cut blouses and tight skirts drifted out onto the floor under the flashing colored lights, and danced with each other to Cameroonian makossa, soukous from Zaire, high-strung electric guitars and dense four-part vocal harmonies built around infectious bass lines and rat-a-tat drums. Near midnight young Gabonese men began coming in, flamboyant sons of the local elites, dressed in the latest sapeur styles from Kinshasa, suits in electric blue, neon orange, pink pinstripes, and fedora hats. Hector eyed them, and the European men arriving singly and in small groups, employees of a transnational railroad project, most of them, saggy-seated wattle-necked older men. All of the men in this place had far more cash money in their pockets than Hector had in his.

The bartender stood expectantly in front of Hector. He said something Hector couldn't hear in the loud music, meaning drink up or get out of his seat, and Hector signaled for a second beer he couldn't afford. At these prices, by the end of the month, he would be scraping by. He turned back to the dance floor, and a stunning girl walked past him, sleepy eyes spaced too far apart, eyes sliding his way as she brushed by on the arm of a smug, pot-bellied European, pointy breasts and bee sting lips, the look on her face telling Hector she'd rather be with somebody younger.

Marimba music replaced an African tune, and the new rhythms surprised Hector to hear. Out on the dance floor in the spinning lights a girl he had assumed was Gabonese began showing the other girls dance steps that made her a Latina. When the song segued into another, Hector summoned the nerve. He walked up behind her on the dance floor and shouted in her ear, "¿De dónde vienes?"

Natalia was astonished to be suddenly addressed in Spanish by a shabby Indio workman. She knew at once that he was an Estadounidense. He looked nothing like the other young Americans she saw around town, the volunteers her colleagues said were building schools out in the villages, young white men driving big camionetas, though one of them was a woman, they said, and another one of them was black.

Outside, Hector's battered old pickup truck with P¢¢r B¢y painted on the doors looked rude beside Natalia's sparkly little Peugeot. They passed tidy bungalows and well-kept gardens as they walked across the CIRMF campus, and Natalia talked to ward off her uncertainties. She enjoyed speaking Spanish with Hector. He was nothing like her, with his calloused hands. One corner of his shirt pocket was torn. His worn tennis shoes were cracking, and his faded jeans were threadbare. He had never been to college, so there was no way to discuss her professional interests with him, and never would be.

Natalia pulled open the door of an icy cold examination room equipped for surgery. She showed Hector the oscillometry unit and anesthesia cart with a monitor that displayed pulse waves and monitored blood pressure and heart rates, and the fluoroscopy equipment, explaining to Hector that to minimize animal stress and the risk of bites, the primates were always brought in under general anesthesia. "It's administered remotely," she said, "using a dart gun."

They went on to the radiology suite, with its adjacent darkroom, and she showed him the ultrasound for monitoring gestation and exploring abdominal disorders and the new video laparoscope for exploration of body cavities. The equipment was better than what the doctors at the Franceville General Hospital had, she said, which Hector was surprised to hear. All this was used only for primates.

What Hector wanted, he reminded her, as they went back outside into the muggy heat, was to see the gorilla. So they started down toward the river.

"We accommodate four hundred primates in twelve hectares of fenced and netted enclosures," Natalia told him. "Only trained personnel are allowed in there. They eat three tons of fruit every week, bananas mainly, but whatever is in season."

They reached the high security main building where individual primates were quarantined during their biomedical protocols, and Natalia pulled open the door. A guard in a green uniform set down the soccer magazine he was reading and handed Natalia the log on a clipboard to sign. Then he got up and opened a steel door, and they went into a corridor of cells, like the L.A. county jail. At the far end was the gorilla.

"This one's name is Caesar," said Natalia.

The gorilla looked at them as they approached. His shiny black face seemed puny beneath his massive brow. He had a prominent belly and tiny ears, and he knuckle-walked to them on the concrete floor. His fingers were the color of licorice. His deep-set brown eyes were inquisitive, looking at their hands, then at their faces, then at their hands again, to see what they had brought him. Deciding they had nothing, he snuffed through wide nostrils, went to the far side of the cage and sat with his broad silver back to them.

"He looks like he's wearing a hat," said Hector.

"That's the sagittal crest."

"The what?"

"It's the ridge of bone from the front of the skull to the back." Natalia indicated on her own head, and the gesture lifted her generous breast, drawing Hector's eye. "The chewing muscles are attached to it."

Hector wondered what it would be like, a guest in her house all weekend long, what would happen tonight after dark. He hadn't known there were black people in Colombia before.

"They can really bite. Their canine teeth are this long." Natalia showed him with her thumb and forefinger. "He could crush your humerus with one chomp."

"My what?"

"He could bite off your arm. He's six times stronger than a human."

Caesar picked up a stuffed animal and sniffed it.

"Just like a baby," said Hector.

Cité de la Caisse

Halfway to Obia, they came to a roadblock patrolled by agitated gendarmes with automatic rifles. Justine had never seen anything like this, traffic backed up both ways. She yelled at her brothers riding in the back of Charlie's Land Cruiser to mind themselves. They nodded, wide-eyed with apprehension, at the gendarmes, the roadblock and the commotion.

A scowling young gendarme came to Charlie's window. "Papers!" he demanded. "Why are you in Gabon? What business do you have on the road today?"

Justine shot off a volley of Téké, startling the gendarme. He retorted, and Justine rattled off another salvo.

Charlie touched her knee, signaling for her not to continue. But she was angry. This was not how things were supposed to be. The young gendarme took her papers as well, to reestablish his authority, and her brothers' identity cards for good measure, and went over to a table and spoke to the officer seated there, recording names. The young gendarme pointed back at Charlie's truck, and the officer looked their way. Justine clucked, and before Charlie could stop her, she was out the door. She marched over to the officer in charge and began gesticulating, pointing down the road toward Franceville. The officer said something, and then handed their papers back.

Justine returned to the cab smiling. "I told him I'm a nurse on a medical emergency," she said as she got in and closed the door. The gendarmes lifted the barrier and waved Charlie through.

There were roadblocks every fifty kilometers, some manned by soldiers. The wait at some was long. Passengers in the taxi buses were ordered off. Everyone's identity papers were examined. Soldiers swarmed all over the trucks, searching through their cargos. Justine had never seen anything like this.

Charlie drove as fast as he dared between roadblocks to make up time. It was late morning when he drove across the bridge over the Mpassa River. There were more roadblocks in the city, one on the way up to the top of the dominant height where the governor's residence was, one along its crest, and then another down the dirt road past the soccer stadium. Finally, they passed the train station and then the police academy and drove into the Cité de la Caisse where government functionaries and schoolteachers were housed. The Peace Corps had a guesthouse there, the *case de passage*. And at the newly painted bungalow on the side of a hill that Hector had refurbished, Charlie turned up the steep drive.

Justine climbed the ladder cautiously to the scaffold affixed in a large tree. Charlie climbed after her, admiring her derriere. At the top, she took hold of the log lintel and inspected the hairy-looking mesh of vines hung from two stout cables of braided vines, like a V- shaped hammock spanning the river. Narrow planks laid end to end in the bottom of the crotch made a footpath to the scaffold in a tree on the other side of the river. Long braided vines tied high in the branches were lashed to the cables along their length.

The twins had clambered right up the ladder and raced straight across, their adolescent voices breaking in squeaks and honks that were audible over the roar of the river, yelling out to the entire world to witness their bravery. The vine bridge twisted and swayed as they went, and now they were on the scaffold on the far bank calling and gesturing at their sister to come on over.

"Your turn," said Charlie.

"No, Charlie, I can't!" Justine hadn't liked the look of the way the vine bridge bounced and writhed beneath her brothers' feet.

"You'll be fine," said Charlie in her ear, and she felt his hands on her waist. Below them creamy froth streamed by on the surface of the river.

"Oh Charlie, je n'aime pas!"

"Don't be afraid. I'm right behind you."

This was pure foolishness. Justine did not want to do this. But there were her twin brothers on the other side calling to her to cross. She steeled herself. Contemplating what she would have to do, she put her right hand on the cable. It was a solid mass of bent and twisted vines too thick to grasp, and then she whipped her left hand onto the other and let her right foot down onto the narrow plank. Gingerly she transferred her entire weight onto the bridge, and it stirred like some creature coming to life. She froze, her feet heel-to-toe, her left foot in front of the right on the narrow plank walkway, and there were her brothers nodding their heads, laughing and waving her on.

"Oh Charlie, what if it breaks?"

"It can't break," said the guide from below. "Impossible." He had seen this reaction many times. "This bridge can support the weight of twenty people, a hundred people."

"You see?" said Charlie. "Look at your brothers."

"I'll be dizzy!"

"I'll be right behind you."

She summoned the nerve to slide her left foot forward. With her palms on the two fat cables, she slid her right foot forward, then her left foot again, then her right foot once more, proceeding in small sliding steps.

Above her clouds floated in a hazy sky. Below, cocoa-colored water flowed beneath her feet. Then suddenly Charlie's great weight came onto the vine bridge, and it began bobbing and twisting. She froze again, her palms pressed hard to the heavy woven vine cables, her fingers trying to grip.

"I can't!" she wailed.

"Keep going, you'll be fine."

"I can't!" she cried, and his two hands were on her waist again. She looked across the length of the bridge, at her brothers waving her on, took a deep breath, and she slid her left foot forward, then the right, shuffling like an old woman along the narrow plank walkway.

She could feel the weight of Charlie following, and she began to adjust to the bouncing and the twisting and the swaying, finding her balance. She willed herself on, gaining confidence. Ahead, her brothers clapped, cheered and waved her forward. Justine laughed. Then she felt like sobbing. She slid her left foot forward, then her right, her hands sliding along the thick knobby handholds. Soon, she was halfway across. She began to anticipate the motion. With a sudden blossoming of courage, she actually lifted her right foot and swung it in front of the left. Then she lifted her left foot and swung it in front of the right, and seeing that she could touch the cables only lightly to balance, she tottered the rest of the way.

Miraculously, she made it across, her brothers cheering as they pulled her by the arms up onto the sturdy scaffold, her knees trembling.

"You were magnificent," said Charlie in her ear, and she felt his voice in her belly.

The twins disappeared with the pocket money into the warren of kiosks, and Justine told Charlie to move away; otherwise, she'd have to pay more for her purchases. Then she went in, and he trailed after her, lurking a short distance behind like her bodyguard. Whenever she stopped, he stopped too, pretending not to be keeping an eye on her, the way she filled out her jeans.

Justine stopped at a kiosk where a woman sold bolts of cloth, and twenty yards back Charlie watched her fingering the goods on offer. When the kiosk owner glanced at him, he looked away, as if watching the people passing by. From the corner of his eye, he saw Justine select one. The market woman unfolded the cloth and held it up, and the haggling began.

A family approached wearing conspicuously new clothes, clearly villagers, ill at ease in the big city. The father led, looking at Charlie warily as he passed. The mother carried a baby on her back. A little girl holding her mother's hand stepped along in a brand new pair of plastic shoes, as light as a cat on quick pink unstained soles.

Mbou Blaise and Mpiga Gérard were among the shrieking boys spilling out into the street, kicking and chopping and wrestling around, imitating the Hong Kong Kung-Fu movie they'd just seen, the only kind of movie Franceville's only theater ever showed. Justine laughed at the spectacle they made. She had enjoyed the experience more than the movie, the audience mostly boys, many of them urchins from the market who snuck in through the emergency exits, whooping and screaming and laughing and talking back to the screen.

They crossed the street to the brightly lit Lebanese-owned pizzeria. Justine and her brothers took seats at a table while Charlie ordered at the take-away window. He came to the table and while they waited, Justine's brothers rehashed the story of the evildoers who slaughtered the students at the Kung-Fu school, the ninja teacher and the five surviving students who hatched the plan for revenge that resulted in the climactic battle.

When the two pizzas came, Charlie drove them all back to the freshly painted house in the Cité de la Caisse. Inside the boys settled at the table in the salon, and Justine found them forks and plates in the kitchen while Charlie adjusted the rabbit ears on the black and white TV Hector had scrounged from his new friends at CIRMF. Justine lingered long enough to make sure her brothers would like the pizza, and when she saw them busily chewing with their faces turned to the snowy picture, she left with Charlie.

She had changed into a rich blue ensemble tailored from expensive Dutch wax cloth, a bodice cut low off the shoulder with a matching long slit skirt and a shawl to ward off the chill. She clattered along the walkway to the restaurant on high heels, and Charlie was conscious of his worn clothes, as the doorman at the Masuku Hotel let them in. The maître d' looked at Charlie dubiously, and when Charlie said he didn't have a reservation, seated them at a table near the kitchen. The clientele were mainly middle-aged white men, a few of them with beautiful young African girls, but most of them eating alone.

A waiter came with menus and took their drink order.

"So the vine bridge and the waterfall, that was your big surprise?"

Justine's dangling earrings set off her eyes. She'd been afraid crossing the vine bridge. Poubara Falls awed her. The waters were at a seasonal high, and when the sun came out from behind a cloud, the drenching spray made a rainbow in the air.

"No," said Charlie, "that wasn't it." Then he hesitated. His news seemed too small now, for the size of her anticipation.

"What is it?"

Charlie reached over to take her hand. "There's a new job they're setting up," he said, watching for her reaction. "They want me for it. I'm going to be assigned to Franceville."

"Oh," she said when she saw that was it. "Is this job something you want to do?"

"I guess so. I'll be moving to Franceville in two months." Charlie told her about the visit from Stu and Harry and Jim, how they really needed him to take the job.

Their order came, and Justine pulled back her hand, her bracelets jingling as the waiter set their plates before them, and wished them bon appétit.

"I'll be living in the house where we're staying."

"Congratulations. Good for you." She sliced her grilled sole and looked around the restaurant chewing, to see what there was to see.

So this is his big surprise, this American named Charlie Sinclair, with his bifteck avec pomme frites. He wants me to move to Franceville and live with him. Why doesn't he just say so? Justine thought of her friend Béatrice who worked at the general hospital, who slept with the Provincial Inspector of Health. Perhaps Béatrice could put in a word about a transfer. But if she did that, what would become of her twin brothers?

14. Faces Peeping Out

Doumboukombi

"What will I see when I get initiated?" asked Dabrian, drinking beer after supper on a moonless and windy night at the table by the window in Johnny Brasseaux's front room.

"If you get initiated!" said Johnny. "It's never sure until it happens. I keep telling you that, Dabrian. You haven't even met the Nima Louembé yet. It may be, when he meets you, he'll see something that makes him say no."

Dabrian grimaced at the thought of Louembé, the Bwiti priest who would initiate him, turning him away. He wanted the spiritual experience intensely, and Johnny knew this. Dabrian wanted to connect to the time before his people were taken from Africa, and Louembé would understand that; he had to. For ten long days in the village of Bambera-Byoko in Ogooué-Lolo Province, Dabrian had helped frame ceilings in Johnny's school, asking questions about the secret ritual. And for ten long days, Johnny had answered, with mounting irritation. Twice, Johnny had driven his truck, Moukongo, down a dreadful narrow trail off the main road to a tiny village called Doumboukombi to introduce Dabrian to Louembé, and twice Louembé was not there.

A powerful gust of wind blew in through the open window, and the yellow flames in the two kerosene lamps flickered. Rain could be heard out in the black of night approaching across the trees.

"Is it possible to have my vision without the iboga?"

"That's not how to look at it," said Johnny. "Bwiti's centered on the iboga, but it's not about the iboga. The iboga is the sacred plant handed down from the first people, the Apinzi, the ones the white people call the Pygmies. I've told you this, how many times?"

The rain came sweeping into the village, hammering onto Johnny's roof. In an instant, a thick sheet of water streamed from the eave, spattering onto the ground, and Johnny got up and closed the plywood window against the billowing spray. It was impossible to speak, and he and Dabrian looked at each other, sipping beer in the thunderous roar, waiting until the rain had eased.

When he could be heard again, Dabrian spoke with his voice raised, "Tell me again about the iboga."

Johnny leaned closer across the table. "Iboga opens your mind. You become super aware, so the vision can come to you, the vision that will guide you for the rest of your life. Once you have your vision, the more you act on it, the more you unlock your atura afou, your inner power."

"Atura afou. My inner power."

"That's right. And the power comes from what?"

"From those who have passed."

"Right." With the window shut, the air in the room soon grew stuffy, and Johnny got up and opened it to a rainy breeze.

"They're still with us," said Johnny, sitting down again, "the ancestors. The afterlife is close by. I've learned that much. The spirit world is like another room in the same house. After I was initiated, I was able to understand what my great granny always knew. The power, atura afou, comes from the ancestors, handed down through the generations. The ancestors are all around us, Dabrian, watching what we do."

As abruptly as it began, the rain ended, and there arose a hoarse throbbing of frogs. In the pulsing chorus, Dabrian could feel them out there, the spirits watching, and he shivered at what was to come.

The third time Johnny took Dabrian to the sacred village of Doumboukombi, a small boy told them Louembé had returned. Johnny switched off his truck by a tiny hut made of palm fronds, a rude memorial to the Apinzi, who first gave iboga to the ancestors. Beyond the hut was a footpath to a crude cinderblock building.

"That's the temple," said Johnny, smiling as Nima Louembé approached. The priest was in his mid-forties, a sprinkling of gray in his hair. He wore a purple smock. He embraced Johnny, then shook Dabrian's hand. Around the priest's neck was a string of teeth on a leather cord.

Dabrian was ready with the things Johnny had told him to bring. He had a hundred thousand franc wad in his pocket, and in Johnny's truck, a mirror, a bucket, a machete, six yards of printed fabric and an unopened bottle of Johnny Walker Red.

"The men here," said Johnny, "are all Bwiti initiates. They're called banzi."

The banzi drifted over from whatever chores they'd been doing to greet Johnny and Dabrian, then filed into the temple. The Nima Louembé led Dabrian down a forest path to a nearby iboga bush, dark green leaves, yellow blossoms and orange-colored fruit. Louembé picked one and handed it to Dabrian, and motioned to taste it. Dabrian sampled the fruit cautiously, like a waxy apricot. It was flavorless.

Louembé laughed at Dabrian's expression. The spirit isn't in the fruit, he said, communicating with his eyes and simple gestures because he didn't speak French. He lifted the iboga's branches, bent down and waved his hand over the ground where the roots lay, to show Dabrian where the spirit resided.

They walked back into the village and entered the temple where a dozen banzis waited on stools with Johnny. The banzis took turns asking Dabrian questions, the same question over and over. "Why should we initiate you?"

The stool was too small for Dabrian's frame. Uncomfortable, frustrated speaking in French, when what he wanted to express was so complicated, Dabrian switched into English, looking to Johnny to translate, Johnny who spoke with his work crew in functional Pounou.

Between translations, Johnny counseled patience. Dabrian studied a painting on the temple wall, ancient Apinzi people handing the sacred iboga to Adam and Eve.

When finally the village men stood up and left the temple, Dabrian asked Johnny, "How did I do?"

"Be patient, brother," Johnny replied. "You got to get into being, not doing."

Outside in the bright light children laughed and shouted. Dabrian wanted to get on with the initiation. He struggled to quiet his desire.

Louembé returned alone, smiling. Dabrian's spirits lifted.

"He says the signs are right," explained Johnny. "Your answers were satisfactory. You are meant to learn of our ancestors, to know our Mother Africa from the inside. You've been sent to Gabon for a purpose that will soon be revealed. You'll be given a responsibility to take back to America to fulfill."

Louembé spoke again in Pounou. Johnny turned to Dabrian and said, "Give him the money." Just then, a lizard went skittering up the wall.

Dabrian's initiation began an hour before sunset. The banzis returned with their faces painted in white clay, wearing red loincloths, animal hides and headbands adorned with feathers. They carried handmade drums, rattles, string instruments and horns. In a noisy procession, they led Dabrian from the village along a slick, muddy jungle path and downhill to a stream. On the bank, Louembé gestured for Dabrian to undress while the banzis chanted and banged their drums, strummed string instruments, blew horns and shook their rattles.

When Dabrian was naked, Louembé motioned to wade out to the middle of the stream. The water was cool, the streambed gritty under Dabrian's feet. He waded in until the water swirled around his waist. Louembé followed, his purple tunic turning red where it touched the water. Johnny was right behind, the acolyte, with a brown raffia sack slung over his shoulder. He handed Louembé a small pot. Louembé scooped out red paste and smeared it on Dabrian's face and then his torso. Johnny handed Louembé a ladle. The Nima dipped chilly water from the stream and poured it over Dabrian. The banzis chanted and played their instruments.

Louembé sloshed ahead of Dabrian and Johnny back to the stream bank where he gave Dabrian a rough raffia loincloth, dyed red, to wear. He draped a stiff animal skin over Dabrian's shoulders. He tied strips of fur around Dabrian's upper arms, and looped a strand of cowry shells about his neck. The men chanted louder when Louembé screwed a red feather into Dabrian's wet hair.

"You have died now, Dabrian," said Johnny, on the banks of a stream in the African rain forest with the sun going down, "and now you will be reborn."

Louembé peeled a pale yellow plantain, sliced it lengthwise with a knife, sprinkled it with white iboga powder and fed it to Dabrian. The raw plantain reminded Dabrian of eating an uncooked yam. The iboga tasted bitter, like aspirin. Dabrian swallowed the first bite with difficulty, then a second bite, and another, until the plantain and the iboga were gone. Dabrian wished he could go to the stream for a drink, to cleanse his mouth.

Johnny produced a small earthen jar containing wild black honey swimming with bits of comb and tiny dead bees. Louembé sprinkled powder on a spoonful of honey, held it to Dabrian's mouth and nodded for him to swallow it, then another, the honey sticky and sweet, masking the astringent iboga, then another, and then another, until the honey jar was empty.

Louembé led the procession back to the village. Barely able to see in the gloom, Dabrian's knees felt shaky. Roots, rocks and twigs hurt his bare feet. There was light ahead in the village. Lanterns on the ground lit the way. Dabrian followed Louembé to a bench outside the temple door. He sat gladly and brushed off the muddy soles of his feet, a keen sensation. He could feel his heart beating as the banzis gathered around him with their instruments. Their chanting and drumming reverberated right into his body. A light began to glow in his belly. He had eaten nothing today, as he'd been told, and he knew the iboga was taking effect. Fleeting glimpses of the essential unity of all creation began to come to him in bursts, and just as quickly flittered away. His vision was opening to him.

One of the banzis sawed a crude bow across a one-stringed harp held against his open mouth. Dabrian became fascinated, watching him, and felt himself smile.

"That's called a moukongo," said Johnny.

Dabrian smiled wider at hearing the name of Johnny's truck, and he beamed with elation and wonder at everyone around him, at the astonishing and pretty marvels flashing in the cool night air. He heard Johnny speaking again, his voice both near and far. "The voices of the ancestors are channeled through the moukongo."

Yes, thought Dabrian, listening to the moukongo, I can hear voices, and they are Chinese! He smiled even wider. But no, they aren't Chinese. Those voices are no language ever heard before!

Louembé placed an antelope tail in Dabrian's right hand, to use as a whisk. Dabrian looked at the coarse tail, the oddest thing he had ever seen, and he roared with laughter.

"Shake it," said Johnny, translating for Louembé, sounding like he spoke from under water. "Keep time with the music," he said.

Again Dabrian laughed, at the absurd suggestion he shake a whisk in time to music. He tried to speak, but no sound came out of his mouth. Then the whisk began shaking in his hand, and he laughed to feel it flicking back and forth with a mind of its own, to see how the shape of it changed as it moved.

Louembé fed Dabrian more iboga powder heaped in a tablespoon, more and more, until the bitter, white dust clogged Dabrian's mouth. He tried to ask for water, but he had no voice. The night, pitch dark, was shot through with every color in the spectrum, moving shapes, trails of sparks, red, green and yellow. The deepest meanings of existence began to open to Dabrian, of a benign and loving, splendid creation eternally unfolding and being revealed.

Several banzis helped Dabrian to his feet. Carrying lanterns, they led him into the temple. The earth sent needles shooting up through his sensitive soles, up deep inside his legs. They helped him sit on a little stool, alone in the center of the room, facing black Adam and Eve taking the iboga from the Pygmy ancestors. The men began dancing around Dabrian, casting whirling shadows onto the walls, where Dabrian saw faces. The faces talked to him, wordless faces, faces that vanished as other faces appeared, talking to him in words he couldn't hear.

Louembé took away the whisk and replaced it with a mirror in Dabrian's hand, and gestured for him to look into it, to see himself for the first time, his face smeared red, the red feather in his hair, the hide around his shoulders, the strand of white shells around his neck. Dabrian didn't recognize the man in the mirror, although he knew he was looking at himself, and he grinned, and Johnny, the Cinnamon Man, magical Johnny, Dabrian's guide said something Dabrian didn't understand. Johnny's face looked so different. It frightened Dabrian. Then it was just Johnny again, and Dabrian wanted to laugh and tell Johnny about the transformation. He just wanted to laugh and laugh at the intricate hairs on Johnny's face. But no sound came from Dabrian's dry mouth. All he could do was smile, and his mouth stretched so wide from the sheer joy of the moment, he felt it would tear apart.

Louembé and the banzis sat on stools in an arc around Dabrian, watching him in silence. They are so beautiful, he thought. I am so happy to be here with them. Their bodies are so sleek and radiant. Do they know how beautiful they are? Do they see? It is all so magnificent, fabulous beyond words. I understand everything.

"If you see a window," said Johnny, through Louembé, recognizing the moment was here; this was Dabrian's epiphany, "you must go through it."

Dabrian felt so happy to hear this, to receive this clue, and he smiled at Johnny, joyous tears sliding from his eyes.

"If you meet people," said Johnny, "you must listen to each one. They will all have a message for you."

Louembé leaned toward Dabrian, his necklace of teeth swinging forward from his purple robe, his face near, peering inquisition itself. Dabrian wondered how Louembé could breathe, his nostrils were so horribly stuffed full of hair. The Nima held a bowl of iboga shavings. He pointed at the shavings, then at his own eyes, and then at Dabrian's mouth. "Eat more iboga," he said in Pounou, "so that you will see things."

Dabrian saw his own hand reach for the iboga. It extended out and out and out. And it went out for a long time. And when his fingers touched the iboga shavings, cool and slippery like red potato peelings, his fingers reappeared in his mouth. He was chewing the vile iboga, and he felt his teeth rooted deep in his jaws grind it into mash. How marvelous, he thought, to have strong teeth to chew with!

Dabrian could feel the spirit flowing out of the juice from the shavings into his mouth, into his body. He swallowed, awed at the muscles of his throat pushing the iboga down into his stomach. He reached for another handful, and another, and another, and another. Then he vomited into the bucket in the sand beside his tiny stool. Weren't they clever, he thought, to have me bring a bucket so I can puke up those glistening little fish for everyone to see.

Now they were helping Dabrian to lie down on a reed mat.

How had there been fish in my belly? he wondered. His mind was everywhere. The young man, the one with a beard like Johnny's

– where was Johnny? – leaned over him, speaking the most beautiful language Dabrian had ever heard, or could imagine. Spinning patterns formed and broke apart and reformed in swirling, brilliant kaleidoscope shapes that made Dabrian want to weep at the sheer beauty, the mathematical precision he could scarcely comprehend, the Structure of Everything, a wondrous geometry of points connected by lines of every imaginable color.

They moved the mirror in Dabrian's hand back to his face. Lying on a mat on the dirt floor, he stared at the amazing sight of his own eyes staring back, and he rose off the ground, and began to float in the air! The drums resumed. He could feel the percussion coming out of the earth, dangerous, pounding, demonic engines of hell. Then suddenly, the banzis sang songs of angelic magnificence, songs of stillness and peace and intelligence and love and clarity, unclouded by any doubt. Hovering suspended off the ground, Dabrian understood. He understood when Louembé told him to look in the mirror and see more. He saw the window of his parents' house on Ezzard Street. He drifted in through the window as Louembé instructed. He passed over the dinner table, dark pink sliced ham on his mother's best platter, collard greens in a ceramic bowl, golden cornbread in a woven basket, tall pitchers of ice tea. In the next room, his aunts, uncles, cousins, nephews and nieces joined hands and bowed their heads. Reverend Thomas stood by the mantel and said, "Heavenly Father, keep your hand on our boy Dabrian out in Africa."

"Yes Jesus, yes Jesus. Amen, yes Jesus."

"We give him to you. Keep him safe from danger. Deliver him from evil. And bring him home again safe in the name of Jesus."

"Yes, Jesus. Yes, Jesus. Amen."

Dabrian watched his father, Leander, look up, and see his son floating in the room. Dabrian loved his father. And he saw God beaming from behind his father, and Leander nodded and said to his son, "You go on now."

But before he could go, Dabrian noticed that his mother, Ulandie, was crying because his cousin Dorell went to jail for shooting a man. And with a terrific shock of recognition, Dabrian knew his purpose. He had the power to free people from the wickedness that held them in bondage. He wanted to tell his mother, below him, down on her tired, aching knees praying for Dorell, but before he could say anything, he saw Tyra, beautiful and slender, loving and intelligent, watching him, and she held up her hand so that his mother would not see him, and she began whispering burning prophesy.

"Your mother fears what you must do! But it is your calling! You must tear the heart of stone from your flesh, and then the scales will fall from your eyes, and you will see, for evil is afoot in the land, Dabrian, and you, with your own hands, will drive it away."

Tyra said this, Tyra who was wiser and finer bred, and Dabrian heard, and closed his eyes at the impossible thought, and lay the mirror upon his chest. He saw a beautiful village with the glorious sun shining down on flourishing green crops in black and fertile soil, children skipping and clapping, happy and laughing. They cried out to Dabrian, to come play with them. He went to them, the ancestors, went into their village, and he heard the women singing as they harvested, as they drew water from the crystal stream. Their singing was pure, and the women stretched out their shapely arms to him, and their singing carried Dabrian on to where the men mended nets in the shade of tall palms. They looked at him and smiled and said in a language he could absolutely understand, "Welcome home, Brother." Dabrian wept freely at long last to be home.

Looking up through his tears into the tall trees surrounding the village, Dabrian saw something leaping about in the branches, a troop of monkeys. Yes! The monkeys emerged from the leaves, and suddenly they weren't monkeys at all. They had dog faces peeping out, claws for hands, and wings! Poised to jump, they spread their wings and flew out, swiftly as bats. The people screamed when they saw them, and began to run. Dabrian hovered helpless, unable to move, watching, calling out soundlessly to the children, "Run! Run!" as the winged beasts swooped in, knocked them to the ground, and squatted on them. And Dabrian saw their long and terrible yellow fangs.

By the time Dabrian reached Ondili, the village was dark. He unlocked his door with the help of a flashlight, and struck a match to light a lamp. He stumbled into the bedroom and climbed straight into bed, exhausted yet wide-awake. He closed his eyes and the face of the Nima Louembé immediately appeared, vivid, nostrils flared, full of hair, sweat beads like studs on his forehead as he smeared the sacred oil on Dabrian, sealing his initiation as a banzi, before each man of the village in turn embraced him, and left.

When everyone but Johnny was gone, Louembé spoke to Dabrian in Pounou, and Johnny translated.

"He says no one must know of your vision," said Johnny.

"That is very important," said Louembé, "very important. You must tell no one."

Dabrian sat once more on a stool too small for him, exhausted from the ritual, yet exhilarated. He nodded that he understood.

"Now tell me," said Louembé, sweat on his face. "What did you see?"

The morning was hot, and Dabrian spoke hesitantly at first, of the window he had floated through.

Louembé wanted to know more. "Who did you see there?"

"I saw my family, and the preacher praying for me. I was inside my parents' house."

"That is normal. Your family is concerned about their son far away."

"I saw God shining behind my father."

"Did anyone say anything to you?"

"My father said, 'You go on now.'"

Louembé nodded. "That is good. Did any women talk to you?"

"My old girlfriend, Tyra."

"What did she say?"

"She said my mother wouldn't want to see me there, because she would be upset. I was sorry I couldn't ease my mother's mind, make her see it was all right. Tyra said I would see a terrible evil in the world, and with my own hands I would drive it away."

Louembé nodded to hear this. "Did anyone else speak to you? What else did you see?"

Dabrian told Louembé about the village of the ancestors, the golden sun, the fertile soil, the women singing, the children at play, and the men who welcomed him home. He hesitated again, uncertain how to describe the winged, dog-faced creatures with claws, how they swooped down like bats from the trees, their mouths yawning wide, baring the yellow fangs they sank into the throats of the little children.

Louembé fell silent for a time, Johnny too, quiet and waiting.

"Do you understand my vision?" Dabrian asked. "It was horrible."

Louembé fingered the teeth on his necklace before he spoke. "You have come here to Africa seeking to connect with the people of your blood. That is what you have done. But your vision will call you to go somewhere. You must do so. There you will witness a great evil; that is true, and then your power will become manifest, and the purpose of your life will become clear."

Lying in cool sheets damp from humidity upon his foam rubber mattress, Dabrian sensed a new power within his grasp, but he would have to purify himself before seizing it. The Nima had told him he would have to remain celibate for six months, in order to be worthy of his vision. He would have to tell Camille to stop coming around. That would be hard; the things she knew how to do. But only then would he realize his atura afou, his inner power, and be able to act on the vision that the Nima Louembé had said would be revealed to him soon, in a dream.

The dream came three nights later. Dabrian dreamed he was adrift on a raft in complete darkness, fearful of being on water because he couldn't swim. He became aware of a noxious smell. He was on a wide and deep river flowing swiftly, and the raft entered some rapids, and began to rise and fall, hurtling faster and faster downstream toward something waiting ahead, hidden in the trees. He knew what it was, the dog-faced bats, dog-faced bats that were men. Instantly, a paddle materialized in his hand. He stabbed it into the water and began pulling hard. Each stroke propelled him an amazing distance toward the indistinct shore. He felt enormously strong, paddling furiously, fighting his way off the river to land.

15. Grim Portent

Libreville

A little more than a year after Ambassador Jones presented her credentials, the situation in Gabon had become volatile. Riots in two major cities following the death of Joseph Rendjambé elevated the risk that Gabon might descend into violent turmoil, and the French flew in an additional regiment of the Foreign Legion to evacuate their nationals.

The initial coroner's report said Rendjambé died of a pulmonary condition and diabetes, but the popular politician's supporters came forward with medical records that gave no indication of any serious health problems. Two days later the state-owned newspaper changed the story, and l'Union ran a banner headline that read: 'Rendjambé dead from drug overdose. Police seek unidentified European woman for questioning'. Two lurid photos from what was by then labeled a crime scene accompanied the article, the first showing Rendjambé dead on his back inside a chalk mark on the floor, his shirt yanked up over his belly. A close-up in the second photo revealed a pinhole in his abdomen that could have been made by a syringe. A month later, the last week of June, the scandal deepened when l'Union reported the lead police investigator assigned to the Rendjambé case had been found by his wife, dead of unexplained causes.

Darlene lacked the tools to fully assess what was happening. She was chief of a backwater mission staffed by junior officers whose contacts did not extend past the middle levels of the Gabonese government. Even direct overtures from her own office went nowhere, ensnared in maddening loops of delay, postponements delivered with buttery regrets, always in impeccable French. The CIA had no station in Libreville. U.S. government interests in Gabon were insufficient to justify the cost. Darlene needed intelligence assets if she was to keep abreast of developments, and she telephoned the Assistant Secretary for African Affairs to request them. Hank Cohen promised to get back to her with an answer. He fixed a day and time for a conference call with the Africa Bureau, and now that time had come.

It was 5:30 in the afternoon and Darlene was at her desk looking out her window at sun showers falling like smoke into a sparkling sea. When she presented her credentials in a ceremony at the Palace, President Bongo strode into the reception room like a gamecock, his chest thrown out, wearing a three-button Armani suit. Darlene was struck by how small the strongman indeed was, even wearing the platform shoes she'd been told to expect. A camera crew flipped on hot lights and a cameraman for the state-run television station taped them for the evening news, President Omar Bongo and Ambassador Darlene Jones smiling and shaking hands. Darlene took her seat on Bongo's right in one of the two Louis XIV chairs. The cameraman moved in for a close up. For a moment, Darlene felt unreal and out of place, the daughter of Isaiah and Clarice Jones from Brooklyn, New York grown up to become an Ambassador of the United States of America, seated beside the shrewd-eyed President of Gabon, with his out-of-date Fu Manchu mustache. They made small talk in French that lasted less than fifteen minutes.

Other countries were making front page New York Times headlines, consequent to the winds blowing out of Eastern Europe and the Soviet Union, winds sweeping south to rattle the coconut trees here in Gabon, where no front page New York Times headlines were being made. Was it possible to raise the visibility of the situation here onto the crowded agenda of Washington priorities, Darlene wondered, remembering the President of the United States coming around his desk to greet her, his new Ambassador to Gabon, being shown into the awe-inspiring Oval Office. We've upgraded your post to a political appointment, he said with his crooked grin. This was to reciprocate, Darlene knew, for President Bongo having been the first African head of state to telephone with congratulations on Election Night, but President Bush made no mention of that. Darlene knew of it from her earlier briefing with Secretary of State James Baker, on the seventh floor at

Main State, where he looked at her levelly, every bit the Houston lawyer. "We intend to rein in the enthusiasts," he said, "and restore a proper realism in our foreign affairs."

That was an instruction, and Darlene was disappointed to receive it, for she shared the enthusiasm of the idealists. The crumbling of the Warsaw Pact and potentially of the Soviet Union itself presented the United States with an unprecedented opportunity to promote the spread of democracy in the world. But she had been given an order, and as a former naval officer who respected the chain of command, she had no choice but to obey.

With Joseph Rendjambé dead, following rioting in two cities, and with the French newspapers full of photographs of fleeing French families, had not the calculus changed? Certainly, it had, and it had changed even further last Friday when the French advisor to the secret police, Gilles Clermidy, met with her RSO Ray Sims and handed over a copy of the toxicological test results. Rendjambé had two thousand milligrams of phenobarbital in his bloodstream when he died, and Clermidy told Ray what the Gabonese police knew. In the hours before his demise, Rendjambé had checked into a room at the Dowé Hotel where he met a mysterious white woman, who left the hotel not long after. It was a set-up, meant to look like a sexual assignation. It wasn't amateurs, Clermidy said, but whoever did it wasn't top drawer; they didn't use a toxin that would leave no trace. The white woman had not been found. In his opinion, she never would be. The case of the dead cop would never be solved either, he said, leaving it to the Americans to draw their own conclusions.

With that, Darlene had telephoned the French Ambassador to accept his longstanding invitation to boat over to Pointe Denis. She and Philippe Berrier crossed in the late morning, on a Sunday, on a twin-engine launch skippered by a Gabonese pilot, flying the French flag. Two young French gendarmes were aboard. The water of the estuary was calm, and the ride across was smooth, and the gendarmes carried the hamper and cooler from the dock into the well-appointed cabin on the beach.

Philippe, tanned, lean and relaxed, served baguettes and pâté with a bottle of Comte Leloup du Chateau de Chasseloir, a Muscadet de Sèvre-et-maine, from the varietal Melon de

Bourgogne, which was a cross between Pinot and Gouais blanc, he said. "At one time the grape of the Melon de Bourgogne was not considered as noble as Chardonnay, and was outlawed in Burgundy."

He spoke as if Darlene shared his knowledge of wines.

"It's nice for lunch because it's very light. What do you think of it?" He made jaunty small talk while they ate. Philippe had a passion for nineteenth century French literature, Baudelaire, Flaubert and Maupassant. Darlene mentioned her love of authors he didn't know, Zora Neale Hurston, Toni Morrison and Maya Angelou.

"But the Russians, oh the Russians!" he said, "Dostoyevsky, Pushkin, Tolstoy, Chekhov! How is it a culture that has produced so much beauty in the world could become such a bloody nuisance?" Philippe swirled his wine glass with a flourish.

With that, the subject turned to the global transformations underway, and Darlene said, "Now you have touched on my passion!" She recited for Philippe the chronology she knew by heart. "Portugal and Greece in 1974. Spain in 1975. Ecuador in 1979. Peru in 1980. Bolivia and Honduras in 1982. Turkey in 1983. Uruguay, Brazil and El Salvador in 1984. Guatemala in 1985. The Philippines in 1986. Pakistan, South Korea and Taiwan in 1988. And beginning last year, Poland, Czechoslovakia, Hungary, and now, maybe the Soviet Union! Can Africa be far behind? Maybe. The whole world was astonished when F.W. de Klerk released Nelson Mandela from prison last February, and last month committed to negotiations with the ANC. With South Africa showing signs of becoming the newest transition to watch, are changes coming to Gabon?" Darlene asked breathlessly. "At the very least, it's impossible to say this isn't a trend."

Philippe raised his hand for her to stop. "Let's go for a walk on the beach."

Shirt unbuttoned, his trousers rolled up, Philippe carried his canvas shoes. Small waves rushed up and rippled back. Gulls hung in the air overhead. As the two ambassadors walked toward the distant point of land, they left behind the gendarmes and the skipper kicking a soccer ball in the sand.

"From now on we must be discreet," said Philippe. "I suspect my activities are being watched. Even in the cabin back there, even in my own office, I must be careful what I say."

"I thought you said President Bongo wants you to keep me informed."

"I am not talking about President Bongo. I am talking about Jean-Jacques Mitterrand. His people are watching me, I must believe. I am a Gaullist. Everyone knows this. I am not supportive of what they are doing, and I tell you, they must be stopped. Their handpicked candidate, Antoine Badinga, who is he? What is the source of his legitimacy? What sort of man is he? He is a thug. This is someone the Gabonese should have as their leader? A man who has trafficked in weapons? Who has profited from blood diamonds?"

"Does President Mitterrand support what his son is doing, grooming this man Badinga?"

"Not so much support, I think, as he is turning a blind eye." Philippe rubbed his thumb and fingertips together, a half smile lifting his mustache. "C'est la politique, n'est-ce pas?"

"Few political transitions are painless," said Darlene. "The Czechs, for example, were fortunate. Not every transition can be as smooth as the Velvet Revolution. Usually change comes through some level of violence. Sometimes it's extreme; look at Romania. My government has one overarching priority: Don't antagonize the Soviet military. Don't gloat. The President wants prudence. What guidance are you receiving?"

Philippe snorted. "None for all practical purposes. Because of the factions in Paris we have no clear guidance at all, which perhaps is just as well. Those on the left are unhappy with what is happening in Moscow, in the Warsaw Pact countries. It seems socialism is being defeated, and so the Socialists don't know how to respond. The best Mitterrand can do is support Thatcher's opposition to German reunification, which cannot be stopped. Have you read the speech Mitterrand gave to the African heads of state at La Baule?"

"Washington faxed me a copy."

"A very weak speech; France will not intervene in the internal affairs of its African friends, he says. He says he sympathizes with the plight of African leaders who must manage the contradictions inherited from their histories. He claims to have forbidden the practices of the past, when France engineered political change, but none of the African heads of state could possibly have believed that. The speech was for international consumption. The Africans know the Socialists are in turmoil and confused and they remember the Gaullists who have always been clear and bold. We want a world in which France plays a leadership role, which African leaders can benefit from. But it is the Socialists who are in power, so where is Bongo to turn? The Foccart network is not the same thing for him as a friendly government. He has turned to your government before, has he not, and your government has never responded. What if he does so again?"

"The Secretary is very clear on this. Gabon lies within France's sphere of interest."

"And there you have it. Where is Bongo to go? To the British who are the handmaidens of you Americans? To the Germans who are busy now trying to reunite? To the Italians? Hah! That would be something! To the Soviet Union when its empire is in revolt? To China when it is busy suppressing its own unrest? Where? The Foccart network is happy to support Bongo. He is our old friend, but the network is not the same as a sovereign government. It is not as in the time of the Master Mind, Foccart, when we Gaullists were in power. It is in the interest of the United States to help defeat this game the Socialists are playing, Darlene, and I hope your people in Washington understand this."

Darlene understood only that Philippe was trying to implicate her, implicate the American ambassador in opposing an intrigue launched by the son of the President of France. The former academic found this fascinating, walking along the beach, but the former naval officer in her found Philippe's disloyalty indecent.

"Bongo sees what he must do," said Philippe. "Tonight he is scheduled to make an announcement on television. Everyone knows he will discuss the political situation. What few people know is he will finally set a date for elections."

"Really? This is certain?"

"Yes, but in the end nothing will change. These so-called democratic forces here in Libreville, they would destabilize this country that is peaceful and reasonably well off and has been spared the many unfortunate, how shall I say, excitements of so many other nations in Africa during the last twenty years, thirty years, to no good end."

"You are sure Bongo is going to announce multiparty elections tonight?"

"Yes, he himself told me."

They reached the point of land, and turned into a stiff wind that wrapped Darlene's skirt around her knees and blew Philippe's unbuttoned shirt from his flat brown belly. Abruptly he folded up and sat, his arms around his knees, facing into the wind, squinting across the breakers of the open Atlantic.

Darlene sat next to him safely a small distance away, braced on one arm, her fingers in the dry sand, her feet tucked under her. "If Bongo calls for elections, will they be credible? Could there be an alternation in power?"

"Of course not." The expression on Philippe's face was adamant. "Bongo will resort to any measure to prevent it. We have already seen that, with Joseph Rendjambé. As for what the son of President Mitterrand is doing, it is only reciprocity. In the past two elections Bongo was a heavy contributor to Mitterrand's opponents, you know that, so the son is repaying Bongo in the same coin. He has supported the university student leaders, urging them to strike. He is paying money to the union leaders, to support the students. He wants to sting Bongo a little. That is all. And with world events trending the way they are, Bongo is in some difficulty. So yes, the elections must be credible, to the casual observer, that is." Laugh lines reached from Philippe's blue eyes into the edges of his wind-tousled silver hair. "But Bongo is clever, Darlene. He has called upon the Foccart network to help. If there must be an election, it will deliver the result Bongo wants."

They sat in the wind without speaking as Darlene absorbed this, looking at the clouds high above in the blue sky, at the white gulls wheeling over the water, and for a while, the only sounds were the roar of the wind and the screech of the gulls and the thump of the breakers rolling in from the west. Then from behind them came a crack and a rumble, and they turned to see black thunderheads piling up over the mainland.

"We must be going," said Philippe, slapping sand from the seat of his pants as he rose. Darlene took his hand when he offered it.

The sun touched the tops of the coconut palms to their right, dropping toward the western horizon as they hurried in and out of the shadows. The wind had swung around and was blowing off the mainland from their left, kicking up whitecaps on the estuary. Philippe's unbuttoned shirt flapped like a flag, and there was a flicker of lightning when they reached the dock, and a sharp crack of thunder. Spume was flying off the whitecaps now, and the black clouds loomed like grim portent over the glittering towers of the city.

One young gendarme stood on the pier ready to cast off. The Gabonese skipper waited behind the wheel, the powerful engines rumbling. The second gendarme braced himself in the rocking boat, ready to help Darlene into the craft.

The telephone rang, startling Darlene. She glanced at her watch and picked up the receiver. The call was ten minutes late.

"Ambassador Jones?" said a voice from across the Atlantic, "Please hold for the Assistant Secretary."

That evening, dressed in her terrycloth bathrobe, Darlene turned on the lamp by the television and reached behind the stand to pull the blue wire from the decoder box. The picture changed to snowy Radio-Television Gabon. The boat ride back had been an ordeal of wind and speed and crashing spray. The small craft stood on its tail going over the waves and plunged its nose into the troughs. Relieved to be ashore and soaked to the skin, Darlene was sopping wet getting into the embassy car. Splashing along narrow Avenue Colonel Parant through the old part of Libreville the deluge had swept every soul from the street. Water poured in sheets from the overlain tin roofs and leaped in torrents through the open sewers. Even on high, the windshield wipers weren't enough, and the chauffeur steered the long Chevrolet with care.

Darlene returned to the couch and the television. Sports, soccer highlights from Europe, Gabonese schoolgirls playing netball followed the news segment. And there were commercials, a brand of tomato paste that would make your husband love you, a brand of toothpaste that would make your children overjoyed, a brand of aluminum roofing that would make you the envy of your neighborhood.

The snowy screen changed to President Bongo at his desk, the flag of Gabon behind him, his expression composed. His was the face on all the money, in the portraits in the banks and the hotel lobbies, the face on the uniforms of the Air Gabon stewardesses, a face that after two decades in power wore a well-practiced expression of serene authority.

Yet, Darlene detected an air of amusement, as if Bongo was about to let everyone in on a secret he'd been keeping lo these past twenty years.

He began as he normally did, sonorously. "Mes chères confrères citoyens et citoyennes," he said, and he swung into the measured cadence that every brave wag could imitate. He began with a review of world events, and explained how faced with these challenges he as their leader and guide had been able to discern the new and legitimate popular concerns of their beloved nation. He had ordered the creation of a Special Commission on Democracy to consult with the people, and make a recommendation to him. Now the Commission had completed its work. It had presented its report with the very recommendation that he, their President, had always anticipated would one day be possible.

"Our far-seeing and all-important innovation of the single-party state has served its intended purpose," said President Bongo. "Our beloved nation is unified and at peace, and the Gabonese people are ready to enter a new phase in their national history. Therefore, in accordance with the heartfelt wish of our people, and the recommendations I have received from the Special Commission on Democracy, I have decided at last to take the step that I have long planned. Tonight I announce to you, mes chères confrères citoyens et citoyennes that measures will be taken to establish a multiparty system of government in Gabon."

Darlene had known it was coming, yet she felt jubilant hearing Bongo say the words. It was actually happening.

Under his authority as Minister of the Interior, he had ordered the preparation of legislation to lift the constitutional ban on political parties, and establish an electoral commission under the authority of the Ministry. He was calling upon the National Assembly to enact this law swiftly. He would sign the bill at once. The electoral commission would be charged with three priorities.

Its first would be to register new voters and bring the voter registry up to date. The second would be to register qualified parties. The third would be to verify the qualifications of all candidates who presented themselves to run. The election would be held the first Sunday in December, six months from now.

"Tonight," Bongo said, looking into the camera, "I announce to you, my fellow citizens, henceforth it will be you, the people of Gabon who shall elect the national leaders of our dear country."

He paused for several seconds, seemingly ready to smile.

"And tonight I announce to you, my fellow citizens, that I will be a candidate for President. And with that I close by calling upon all the brave patriots of our beloved land; I call upon all of Gabon's sons and daughters; I call upon all who love our dear Republic, to unite with me in this historic endeavor." And with that, it was over, and an instant after the image of President Bongo faded from the screen, the telephone in the residence rang.

16. Sacrifice of Souls

Otou

Bongo's amazing speech left Rebecca feeling as giddy as a little girl. She clapped her hands listening to it on La Voie de la Rénovation with her boyfriend Philbert and the schoolteacher Gustave, whose students would one day attend the school she was building. Philbert listened in silence, his muscular arms folded, showing no surprise at the announced shift to multiparty democracy. Gustave, with his shaved head and goggling eyes, was skeptical. "Bongo is very tricky, Rebecca," he warned, "Elections will distract the ordinary Gabonese, but in the end, nothing meaningful will change."

Rebecca begged to disagree. "There will be multiparty elections, Gustave! That alone is a huge change!"

Bongo's announcement still thrilled her two days later. Cutting up a chicken as her mother had taught her, Rebecca couldn't stop thinking about the opportunity to observe a transformative African election firsthand, and to gather material for a first-class doctoral dissertation. Before her stretched tantalizing career possibilities that made her breathless as she twisted the slippery chicken legs up and out of the joint, dislocated the hips, sliced through the skin and cartilage with a knife and cut loose the drumsticks. It pleased her down to her toes to wonder which of the three graduate schools she would ultimately select. UCLA, Wisconsin and the University of Florida had all agreed to defer her admission, to permit her to serve two years in the Peace Corps. Her journal was now nine full notebooks long, and the thought of the scholarship she would produce made her simply joyous.

Rebecca felt good about what she was doing in the village of Otou. She dislocated the first knee and cut through the joint, confident in her view, which was the correct view, that construction volunteers should spend time to build consensus, before they began building their schools. That, Peace Corps had told them back in Philadelphia, was the Peace Corps way. The point wasn't to work fast. The point was to work smart, and that was how Rebecca did things in Otou, except for the week of disruption, when Hector brought the riotous stagiaires from Obia, on orders from their APCD, according to Hector, to lay out the construction site and pour the footings. Harry Bowman, for assuming she needed Hector's help, was thereby diminished in Rebecca's eyes.

Nothing had changed. With Harry's support, Hector continued to train stagiaires to work at the speed of general contractors, and Rebecca continued to insist Hector was a walking violation of the basic principles of sustainable development. Rebecca was a lone voice in the wilderness.

She twisted the wings away from the slippery carcass. In Otou, of all the Peace Corps sites, she alone was doing things right, working at the appropriate pace, and with full village participation. She had hired every physically able person who wanted a job, women included, by far her most radical step. Of course, that meant she had to overcome the challenge imposed by the payroll limitation of ten full-time jobs, sixteen hundred man-hours a month. She cracked that problem by paying everyone the same wage, and no one could work full time. Each month, she calculated payroll by dividing the number of villagers who'd worked into the total permissible hours, with one exception. Her foreman, Ongongi Faustin, worked full time. A forceful man of forty with remarkable pale brown eyes, Faustin had directed the improvements on her house, and then had directed the building of the teachers' houses. When it came time to start work on the school, it was only natural that Faustin should direct all four crews. No one objected, and Rebecca quietly paid Faustin more than she paid the others.

Humming, near to euphoria, Rebecca cut through the shoulder joints and detached the wings. She dislocated the elbows, flipped the chicken over and cut straight down through the ribs to separate the breast meat. Each of the four crews had at least two women, and each had selected a name for itself. There were the Lions, the Gazelles, the Leopards and the Airplanes. The workers understood that Rebecca was the boss, and that Faustin was essential to her system. He made sure all four teams stayed on task, while she acted as cheerleader and jokester. The Batéké loved insulting each other, and whenever she insulted one of them – "O! Ce n'est pas comme ça-o!" or "Regards sa tête!" or "Tu sors d'où comme ça?" – they laughed deliriously, happy on the job, happy to have an income.

She cut deftly through both shoulders and the sternum. Well before work on the school began, she started discussions with Chief Petie and the village elders about forming a school management committee to keep the school in good repair after she was gone. It came as no surprise when the elders nominated Faustin to lead the committee, but Rebecca said no, without explaining her concern about showing too much favoritism toward Faustin. The elders then nominated Chief Petie, which came as no surprise either. But Chief Petie was an alcoholic. No, she thought to herself, rinsing the pieces of chicken in a bowl of water and patting them dry with a cloth, Chief Petie could not be trusted to take care of the school.

"Bonjour, Rebecca," said Philbert, sauntering into the kitchen. He was back from his bath, her black Adonis, bare-chested in green gym shorts and a pair of red flip-flops.

"Who do you think should lead the school management committee?" she asked, rubbing dried spices on the chicken and placing the pieces one by one in a baking pan.

"'Sais pas," said Philbert. He slipped his arms around her from behind and put his chin on her shoulder, to watch what she was doing. She opened the oven door and bent into the radiating heat to slide in the pan. Philbert gripped her waist with both hands and pressed himself against her bottom. She went slack. Her eyes shut. She gasped and felt her body responding, but then she straightened and broke away.

"Après," she said, and licked her lips.

Philbert grinned, careless about who might have been looking in through the window. The muscles of his arms, his chest and his belly looked like they'd been cut with a wood chisel. He went into the bedroom to dress, and Rebecca watched him go, and then checked her watch to make sure the chicken baked no longer than thirty minutes.

When Rebecca put her hiring plan into action, Philbert did not sign on for a job. It would have been awkward, working for his girlfriend. He had it pretty good as it was. Rebecca gave him walk-around money, kept the pantry stocked, did almost all the cooking, and at night she took care of his needs. And he certainly took care of hers. He could make her go limp in his arms. He could make her tense up as tight as a coiled spring. He could bring her right to the edge and hold her there, before making her erupt into a quivering puddle.

Rebecca smiled and started peeling potatoes imported from France, an extravagance available at the supermarket in Franceville. Philbert's sexual advances sometimes annoyed her, especially when she was cooking or cleaning the house. He was the most beautiful man she had ever taken into her bed, and she smiled as she dropped the first peeled spud into the pot of salted water. It was, as Eric Slidell and Buck Buford had said back in Boundji, free love over here. White male expatriates held out the promise of wealth, status, and material goods that were otherwise unattainable for the average village girl. Rebecca enjoyed the role reversal immensely.

All the young Peace Corps volunteers found themselves in a situation most had never encountered back home, and most never would again. They were in high demand. New college graduates for the most part, none of them wealthy, or powerful, and most of them not particularly good looking, Gabon was a fantasy come true. The most beautiful Gabonese girls and the most handsome young Gabonese men came after them, like yowling cats curling about their legs. Even on a volunteer's stipend, the Americans could afford what was expected in return, but most were ill prepared for the situation. Nearly every volunteer jumped headlong into sexual adventures without fully thinking through the consequences.

Polygamy was legal in Gabon. Men could have multiple wives, and wealthy men could have both wives and mistresses. Women expected financial compensation for their favors, and men knew they had to provide it. Sex was a transaction, and both men and women were free to break off a relationship at any point. The unbridled promiscuity resulted in elevated rates of sexually transmitted diseases and teenage pregnancies. President Bongo publically celebrated fecundity with gifts of money and medals to all mothers who gave birth to ten children, but one out of every hundred babies died at birth, while widespread disease meant the odds for the rest were bleak. One out of every ten Gabonese children did not live to see their fifth birthday.

Les bébés métis, mixed race babies, were highly prized, and considered especially beautiful. "And when you leave," villagers would say, "il faut nous laisser un souvenir." The souvenirs volunteers were expected to leave could be anything, from a new roof on a village clinic to a set of drums for the village dance group. But a baby was the best souvenir of all. Rebecca found the very idea abhorrent. She could not imagine leaving a child of hers behind, and her stock of Tahitian Treat condoms was running low. New supplies were promised at the construction program conference, scheduled in a month for early August.

The sound of an approaching vehicle broke her reverie. Milla's bush taxi slid to a stop in front of her house, the clattering engine adding volume to the yelling of passengers climbing down. Philbert came out of the bedroom in jeans and a tee shirt to see who had arrived, and shouted in joy and went outside. A moment later, he came back in leading a man in a black leather jacket and a very white pair of basketball shoes.

"Here he is," said Philbert, bringing the man into the kitchen. "This is the one I told you about, Rebecca, my brother who studies engineering in Romania."

Philbert's brother had a trim mustache and small ears that lay flat to the skull, wide nostrils and careful eyes. He had Philbert's ears, but those were not Philbert's eyes. His were the eyes of a man who had seen something of the world. Rebecca was accustomed to the fact that the Batéké normally introduced people by their relationship, not by their name. "Comment vous appelez-vous?" she asked, drying her hands.

"I am called Georges Kassélé."

"Not Kassélé Georges?" Rebecca teased. "You have adopted European mannerisms, alors, along with their fashions, that black leather jacket and basketball shoes."

"I could say the same about you," said Georges. "You wear a pagne around your waist like a village woman. We all must adapt to our environment, n'est-ce pas?"

Rebecca bowed her head in acknowledgement. "Touché," she said.

239

Philbert got a bottle of beer from the kerosene refrigerator and two glasses from the shelves. Georges' black leather jacket creaked as he took a thirsty gulp.

"I believe my brother has told you about me?"

"That you study engineering in Romania, yes."

"And is interested in politics," said Philbert. "Tell her."

"I am also the secretary-general of the youth wing of the Parti National Démocratique, the PND. You have heard of us?"

Rebecca smiled. This explained why Philbert had not seemed surprised by President Bongo's announcement. He must have known something ahead of time, from his brother. There were so many parties forming up, more than a dozen already, and she couldn't keep them straight. She could only imagine what the ordinary Gabonese made of them all.

"Mon parti m'a nommé candidat pour l'Assemblée Nationale dans la circonscription d'Akièni."

Georges Kassélé was a candidate for the National Assembly in the constituency that included Otou. The fates had delivered Rebecca another sign, this man in a black leather jacket.

"What do you think your party's chances are?"

"We are more multiethnic than the Bûcherons. They're Fang chauvinists. And no one knows the Parti Gabonais du Progrès. We are the ones who can reach all elements of Gabonese society. And we have major backing."

"Oh? Who is your backer?"

Georges answered a different question. "The Parti National Démocratique will open the people's eyes to what has been happening."

"Who is your backer?" Rebecca asked again, ushering the brothers to the table in the front room where she opened her current notebook to make jottings.

"The PND will put an end to neo-colonialism," said Georges, ignoring her question a second time, "this corrupt government stealing the people's money; that man Little Pepper."

Rebecca smiled at the nickname for President Bongo, diminutive like Napoleon, but like Napoleon, also quite dangerous. The schoolteacher, Gustave, had told her of the time when Bongo was still consolidating power, when people who opposed him died violently, often in plane crashes in the jungle. Gabon was entering into a democratic transition, and Rebecca was happy to be smack dab in the middle of it.

"Who is your backer?" she asked once more.

"He is a very big man in Europe who does not wish his identity to be known."

"That's interesting," said Rebecca, wondering who that might be, and why he wanted to remain anonymous. "You were in Romania at Christmas?" she asked, as Philbert refilled his brother's glass, and then his own.

"What you are asking is was I there for the democratic revolution. Yes I was, and what I saw opened my eyes."

"It must have been dangerous, the violence."

Rebecca had listened to the BBC reports last December on the pitched battles between the regular army and Ceausescu's Praetorian Guard. She had been newly arrived in Otou at the time.

At that very moment, transistor radios turned on all across the village. An organ began groaning out a funereal dirge while a mournful-sounding woman read the day's obituaries. It had been Eric Slidell's second-favorite radio program back in Boundji. "Death Report!" he would call out, turning up the volume. "Come on you guys, pipe down! The Death Report's on!"

Suddenly there was a shrill scream nearby, and several more from further way. Philbert set down his glass and went to the door. There was another scream, and Georges followed his brother outside. They were talking in Téké when someone rushed past them babbling.

Rebecca went as far as the doorway. Her neighbor had hurled herself to the ground and was flopping like a fish in the sand. Another woman raced by shrieking. Her neighbor got up and hurried on wailing. A dog slunk past with its tail between its legs, and howled at the ungodly noise.

Faustin trotted up with anguish on his face. "Obouyi Joseph has died in the hospital in Libreville!"

Rebecca didn't know who Joseph was and didn't have time to ask before Faustin rushed off in the gloom. Globes of light emerged from houses around the village, bobbing toward the home of the bereaved family, the air full of the keening sound of grief.

Okouya

Édouard heard splashing inside Charlie's house. He knew Charlie had recently built a small douche in the corner of his bedroom for when the schoolteacher's sister, Justine, spent the night.

Sometimes Charlie drove to Akièni and brought Justine back to Okouya; sometimes she took Milla's taxi. She made no secret of her presence; she did not hide in the otangani's house. In the morning, after spending the night, Justine was there for all to see. And sometimes Charlie spent the weekend with Justine in Akièni. During the week, Charlie worked with the crew long days at the chantier. The block walls were nearly done, a sure sign to everyone that the otangani was in a hurry to finish, and leave them.

When the splashing stopped, Édouard knocked again. Charlie opened the door wearing only a towel, slimmer than when he first arrived, and clean-shaved now, because Justine didn't like beards.

Embarrassed to disturb him, Édouard said, "The ngaa-bwa Okorogo René is back from the Congo with very powerful skills. He's down at the little grove. You must come see what he is doing."

Charlie's first impulse was to say no. He was hungry and wanted to start supper, but he had learned the hard way to consider things carefully before acting. Édouard had given him an order only once before, when he told him to obey Chief Oyamba's decision who to hire. Charlie had ignored Édouard then, and now half the families in the village no longer spoke to him. Women stopped bringing him free food, and the girlfriends stopped coming around. He didn't care much about that. Justine was in his life now, but he had to cook all his own meals. Charlie looked at Édouard, with his pencil mustache and chipped front tooth. He was just one of the masons on the worksite, but among his people, Édouard was the future land chief of the westernmost Louzou, the man who had watched over Charlie from the very first day, and ever since the disastrous second palaver about hiring workers, Charlie had become more solicitous of Édouard's views. So Charlie decided to do as Édouard asked. He went to the bedroom, put on a tee shirt, shorts and a new pair of blue flip-flops too small for his big feet. Charlie followed Édouard, the cheap flip-flops from a shop in Akièni snapping in the deep sand.

"Who is this guy, anyway?" Charlie asked.

"He's the ngaa-bwa I told you about before," said Édouard, "the one who has been in the Congo, a guérisseur," which Charlie recognized as the word for a healer, a medicine man.

As they drew near, Charlie could see nothing out of the ordinary about Okorogo, a thin man in his early fifties. Like all the other village men, he wore used clothes sold in the urban markets by the bale. The distinctive blue yachting cap on his head amused Charlie as he reached the line of people waiting to see the shaman.

Chairs materialized for Charlie and Édouard, as Édouard explained what they were seeing. Okorogo was practicing ati, he said, which meant traditional healing. Okorogo listened to each person in turn describe the complaint: coughs and sore throats, headaches, backaches, sleeplessness and a variety of problems of the bowels. Many of the women had colicky babies for the ngaa-bwa to diagnose, and when it came to explaining what ailed a few of the older men, people chuckled, and Édouard left what was wrong with those old men to Charlie's imagination.

With the tougher cases, the ngaa-bwa would lay on his hands. For most, he prescribed combinations of roots and herbs to gather, and he told the sufferers how to concoct the cures. For those who came with such problems as dying goats or poor quality crops, a sacrifice of some sort was appropriate, to appease whichever ancestors were unhappy.

One case involved a small delegation that included Oyamba Jacques, the bar owner, and his brother, Oyamba Benjamin, one of Charlie's masons.

"They have asked Okorogo," Édouard explained, "to help their older brother, Oyamba Hilaire."

Hilaire was the man stricken blind and speechless Charlie had seen on his first day in the village, led outside by his wife. Villagers claimed Hilaire was stricken for having thrown away the bones of a dead twin.

This particular consultation went on for some time. Finally, the ngaa-bwa Okorogo René delivered his prognosis.

"The problem of Hilaire," said Édouard, "is sufficiently serious that the entire village will have to help, tonight, once the sun is down."

Édouard knocked on the door when Charlie was washing the dishes. "It's time," Édouard said.

Charlie walked with him to the middle of the village where Hilaire sat blank-faced in a straight-backed chair next to a fire. The ngaa-bwa Okorogo had formed the men in a circle inside a surrounding circle of women. The men moved slowly clockwise with a kind of dance step, their faces lit by the fire. The women sidled in the opposite direction, an eerily silent ritual with no drums or chanting. The ngaa-bwa stood in the middle with a stick worn dark and smooth in his hand, a bit of red cloth tied to one end. He was wearing his blue yachting cap and was yelling into the sky.

Édouard explained. "He is calling upon the ancestors to help Hilaire, to make Hilaire sound again. First, they must find the bones. You understand?"

"No," said Charlie, "I do not understand." Or rather, he understood, but didn't believe.

Okorogo fell silent, and for a time the only sound was the crackling fire. Then the ngaa-bwa seemed to shudder. Paroxysms swept through his lean frame. People gasped to see him tremble and twitch. Charlie thought Okorogo was putting on a show, then worried he would fall over, but the ngaa-bwa recovered and looked around the circle of men. He spoke in his loud rasp.

"He is going to hand that stick," said Édouard, "to a man who will pass it to another, and it will go around the circle until it comes to the man who will know where the bones can be found. That man will lead us into the forest to retrieve them. We will put the bones in an ndjo okira and that will cure Hilaire."

Okorogo handed the stick to a frail old papa Charlie didn't know by name. The old papa took the stick with evident fear and passed it quickly along. Each man in turn handed it swiftly away. The stick raced around the circle until it came to the hunter Ndebi Marc. The moment he took it, Marc dropped to his knees and began jittering as if electrocuted. It all seemed like play-acting to Charlie. What could possibly make a man do that?

"Mi ndjayi biri ye libo!" Marc wailed in distress.

"He knows!" Édouard cried. "He can see the bones!"

Okorogo helped Marc to his feet and shouted out a long stream of words.

"We are to follow," said Édouard. "We will go to where Hilaire threw away the bones, right now!"

The men were hollering, milling about, and the women moved out of the way as Okorogo pulled Marc with him toward the woods, the stick in his hands like a divining rod.

Charlie didn't want to go out into the woods at night. There would be bugs. He resisted when Édouard tugged on his arm, and then again a second time. With a backward reproachful look at Charlie, Édouard followed the men toward the forest, and Charlie headed back to his house behind the women, chattering about what they had seen.

At the chantier the next morning, Charlie's work crew could not stop talking about the night before. Marc had actually found the bones. The men had brought the bones back to the village and put them in an ndjo okira. The men were worn out from staying up so late, dragging from fatigue, spending more time talking than doing their jobs, sitting on blocks, leaning against the walls, listening to Marc recount once more what the experience had felt like. Charlie finally told everyone to knock off early.

After they cleaned and put away the tools, Charlie went down to the stream for a bath. When he got back to the house, two little girls, Marguerite and Sylvie, were waiting by his door. Once or twice a week, they showed up to root through his garbage pail for valuable items to sell to the boys as raw materials for the manufacture of their inventive toys. Charlie especially liked the yard-long bamboo cars the boys constructed, with headlights engineered from flashlight bulbs and D cell batteries, wheels carved from bamboo, axles slung on strips of old inner tubes, steering wheels made of bent and lashed twigs fastened to long sticks with a fork in the end. The boys would place the fork of the stick against the front axle of the car. Walking while twisting the wheel to steer, making motor noises with their lips, each day after school they spent their afternoons cruising the village like high school boys in America.

The girls of the village didn't have anywhere near as much leisure time. After school, they had to help their mothers work. They helped take care of their younger siblings or went with their mothers to the fields to tend the crops or to the stream to wash dishes and clothes. The women worked all day, every day of the week. The girls helped in the fields, weeding and collecting food. They helped in the forest, chopping and gathering firewood. They helped at the creek, fetching water, doing the laundry, washing dishes. The girls hauled heavy loads back to the village on their backs each afternoon, then helped prepare the evening meal, tending blackened pots on three stone fires in the smoky cook huts. The men ate first and then the kids. The women ate what remained, or did not go to the dogs. After dinner, there were bucket baths to give the littlest, finally getting all the kids off to bed, three and four to a foam rubber mattress.

As the two little girls walked off with an egg carton and all the empty tin cans, Charlie saw a small crowd of men approaching. In front of them was Édouard.

"It worked!" Édouard shouted, hurrying forward to shake Charlie's hand. Certainly now the otangani would comprehend the formidable power Okorogo had acquired in the Congo, for coming along slowly behind him was none other than Oyamba Hilaire, walking feebly, supported on one side by his brother Jacques and on the other by his brother Benjamin. He had to be helped over the threshold and into Charlie's front room, where Benjamin and Jacques helped their brother sit at Charlie's table. Hilaire wanted to greet the otangani.

The blind man was actually looking at him, and smiling. His brothers and the other men were all talking loudly about the miracle that had occurred. The only thing Charlie could think to do was to serve Hilaire some cold water and say, "Nice to meet you."

"Thank you," replied Hilaire in a voice rusty from disuse. He hadn't spoken in over a year, and with obvious pleasure at being able to grasp the glass himself, he took it from Charlie's hand.

Otou

Two Nissan Patrols with dark tinted windows powered through the dirty sand into the village. Antoine Badinga got out of the second car, idling with the air conditioner on, an older woman inside. He was a bulky man in his late forties wearing a khaki short-sleeved suit, a roll of flesh beneath his bullet skull. His bodyguards emerged from the first car in jogging suits and mirror sunglasses. The presidential candidate looked around at the crowd that began to gather and started shaking hands, rubbing the boys' heads, making them grin, pinching the girls' cheeks, making them smile.

Grilled by Rebecca in bed the night his brother Georges arrived, Philbert revealed that Antoine Badinga was their older cousin. Rebecca immediately demanded to meet him, the founder of the PND, the party Georges belonged to.

Badinga wanted to meet Rebecca as well. Previously informed that a young white woman was living alone in the village, he looked at Rebecca with more than a little interest as she approached him.

"Can you sign a copy of the PND manifesto for me?" Rebecca asked him. "I would like to study your party's platform, and keep it as a souvenir."

Badinga considered her request for a moment. "I'll have one sent to you," he replied.

Rebecca should have known then that no such document existed.

Okouya

Birdsong and the sweet smell of cut vegetation filled the kadigi, the clearing in the woods forbidden to women. Okorogo René was on his feet in the bright blue hat he always wore. Wide-eyed young boys who the day before had cleared away the brush squatted inside the semicircle of men seated on logs, as in the old days.

Okorogo gestured at the one among them conspicuous for his expensive black shoes, twice the weight of any man present, Antoine Badinga, clearly accustomed to eating his fill. "This man is a son of our village," Okorogo rasped. "You knew him as a child who was sent away to France. There he gained great knowledge, and he has returned to us as the grand man you see here before you, a grand man who knows very powerful etangani."

The assembled men murmured to one another and studied Badinga intently, a wealthy politician who had returned to the village of his birth from the fabled land of the whites.

"You know this man's mother, Assélé Brigitte, the childhood

friend of the former First Lady. You know she married Epolo Calixte, who held an important post in the government, before they took it away from him."

The assembled men buzzed with discussion about the important government post Epolo Calixte had once occupied, that once had yielded valuable prébendes he shared through his wife with the Louzou clan, until Josephine Bongo absconded with a fortune and ran off to America with a guitar player, and President Bongo purged all Louzous from his government, including Epolo Calixte.

"This man Badinga is a man to be reckoned with!" Okorogo shouted. "He may well be elected the next President of Gabon!"

That caused an outburst of debate about the extraordinary notion that someone other than Omar Bongo could somehow actually be president.

When the voices died down, Okorogo said, "Badinga will soon be in a position to do great things for this village, for everyone here today, for each of you individually!"

The noise rose again, the men watching Badinga, who kept his face carefully composed.

"That is why I have called you select few here today," said Okorogo, and the voices subsided. "I have picked you to share in the good things to come. The good things to come will not be for everyone, only for us. But to have a share, you must help assure they materialize."

Édouard listened grim-faced in the reassembled secret society of men. He was here only because his father, the land chief Oyamba, was bed-ridden and too infirm to attend. Édouard knew exactly what Okorogo was doing. He had just revealed to the reconstituted secret society that he was more powerful than any ordinary ngaa-bwa. He was more than a shaman. He was in fact an ngaa-mpiaru, a sorcerer. Okorogo had picked the men because each of them was aggrieved. Édouard knew what Okorogo meant when he said these men must help. They would make unkébé, a powerful spell to assure the success of Badinga in the elections, in exchange for a share of what would come.

Édouard knew another thing about Okorogo. The man aspired to displace him, and become the next nkani-ntsie. Oyamba

Benjamin had told him this. Benjamin had learned of it from his brother Hilaire, who Okorogo had just recently cured. Part of Édouard welcomed the idea. Part of him very much wished to hand the chieftaincy to Okorogo. Édouard wanted to move away with his wives and his children and leave the old ways behind. But Okorogo was a newly revealed ngaa-mpiaru who intended to use the bitter men he had assembled to make unkébé. A land chiefdom led by Okorogo would mean sadness for many households in Okouya, as well as all the other villages in the ntsie. Okorogo intended to harvest human lives to expand his power.

The sorcerer had summoned the men here on behalf of Assélé Brigitte, Badinga's mother, who waited in the village like a spider. She, her son and her nephew were staying at Okorogo's house, and the night before, the three of them had gone in the dark so no one would see them to sit with old Chief Oyamba, and explain their purpose, and secure his promise not to interfere. Chief Oyamba had sent for his eldest son before answering. He was tired, he said when Édouard joined them; his time was over. He would not interfere with the reintroduction of the old arts, nor would his son. Neither he nor his son could oppose President Bongo, for back long ago, the President had sent a machine from out of the sky that flew Oyamba over the forest faster than any bird, delivering him to the Palace where the air burned like fire, where they made him swear blood fealty.

"Your position is reasonable, Chief," said Brigitte. A realist, she knew the odds were against her son being elected president, but she wanted to be sure that Oyamba would not stand in her way. "We have a plan, and we would like your support, but if you cannot give it, I understand. We have resources from a very influential Frenchman, who I cannot name. We have other resources as well." The old woman eyed the dying land chief, sitting on the edge of his filthy unmade bed. Bongo had promised to appoint her son to head a powerful ministry, and she wanted it assured, and wanted assurances as well that her nephew would be elected deputy to the National Assembly. Okorogo, the ngaa-mpiaru was going to help her carry her plan through, and he was not the only ngaa-mpiaru Brigitte had recruited. She had enlisted the aid of every ngaa-mpiaru in the Louzou clan, and in Libreville, there was even a powerful marabout from Senegal. "I ask only that you do not oppose us, Chief."

"Agreed," said Oyamba wearily.

Édouard had grown up with the youngest of the men assembled in the kadigi. He'd gone to school with some of them, played soccer with many, hunted with others. The youngest were the ones who hadn't gotten a job building the school. The oldest were his fathers and his uncles who had taught him how to set snares and track game. Pinched financially, now that the money from the former First Lady and her associates had dried up, many disliked that Édouard had become the favorite of the otangani. In fact, all the men there had become hostile to everything Charlie, the otangani, stood for, and for that reason, they sat closest to Antoine Badinga.

Okorogo had called them to the sunny clearing, abuzz with insects, where the secret society had met in years past, because this was where their land chief, their nkani-ntsie, Oyamba Paul, had practiced ndjobi, the newest of the dark arts, and the older ones as well, ongala, okani and ondjandja, when he was young, and building up his power. In those days, Oyamba had led the initiates in the practice of the most powerful conjurations that required the sacrifice of souls. This was well known. Ngawanaga Bernard, the Christian had persuaded Oyamba to cease the sacrifices. Entering his declining years, Oyamba had completely given it up and the practice of unkébé fell into disuse. The meetings of the secret society in the kadigi ended.

After nearly a year in the Congo, where he learned the dark arts anew, Okorogo returned to Okouya to reveal his power, to revive the secret society, to refill the village with bisemo unkébé mudzira, powerful talismans that would impel his rise as they had impelled the rise of Oyamba, who lay dying in his bed up in the village. Okorogo would call each man who volunteered here today to his house in the dead of night, and one by one he would administer powerful medicine, and initiate each man into complicity.

Badinga finally stood in a shaft of sunlight that gleamed on his shaved skull. "Thank you, all," he said. "I apologize for my poor Téké. It has been years since I have regularly spoken our language." He spoke haltingly, pausing for long moments to recall the precise word he wanted. "I want everyone here to remember how once

Okouya was a center of power among the Louzou clan. Do you remember how once we were a great village?"

The men shouted in affirmation.

"I want to restore Okouya to its former preeminence. I want to rebuild the power of the westernmost Louzou, and I will need your help," he said, looking around the circle, at each man among them individually, and Édouard could see everyone here understood exactly what this meant. Okorogo would be making the most powerful unkébé of all, but Badinga could not discuss the details, not in front of the young boys, for they had not been initiated, because the rituals had been neglected for so many years. The working of it would come secretly, in the night, and all the men here understood this, and understood it would require eating a human soul.

Charlie's bones were broken. Toxic worms crawled through his veins. His skin felt cold, yet he burned inside. Cars rumbled by in his delirium with their windshield wipers clicking, trailing cottony spumes of exhaust. Their headlights cast a diffused glow in the silence of the heavy snowfall. Taillights tinged the thick snowflakes swirling in their wake. Snow piled up on the rooftops and windowsills, smoothing hard edges from cars parked on the street, settling like a mushroom cap on a birdbath in a side yard, clinging to bare branches in delicate patterns like lace, transforming the city into a hushed and enchanted place.

Glorious Justine walked beside him, her hands deep in the pockets of a blue cloth coat, snow powdering her shoulders, glistening on a knit cap pulled down to her eyes, a scarf pulled up over her nose. Snow squeaked under their boots, and Charlie shivered with a glowing wracked joy at the fact of Justine walking beside him. He grabbed her elbow, and they stopped for a second on the sidewalk. "Listen," he said, "can you hear it? Can you hear the sound of the snow?"

Justine pulled down her scarf, tipped back her head, closed her eyes and smiled at the unfamiliar sensation of snowflakes on her face, settling white on her eyelashes, wetting her black cheeks like tears.

Otou

A heavy orange truck with an Akièni travaux publique logo on the door crawled onto the worksite, a crew of muscular men riding atop a cargo of white sacks. Rebecca's crew, called the Airplanes, twelve men and three women stopped laying block to watch.

"What's this?" Rebecca asked Faustin.

A pickup truck with tattered green, blue and yellow bunting hanging from its sides followed the orange truck onto the chantier. Scratchy soukous music blared from a loudspeaker affixed to the pickup truck's roof. The ruling party emblem, the palm of a hand held up in peace, was plastered on the passenger's door. Pretty girls wearing pagnes with the same logo stood in the back, waving to all and sundry.

The music switched off and a fat man wearing a PDG shirt got out of the pickup and raised a bullhorn to his mouth. "Venez voir! Venez voir! Venez voir, mes amis, ce que Président Bongo et le PDG vous amènent!"

"What are the party and the president bringing us?" asked Rebecca.

"That's our Deputy, Onkouma Alphonse," said Faustin. "It looks like rice."

Onkouma Alphonse, a member of the National Assembly, was running for reelection. The Airplanes dropped their tools and hastened to join the people coming on the run, paying no attention to what Onkouma Alphonse was saying through his scratchy bullhorn, or to the pretty girls waving at everyone.

"Votez massivement pour moi et pour le PDG!" Onkouma Alphonse yelled, "pour le parti qui vous assure à bien manger!"

The muscular men in PDG tee shirts began handing down heavy sacks of rice to the first arrivals. More and more villagers joined the crowd, swiftly growing unruly.

"Do you see what I'm up against?" said Georges, suddenly at Rebecca's side. "He's using a state-owned truck! Who paid for an entire truckload of rice?"

"Le parti du progrès, le parti de la paix, et le parti de la prospérité!" Onkouma Alphonse cried. Villagers continued to stream to the back of the truck and jostle for a sack of rice, handed down by the men in white tee shirts.

Then a second public works truck appeared, roaring through the deep sand. It crept onto the worksite with the horned heads of roan-colored cattle hanging over the sides. The truck stopped by the rice truck. Three men got out and lowered the tailgate revealing the small cattle, lowing and foaming with thirst, scraped and covered with dung from having fallen repeatedly. Rebecca knew these had to be cattle from West Africa, a breed resistant to tsetse flies. She watched the men pull down a wooden ramp.

Standing beside the Land Cruiser, Onkouma Guillaume continued shouting into the bullhorn, "This is why everyone should vote PDG, the party of peace, the party of prosperity, the party that assures everyone will eat well!" He had noticed Rebecca, and gestured for the men to hurry so they could leave.

Two men used switches to isolate one bawling steer and drive it down the ramp to the driver who slipped a noose around its neck. From their skill handling the steer, Rebecca knew these men were not Gabonese, and asked who they were.

"They're Fulani," said Georges.

Faustin, who had disappeared from Rebecca's side, led the steer away. Children followed, laughing and slapping the steer's rump.

Men with machetes joined the procession toward Chef Petie's house, where the first cow in Otou Rebecca had ever heard of was going to be immediately slaughtered.

Onkouma Guillaume had finished his speech and got back in the Land Cruiser. The loudspeaker began emitting scratchy soukous music again, and the two pretty girls ceased waving. The Fulani slid the ramp back up into the cattle truck and raised the tailgate. The two drivers started the trucks, and the two great orange Mercedes began belching smoke as they pulled away.

Empty-handed villagers cried out, angry for being overlooked. Boys ran alongside the trucks as they ground away through the sand, yelling at the drivers to stop for the ones who hadn't gotten any rice. But the distribution was over. The ruling party reelection campaign was on its way to Okouya, the pretty girls holding onto the pickup truck's roll bar like water skiers, the two orange Mercedes crawling off with the heads of the forlorn cattle hanging over the sides of the rearmost one.

"My good people do you see?" Georges shouted at the villagers.

"That is the politics of the PDG! They come here with rice that they don't give to everyone! Who do you think paid for that rice? Where did the money come from? And that cow?"

People were beginning to look at Georges, in his black leather jacket and his white basketball shoes.

"Don't you see what they're doing? They're trying to buy your vote with a little bit of rice and some meat bought with money that rightfully belongs to you! They think you're not smart enough to see! My good people, I tell you, go ahead and take that rice! Go ahead and eat that cow! But when it comes time to vote, vote for the ones who won't trick you, or steal from you!"

Georges switched into Téké, his voice rising. There were a few ehs and ahs of affirmation. His fists clenched, he began rocking up onto the balls of his feet, punching the air, slashing with the heel of his hand.

Rebecca thought to herself, This guy is a natural.

But Georges had nothing to give away and the people drifted after the lucky villagers carrying bags of rice to their houses. Sharp arguments were breaking out. Standing a short distance away, an unsmiling man, new to Otou, watched Rebecca intently.

Plateau

Dabrian sat behind the steering wheel of Air Afrique, looking in dismay at the dozens of furrowed tracks leading northeast. It seemed impossible that his worn out old truck could get through the deep sand. He had to assume that bush taxis managed the route, so therefore must he. He had to trust in the power of his vision, trust in his truck, and he pulled back the transfer box lever. It growled, but didn't want to go. He pulled again, and it clunked into four high. Air Afrique was ready to try. Dabrian drew a breath, gritted his teeth, and then eased in the clutch, and sent his truck into the sand.

The old truck labored, waddling over the broken ground. It groaned and creaked and the engine blew smoke, and the tailgate chains slapped back and forth. Dabrian's determination grew with each hundred yards. He had been called here by his dream, and he would not succumb, not to any fear of getting stuck, or breaking

down. He was coming to make the power of his vision take hold, and Air Afrique was going to get him there.

The dream had come to him again this morning, clear as day, in the early hours before dawn. He was on the river of danger, drifting along on the raft, moving easily at first, until he became aware of the foul smell, and saw the darkness ahead. The current began to pick up, and he knew he was being swept toward what lay ahead, the menace hidden in the trees. He knew what was there, and he began paddling his way off the river, fighting his way toward the bank, paddling with tremendous strength out of the current. He reached the shallows, jumped into the water and sloshed ashore, and he fell to his knees exhausted. He crawled up the bank. Suddenly, dozens, then hundreds, then thousands of small lights floating in a flickering cloud illuminated the pale face of big Charlie Sinclair lying unconscious, on his back, on the ground.

Okouya

Her breasts sprouted sharp thorns that stabbed into his palms, and he shut his eyes not to see the strands of drool hanging from the long red tongue lolling from the side of her snout. Then a noise brought Charlie to his senses. The dog-woman straddling him was gone and the aluminum roof popped like firecrackers in the heat. A fierce afternoon light blazed in under the eaves. There was an engine outside growling louder until it pulled up right in front of his house and turned off.

Milla's taxi, he knew, but instead of a clamor of Téké from arriving passengers, he heard someone pounding on his door. An American called his name.

Charlie rose from his bed, sweat freezing on his skin, his body inside an inferno. He shuffled into the front room with a pagne around his waist.

The light shot into his eyes when he swung open the door, and there tall and black in silhouette was his friend Dabrian.

"Jesus," said Dabrian.

Édouard rushed through the door as Charlie slumped into a sling chair.

"What's going on? Your whole village is going nuts."

"I've got malaria." Charlie croaked. "Can you get me some water?"

Dabrian went to the fridge, came back with a bottle and sat with Édouard at the table while Charlie guzzled down half the liter. Charlie could hear Édouard saying something about a woman, an ngaa-bwa, and something about his senior wife, Nadine. Charlie wiped the sweat from his brow and felt his sopping hair was ice, and then his blood began seething in his arteries; the pressure was building again, stretching his skin to the bursting point, and he closed his eyes not to see his gore spatter the wall.

"Man, you look like shit."

Charlie drained the rest of the water. "I feel like shit."

"I got to take you to a doctor."

"I think I'm over the worst," said Charlie, but the fever was spiking once more. He was addled, and sinking.

The dream was prophetic, Dabrian could see. It was as the Nima had told him. The dream had shown him Charlie in trouble, and it was true. Dabrian would not doubt his vision for the rest of his life. The old woman he had seen as he drove up came through the door with a face painted white, the clay crinkled around her eyes, barefoot and naked above the waist, her arms and legs painted red. White cowry shells, red feathers and bird claws covered her withered breasts.

"You come from far away," she said to Dabrian. Dabrian looked at Charlie in amazement to see if he had heard the old woman speaking English. But Charlie had nodded off, streaming sweat. Dabrian looked at the man with a chipped front tooth. Judging from his expression, the ngaa-bwa had spoken in Téké.

"You must come with me."

She is the one who called me here, Dabrian realized. She was aware of his power, his atura afou. She knew it was about to become manifest, and she needed it outside.

Dabrian got up and pulled on Charlie's arms. His destiny was calling. "Come on, my man. We got to get you back in bed."

Charlie groaned, beefy, hot and slippery, and Dabrian put Charlie's heavy arm across his shoulders, and with his right arm around Charlie's waist, he helped him unsteadily in through his bedroom door, and he flopped back onto the tangled sheets.

The painted woman led the way into the sunlight. Three grandmothers sidled around a barrel in the middle of the village, chanting and huffing and raising their arms above their heads. The painted woman shook a rattle as she approached them, and the old women ululated in a shrill cheer, and somehow Dabrian knew the painted woman had given all the grandmothers of the village the power to see where evil was hidden. That explained the young girls racing about in the village. They were uncovering the fetishes the old women were seeing, digging things out from the roots of trees, pulling them from the rafters of smoky old cook huts, lumps of knotted rags and wood containing the fearsome things the village grandmothers had sent them to find, carrying them to the grandmothers who dumped them into the barrel of water.

"You come from far away," said the diminutive woman, looking up into Dabrian's face and smiling mildly, her white-painted face, her necklaces, her white shells, her red feathers and claws.

No question; she had said it in plain English. Or was Dabrian somehow able to understand her?

"You have something," she said, speaking straight into his soul, and she led the way past the barrel just as two old women dumped in two fetishes, and Dabrian expected to hear a hiss and see steam rise into the air.

There were men in the near distance looking on with stony expressions. They were the proprietors, Dabrian knew. Those men are man-bats.

The painted woman led Dabrian around the corner of a house to where, with a shock, he saw a body wrapped in a sheet. It was a woman's face, laid out in the sand, lying on a woven mat. Was she dead?

Women squatted in a circle around her mumbling a chant.

"You have something," the painted woman said again, and she knew what it was, and was going to show Dabrian, smiling as she took hold of his wrist and pulled on his arm for him to squat down by the woman wrapped in the shroud. "Here," and she stroked the palm of his right hand to show him the thing he had, the outlet of his power, his atura afou.

The eyes of the woman in the shroud were peacefully closed.

257

Perhaps she was asleep. The man with a chipped tooth, whose wife it seemed this was, looked fearful.

"Touch her," said the painted woman, guiding Dabrian's right hand to the forehead.

Men and boys leaned in over the heads of the squatting women to watch as the painted woman placed Dabrian's hand on the woman's cool forehead.

"Now, put the other hand on her too."

The moment the painted woman guided Dabrian's left hand on top of his right, he felt his atura afou stir. It flowed from his backbone right up through his shoulders and down both his arms. And there came a shout that startled Dabrian. Dozens of orange scorpions scuttled swift as mice from the bottom of the winding sheet, their tails raised ready to sting. The bystanders scattered. Dabrian felt a shock wave burst from his head. Chickens ran like torpedoes from every direction, pecked at all the scorpions and gobbled them down.

Two hours later, Justine rode in silence beside Dabrian as Air Afrique roared through the sand. He had brought her a note sealed in an envelope addressed in Charlie's hand to nurse Ntchaga Justine, care of the Akièni Hospital. Once in Okouya, she craned her neck at the old women by the rain barrel. Up ahead she saw Charlie filling the doorway to his house. When Dabrian pulled to a stop, Justine got out and went to him at once, pushing Charlie back inside. She sat him down at his table and opened the kit she had with her, which included the artemisinin. She pricked his finger, drew blood into a pipette and transferred the drop onto a paper gauge.

"See if you can find him some broth to eat," she said. Dabrian went into the kitchen and found a yellow packet of Knorr soup mix on a shelf. While the instant soup heated, he refilled all Charlie's water bottles from the faucet, admiring the kitchen sink.

Back in the salon, the colored paper gauge soon indicated positive for malaria. Justine went to the kitchen and wet a towel to bathe Charlie's face. "We have to cool you," she said.

Charlie looked haggard, but in momentary remission, felt animated. He wanted to tell Justine what he'd learned while Dabrian was gone, of a painted woman who had walked into the village from out of nowhere, just like that, called here by evil generated in this village, she said. The painted woman summoned all the grandmothers. They set up a barrel of water. The grandmothers began to see fetishes buried in the ground and wedged in crannies in cookhouses. They directed the girls of the village where to go find the fetishes, root them out, bring them to the barrel and throw them all into the water.

Because of a spell, Édouard's senior wife had been finding scorpions everywhere she turned. The painted woman wrapped her in a white sheet and told her to sleep, then she brought Dabrian to her.

Charlie turned to Dabrian. "Édouard said you put your hand on her forehead and scorpions came out of the sheet, and then chickens came running and ate them all up. Édouard says you broke the spell. Is that true?"

Before Dabrian could answer, there was a rap at Charlie's door. There stood the ngaa-bwa herself, Édouard behind her.

Justine greeted the painted woman politely as grandmother. She asked Édouard in Téké, "What happened?"

"Bourou ma lo ndé eboulou," he said. "Someone put a curse on my wife and this old woman freed her."

The ngaa-bwa spoke to Dabrian.

Justine translated. "She says she will be leaving tomorrow, at dawn. She is going back to where she lives. Her village is at the foot of the mountain called Amaya Mokini, and she wants you to know, Dabrian, that she will see you again."

"You wouldn't believe how much better I feel," Charlie said as he came into the kitchen to find Justine preparing breakfast with Dabrian. "That stuff really is something. What's it called again?" He remembered the Peace Corps nurse telling them about it, years ago, it seemed.

"Artemisinin," replied Justine.

"Man, this smells good," said Charlie. He served himself a heaping plateful of scrambled eggs and manioc and smothered it in ketchup. "The water barrel is almost empty," he said with his mouth full. "I have to go get water. I'll need help."

"I really have to get back to work," said Justine, having spent two nights in Okouya nursing Charlie.

"It won't take long. I need at least one other person to fill the barrel." Charlie looked at Dabrian. "You want to come? You don't have to. You can leave if you want to."

Dabrian knew the correct answer. "I didn't sleep so good last night," he said. In fact, uneasy dreams had troubled him. "I think I might catch a little more shut-eye, before I head back."

"Suit yourself," said Charlie. He gave Justine his special smile. "I really need your help, chérie."

Twenty minutes later Justine was beside Charlie in his truck, with a barrel in back, on their way to Aliga Creek. He had never felt more alive. The clouds in the sky were beautiful. White egrets feeding on insects in the tall grass turned brown now in the deep dry season leaped into the air and flapped away when the truck drew too near. The world was sublime, and beside him was the woman he loved. He described for Justine his feverish dreams, the acid worms in his veins, the woman with a dog's face, thorns on her breasts. He reminded Justine about the evil thing coming for him in the woods he had sensed, how he hurried out from the lashing trees into the wind and saw an eagle fly away carrying a snake. A few days later, a woman appeared half-hidden in trees. She tried to tell him something urgent, but he couldn't hear her. Then she vanished.

"It's all intertwined," he said, "with everything that's happened in the village the last several days while I was sick. Justine, I have a bad feeling about Okouya now. I'm really looking forward to getting out of this place. So what do you think about moving to Franceville with me?"

Justine did not respond.

It bothered Charlie the way she could do that; withdraw down inside, rather than answer a question. He knew better than to insist, however. That just drove her deeper into silence. This was something about her he didn't like. Justine could disappear in his company. But that had once been his way too. When the time came, he would leave Okouya with mixed feelings, because he had friends here, especially his workers.

"What are you thinking? What about my idea, moving to Franceville with me?"

Once again, Justine did not respond. For a time, the two of them were silent as Charlie steered the truck eastward across the tawny hills. Justine watched Charlie surreptitiously. His face had become so drawn. There were sharp angles in his cheeks that hadn't been there before. The fever had burned flesh off him; the man her brothers liked so much, the twins especially, and Jonas. No Batéké man would have her for a wife, people were saying, a kakouma woman, unable to bear a child.

They descended a hill toward an opening in a bosquet. Charlie swung the truck around and backed it down into the trees. He stopped, they got out and he lifted Justine lightly under the arms up into the pickup bed. She watched him go down to the creek with two buckets, awed at his strength; the fever hadn't diminished it. He lugged the buckets back full of water and she emptied them one by one through the large blue funnel. It took fifty buckets. When the barrel was full, Charlie jumped up into the bed and screwed on the cap, and then he lifted Justine down and they went hand-in-hand to the stream and undressed in a cloud of flittering butterflies. They waded down into the clear clean cold flowing water to the side of the moss-covered logs of the old bridge, and there Justine turned to Charlie, reached up to put her arms around him and they kissed in the golden light.

The young girls Marguerite and Sylvie scampered away from Charlie's house with a few items visible in their hands as soon as they heard his truck roar into the village.

"Who's that?" Justine asked sharply. "What are they taking?"

"They just take things from my garbage pail," said Charlie. He explained the longstanding routine as he pulled alongside his water barrel.

Dabrian came outside with a book in his hand as Justine got out of the truck. She clucked her tongue at him, pushed past and went inside.

Dabrian watched her enter the house, surprised at Justine's hostility. He shrugged it off and went to watch Charlie siphon water from the barrel in the back of his truck, through a length of hose into the barrel next to his house.

"You know, Dabrian," said Charlie, "I was thinking I could

drive Justine to Akièni, but now I'm not sure I can manage it. I'm feeling kind of weak. I'm still not a hundred percent. Could you take her?

"Sure, no problem," said Dabrian. "It's on my way back to Ondili, anyway."

Justine gestured furiously from the bedroom when Charlie went inside. "Come here!" she demanded.

Her overnight bag sat packed on the bed. "What's the matter?" he asked.

"Where are my panties?" she hissed, so Dabrian wouldn't hear.

"Panties?"

"The panties I wore yesterday. Where are they?"

Charlie didn't know what to say.

"Someone has taken them!"

"Who would do that?"

Justine clucked and went past him into the front room.

"Did you watch those little girls the whole time they were in the house?" she demanded of Dabrian.

"I may have been dozing in the sling chair," he said.

"And you left the door unlocked?"

Dabrian blinked. "I didn't know I was supposed to lock it."

Justine glared at Charlie. "I need to go," she said, and went back into the bedroom and came out with her bag.

A man standing a short distance off smiled when he saw Justine coming out of Charlie's house, and he began to approach.

It was not a pleasant smile Dabrian saw. The man wore an old suit jacket and a powder blue yachting cap. This man isn't right, thought Dabrian, and he instantly saw why. This was a man-bat coming to greet Justine with fiendish thoughts up his sleeves.

17. Whistling Along

A fter weeks spent bed-ridden in gradual decline, Oyamba Paul died peacefully in his sleep. The next day, Charlie halted work on the school out of respect. Mourners poured into Okouya from miles around. It amazed Charlie to see how fast word spread in a part of the world with no telephones, and very few motor vehicles. The numbers of people coming to grieve for the great land chief of the westernmost Louzou soon tripled the population of the village. Informed that mourning would continue for an entire week, he drove to Akièni to spend the time with Justine.

Charlie had nothing to do during the day when Justine was at work and her brothers at school. The twins were taking summer preparatory courses to improve their chances of admission to Lycée. He felt awkward around the boys, unsure of what they thought of him being in their home, using their bathroom, sleeping with their sister. He cooked breakfast and dinner but had no idea what they thought of his meals. The boys, in fact, liked having him around. They liked spaghetti, omelets and toast. And as for affairs of the heart, these were not serious matters in Gabon, as Buck Buford and Eric Slidell had said back in Boundji. It was true, Charlie learned with the girlfriends. But Justine was different, unlike any girl Charlie had ever known. He wanted to get serious with her, if only she would let him.

Saturday night, he invited her to the Bottle Cap Bar. She didn't want to go. She was tired from a hard week at work. She didn't like going to bars. But he insisted, and her brothers insisted, that she go. The owner, Papa Clément, had recently installed a new deep freezer for the drinks, and a powerful new sound system for the music, and there was a much larger clientele in the evenings Charlie found a seat against the wall for the two of them and went through the crowd to the bar. He came back with a bottle of orangeade for Justine, a bottle of Régab beer for himself. She wore the same yellow sundress she'd worn on their first date, and Charlie leaned close to her, smelling her scent.

"You look fabulous."

"Thank you."

"We can have the Franceville house to ourselves, you know, chérie," he said, nuzzling her ear through her braids, speaking loud enough to be heard over the music. They had slept there, the night of the movie and pizza for the twins. "What do you think? Hector's moved out. He's living with a South American researcher at CIRMF."

Justine frowned, a pout pulling down her lower lip, and turned from him to watch the dancers. "The music is too loud," she said.

"If you apply to transfer to the general hospital in Franceville," he said, "I know they'll take you. You'll probably get better pay. And for certain, the work will be more challenging. It would be a good career move for you."

She gave him a dubious look, and sipped her orangeade.

"I can tell what you're thinking. You can't abandon your brothers in the middle of their studies." Charlie waited until she nodded. "So, how about if the twins come live with us too?"

The question startled Justine, and she leaned away to look at Charlie better, with her wide-set almond-shaped eyes. But she made no reply, and turned back to watch the rhythmic motion on the dance floor.

"I'm serious, Justine!" Charlie grabbed her hand and squeezed. "The twins could transfer to the collège in Franceville. It's a better school. They'll be admitted. They're the best students in Akièni. You've told me that. They have the best test scores, and their scores are legitimate. You don't pay bribes. You told me that."

She turned to look at him again, this time with a smile playing on her lips. She hadn't said yes, but she hadn't said no, and she was so beautiful it made his heart swell.

"Do you want to go somewhere else?" he asked in her ear, with a grin she couldn't see. "It's way too loud in here."

Okouya

With the block laid, time had come to pour the concrete ring beam to bind the walls together. The day they started, Lalish stumped about the chantier in his oversized platform shoes, broken watches clattering like bracelets on his skinny wrists, writing in his blank notebook, waving his dry pen around, shouting orders in gibberish as he directed in his mind the biggest project the village had ever seen. Charlie and Albert made concrete as fast as the mixer drum would turn. Two laborers trundled wheelbarrows along splintered planks back and forth to the walls. Another two laborers shoveled concrete from the wheelbarrows into heavy gauge black plastic pails they boosted up with both hands. The masons on the scaffold poured each bucket of concrete into wooden forms, and then tossed the empty buckets down. Periodically they jammed the concrete down into the hollow cells with short lengths of rebar and smoothed the concrete flat with wooden floats. As soon as a section of ring beam was finished, the masons jumped down, and everyone scrambled to move the scaffold. Fresh concrete soon wet through the tops of the gray walls like sweat stains, and one-meter tufts of rusty rebar tie-downs bristled upright like marsh reeds.

Charlie loved the cocky attitude of his crew at work, the pride shining forth from their eyes. He loved the way they bantered with each other over the roar of the mixer engine. Each worker focused on the task, anticipating what to do next, wasting no motion, working with the practiced unity of action of a well-drilled football team. Charlie's pleasure at the sight made him feel guilty about the secret he was keeping from the men. No one in the village yet knew of his decision to accept the logistics coordinator position in Franceville.

The day after completing the ring beam, Charlie set the crew to work mounting the ten roof trusses that had been leaning against the outer walls of the green teacher's house. Laborers carried the first heavy wooden truss to the scaffold positioned along the front wall. Charlie helped them lift one end and shoved it upward and forward in heaves, until it reached its tipping point. Jean-Paul, Benjamin and Édouard on the scaffold pushed the truss across into the waiting hands of Albert, Bruno and Jean-Luc on the scaffold along the back wall, inside the classroom. Charlie joined them, and the men on both scaffolds pulled the truss along, un, deux, trois, until Jean-Paul on one end and Charlie on the other measured and determined it was in the right place. Then they all pushed the first truss erect onto its tie-down on the ring beam.

At opposite walls the workers bent paired strands of rebar up and slid the ends of the tie-downs into holes predrilled into short two-by-fours. They turned the two-by-fours, twisting the strands around the bottom cord tight enough to bite, before bending the iron braids over and nailing them fast to the truss.

All morning long, they repeated the process, until the ten trusses stood upright on the walls, cross-braced with two-by-fours. Pleased with the sight, Charlie yelled, "Lunch break!"

Édouard fell in beside him. "Can you come eat at my house?" he asked quietly. "I have something I need to tell you."

A basin and pitcher of water sat on a small table outside Édouard's house, beside a clean towel and a new bar of soap. Inside, Édouard's senior wife Nadine greeted Charlie with a handshake and a curtsy, and showed Charlie into the salon where she had set the table for two.

"I have wanted to talk to you for some time," said Édouard, as Nadine brought the food in covered dishes. "I want you to know what was done to my wife. Tell him," he said to Nadine.

In perfect French, Nadine – clearly a star pupil in her school days – told Charlie how she began finding scorpions everywhere in the house. She found them in numbers and places out of the ordinary, in her cook hut, climbing the walls, up in the rafters, in a hole in a log she pushed into the fire, under her pillow when she turned down the sheet. Most terribly, she found a scorpion inside the strap of a sandal she was about to put on her daughter's foot. Then from out of nowhere, an ngaa-bwa came to Okouya, as Charlie knew, the old woman painted all red and white, and the ngaa-bwa wrapped Nadine in a white sheet and told her to sleep. When Nadine awoke, the black American was there. The ngaa-bwa had caused the black American to put his hands on her forehead while she slept, and scorpions came out from the sheet.

"And then chickens ate them all up."

"Thank you," said Édouard. Nadine curtsied and left the room.

"So now you know," he said to Charlie, as they served themselves nkoumou, goat stew and piping hot fou-fou.

"It's quite a story."

"And it's why I asked to talk with you. I want to know, when the job is over, will we get work certificates?"

"Of course," said Charlie. From the question, and from the look on Édouard's face, Charlie suddenly realized that his first friend in the village was quitting.

"Is it possible I can get my papers before the school is finished?"

"I suppose so," said Charlie, disappointed at what was happening.

Édouard chewed, choosing his words carefully.

"You know it is expected that I will succeed my late father as nkani-ntsie," he said, "but as you just heard from my first wife, sorcery is aimed at my family. I've told no one except my wives what I'm about to tell you."

The hot food brought beads of sweat to Charlie's forehead. He didn't want to hear this.

Édouard drank some water. "I'm not sure how to express this in French. Bari ali ma mpougou yi ba bouma abouga ma ati. Do you understand what that means?"

"Something about people trying to kill others."

"I'm going to tell you something you may find hard to believe, Monsieur Charlie. Do you remember the politician who came here with his mother?"

"Badinga?"

"Yes, Badinga. And you know the man Okorogo René?"

"The medicine man, of course."

"He is more than that. You know, there are people in the village who are very jealous because you gave jobs to some and not to others. They resent you and me and everyone else who works for you. They resent everything you do."

There it was, finally out in the open. Édouard was the first person to say what Charlie had been sensing for months. Some of the villagers actually hated him because of the way he had hired the work crew. It saddened him, made him angry, made him want to

267

pack his bags and go away, head for the new job in Franceville and the chance to live there with Justine.

"Okorogo René works for Badinga," Édouard continued, "and Badinga has promised to reward all who support his political campaign. Okorogo and the jealous ones want Badinga to succeed, so that they can profit from his rise. They are taking measures to assure it happens. This is a secret, Monsieur Charlie, and you must tell no one."

Charlie chewed his food and listened, taking scant pleasure in this new clarity, but giving Édouard all the time he needed to come out with what he had to say.

"I will not be the next land chief," said Édouard, and it did not seem to pain him to say it. "This is the best decision for me and my family. I have saved money, and as soon as you can give me papers for this job, I intend to leave Okouya. I will move to the city and look for work."

"I'm sorry to hear that," said Charlie, and he meant it. He swabbed up nkoumou with fou-fou. Okouya without Édouard was something he hadn't imagined. His own plans now had a problem. All along, his resolve to take the Franceville job was based on the assumption that Édouard would help in the transition to a new volunteer. Now, it turned out, both of them had been planning in secret to leave before the school was done. For Charlie, the irony was heavy. He had assumed Édouard would provide continuity to the project when a new volunteer came to finish the school. At least Jean-Paul would remain. Perhaps it would not make much of a difference, when another American replaced him. Maybe it would even be better. The former girlfriends would likely welcome a new American, a new source of cadeaux.

Charlie's thoughts turned to what was going to happen next. In the morning, Rebecca expected him to pick her up, to go to the annual construction volunteer conference in Franceville, where Charlie's transition would be announced. Though Charlie hated to betray his crew, his loyalty to them was not enough to keep him in the village any longer. Édouard's choice would change nothing. Okouya had become a nest of deviltry.

"Monsieur Charlie, there are bad things happening in this village," said Édouard. "There are people making powerful unkébé, and these people are not your friends."

Franceville

The short wave radio signal was at its worst during the heat of
the day. Waiting for Charlie to arrive, Rebecca patiently fine-tuned
the dial, seeking the BBC noonday news. She and Charlie had
agreed there was no reason to take two trucks to the annual
conference that each year coincided with the induction of the
annual cohort's new construction volunteers. Rebecca looked
forward to the chance to argue her case in front of the stagiaires
who would swear in. Hector Alvarado's furious pace of work
violated the Peace Corps principles of sustainable development. She
would choose her moment to say this plainly to all the volunteers,
in front of Hector and Harry, in the presence of Stu. All of them
needed to hear it.

The short wave signal swelled, then faded, then swelled again,
and at last, it came through clearly.

"…troops entered Kuwait at 2:00 am, local time," crackled a
plummy accent in London. "There are reports the invasion has
been carried out with the support of Teheran, part of a common
response to Kuwait and the United Arab Emirates for violating …."

The signal was lost in a hiss of static. Astonished at what
seemed to be happening, Rebecca turned the radio dial in tiny
increments, frowning until she got it back.

"…believed that some among the four hundred thousand
Palestinians who live in Kuwait lent active support to the…"

The signal faded again. Rebecca frowned once more. "What's
happening in Kuwait?" she muttered. She eased the fine tune dial
until she got the signal back, eager to know.

"…unlawfully created by imperialist powers to limit Iraq's
access to the ocean, according to a statement issued today by the
government in Bagdad. The invasion comes at a time when
Palestine Liberation Organization militants have sharply
criticized…"

A rising electric ring swamped the signal, and Rebecca fought
down impatience, fine-tuning the dial gently until she could make
out a British woman's voice.

"…the United States and Kuwait are jointly drafting a

resolution demanding that Iraq withdraw all its forces from Kuwait immediately and unconditionally. Here in New York, the spokesman for the president of the Security Council said that the vote could be held as early as…"

A skirling sound drowned out the woman's voice. Again, Rebecca turned the dial gently, aware now that war had broken out in the Persian Gulf.

"Let me tell you both a story," said Justine, squeezed on the Land Cruiser bench seat between Charlie's hulking frame at the wheel and lanky Rebecca by the window. Justine wore white shorts, her shapely legs turned sideways to make room for the stick shift. The last time she and Charlie had gone down this road, the twins were riding in the back, and there were roadblocks. Today the highway was open, and they whistled along trailing a stream of dust. "One time I went to the field with my grandmother," Justine began. "My grandmother told me to go pick nkoumou while she gathered pineapples. So I walked toward a tree where vines of nkoumou grew, but I saw a snake."

"Sssssss!" Charlie hissed.

Justine and Rebecca both looked to see if Charlie was joking with that sharp hissing sound.

Earlier, when Charlie arrived to pick up Justine, she had come running out of her bungalow and kissed him hello in broad daylight, heedless of anyone watching. Charlie loved Justine's moxie. He loved hearing stories from her childhood. He loved Justine, and he hated snakes.

"It was coiled in a patch of sunlight," Justine continued, "and I picked up a stick and hit it."

"E-e-e-e," said Charlie, and again Justine and Rebecca looked at him.

"What kind of snake was it?" Rebecca asked.

"I don't know the name in French. We call it nyedi. It's green and has chubby cheeks."

Charlie laughed. It sounded like a gag. "Chubby cheeks."

"Green? A green mamba?" asked Rebecca.

Charlie twitched in his seat, recalling the very slight thud on the ground close by him one evening at the Shade of the Mango Trees

Bar, frequented by volunteers in Franceville. He was sitting in a metal chair with several other volunteers under the spreading mango tree when he heard a very slight thud close beside him. He glanced down. A green mamba had fallen from the tree and whipped away in the dust. In an instant, Charlie's chair lay on its back, his beer bottle tipped over, and Charlie was twenty yards off and moving.

"No," said Justine, "A nyedi is not a green mamba."

"A nyedi, is it poisonous?"

"Yes."

"So you threw a stick at it and hit it?"

"No, I picked up a stick and whacked it on the head to provoke it. I wanted to see what it felt like to get bitten by a snake."

Charlie made a mewling sound. This was beyond imagining.

"Charlie, are you all right?" Justine placed her hand on his knee.

"Yes," he said through gritted teeth. No, he wasn't all right. He really hated snakes.

"What were you thinking?" asked Rebecca. "You wanted to get bitten by a snake?"

"I was just a child. I didn't know any better. I picked up a stick and whacked it on the head and I said to the snake, 'Bite me.'"

"Argh!" said Charlie, and he shuddered. Justine looked at him once more.

"What did the snake do?" asked Rebecca.

"It just looked at me. A nyedi counts to nine before it bites you. That's what they say."

Rebecca laughed. "You counted to nine?"

"No, I was just a little girl. I kept whacking it."

"Aw, Jesus!" cried Charlie, speeding downhill to the Mpassa River. Beyond was the provincial capital, Franceville, and Charlie raced across the bridge into the city, fleeing the thought of snakes.

Volunteers milled around in the parking lot of l'Hôtel du Plateau taking pictures of all the Land Cruiser pickup trucks. Timo, the transport driver, stopped cawing like a crow the minute he saw Rebecca getting out of Charlie's truck. He hurried over and kissed her on both cheeks.

"Look at dem, all de trucks in one place!" cried Timo, and he

271

swept out his arm in sheer elation.

Several volunteers noticed the pretty girl sitting in Charlie's truck, and two came over to see who she was.

"Bonjour," drawled Cleon Renfrew with a grin, pushing up the brim of his cowboy hat as he reached his tattooed arm through the passenger's window to shake Justine's hand, "quel est ton nom?" he asked in bad French.

"No guests," said Jim Bonaventure at the driver's window. "She can't stay here with you, Sinclair."

"Jesus, Jim," said Charlie. "I'm just dropping Rebecca off. Justine and I are staying at the new house."

"Her name is Justine?"

"Yeah, I'll be right back."

"You better be," said Jim, "The Ambassador's here. She flew in a couple hours ago."

"Truly, Justine," Charlie said as he pulled up into the driveway of his new house, "what do you say about going to Mayumba?" She didn't reply, and he asked it once more as they went inside.

"Just the two of us, a week alone. We'll have a romantic adventure while you make up your mind about moving to Franceville with me. They say the beaches there are the most beautiful in Gabon."

"I have to pee," said Justine.

Frustrated, Charlie took their bags into the bedroom. Back in the salon, he saw a note lying on the table.

"Dear Charlie," it read. "I'd like to have you and Justine over for dinner tonight. I hope you say yes. I'm looking forward to meeting you both. Natalia." Below her signature, Hector had scrawled, "See you at the swearing in!"

Charlie translated the note for Justine when she came out of the bathroom. "What would you rather do. We could have dinner at CIRMF with Hector and his girlfriend. Or we could go to a restaurant. It might be fun to meet new people at CIRMF."

"Yes," said Justine.

"Which do you mean, go to CIRMF, or go to a restaurant?"

"I mean yes, I'll go to Mayumba with you."

Charlie howled and swept Justine into his arms. He squeezed her until she squawked, then he leaned back to look at her face smiling up at him. He wanted to shout to the heavens; he wanted to swallow her into his soul. He kissed her instead.

She pushed him away, laughing. "I have something to tell you."

"What?"

"I called my friend Béatrice from the post office in Akièni. She works at the Provincial Inspectorate of Health. She sleeps with the Inspector."

"Oh? Oui?"

"I told her I'll be in town. I told her I want to ask about a transfer to Franceville."

Justine yelped when Charlie lifted her and swung her round and round.

Jim happened to be at the reception desk checking with the clerk to make sure that everyone was accounted for when Charlie walked whistling into the lobby.

"Where's your luggage, Sinclair?"

"Christ, Jim, I told you, I'm staying at the new house, jeez," said Charlie, on his way to the men's room, where Harry Bowman happened to be standing at one of the two urinals. Charlie said hi, and unzipped.

"You excited?" said Harry. "Today we're announcing you'll be taking the Franceville job."

"That's something I wanted to talk to you about."

Harry looked at him. "You're not backing out, are you?"

"Well, I never really said I'd do it."

"You better frigging be joking," said Harry, as he zipped up and went to the sinks. "We're counting on you."

"Which is why I want to ask if you'll do something for me."

"Yeah?" said Harry over the noise of running water.

"I want to take my annual leave before I finish my first twelve months of service."

"We can manage that."

Charlie joined him at the sinks. "There's a girl."

"Oh yeah?" said Harry, drying his hands with a paper towel.

"Yeah, and I want to take her to Mayumba."

"Where you go on leave is your own business."

"I want to take my truck."

Harry scowled. "You know the rules, Charlie."

"I'm asking you for special permission. I'll make sure no one else knows."

Harry shook his head. "I don't want to hear anything about it," he said, starting for the door.

"Then maybe you should find someone else to take the Franceville job."

Harry turned. He didn't like being threatened, but then he saw Charlie grinning. "I said I don't want to hear anything about it," said Harry, and he winked and walked out of the restroom.

Ambassador Jones stood before the bathroom mirror in the Presidential Suite at l'Hôtel du Plateau, fighting off the familiar dread. She was failing her son Calvin Junior, trying to raise him in the interstices of her career. Just a child, her son hadn't been able to object about what might happen when General Colin Powell telephoned Darlene from out of the blue with the offer of a position on the National Security Council, a job that would put her right in the cockpit of U.S. foreign policymaking, Special Assistant to the President and Senior Director for Africa. Darlene went to work almost immediately, at the Eisenhower Executive Office Building, where the waves from the world's most troubled continent rolled in. Tough issues brought out her tough work ethic, which garnered her favorable notice in the Vice President's office, and led to her nomination to become ambassador. And that ambassadorship eventually led to the conference call on a secure line with the Africa Bureau staffers chaired by Assistant Secretary of State for Africa, Hank Cohen.

"The Gabon team is all here," said Cohen. There were no introductions of who else was on the call. The Assistant Secretary was abrupt. "Tell us for the record what you're requesting, Ambassador Jones."

"Sir, I need a CIA case officer and a qualified election analyst in Libreville as soon as possible. The details are in the cable."

"You know, Ambassador," said Cohen, "there are many

competing priorities, and to be blunt, Gabon is not a priority." He did not give Darlene a chance to respond. "There's no way the CIA is going to open a station in Libreville, at least not in the timeframe you're dealing with. And no one here has ever heard of the CIA deploying a case officer on TDY. That being said, you're facing some unique circumstances, we all agree, so we're prepared to pass your request on to them. We're going to ask the CIA to send someone to you on covert assignment."

"Thank you, sir."

"On the request for an elections analyst, let me turn that over to the desk officer. Cindy?"

"Hello Ambassador Jones, this is Cindy Tomkins." The desk officer's voice sounded like she was a teenager. "I've looked into your request, and I have good news. It turns out USAID has a standing agreement called the CEPPS mechanism with an organization that specializes in election support called IFES. State could transfer ESF through a PASA to USAID, who could put the funds into the CEPPS mechanism, and IFES could draw on those funds and send you an elections analyst. Based on your cable, Ambassador, I can draft the scope of work for the analyst."

The young desk officer clearly knew her business, how to make money move through the complex plumbing of the federal bureaucracy.

"So we're approving your request, Ambassador," said Cohen. He paused before hanging up. "Good work, Darlene," he said. "And good luck."

Leaning closer to the mirror to apply mascara, Darlene saw in her mind's eye the picture on her desk in Libreville, Secretary of State James Baker administering her the oath. Calvin Senior, her husband, held the Bible. Little Calvin Junior stood by his father's side, looking on. Darlene's husband had no interest in becoming a trailing spouse. Not for one moment had he considered accompanying her to post. The moment she first laid eyes on him, she thought Calvin the handsomest man of the NROTC scholarship midshipmen reporting for shore assignment that summer, resplendent in his service dress blues. That was the year President Carter revoked an unwritten Navy policy preventing black and women midshipmen from being assigned to summer cruises.

Darlene counted fifteen years since Calvin first went to sea, working to qualify as a Tactical Action Officer. They were married just days before he shipped out, and she reported to her duty location at the Office of Naval Intelligence. Five years in Naval Intelligence opened a door to Princeton for her, a door into the world of the mind, and a pathway to an assistant professorship at Howard. Then came the birth of their son. Darlene looked deep into her own eyes reflected in the mirror. Oh how her mother had smiled, holding the grandchild she'd been awaiting so long. They didn't know it yet, but the cancer that would kill her mother was already burning inside.

Then came the two-story brick house in Fairfax they bought the year Calvin left the Navy for the new job at HUD. They were the first black family in the neighborhood, their son the only black child in his kindergarten class. She remembered her little boy on his first day of school trying so hard to look brave for his momma. Darlene's eyes whelmed up at the memories, threatening to ruin her mascara. She took a deep breath, patted her hair, and inspected herself one last time.

It was almost five o'clock when the Ambassador walked in. The construction volunteers were chatting with each other, some of them standing, some of them sitting around the white linen-covered tables arranged in a horseshoe. The more senior volunteers watched with supercilious good humor the twelve rowdy stagiaires, soon to swear in, as the Ambassador strode into the conference room.

Peace Corps Country Director Eaton followed next. "Quiet down, everyone, and get on your feet."

Ambassador Jones took the chair held vacant for her at the head of the tables. "Be seated," she said.

Stu went to a podium at the open end of the tables. He tapped the microphone, which squeaked while he read the agenda. Then he introduced the Ambassador. "Dr. Darlene Jones."

Darlene walked smiling to the podium, a petite black woman with the posture of a gymnast wearing blue jeans that showed off her slender figure, and she turned off the offending microphone with a broad and friendly smile.

"Can you hear me? Thank you, Stu. I'm not going to give a

speech. First, you have all heard the news, am I correct? Iraq has invaded Kuwait." Darlene looked around the room, waiting for the buzz of voices to subside. "Here is what we know. About an hour ago, the U.N. Security Council passed a resolution demanding that Iraq withdraw its forces immediately and unconditionally. There's no way of knowing if Iraq will comply. We all hope they do. President Bush has said this aggression will not stand. We're not sure what the ramifications will be, but I want you all to know when it comes to the Peace Corps in Gabon, your safety is my number one concern."

The volunteers, most of them seeing her for the first time, studied her closely.

"I'm not going to speculate on what might happen. We will do all we can to keep you informed. As all of you know, this is happening right in the middle of a global political transformation that is having an effect here in Gabon. The elections scheduled for this coming December are a major concern, obviously. I won't sugarcoat things. There were riots last May after the death of an opposition political figure named Joseph Rendjambé, and those of you who were here when it happened have been getting worried letters from your families, I'm sure. With the mail being as slow as it is, some of you are probably still getting those letters."

The Ambassador's jab at the Gabon postal service provoked laughter from the volunteers.

"We handled a lot of calls from your parents, so I want to ask you, when you write to your folks or call them from the post office, please tell them the Embassy is monitoring the situation very closely, and at this point we don't believe there is any credible threat to your personal security."

Darlene surveyed the faces around the tables.

"Clear enough? It's possible there will be more disturbances as we get closer to Election Day. No one can be sure what's going to happen, but there's going to be campaigning and people will be getting excited. Now, I'm going to sound a little legalistic here, but your obligations as Peace Corps volunteers are important for you to understand. Pursuant to a law passed by Congress in 1966, we have a treaty with the Government of Gabon that allows Peace Corps to send you volunteers here. The first article of that treaty requires a separate framework agreement, and that agreement lists all the activities that volunteers may engage in, as well as the sorts of things volunteers may expressly not do. One of the things you may not do is get involved in domestic politics. Those of you who were here over the summer received a letter from me reminding you of this."

"We sent it to them by registered mail," said Stu from his seat.

"And those of you who are about to swear in have a copy in your packet, I'm told. This is a condition of your service. It is not open to discussion. Am I clear?" She looked around the tables. No one said anything, so Darlene said, "All right then, do any of you have any questions?" Still, no one said a word. "This is your chance to ask me about anything that might be on your mind."

Rebecca raised her hand. "Suppose there's a political rally," she said. "A speech or whatever, are we allowed to go, just to watch?"

"You'll have to use your best judgment, of course. Be careful about getting into risky situations. We don't want you in crowds that could turn riotous."

"Just stay away from anything like that," said Stu, "political rallies and whatnot."

"But Stu," Rebecca argued, "this is history in the making, and we're Peace Corps volunteers. Part of our job is to learn about the local culture. Isn't going to watch a speech or a rally part of what we're supposed to do?"

"Fair enough," said Ambassador Jones, "but let me be very clear and underscore this point once again. You are not to participate in any election campaigning."

"If any of you disobeys," warned Stu, "you will be sent home, period."

Rebecca smiled. She had received her copy of the Ambassador's letter and found it pompous. She flipped open the conference packet. The date was Monday, August 6, 1990. In less than four months, it would be a year since her own swearing-in. And not long after her anniversary, she would have to decide which university to attend when she returned home. Her plan was still half-formed. It started with the fact that her boyfriend Philbert had a brother named Georges, recently returned from Romania, who was an opposition candidate for the National Assembly. She was curious about the contours of a government the opposition might create. The election was an opening for a new generation of Gabonese political leaders to emerge. She felt drawn to what was admittedly a quixotic campaign to unseat a member of President Bongo's ruling party. It was an interesting challenge, and an amazing opportunity for her future graduate work. In fact, what she was considering actually had a name in the book on social science research methods she'd read, that one of her former professors had sent. She would be a participant observer. No American need know. She could keep it secret. With the election experience, and her field notes that filled twelve notebooks, what a dissertation she could write!

"Any other questions?" Darlene asked. "No?"

"Thank you, Ambassador Jones." Stu led a round of applause as he walked to join her at the podium.

Stu handed the Ambassador a copy of the Peace Corps oath. He asked the stagiaires to come forward. The sun-darkened, work-hardened young Americans formed a semicircle around Darlene.

"Raise your right hands," she said, smiling, "and repeat after me."

After stating their names, the twelve young Americans swore to support and defend the Constitution of the United States, and faithfully discharge their duties to the Peace Corps. "So help me God," they all said.

CIRMF

A delicious aroma wafted from the kitchen. Natalia, a black woman who looked like an African but was not, twirled into the salon wearing a colorful dress with a long gathered ruffle cut low off the shoulders. She sat on the arm of the couch by Hector, who Justine supposed to be a red Indian because of his skin color. She'd learned about red Indians from American movies on television, dressed in leggings and headdresses, shooting flaming arrows from horseback at white men with rifles firing from behind covered wagons. Hector spoke Spanish with Natalia. This was something new for Justine. Not all Americans were white, and they didn't all speak English.

Natalia had invited two other guests, a very pale Frenchwoman named Geneviève, and her husband Yves, a doctor performing his national service at the General Hospital. Geneviève's straight blonde hair hung halfway down her back. Justine thought how nice it would be to stroke that hair. Yves was a slender man with gray eyes, and he held himself very erect. He spoke Spanish with Natalia and Hector. When Justine asked if he was from Colombia too, Yves laughed and said, "I come from Bayonne, in the southwest corner of France, very near the border with Spain."

"What brings you to Franceville, Justine?" Geneviève asked, having learned Justine worked as a nurse in Akièni.

"I'm inquiring about a possible transfer to the General Hospital. I have a friend who works at the Inspectorate. I hope she can schedule an appointment for me with the Inspector."

Yves turned his gray eyes to her. "I know the Inspector," he said.

"You'll like Franceville," said Hector. "The tap water is safe to drink. There's electricity from the dam near Poubara Falls. There's a vine bridge there you have to pay to cross. It's like walking on a thirty-meter hammock." He stood up and imitated, bouncing, swaying and twisting. "Have you seen it?" he asked.

Justine shared a smile with Charlie. "Yes, I have seen it."

"You're going to like living here," Hector said again.

"Tell me, Natalia, about Colombia. Is it anything like Gabon?" Justine asked.

"Where I come from is like Gabon," said Natalia. "Even the people. We were taken out of Africa as slaves. For many years, we were ashamed of being black, but that is changing now. We are more proud of our heritage, and we are having an influence on the broader culture. Partly this is because of our music. Let me play you some."

Natalia went to her stereo and selected a cassette from a rack of tapes. "This is Grupo Socavón." She punched the stop button and ejected the tape Hector had put on, *La Pistola y El Corazón*. She slipped the new tape in. "You will hear how the marimba exactly resembles the African balafon. We use an assortment of drums and a rattle called a guasá."

As soon as Justine heard the balafon, she started nodding her head with a smile. Listening to the loping drums and rattles, a woman's voice calling out and a chorus of women singing in response, Justine closed her eyes. For a second, she was a child back in Onga again with her people, dancing and singing under the stars.

Natalia got up and went back to the kitchen to check on dinner, and Justine and Geneviève followed, to see what the meal looked like.

"These are traditional dishes from my homeland," said Natalia, "like my dress. The first course is called ajiaco." She lifted the lid from a large pot simmering on the stove. "It's chicken soup made with potatoes, corn, sour cream, capers, avocado and guasca, which is an herb I brought from Colombia." She ladled out a steaming spoonful for each to taste. "Guasca is what gives it the distinctive flavor."

Justine liked Natalia. She had a bright personality. Justine liked Natalia's green and blue dress. Natalia seemed like a person it would be easy to befriend.

Natalia asked Geneviève, "Do you eat manioc?" Geneviève shook her head no. "We eat it in my country, too," Natalia told Justine. "This is patacones," she said, motioning to a platter on the counter piled high with golden brown patties of fried mashed green plantains. "The main course will be fritanga." She opened the oven to show a platter of grilled beef, chicken, ribs and sausages. "And for dessert, there will be arroz con coco." She opened the refrigerator to show them coconut rice pudding with lemon zest and cinnamon.

Justine and Geneviève carried bowls of soup to the table and Natalia called the men to dinner. Yves went to the kitchen to open the chilled bottle of pinot gris he'd brought.

Justine had never tasted wine before. She didn't like it much. She had never eaten in such diverse company. She sipped her soup, aware this was a glimpse into a possible future with Charlie, and the knowledge pulled at her in a way that made her feel both excited and afraid.

Okouya

The workers sweated, paired off on either side of the last hardwood log, gathering their strength. Jean-Paul crouched opposite Charlie. This was the tenth log they had lugged out of the forest, using slings. The logs were so heavy, the workers could carry them only a few steps before they had to set them down and rest.

Charlie had returned to Okouya from the conference to pack up his stuff and decided to put in a last day of work and help with the job of moving logs. In the morning, he would turn his former chantier over to a new volunteer, Sharon McGuire, and drive away to Franceville. Rebecca and Sharon brought to two the number of women in the school construction program. Nearby, Sharon's new Land Cruiser pickup faced uphill on the flank of the plateau.

Jean-Paul had personally selected ten trees for the exterior columns that would support the roof over the school's deep veranda. While Charlie was at the conference, the workers had felled the trees, lopped off the branches, and topped the logs with saws.

Up in the village, Édouard directed the workers stripping the bark off the ninth log, taking care not to gouge the wood. Eight peeled logs lay drying on leftover cinderblocks.

Charlie had expected it would be hard to break the news to the crew that he was leaving, but none of them showed much emotion. He suspected they'd somehow guessed what he was planning. They were curious about Sharon, his replacement. Charlie figured that many of the villagers were probably glad to see him go.

With the last log nearly out of the woods, Charlie imagined how beautiful the hardwood columns would look in place on the veranda, the rustic effect they would give the school. This last log and one other were padouk, deep red in color like the three ongoumou logs. Three were étogo; wood the color of roasted peanuts. The dark chocolate log was lengiyé. The final log, almost white, was iyandja.

Charlie had a moment of melancholy, musing, I won't be here to finish the school. He and Justine were going to the coast. "Fuck it!" he said. Sharon and the workers looked at him. They still had ten meters to go. "Okay!" he shouted, spit on his palms, rubbed them together and grabbed his end of the sling. "Un! Deux! Trois!" They lifted together with a shout and lurched to the rear of the truck where they dropped the log with a thud.

Sharon climbed into the driver's seat. Charlie helped Jean-Paul,

Bruno and Alphonse chain the end of the log to the back hook of the truck. They'd done this nine times now.

There was one thing that made Charlie uneasy about leaving Sharon McGuire on her own in Okouya, something she didn't know about; something he wouldn't tell her about, because he wasn't sure how to bring it up. Certain of the men in the village were still so angry about the way Charlie had selected the workers they planned revenge. It involved witchcraft. This was why Édouard had abdicated the land chieftaincy. Councils of elders in all the surrounding villages were debating how to fill the vacancy.

Charlie had introduced Sharon to the man who wanted the post, the shaman, Okorogo René. When he understood this woman was taking over the site, Okorogo scowled, as if trying to figure Charlie's angle.

Sharon's truck bounced as the men clambered into the bed. Most of them sat on the sidewalls. Jean-Paul sat on the tailgate. Charlie nodded at them, and got in the cab.

"Okay," he said to Sharon. "All set."

He looked over his shoulder through the window at the men. Jean-Paul would keep an eye on the log. A couple logs had tried to burrow into the ground. Jean-Paul would signal if this one began to nose down.

Sharon's short sweaty hair stuck to her temples and to the nape of her neck. She started the engine with the emergency brake engaged. She put the truck in first gear. The transfer case gears growled as she pushed the lever toward Charlie into four low. Charlie had dragged the first log, so Sharon could watch how he did it. She had handled each one after that. Confident she knew what she was doing, Sharon pushed lightly on the gas, easing in the clutch, then she released the emergency brake and the truck inched uphill, taking the slack out of the chain. When she felt the full weight of log, she gunned the engine, and its noise rose to a roar. The four knobby tires dug in, and the truck began to claw its way up the hill. Charlie watched the men in back hanging on tight as Sharon swung the wheel to thread a path between two stunted trees. At the steepest spot, the truck began hopping on its springs, and the men laughed to see the ragged torn furrow they were leaving behind.

18. To the Sea

Okouya

Orange sparks rose from the crackling fire, borne aloft in smoke. Shadows danced in the surrounding trees, excited with spirits. The secret society of ndjobi gathered again in the kadigi, at night, as in the old times.

"She has no relations among us," said Ongouya François, an embittered and childless man. "She is not from our mpugu. None from our village will mourn her. And she is kakouma, of no value to anyone."

"Eh," said a chorus of voices.

"What is more," added Assélé Laurent, the mason who had not been hired, "she has become the woman of the otangani, and he should be made to pay for giving jobs to so few of the men."

"I agree," said Owaga Charles, once a well-placed functionary and a favorite of the former First Lady, forced by the purge to return to a life of reduced circumstances in the village of his birth.

Everyone in the assembly nodded, and the consensus pleased Okorogo René to see. The otangani Charlie Sinclair had delivered a woman of no social value into their hands. It was perfect. Eating her soul for the unkébé to assure Antoine Badinga's success in the coming election would punish the otangani for his injustice as well, yet it would not cost the life of a single inhabitant of Okouya. No man in the kadigi could find reason to oppose this perfect plan.

Except Oyamba Hilaire. Although he owed Okorogo René allegiance for restoring his eyesight, the murderous course they were embarking on disturbed him. He spoke up, giving the men pause. "What about the ngaa-bwa from the south?"

The men looked at each other, muttering about this unknown element, the celebrated witch from Amaya Mokini, who had mysteriously walked into Okouya one day painted red and white, and then just as suddenly left. She apparently had summoned a black American who arrived shortly after her, and the ngaa-bwa used him to break the spell inflicted on the senior wife of Akoa Édouard. "That woman did great damage to your plans, Okorogo," Hilaire said. He wanted to stop the men from going any further. "The ngaa-bwa revealed the bisemo unkébé mudzira to the grandmothers, and broke the power of all the talismans."

"Our potency has been diminished, not broken," said Okorogo René. "It will require building up again, that is all."

"The woman said she would return one day," Hilaire warned them, "to finish what she started."

"And so we will act swiftly," said Okorogo. "Nothing can stand in our way."

The bitter men in the kadigi wanted to believe the path was open for Okorogo René to become the next nkani-ntsie of the westernmost Louzou. They wanted to believe Antoine Badinga would become a commanding politician, and would handsomely reward them all. They did not want to listen to Oyamba Hilaire.

Okorogo bent down, reached inside a sack at his feet and lifted out a pair of lacy pink panties, stolen at his bidding from the kakouma woman, Ntchaga Justine.

"Let us begin," he said.

Libreville

Marcel Marais stood in the conference room of the American Embassy prepared to deliver his exit briefing. It was far from ideal to have given such a sensitive assignment to a Canadian, but Marais was a retired chief electoral officer from Quebec, and the best French-speaking elections expert IFES could find on such short notice.

"Mr. Marais has to leave in about forty-five minutes to catch the UTA flight to Paris," said political officer Hughes, handing copies of Marais's outline to the three people in attendance, "so this exit briefing will be, well, brief."

"I'll just be giving the main points," said Marais. Tall and stooped, his thinning gray hair carefully combed, he wore a blue blazer, striped tie and tan slacks. "The details will come in the full report."

"No copies will be circulated other than to us," said Ambassador Jones. It wasn't a question.

"Correct," Tom assured her.

"Understood, Madame Ambassador," said Marais. "I will start by saying, after two weeks of fieldwork that Gabon is in many ways far in advance of its neighbors, and that is good." He spoke English with a slight accent. "There are a number of problems I will brief you on today. The first point that you see there – and perhaps the most serious – is that the electoral authority is housed in the Ministry of the Interior. This is a problem, because the Ministry of the Interior is the line ministry for the police, and the President holds that portfolio."

"And the Ministry of Defense as well," said Ambassador Jones. In addition to Tom, the caustic DCM Jerry Andrews and the USIS director Pamela Rossow were present.

"Why is that a problem?" asked Pamela.

"It isn't necessarily a problem," Marais answered. He had a nervous habit of smiling at nothing in particular. His teeth were very yellow. "France uses the same system, for example, and the United States as well. State governments, each overseen by the secretary of state, administer your national elections. In countries where the institutions are not widely trusted, the system becomes a problem. Perhaps people here have reason not to trust the police?"

"You can say that again," said the DCM, stroking his beard.

Marais waited for a moment, to see if Jerry had more to say. Then he continued. "There has been registration of new voters, which is fine, but they have been added to the existing roll, which was highly suspect to begin with. There are no provisions for purging the ghosts."

"The what?" asked Darlene, wanting to be sure she had heard right.

"Ghosts?" echoed the DCM.

"Ghosts, yes, purging the ghosts," said Marcel Marais. "When a family member dies, who thinks to have that person's name removed from the electoral roll? When a family is planning to move, who thinks to go tell the electoral authority? This is a constant problem in all democracies, and the means for purging an electoral roll of so-called ghosts are limited."

"How is it done?" asked Pamela.

"Typically, in a mature democracy, the electoral authority will expunge a name if the person has not voted for a certain number of consecutive elections. But then, there has to be a provision for such persons to be immediately re-registered if they show up at the polls again. In new democracies, typically voter enrollment takes place only during a limited registration period. The roll is not permanently open, you see. Generally, it is closed long before Election Day in order to permit the electoral roll to be printed and the correct sections distributed, even to the most remote polling stations. Purging the roll to remove the ghosts is a particular challenge in countries such as Gabon."

"I'm shocked to hear there is a problem in Gabon," said the DCM.

Marais wasn't accustomed to hearing sarcasm in such settings. He waited a moment, looking at Jerry, before he resumed.

"Second point, the Government has no plan to provide the political parties with a copy of the voter roll, so the opposition parties will not be able to check if voters are registered at more than one polling station. Third point, there are no meaningful provisions against fraudulent voting. Voters will simply present their national identity cards." Marais handed Jerry an ID on heavy green paper. A black and white photograph with an ink stamp on it showed a middle-aged man looking uncertain about having his photo taken. The information was typed. A second ink stamp at the bottom covered the signature of a minor authority. "This is an actual Gabonese national identity card, which you can see is very easy to forge. It's the only identification required at the polls. Parties could make false identity cards in the names of registered voters who have died, or moved to another district, and give them to supporters, so they could vote at more than one polling station."

"I always wondered how they do it in Chicago," said Jerry.

"Tom," said Darlene, studying the card, before she passed it to her political officer, "I don't suppose we have any way of tracking the sale of green card stock in Gabon."

Tom laughed. "Not a bad idea, Ambassador, but I doubt there's any way we could."

"This particular problem can be overcome," said Marais, "through the practice of staining the finger or thumb of each voter with indelible ink, but that will not be done here. There will be no ink at the polling stations. So there will be no safeguards against multiple voting."

Tom handed the identity card to Pamela. "These cards definitely would be easy to duplicate," he said, watching to see Pamela's reaction. The mechanics of an election was something he had never thought about before, and he always enjoyed the chance to look at the Information Service chief, her thick blonde hair and green eyes.

"Next point," continued Marais, "there will be no party agents at the polling stations or the collating centers to verify the count. This means there will be no safeguards against fraudulent vote tallies. The international best practice is for party agents to be present at the polling stations while ballots are cast, and at the collating centers where the results from polling stations are tabulated, as well as at the national election returns center where the results are announced. The international best practice is for party agents to certify the returns at all three stages of the vote count."

"One for me," said the DCM, drawing hash marks on the tabletop with his finger. "One hundred for Badinga. One hundred thousand for Bongo."

Marais smiled uncertainly, and glanced at his watch. "If I may continue, the problem for opposition parties in new democracies, even when they are permitted to send agents to observe, they seldom have adequate resources to send party agents to cover all polling stations. Being new parties, candidates are not necessarily able to trust the agents their parties can afford to recruit. The lack of committed volunteers is the Achilles heel for opposition parties in new democracies. But that's neither here nor there, because in Gabon there will be no party agents allowed at all, anywhere in the process. Am I going too fast?"

"No," said Ambassador Jones.

"The next problem I foresee is the ballot box design. The emerging best practice is to use clear plastic ballot boxes so that when the polls open, everyone can see that the ballot box is empty. The ballot boxes I saw were made of wood. There is no standard design. On Election Day, there will be no way of knowing if the boxes have been delivered to the polling stations with pre-marked ballots inside. Related to that is the last problem I will mention, the printing of ballots. The international best practice, for the initial election at least, or until such time as the parties learn to trust the system, is for the printing to be handled in a different country. The ballots should bear serial numbers and the political parties should be allowed to inspect the ballots when they are delivered, to verify the serial numbers are sequential. That is not being done here. The ballots are already being printed at the government printing office. No one has been allowed to inspect the ballots, or even verify how many ballots are being printed. This raises the possibility that ballots marked outside the polling station could be put in the ballot boxes, which as I already mentioned will not be transparent, ahead of the vote. Those are my main findings. Questions?" said Marcel Marais, and he looked at his watch again.

"It seems to me there are three vulnerabilities," said Pamela. She turned back a page in her notes. "First is fraudulent voting. The voter roll is full of ghost names, as you say they're called. The national identity card is easy to forge. Cards can be forged using the names of dead people still on the roll. Since the voters' thumbs won't be stained, there's nothing to prevent people with multiple identity cards from voting more than once."

"Correct."

"Number two, there's no control on how the ballots are being printed, and the ballot boxes aren't going to be transparent, so there's nothing to prevent ballot boxes from being stuffed ahead of time." She turned a page.

"Yes, that's correct."

"And number three, there will be no party agents at the polling stations, or at the collating centers, or at the national returns center to verify the count, so the government could fiddle with the vote count at all three places."

"Right again."

"So what's the conclusion?" asked Jerry, "as if we don't know."

Marcel Marais answered the DCM directly. "My report will conclude this is an electoral system expertly designed for rigging at multiple levels."

Franceville

It was a cruel blow to Charlie when Toad drove his Land Cruiser away. Justine sat on the front steps of Charlie's new house watching with displeasure.

"Il fallait refuser," she said, and spat at the sight of Twisted Sister in the driveway, the ugliest truck in the program, the truck Toad had left behind.

"I wasn't given a choice!" Charlie protested. Justine made it sound like he'd cravenly caved. "It was Harry Bowman's decision. Toad needs a reliable vehicle for his new site, and you know how bad the road to Onga is. It's your home village, Justine. I just didn't think they'd give him my truck."

Justine sucked her teeth. She had good reason to be upset. No sooner had she decided to take three weeks of her ample accrued leave to go to Mayumba with Charlie, than the truck they'd planned to travel in sped away, with someone else driving.

Charlie flipped through the new spiral bound truck maintenance handbook that volunteer leader Bonaventure had handed out at the conference, glancing through sections on lubrication, valves, brakes, the drive train, pausing at an illustration of how to pull an engine.

"I guess that mechanical drawing class finally came in handy," said the author, Ronnie Clavelle, assigned to finish the *stage* site at Obia and on Harry's order here to help Charlie fix up Twisted Sister. "Let's take the beast for a ride."

Charlie got in the passenger side as Ronnie slid behind the wheel. Ronnie's beard was so long, Cleon Renfrew once asked him if he used a currycomb to brush it. Ronnie looked at Charlie, cocked his head and said, "Here goes." He turned the key. The engine started. "That's a real good sign," he said, and backed down the driveway.

The condition of the cab distressed Charlie. It stank. The gray vinyl seats had burst at the seams, and leaked yellow foam. The headliner had been removed.

Ronnie pulled out of the Cité de la Caisse onto the dirt road and headed up the hill. Twisted Sister began rattling like a coffee can full of nails.

"Hang on. I'm going to check the brakes," said Ronnie, and braked hard. There was a scraping squeak. Then Ronnie let in the clutch, hit the gas and accelerated, and there was an audible clunk.

Out on the asphalt highway to Moanda, Ronnie reached cruising speed. "You feel that vibration?" he asked. "Not too bad, but we'll need to check the driveshaft when we get back."

After about fifteen minutes, he pulled to the side of the highway. "You drive back," he said. "Tell me what you think."

Charlie passed Ronnie at the front bumper and got in. Cars and trucks raced past from both directions. Charlie waited for a gap in the traffic and flipped on the turn signal. The indicator didn't work. He shook his head and grimaced at Ronnie, looking at the long pale scar that emerged from Ronnie's hairline, descended his brow, gouged through his eyebrow, crossed his cheek, and disappeared into his mustache. "How'd you get that scar?"

"Car wreck," said Ronnie. "I hit a bridge abutment."

"Wow. How fast were you going?"

"They think about a hundred and ten. I don't remember a thing. I went through the windshield. Probably would have been killed if I'd had my seatbelt on. They found me about a hundred feet from my car, a '70 'Cuda. Had that 426 hemi with the hydraulic lifters and twin Carter AFB four-barrel carbs. When you put your foot down, Jesus that car would fly! Want to see it?"

"Sure," said Charlie, expecting Ronnie would reach for a snapshot in his wallet. Instead, he popped his blue eyeball out into the palm of his hand and held it for Charlie to see.

Justine came out the open front door when she heard Twisted Sister pull up the driveway.

"Ronnie says it's not so bad," Charlie called to her. He caught a whiff of the delicious smell of stew as he and Ronnie got down on their backs and crawled under Twisted Sister. Ronnie grabbed the rear driveshaft and pulled on it.

"See that?" he said. "See how it slops back and forth? Shouldn't move like that. Universal joint will have to be replaced." He looked around. "A lot of the bolts holding on the bed are shot. You'll need a new set. Probably have to cut the old ones off with a torch. No sign of the engine leaking. That's good. Nice and dry around the main seals. The oil pan, tranny and transfer case aren't leaking. Seals on the two differentials seem okay."

292

They crawled out. "So it's not as bad as I thought?" Charlie asked hopefully.

"I'm not done looking," said Ronnie. "Get in behind the wheel and crank it from side to side." He squatted beside the front bumper to watch what happened as Charlie turned the steering wheel one direction, then the other.

"Tie rod ends are worn," said Ronnie. He moved to the left fender, grabbed the top of the tire and pulled on it hard. "Hear that?" He pulled and pushed. The truck swayed. Charlie could hear a thumping. "Bearing needs to be tightened," said Ronnie, "probably on both sides. That's not too hard a job."

Charlie got out as Ronnie lifted the hood. Serious problems were immediately evident. The battery moved back and forth. So did the radiator.

"Bolts to those mounts are sheared off," Ronnie said. "See there? Going to have to weld the struts to the frame." Some of the problems weren't so obvious. Ronnie pointed out the wobbling fan. "Water pump's about to go."

"Well shit," said Charlie, despairing about the number of things that were wrong. His trip with Justine now seemed impossible.

"All in all," said Ronnie, "not too bad."

The first day of the repair job, they took the truck to a welding shop to use an acetylene torch to cut off the bolts holding on the bed. They installed new bolts and used an arc welder to secure the struts holding the battery and radiator in place.

On the second day, with Charlie helping, Ronnie replaced the tie rod ends and the brake shoes and cylinders all around, and tightened the front wheel bearings and adjusted the valves.

Day three, in the morning, they replaced the water pump. In the afternoon, they removed the drive shaft. Ronnie knelt with Charlie on a piece of plywood and pulled it apart at the slip joint, exposing the spline. Installing a new universal joint was the last job before Ronnie would pronounce Twisted Sister ready to roll.

All the Americans knew Charlie intended to take Twisted Sister on a tour around the school sites to familiarize himself with their situations, as part of his new job. Only Justine knew what he planned to do after that.

"Donnes le jus magique," Ronnie said, and Charlie handed him the can of WD-40. "The secret ingredient," said Ronnie "We'll just hose her down real good. In a pinch, Coca Cola works too. Hand me the needle nose pliers and a flathead screwdriver."

Charlie found them in the toolbox. He had never tried his hand at any major auto repairs. He was learning a lot from Ronnie, and acquiring a huge debt of gratitude for saving the trip that he could not tell Ronnie about.

"First thing we do is remove the c-clip at the end of each arm of the center cross. They hold the bearing caps in place. See? There's four of them: here, here, here and here. They're wedged into grooves. See? So to pop these c-clips out, I'm going to use the needle nose to pinch, like this, and the flathead screwdriver to pry and sort of hook them out."

The first c-clip popped out. "See? That's one. It's not always that easy. Sometimes it helps to know the secret word." Ronnie grinned. The long scar from his hairline to his mustache never tanned, and the socket of his glass eye was watering.

Twisted Sister was strong. She creaked and rattled and the engine smoked, but when Charlie called on her for power, the old girl responded. They passed through Otou, Okouya, Aliga, Ossiélé, Olou, and in the late afternoon neared Justine's home village, Onga. Grudgingly, Justine's affection for the battered old truck grew.

Some of the volunteers were just recently installed, others had been at their sites long enough for construction of teachers' houses to be underway. Some were finished. Charlie and Justine saw new schools being laid out, some rising from the ground in the string of villages along the sandy track that ran east from the western edge of the plateau.

Charlie stopped for perhaps an hour in each village, long enough to speak English with the American volunteers. He took notes and made a show of familiarizing himself with both the road and the supply needs of each project. At every village, when Justine got out of the truck to stretch her legs, the young male volunteers looked her over. She was easy on the eye. After that first trip, the volunteers all knew Justine was Charlie's girl.

They found Toad setting up his house in Onga, guiltily pleased to be driving Charlie's truck but tickled to see Twisted Sister out so far on the plateau. Charlie smiled ruefully. Like Justine, he was beginning to grow fond of Twisted Sister. The old crate would soon take him and his lover on a furtive adventure to the sea.

That night Justine told her mother where they were going. Mama Angélique had heard of Charlie's existence, but this was the first time she had seen him. She had a lot to say to the hulking young white man who had taken up with her daughter. She was a work worn woman with a strong face and a keen eye, a widow wearing black, still in her year of mourning.

The jagged sand walls looked like ancient ruins. Trees wound around their bases, and quite a few grew right atop them. Far off in the bottom of the canyon was a winding lake.

"What's the name of that lake?" asked Charlie. He held Justine's hand, their fingers entwined, sitting on the canyon's edge in the grass.

Justine did not know its name. She had never been to Lékoni Canyon, although she knew it existed, out here in the remotest part of the Batéké Plateau. To their south and east was the Congo.

"This is something to see."

They were quiet for a while, enchanted by the view. Then Justine asked, "Comment est-ce qu'on dit 'je t'aime' en anglais?"

Charlie was surprised to hear the question, and very pleased, he smiled and touched her face.

"I luff you," she repeated.

"Love," Charlie corrected. "I love you."

"I love you," she said, and they were kissing.

By mid-morning the next day, Charlie and Justine were far into the province of Ogooué-Lolo, en route for the city of Tchibanga. They had left Franceville hours before dawn. It was the beginning of the autumnal rainy season. All along the muddy ribbon of road, the villages were festooned with ruling party flags. They came to a section where heavy engines were putting in a new culvert, yellow machines moving about in the flittering jungle, snorting black smoke from their pipes. Charlie had to follow a sloppy temporary road that made him nervous.

When the detour rejoined the road, Charlie faced a muddy red lane. He shifted the old truck back to high range and going to third he asked, "Can I ask you a question, Justine?"

It was something he'd been thinking about.

"Would you consider studying in America? That subject you're interested in? Pharmacology?"

From her expression, Charlie guessed she was thinking of the story he'd told her, going ice fishing with Coach Dawber and Uncle Vince in one of the huts that sprang up like villages on the frozen lakes of Minnesota.

"It wouldn't have to be in a cold weather state," he said. "It could be someplace like Florida or Hawaii. There are places where the weather's like Africa."

Her sweet, dark eyes fastened on him.

They approached a log bridge and Charlie slowed. Justine no longer insisted on getting down and walking across them, but the log bridges still made her nervous.

"Think about it," Charlie said. "Studying in America. It would be an opportunity."

Justine saw the assumption he was testing, that she wanted to go to America with him. She was not ready to have this discussion. She wasn't even sure she would be moving with him to Franceville. She had met with the Inspector and had submitted a formal request, but she had not yet received a reply.

"Do you believe in ghosts?" she asked.

Justine was always doing this, changing the subject. "I don't know," Charlie said, annoyed. But he went along with her. "There was the woman I told you about, who appeared in the woods. She looked like she was trying to tell me something important, but I couldn't hear her, and then she vanished. Was she a ghost?"

"Maybe. I'll tell you a story. It was mushroom season and there was this woman named Henriette. This was in Onga and she was the mother of two boys, and she was pregnant. She was hoping it would be a girl. She had been to an ngaa-bwa, who told her it would be a girl. Henriette was very happy, and told everyone. One morning she went with a friend to the forest to pick mushrooms. The friend was my aunt, whose name is Simone, and Henriette began to have contractions. You know what those are? She was starting to give birth. She gave birth there in the forest. Simone was there to help her. Henriette gave birth to a little girl, and Simone said, 'Your wish has come true.' But Henriette couldn't look at the baby girl. Something was wrong. Henriette was in too much pain. She couldn't walk. She was bleeding too much. It was getting dark, and Simone said, 'I will go get help.' And she left Henriette there with the baby."

"In the woods."

"Yes, and as she was leaving, my aunt Simone saw two baboons in a tree, not far from Henriette. She ran as fast as she could back to the village. She told everyone Henriette had given birth to a little girl, but was in serious pain, and couldn't walk, and there were baboons nearby. Henriette and her newborn baby girl were in serious trouble. The women got blankets, water and towels, and the men took flashlights and their shotguns and they hurried to where Simone had left Henriette with the baby. When they got there, it was too late. Henriette was dead, and so was the baby."

Charlie made a sympathetic noise. "Did the baboons kill them?"

"No. No one could tell how they died. They just died, like that."

Charlie had heard dozens of these sorts of tragedies since he'd arrived in Gabon, a year ago this month.

"So the people had to make a decision whether to bury them in the woods or carry them back to the village. They decided to bury them where their bodies lay. Some of the men went back to get shovels. When they returned, they buried Henriette and her baby where they died. And ever since then, when people pass by that place, sometimes they can hear that baby crying, and they can hear Henriette singing, and trying to comfort her baby girl. And sometimes when I've walked past that place, Charlie, I have heard that sound myself."

Charlie reached over to take Justine's hand. He had goose bumps. They were entering a stretch where it had been raining heavily, and the road was slippery. He put both hands back on the wheel. Ancient dripping wet trees reared up like canyon walls. Coming to a curve, he slowed. As he rounded the turn, up ahead he spotted the undercarriage of a truck that had tipped over and lay on its side with its nose on the road. Cargo had spilled. Someone had covered it with a tarp. As they approached, glum looking boys appeared from under the tarp. They were the truck's boy chauffeurs, as they were called, and they were covered with bees.

Instantly, Twisted Sister filled with bees, yellow bees buzzing, the soft tickling of bees on their skin.

"Try not to move too much," said Justine. "This is the Forest of Bees." She had heard of this place, le Forêt des Abeilles, a forest of bees that didn't sting.

Charlie did what she said, enduring the sensation of bees on his face as he steered, driving slowly to pass around the overturned truck blocking the road, bees on his arms, crawling up inside the sleeves of his tee shirt. He shook his head to shake off the bees that explored too near his ears, snorted bees from his nostrils, edging Twisted Sister around the nose of the truck. One of the boys waved him forward, guiding him. As Charlie passed, they looked at each other, their two faces covered with bees. Charlie handed the boy a thousand franc note for his trouble and accelerated away.

Justine laughed at the experience as she batted and waved the bees out her open window. It was several miles before the last bee was gone, but the ghosts of a newborn baby crying and her mother singing to soothe her would stay with Charlie from that moment on.

They passed through a village where a dead mandrill hung on a stake for sale. It had a vivid blue and pink nose. A naked little boy waved at them in the midst of bees. Charlie honked the horn and the boy ran for his mother. How did people live out here with all the bees?

Nearing a signpost for Tchibanga, they came to a long rust-red puddle that would be a lake by the end of the rainy season. Charlie slipped Twisted Sister into four-wheel drive and eased her into the water, and when he saw how deep it was going to get, he hit the gas. Water lapped over the hood and up the windshield and the truck bounced and slithered and Charlie gunned it, and as they came up out of the water on the other side, he reached over and squeezed Justine's knee.

"Road trip," said Justine, with her thousand-watt smile.

This was their joke now, an expression Charlie had taught her. Justine was excited at having seen the mythical Lékoni Canyon, at passing through the legendary Forest of Bees, at being on this trip with Charlie to the sea, and his heart went out to her in a new rush of love.

"So answer my question," he said, rounding a curve that opened to a good stretch of road, shifting to fourth. Before he could say another word, Justine screamed.

"Elephants!"

Charlie jammed on the brakes and the four wheels locked up.

Two elephants stood partly emerged from the trees. They shied at the sight of the Land Cruiser sliding to a stop. But more and more elephants came forward in a great crackle of breaking branches. Suddenly the herd pressed across the narrow road. They flowed past flank-to-flank, sinuous trunks in the air, gleaming brown eyes regarding the Land Cruiser wildly, jetting urine, flicking their little wire-haired tails aside to dribble out grand clods of dung. They crossed in quick strides, the curved, knobby ridges of their towering backs like a moving gray mountain range, wrinkled hides, heavy feet padding silently by, the smell earthy and musky. The cows strode past between the car and the calves. Young bulls turned to face the Land Cruiser, swinging their massive heads menacingly, their long narrow pink mouths open, tossing their white curved tusks, flapping their ears and coiling their trunks. Then they turned and followed the herd crashing into the trees on the other side of the road. As quickly as they had appeared, the elephants vanished.

Charlie looked at Justine, his heart racing. "Wow." He inched the truck forward, stuck his head out the window and looked down at the elephant tracks.

"Don't get out," Justine said, when he opened his door. "No, Charlie, don't! Elephants are too unpredictable!"

"Have you ever seen elephants before?"

She hadn't.

"Then how do you know?"

He stepped down into the mud. His size fourteen sneakers fit easily inside each track. He walked to where the elephants had entered the forest and contemplated the broken branches and trampled vegetation already bending back.

Justine honked the horn. She was worried the elephants might come back. Charlie smiled and walked to the truck and got in. She berated him for having taken such a risk, and he drew her to him and kissed her.

"This is another thing," he said, looking into her eyes, "that you and I will remember for the rest of our lives."

Mayumba

At dusk, they waited at the end of a miserable road. A light rain fell. They watched the ferry coming toward them across the lagoon, coming to take them to the peninsula where Mayumba lay. They had almost arrived.

"Tell me another story," Charlie said. "But not about ghosts."

After a moment, Justine began. "One time I was in the woods with my mother and I came to a snare. Do you know what that is, a snare?"

"Yes."

"I put my foot in it."

"What! Why?"

"I wanted to see how the animal feels."

"Are you always wondering how other things feel?"

"Whoosh! The snare swung me up in the air, and there I was hanging upside down, yelling my head off, until my mother came and cut me down."

"Served you right. What did she say?"

"She asked me what happened. I told her I put my foot in the snare. She said I was a fool."

"You were," said Charlie, and he leaned over to kiss Justine. "You are a very brave fool."

The rain fell harder as the crossed on the ferry. Mayumba wasn't much bigger than Akièni. Charlie drove along unpaved sandy streets looking for l'Hôtel Club de l'Océan, the hotel that was farthest from town. They found a handmade signpost, and Charlie followed the road out of town to a cement-block beach house. His headlights were on when they came to the open Atlantic.

Justine had not seen the ocean since her days at the nursing school in Libreville. The little hotel didn't have much in the way of amenities. Their room was clean, with a ceiling fan, an air conditioner built into the wall, and over the bed a mosquito net. Until they turned the generator off at eleven, there would be electricity.

Justine took her cold shower first, and after Charlie took his, they went to the restaurant. It was pitch dark outside and the rain fell steadily. The owner's name was Lorraine. She was a friendly woman, anxious to know if they found her accommodations comfortable. She poured Justine an orange soda pop and Charlie a beer. She had been open for two years, she said, and hoped tourists would soon discover Mayumba.

Charlie worried they would have bad weather for their whole stay.

"This rain won't last," said Lorraine, and she took their orders. Fresh grouper was on offer, and Charlie was starving.

"What are some things we can do?"

"Our beaches are very beautiful. They go on for miles and miles."

"So we have heard. What else?"

"Do you like oysters? This is the time of year for oysters, from June to September. This is the last month this year when Mayesiens go diving for oysters."

"Who?"

"Mayesiens, the people of Mayumba. Would you like to go oyster diving?"

Charlie stood up in the pirogue. He wore his swimsuit and sneakers and held the short gardening rake they'd given him, and a woven plastic sack. The boy in back grinned, and then Charlie jumped over the side. Justine cried out and clutched the low gunwales as the canoe rocked crazily, and the boy laughed like it was funny.

Charlie surfaced and smiled at Justine, and her heart reached out to him. He took a deep breath and disappeared. Last night she had clung to his bunching muscles, needing his huge and essential strength, holding onto him as he pressed himself into her, opening herself up to the things that were good, letting herself rise, letting it build, tighter and tighter at the good of it all, until the release came in shattering waves.

The water was nowhere more than ten feet deep, and in many places Charlie could stand on the jagged bottom, hence the sneakers that Lorraine had told him to wear. He found that it was best to float to a spot where the water was clear, and then dive head first with the small rake and the bag and rake the oysters loose and gather them, until the water became too cloudy to see. He could rake a dozen or so oysters into the sack at a time before he had to come up for air. When it was too cloudy in a spot to see anymore, he clung to the canoe, and the boy paddled them to a new place. Other boys in pirogues, seeing a white man diving for oysters, paddled over to watch this unusual spectacle, and get a close hand look at the beautiful woman with him. They dove in with Charlie, bringing more and more oysters to the canoe, until there was a clattering wet rank pile of them glistening at Justine's feet, and Charlie surfaced for the final time with a bleeding cut on his palm.

That evening Lorraine's staff lit a fire to grill the oysters, a feast for Charlie, but Justine had a quiet word with one of the staff, and they brought her goat stew with ripe plantains as the sun sank into the ocean. After they had eaten, the staff brought them sling chairs, and Charlie and Justine grew quiet, reclining side by side in the sound of the surf, holding hands under twinkling stars.

The beach to the south was empty as far as the eye could see. It was a cloudy morning as Justine and Charlie started out. She carried a plastic bag to collect seashells, wearing gym shorts with one of Charlie's tee shirts knotted at the waist, and a straw hat. By mid-morning, they had lost sight of Mayumba. Out on the ocean were fishing canoes.

"Tu sais, je suis jaloux de mes rivaux," said Charlie. The sores on his legs were closing up, healing thanks to the salt water, leaving pink puckers amidst all the black hairs.

"Jealous of what rivals?"

"It seems I have many rivals for your affection."

"What are you talking about?"

"I saw them, yesterday, harvesting the oysters. There are lots of them, and I could see they all have a crush on you."

"Those were little boys!" Justine exclaimed, and she slapped

Charlie on the chest, dropped the bag of shells and ran on her good legs into the surf, younger than her years, old as the sea. He pulled off his tee shirt and ran after her. A wave broke around her thighs and her hat blew off as he caught her, and he wrapped her in his arms and kissed her, and a wave rose up to her breasts, and then he released her, dove in and swam away.

When he waded back out, she stood, bent over, looking at a small orange crab waving one claw in the air. Charlie took Justine's hand and they walked on southward, the sand squeaking under their bare feet, the waves running in with a chuckle, running out with a sigh, rippling about their ankles.

Overhead, a lone gull hung in the air screeching as they came upon a hole on the beach partly filled with drifted sand.

"That was a sea turtle's nest," said Justine. "An animal dug it up and ate the eggs."

"How can you tell?"

"What else would make a hole out here on the beach?"

He didn't have an answer.

The sun came out, instantly blistering. It was nearing noon, nearly the equinox, and the sun straight overhead was so intense they retreated into the shade of some coconut palms.

"Over there is America," said Charlie, leaning back braced on both elbows, looking into the hot wind. "Won't you answer my question about someday maybe studying pharmacology there?"

Justine sat with her legs curled under her. She liked watching how the wind riffled Charlie's hair. When he turned to her, she looked out across the sea. "Not today, Charlie," she said. She opened her plastic bag and laid out the seashells she had collected, and examined them one by one.

"Look," said Charlie, and pointed into the sky at a twin-engine propeller plane banking over the ocean. He shaded his eyes. It bore the Air Gabon markings. The plane turned toward the shore and leveled out, going in for a landing.

They lay back in the shade, and for a while they dozed, and when they awoke the wind had died away, and the flaming sun was halfway down the sky.

"We should start back," said Justine. "Or it will be dark before we get there."

"All right," said Charlie. They got to their feet, but something in the distance further south caught Justine's eye, a quarter mile down the empty beach; there, something coming out of a palm grove, crossing the sand, two, three, then four of them, and a calf, hippos going into the sea.

"Yes, those were hippopotamuses," said Lorraine at dinner. She sat with Charlie and Justine while they ate the sliced sweet bananas and papaya she had brought them for dessert. "It's a good thing you didn't approach them. They're very dangerous if you get between them and the lagoon."

"Do you see them often?"

"No, I don't ever go out on the beach, but others tell me of them."

"I never heard of hippopotamuses going into the ocean," said Charlie. What he knew of hippopotamuses came from American TV.

"Maybe the salt water gets rid of skin parasites," said Lorraine, and she looked into the dark, in the direction of the ocean, toward the plump and crash of the surf.

After a time she asked, "Have you ever seen whales? This time of year they come around."

"Really?"

"Yes. There's a white man who comes this time every year to study them. September is the beginning of the breeding season. He came in on the plane today. He's staying here. He should be coming for dinner any moment now. He'll be going out on a boat every day. Perhaps he could take you along."

The Zodiac banged over the waves, its twin engines screaming in perfect tune. Justine hunched down, out of the spray in the back, looking miserable in an orange life vest.

"Doesn't like boats, does she?" said Tim at the wheel.

"She'll be okay," said Charlie. "She'll admit she enjoyed this, when we're back on dry land, if we see whales."

"Oh we will," said Tim. "It's the season, mate. Humpback love is in the air."

Raised around boats, Tim had grown up in Darwin, a port on the Timor Sea. His weather beaten face showed it. At the bow stood his Gabonese assistant Jacques, hanging on a line and scanning the waters ahead.

"Ten percent of the world's humpbacks migrate through here, near as we can tell. They come through twice a year, to and from the South Atlantic. We've been able to count about two hundred of them each year."

Charlie liked Tim's accent. He worked for the Australian Institute of Marine Science, and his wrinkled brown face was full of stories.

"The aim is to photograph as many flukes as we can spot," said Tim, "and if we get close enough, take DNA samples with a crossbow."

"How do you get a job like this?" Charlie asked, only half kidding.

"Sad to say, you have to get a lot of schooling," said Tim. "A lot more schooling than I ever thought I'd go through. I was a bit of a hell raiser, in my youth. Now I'm a rainmaker. Writing grants is what keeps me out of the classroom."

His teeth flashed bright beneath his sunglasses, against his deep-water tan, and he returned to scanning the horizon.

"It's a game of push and shove out there. Three, four, five males will court a receptive female at one time. They jostle for the prime position alongside her. It'll be a regular scrum. They'll take no notice of us."

"Is it ever dangerous?"

"Pretty hard to flip over a Zodiac, but I promise to keep my eyes peeled. What we're hoping to see is a –"

Jacques sang out and pointed, and Tim swung the wheel to aim the Zodiac at a black and white fin sticking out of the water, and throttled down. As soon as Charlie saw it, the fin slapped the surface of the ocean, and the whale disappeared.

A few seconds later, thirty yards to the left, the back of a whale broke the surface and disappeared again.

"Humpback, all right," said Tim. "Did you see the dorsal?"

"Is it the same one?"

"Pretty sure."

The long black and white fin emerged from the water to the right. Splat! The whale slapped the water with its fin, and disappeared.

Charlie tottered aft, clutching the backs of the seats fixed to the Zodiac's deck to the stern where Justine huddled with her chin tucked into her life vest. "A whale, chérie," he said. "Look."

There it was again, far from them now, the fin moving back and forth, as if waving in greeting. Then the whale slapped the surface and disappeared as the sound came across the water.

Charlie gave Justine his hand. She got up and he helped her make her way forward, balancing in the swell.

"A lone male," said Tim.

Charlie translated. Justine watched where the whale had been, and suddenly a hundred yards to the left, white and black flukes reared hugely above the gray waves, and remained upright, twenty feet high, moving back and forth.

"O-o-o-o," said Justine, in wonder.

"Tail sailing," said Tim.

The whale slipped beneath the waves.

"I bet we got a singer. He'll be diving now. He'll hang upside down, singing his fool head off. Lower the hydrophone, Jacques!" Tim put on a headset and waited, adjusting some dials. Then he grinned. "Want to have a listen?"

He handed a second headset to Justine and gave his own to Charlie.

Coming through the padded earphones was one of the most haunting sounds Charlie had ever heard, a sort of cooing and whooping, the pitch rising and falling, louder, then softer, clicks, then silence, and then the song resumed.

The expression on Justine's face was pure fascination at the fact that a living whale was making this sound.

"Wooo-oooo?" came through the earphones, like a question. "Eeee-yun click-click-click," like an answer.

This was wonderful.

Then nothing, and after a moment Charlie handed the headset to Tim. "Did it stop?"

Tim listened. "Yep," he said. "Get ready, now. We might see a breach."

He turned off the tape, and at his signal, Jacques began reeling in the hydrophone.

"The whale might be getting ready to jump out of the water," Charlie told Justine. She had taken off her headset too.

They waited, the Zodiac bobbing. Jacques and Tim readied expensive-looking cameras with long lenses.

Charlie saw the whale out of the corner of his eye, over Tim's shoulder, far off. It shot out of the water like a missile into the air, and hung for implausible seconds before it crashed into the water on its side in an explosion of spray.

Justine's mouth opened with awe.

Tim had not been fast enough, but Jacques signaled with a thumbs-up that he had gotten the shot. Tim made a mark with a grease pencil on a plastic sheet on a clipboard by the wheel.

"What'll happen now?" asked Charlie.

"I don't reckon he's done yet."

The next breach was closer. As it came out of the water, the whale looked like it was smiling before it splashed back into the sea with a boom.

Tim had gotten that photo, and Jacques had too.

"Quite a way of impressing the gals," said Tim.

The next sight of the whale, it was to their right, on its side with its fin in the air as if waving to them. Then it began slapping the water. Whap! Whap! Whap! Then it disappeared.

"Hope we can get close enough for Jacques to hit him with the crossbow," said Tim. "Be nice to get a DNA sample."

Jacques yelled and pointed just as the whale burst from the water thirty yards from their boat, and Justine cried out at it rising into the air, at its immensity as it rolled, showing its white belly, and then it crashed into the waves with a thump that shook them, and droplets showered down like rain.

That night in their room, the lantern turned low, the window open to the sound of the surf, Justine lay with her face on Charlie's chest. He stroked her flank, her hip, with his hand, nearly healed, the hand she had tenderly bandaged, his nurse. He asked her, "So what do you think?"

"It was good," she said, twisting whorls of the hair on his chest with her forefinger.

"Not that," he said. "I mean about America. Studying pharmacology."

She sighed, a greedy lover. With his left hand, he traced a line to her perfect navel and poked it like a little button.

"So answer me."

Justine came up on one elbow, her breasts bobbling. "Why don't you ever ask what I think about you staying here in Gabon with me?"

"What would I do?"

"Exactly my point," she said, and laid her head back on his chest, lazily smiling.

He was quiet for a while. He saw what she was saying.

"You ask too many questions," she said.

He frowned at the way she had of putting him off. Often, right when he most needed her to be serious, she answered his questions with belligerent questions of her own. It got on his nerves, when he was edging around the biggest question a man could ask a woman. He did not want to imagine ever resuming his life without Justine.

How dark he has become, Justine observed, a dark red-brown, like an old cola nut, except where he wears his shorts, where he remained white as bone, the color he was born to be. His little brown bangala flopped over in his thatch of hair was surprisingly small for such a big man. She liked being with him like this, wearing nothing at all. At first, she hadn't liked him seeing her with the lights on, but she was learning to like the look he got on his face, the look that never changed.

"Why was it so hard for you to say you love me?"

Justine took a moment; long enough for Charlie to think she wasn't going to reply. "It isn't our way," she finally said.

"What do you mean?"

"We are a matrilineal people."

The Batéké traced their descent through the maternal line, a natural outcome in a promiscuous society, where you could never be certain who your father was. Justine had explained this to

Charlie, but why was she bringing it up now?

"What's that got to do with us?"

"Maternal uncles decide the fate of girls."

Was she telling him she couldn't make her own decisions, in her own right, without her mother's brothers involved? If so, he didn't want to hear it.

"Batéké women have many reasons not to express love to a man, Charlie. Men keep us as virtual possessions."

He knew what she was saying. He had seen how some of the village men treated their wives, beating them with impunity, sometimes with sticks. Women could be abandoned, supplanted, cherished or abused, according to the whims of their men.

"Mothers counsel their daughters never to say it. I can't remember once in my life ever hearing the words."

"What words? I love you? You've heard me say it a million times." Charlie stroked one of her nipples with a fingertip.

She lifted her head to him. After kissing a while, she lay down on the pillow beside him. He grew curious, looking at her. "Your mother never once told you she loves you, really?"

"Not that I can remember."

"No one ever did?"

Justine shook her head.

"Ever?" He knew what that was like, to grow up that way. It was something they had in common.

"It's not what you're thinking," she said. "It's not that we don't love one another. It's just that we don't express it."

"Seriously, you're telling me that people don't even say it to their children?"

"No," said Justine. "They say it weakens the child."

Parents did not declare their love to their children, nor praise them for grace, nor quickness, nor strength, nor pluck, nor wit, the very thing they'd taught Charlie in psyche 101 that children had to have, lest they grow up emotionally impaired, which meant he'd grown up emotionally impaired.

Justine was telling him, for a woman to express love to a man was to make herself that man's slave. For a man to say it to a woman was to place himself in her power. This would explain why in the village Charlie had never seen lovers kissing or holding hands or cuddling or gazing moon-eyed at each other, and why the girlfriends back, it now seemed a hundred years ago, behaved the way they had, clambering into his bed and getting the deed done, and then leaving with expectations of a gift. Lying in bed with Justine in a little hotel on an African beach three hundred miles south of the equator, Charlie was seeing deeper into her culture than he ever had before, the means by which, and the reason why Batéké women tried to maintain their independence from men.

"What about us? Can't we be different?"

Justine changed the subject, as she so often did. "Soon my mother will come out of mourning," she said. "Do you know what they will do to her then? They will shave her head. And then they will tear down the house she lives in."

Charlie grunted. "That's stupid. What a waste."

"I am worried for her. Where will she live?"

He was silent, and then he understood why she was bringing this up. She was telling him why she couldn't go to America.

Justine sensed his sudden distress and began stroking his hair. "I have a responsibility for my mother, as I have for my brothers, the twins." She kissed him softly on the lips. "Now I have a question for you."

"What is it?"

"Why do snakes bother you so much?"

Charlie involuntarily drew a sharp breath, like a hiss. "Bend over and show me your asshole." What did little Charlie know? Six years old, living in the horrible house of his earliest beastly memories. "If you tell my mom, I'll kill you!" The older boy with his arm around little Charlie's neck began choking him, his pajama bottoms down around his ankles. It hurt. But it was her bowling night, when she went out with Clyde. They always came back late. He would wake up in the middle of the night, that cold thing slithering along his thigh. A shriek, like a whistle, and he was out of bed, on the floor, frantically pulling off his pajama bottoms. And the thing went flying across the room in the dark. The older boy who kept it in a glass cage flicked on the light, laughing at him. And he picked up the snake and cuddled it writhing by his face and said, "Remember, if you tell my mom, I'll kill you," looking every bit like he meant it.

Justine groaned, and for the briefest instant, Charlie marveled that, somehow, she was experiencing his very worst memory. Then she rolled onto her side, pulled up her knees, curled into a ball and groaned a second time.

"What's wrong?"

Charlie's hand rested on her shoulder, her question forgotten when he saw her stomach clench.

19. The Promise of Heat

Libreville

T he first streaks of dawn lit the eastern sky when Darlene
pulled into the residence driveway, back from the gym. She
liked to drive herself, no chauffer, before morning traffic grew
hectic. Awakening birds chirped in the trees when she got out of
the car and entered through the kitchen door. Bernice in her blue
uniform and white apron was grinding coffee beans. The smell of
bagels filled the kitchen.

"Oh what a lovely aroma," said Darlene. Bernice laughed
proudly. She carefully guarded her baking recipes: bagels, bread,
cheesecake and pies, her ticket to continuous employment as the
Ambassador's chef, though her delights were wasted on Darlene,
who took but the one bite or two she permitted herself before
taking the treats to share with Embassy staff.

In the shower, Darlene found herself thinking about the cable
that had gone out requesting guidance for dealing with the coming
election. The IFES assessment report prepared by the Canadian,
Marcel Marais, concluded that, in all probability the ruling party
intended to rig the election. What should be the official U.S.
Government position? Two weeks had passed since the cable went
in, and still there was no response. A reply was no doubt working
its way through the queue of noncritical clearances, noncritical
compared to the potential war brewing in Kuwait. Crooked
elections in an obscure African country would be on no one's but
the Gabon desk officer's list of priorities.

Darlene debated what to wear to work. She held up a dark
green wool pantsuit in front of a full-length mirror and judged how
it went with different blouses on hangers. Suddenly, a panorama of
American citizens waking up in Gabon rolled past her mind's eye:
oil workers on rigs off the coast, evangelical missionaries at prayer

in their remote stations, a dozen or so businessmen awakening alone in their Libreville hotel rooms, some seventy-odd Peace Corps volunteers emerging from their mud huts. Darlene sensed that one of the volunteers was in danger. Then she shook her head and chose a white silk blouse before contemplating the contents of her jewelry box. The feeling lingered. Someone was in danger. Such presentiments came to her from time to time. She selected a necklace of Ghanaian beads. She did not believe in premonitions.

Franceville

Mist hugged the ground. The morning sun rose above the trees, dull red and promising heat. Never sure which of his keys opened which padlock, Hector got it wrong again. Once more, he promised himself to mark the keys with paint. Theft was a problem in the provincial capital of Franceville, unlike the villages of Boundji or Obia. He'd welded rebar burglar bars on the magasin windows and affixed multiple padlocks to the door. He tried a different key, and the first padlock dropped open.

Timo watched, rubbing his bare arms to ward off the chill. "Il fera chaud," he said with a yawn, predicting a hot day.

Caterpillar, the long-snouted yellow dump truck loomed on the school grounds, crammed to capacity with lumber and beaded with dew. Chickens and goats wandered about, and a cock crowed. Schoolchildren, still at home eating breakfast, would soon arrive, and soon the air would be full of their voices. Timo had arrived late the night before from the lumber mill down in the Ogooué-Lolo town of Bidoungi.

"Je vais benner," said Timo, suggesting he'd dump all the two-by-fours and planks like a load of gravel.

"No," said Hector. "Too many boards get broken that way. We'll wait for the crew to arrive, and unload the truck by hand."

Timo shrugged. He did whatever the volunteers directed him to do with the load when making deliveries. And for the time being, while Charlie was gone on the trip to familiarize himself with the logistical needs of the school sites, Hector was in charge of Timo's schedule.

"Notre frère a fait longtemps."

"You mean Charlie? He has been gone a long time, now that you mention it."

"Because of the girl, maybe."

"Yes," said Hector, smiling at the thought of the beauty Charlie had landed. "Maybe they ran off and holed up somewhere. Can't say as I'd blame him if he did."

Three workers approached. Two more men rounded the corner of the school from the other direction. They shook hands with Timo.

Hector shook each worker's hand. "Good morning," he said. "Let's start unloading."

Plateau

Rebecca drove north toward Okouya in the early morning light, the sun rising red to her right. During the rainy season, she had learned, a red sun in the morning usually meant that by midday thunderheads would fill the sky, bringing a deluge in the afternoon.

"C'est déjà octobre," she said. "Incroyable." Somehow, living in a village where the rhythm of life seemed so slow, each unchanging day filled with small repetitions, the seasons a constant cycle, the months were speeding past.

"Yes, October already," said Georges.

"This time last year I was a stagiaire in Boundji."

Georges sat by the window. A girl named Lucille was between them. Rebecca's boyfriend Philbert rode in the back, angry that his woman had not insisted he ride in the front with her. In fact, Philbert felt he should be driving, and it made him even angrier that Rebecca never let him drive.

Rebecca didn't know how much longer she would keep Philbert around. He had begun to bore her. To make sure he couldn't take the truck on joyrides, just to show her he could, show her who was boss, she hid the keys. Philbert fancied himself quite the big shot, and told his friends, who else in all the Batéké Plateau could boast of having a white woman? His brother Georges was infinitely more interesting to talk to. And Lucille had a role to play as the leader of the Otou dance group. It had taken a lot of persuading to get her to agree to work on Georges' election campaign. Then Lucille had to convince the rest of the girls to become the animatrices. The girls would be paid out of the meager funds from the Party that Georges had recently received. This was quite a step up for Lucille. Her previous work experience had been limited to running the village bar for her father, for which she wasn't paid. She was the prettiest girl in Otou, with a high forehead and a strong jaw, an impressive bust and an hourglass figure, a bottom that drew men's eyes whenever she walked by. Rebecca was mildly amazed that Lucille had no child, or boyfriend. "I wonder where Charlie is anyway?" said Rebecca.

"Who?" asked Georges.

"The giant American who used to live in Okouya. You know him, Lucille."

"Yes," said Lucille. Charlie had once made a pass at her. "He is travelling with the kakouma woman, the nurse from Akièni."

Rebecca didn't bother to ask what 'kakouma' meant. Her mind was racing ahead. The promised Party pagnes hadn't arrived, so the troupe riding in back didn't have a campaign outfit to wear. But the girls, the drummers and Philbert were ready for the speech in Okouya. Rebecca had written it and had helped Georges rehearse. He hadn't needed much coaching. Like most African men, once he got going, he could talk nonstop. Even so, Rebecca drew on everything she could remember from her high school debate club to get Georges ready. He was a natural orator with none of the usual problems. He stood with his feet planted shoulder width apart and didn't shift his weight from foot to foot. He projected from his diaphragm and wasn't awkward with his hands. He didn't stumble over words and he made eye contact with his audience. He could pitch his voice high enough to be clearly audible, but not so high-pitched as to sound strained. His rhythm was musical and his cadence measured.

"Remember your timing," she said. "Remember all the places in the speech where you want people to applaud, and especially where you want them to laugh. Don't rush it, Georges."

"I won't." Georges was relaxed. He knew he had a natural gift. Rebecca had first seen it when he made the impromptu speech in Otou when the ruling party was delivering the rice and a cow, and then a second time when he gave the version she had worked with him to polish in front of a much larger crowd in Akièni. Georges knew instinctively that laughter was the best way to win people over, which he had to do before he shocked them with the forbidden things he had to say, the things in the speech Rebecca was becoming so proud of.

On her advice, Georges had stopped wearing the black leather jacket and the white basketball shoes and started carrying a small whiskbroom, a symbol that connected with the women. The speech made the crowds drawn in by Lucille and the Otou dance group nervous at first. Her candidate was breaking a taboo by denouncing Bongo's culture of corruption. He promised them that the PND was a new broom.

"A new broom always sweeps clean! We need a new broom to sweep out the corruption!" Georges proclaimed, provoking shouts of frightened laughter from the crowd, surprised to hear anyone say through a microphone what everyone knew but had always been afraid to say because it was forbidden. "A new broom!" Georges yelled. "A new broom!" waving the broom. "A new broom! A new broom!"

Lucille and the prettiest girls from Otou clapped, gestured and smiled at the young men in front as they took up the chant. Georges waved the broom back and forth over his head, "A new broom! A new broom! A new broom!" More and more people began chanting, until the whole crowd roared in unison, "A new broom! A new broom! A new broom!"

Rebecca had a cover story. She was going to Onga with her travelling mattress lashed to the roll bar to visit the other Americans along the way. According to plan, she would stop in every village with a Peace Corps school under construction and spend the night with the volunteer posted there. That would give Lucille and the Otou dance group plenty of time to draw a crowd with their dancing, singing and drumming. With the crowd in place, Georges would deliver his speech. Anyone who asked, Rebecca would say she was en tournée visiting volunteers. She had simply given these people a ride. That was her story, behind the wheel of her truck on her way to Okouya, with the sun rising red to her right.

Franceville

Dabrian navigated the curving streets of the Cité de la Caisse in irritation. Ten minutes and he still couldn't find Charlie's new place. He'd had the dream again, in the hours before dawn, drifting down the river of danger on a raft artfully carved, ringed all around with fertility figures, floating easily in the gentle current, until he rounded a bend and the foul smell greeted him. The current grew swifter, sweeping him downstream and he could hear rapids up ahead. He sensed the winged, dog-faced creatures with claws waiting, and leaped overboard and sank, expecting to drown. Miraculously, he bobbed to the surface and began to swim, expertly, with the power of an Olympian, two yards toward the riverbank for every ten the river swept him downstream. He swam closer and closer to land until he could feel his feet touch the muddy river bottom. He sloshed ashore through water up to his chest, up to his hips, up to his knees, and fell to all fours and crawled out of the river gasping for breath. He needed a place to hide, and wriggled underneath a bush, pushed a branch from his face, and saw Charlie's girlfriend, Justine, lying there.

Dabrian reached an intersection he'd already been through and braked. "Where the hell's Charlie's damned house?"

Charlie hurried up onto the front porch, unlocked the door and raced back to the truck for Justine. He had driven through the night, stopping repeatedly so she could vomit, though she'd managed to sleep the past couple hours, until just before they reached Franceville. She shrugged off his hands, got out of the truck on her own and walked onto the porch, weak, bent slightly at the waist from the cramping.

When the first sharp cramp struck her like a punch, Justine feared another miscarriage. Then the nurse in her head took over. The pain associated with a spontaneous abortion began in the lower back; this was in her abdomen, and was she even pregnant? After the first spasms subsided, it wasn't that bad, and she managed to sleep. In the morning, she felt good enough to sit in the shade of the coconut trees and watch the waves. That night, the pain and cramping returned.

Charlie said, "That's it. We're going to see a doctor here in

Mayumba."

Justine didn't want that, so they checked out and he drove straight through the night to Franceville where Charlie insisted he would take her at once to see Dr. Yves. But Justine didn't want that either.

"All I want is to get to Akièni where I can rest in my own bed. The twins need me, anyway. I'll shower and then rest for a while. A hot shower will make me feel better. You go gas up and get more money. Your money order should be waiting for you, isn't that what you said? You need a few hours' sleep too."

She went into the bathroom and turned on the shower just as a diesel came roaring up the driveway.

It's Hector, Charlie thought, until he saw Air Afrique, Dabrian behind the wheel.

20. Bongo

Libreville

The Ambassador strode out of the chancery dressed in a charcoal gray business jacket and skirt with a cream blouse. She descended the Embassy steps in high heels and settled into the principal's seat of the Chevrolet, on her way to meet with President Bongo for the first time since presenting her diplomatic credentials eighteen months earlier. USIS Director Rossow slid across the backseat next to Darlene, followed by Harry, the Peace Corps APCD, taking the place of director Eaton, who was out of the country on annual leave. Tom Hughes sat in front.

A Gabonese motorcycle cop waited outside the Embassy wall. He turned on his siren and blue lights as the black iron gate began to slide open, and led the way for the dark Chevrolet coming out with an American flag snapping above the front fender, signifying Ambassador Jones was inside, the car itself American territory.

The Presidential Palace was located not far from the U.S. Embassy. The gate in front of the five-story structure of weather-stained marble swung open, and the Chevrolet followed the motorcycle up a circular drive to a red carpet where a twelve-piece brass band waited. An official opened Darlene's door. As soon as she stepped out, the musicians sweating in red wool uniforms struck up a rendition of the Star Spangled Banner. Darlene and her entourage stood at attention until the band had finished; then the chief of protocol led them to the great front entrance flanked by guards wearing tall military shakos festooned with ostrich feathers, dark tunics cinched at the waist with chalk white belts, and dress puttees above black boots spit-shined to a mirror gleam.

President Bongo's Palace had been built during the oil boom of the 1970s at a cost of nearly one billion dollars, paid for with windfall revenues. The interior décor demonstrated very little evidence of restraint, or taste. Nothing was understated. Ranks of white plaster replicas of ancient statues of Greek and Roman gods lined the vestibule walls. The chief of protocol led them up a marble stairway and down a hall gaudy with red velvet and gold foil wallpaper, past a darkened, cavernous ballroom. At a door that slid open like a supermarket entrance, he bowed Darlene into a waiting room furnished with brown naugahyde sofas and chairs. Framed tourism posters adorned the walls. A large color television beside a sickly potted palm played French music videos, the volume turned low. A second sliding door remained closed.

Darlene had warned the three young Americans to say nothing careless in the Palace, where the rooms were likely bugged. Still, the three young people with Darlene could not help exchanging snickering glances.

The icy air bore the faint odor of mildew. Tom wore a light gray suit with a conservative tie. Pamela looked competent in a taupe pantsuit. They would take the official notes. Harry wore a suit he might have owned in high school. His wrists hung out the sleeves. The jacket was too tight in the shoulders. But the Ambassador had expressly ordered him to dress formally, so he had rushed to Marché Mont-Bouët to buy the ill-fitting suit he had on. With his moth-eaten haircut and ragged beard, Darlene regretted having him along, but the Office of the President had been clear whom she should bring. Bongo wanted the Peace Corps represented.

Time passed without discussion, in silence save for the French musicians gyrating to muted rock and roll on the color TV. The Americans studied the tourism posters, each slightly askew, each bearing the parrot logo of Air Gabon. There was a man paddling a dugout canoe across placid waters, coconut trees leaning out over a white sand beach, smiling little girls carrying wooden bowls on their heads, a small herd of short-tusked forest elephants curling their trunks.

After ten minutes, Darlene said quietly, "This isn't normal. Someone of appropriate rank should be here in the room with us."

No sooner had Darlene voiced her puzzlement than the interior door whisked open, and the chief of protocol gestured them into a high-ceilinged room filled with ornate Louis XIV furniture, the walls adorned with giant gilt-framed paintings of cavalry charges and naval battles from the age of sail, all of it authentically old, and priceless. Tinted picture windows draped with heavy mauve curtains held open with silk ropes overlooked the estuary. Strangely, there were many dozens of clocks on the walls, all shapes and sizes, each bearing the portrait of Omar Bongo.

A door opened and the President entered, a diminutive man dressed in a costly grand boubou of pale blue brocade that rustled as he moved toward them past an over-sized desk trailed by three men in dark suits.

"Bonjour, Madame l'Ambassadrice," said President Bongo, shaking Darlene's hand. "Permit me to say how nice it is to see you again."

"A pleasure to see you as well, Monsieur le Président."

Bongo's cabinet had nearly fifty ministers. Three accompanied him, the ministers of Foreign Affairs, Culture and Sports, and Rural Development. After the chief of protocol introduced them, Darlene reciprocated, introducing her Political Officer, her Cultural Affairs Officer, and the acting head of the Peace Corps. With the formalities over, the chief of protocol left the room.

Bongo looked pleased shaking Pamela's hand, such an attractive young woman. "The English language lab your cultural center donated to the Palace has proven very useful," he said, speaking French, for his own well-publicized attempts to learn English had not yielded results.

Pamela smiled, "I'm glad to hear that, Monsieur le Président, but the donation was made many years before I arrived in Libreville."

Abruptly, Bongo told his ministers, "Show your counterparts to the next room. I want to speak with the Ambassador alone."

The ministers accompanied Tom, Pamela and Harry into an adjoining conference room, and as the door slid shut, Bongo motioned for Darlene to sit in an elaborately carved armchair, very old and fragile, embroidered with worn tapestry in a lion motif. It didn't look comfortable, and was not.

The President's boubou crinkled like a paper bag as he took a seat on a mismatched couch beside her. "I trust you have been well, Madame l'Ambassadrice."

"Thank you, Monsieur le Président, I am quite well. Thank you for asking."

"I understand," he said, his melodious voice suddenly soothing, "that you are here without your husband. That must be very difficult for you." His soulful eyes searched hers for a sign.

The question was inappropriate, and Darlene met the President's gaze head on. "Pas du tout," she said coolly.

Bongo possessed a strong face, handsome enough, although Darlene thought his Fu Manchu mustache out of date and rather ridiculous on a man his age, a head of state. For a quarter century, the President had wielded unquestioned power. He wore his authority easily as he peered at her in a way that made her as uncomfortable as the chair upon which she sat.

"Madame l'Ambassadrice," he said, "I hope we can have a frank conversation."

"Of course," said Darlene. From his comment about her absent husband, she worried what he might say next.

The President's smile stretched the arc of his mustache wide, and he slid closer and leaned to her across the arm of the couch. "I wish to know how to develop closer relations with you."

Darlene groaned inwardly and thought instantly of the former Miss Venezuela, who accepted an all-expense paid trip to Gabon on the pretext of hosting a beauty contest, and ended up trapped in the Presidential Palace for two weeks. The poor woman's ordeal was a legend on the diplomatic circuit. Darlene focused on her hands folded in her lap. Can this really be happening? she wondered in dread.

The President waited for her to reply.

"It goes without saying," said Darlene, and she looked at Bongo, "that the United States seeks good relations between our two countries."

"I am very glad to hear it," said Bongo. "I wish to speak truthfully with you, Madame l'Ambassadrice."

"By all means," said Darlene. She hoped she had misapprehended the President's intentions.

"I am weary of the weight of France on my back," he said. The broad smile left his face. "I want to know what it would take to form a closer relationship with the United States."

Then it clicked: Shaft! Darlene could barely keep from laughing out loud. Bongo looked like Hollywood's first black action hero, of almost two decades ago. Trying hard to conceal her amusement, Darlene said, "My government is pleased, Monsieur le Président, with the excellent relations we have always enjoyed with Gabon."

Bongo's smile twisted into the smirk of someone seeing through pretense. "You should know, Madame l'Ambassadrice, that my first position in government was in the Ministry of Foreign Affairs. I learned how the game is played at a very young age. I know your government's policy. You have consigned my country to the French sphere of influence." He waited for Darlene's reaction. When she made none, meeting his rather small eyes, he said, "I would like to know how we can change that."

"What changes do you have in mind, precisely, Monsieur le Président?"

"As I'm sure you well know, Madame l'Ambassadrice, geopolitical structures being what they are, we dare not make a move without assurances beforehand."

"Could you be more specific?"

"I would like a sign from Washington."

"What sort of sign, Monsieur le Président?"

For a moment, Bongo stared at the backs of his hands resting on his knees. It gave Darlene an opportunity to study the famous face printed on the currency, the face gazing out from the walls of all the banks and hotel lobbies, the face seen every night on national TV, the face on the many dozens of clocks displayed in the room.

This is a man of cunning and power, she reminded herself. He is capable of great cruelty. "What sign do you seek from Washington?" she asked.

"You were an officer in naval intelligence," he said, lifting his gaze, "and you have studied international affairs at a renowned university. You are the author of an important book. I know you understand global politics very well. You are a citizen of the most powerful country in the history of the world."

Darlene inclined her head, a small bow of acknowledgement, but she made no reply.

"And you are also a daughter of Africa." The remark struck a chord with Darlene. Seeing the reaction in her eyes, Bongo smiled again. "As such, you are my sister. And, my sister, you cannot dispute that we live in an unjust world, an unbalanced system, strong nations that exercise hegemony over weak nations carved out by the imperial powers. African nations are mere fragments of territory, really," he said, compelling her sympathy. "Our national aspirations are constrained by arbitrary borders we did not design. In the grand scheme of things, we are powerless. Gabon has few instruments at its disposal. Perhaps the most potent tool we have is nationalization." He drew the word out, watching for a reaction that Darlene was careful not to make. "Of course, wholesale nationalization would be a calamitous step, I know, for I am a believer in free markets. I have always been a staunch anticommunist."

Darlene could not resist. "Gabon is a member of the Nonaligned Movement. That is hardly an anticommunist organization. And Gabon is a member of OPEC, a cartel that is hardly supportive of free trade principles, Monsieur le Président."

Bongo chuckled. "Certainly you understand the politics behind the reasons we join such organizations, Madame l'Ambassadrice. We are a moderating voice in both institutions. We are a friend of the West."

They stared stubbornly at one another, until Darlene said, "I assure you, Monsieur le Président, the United States values its friends."

"And we value the friendship of all nations that support our aspirations. As I said, Madame l'Ambassadrice, quite simply I have asked you to come because I seek to strengthen our bilateral ties."

"Well, Monsieur le Président, with respect," said Darlene, "a good way to start might be greater transparency."

Bongo's smile collapsed into a frown. "Transparency is a Western term."

"Ah, but is not accountability to the people an attribute of traditional African societies? Were not all of the great African chieftains of yore accountable in this sense? I think of the great Makoko, for example, the last leader of the unified Batéké."

"Such terms do not translate well, from one time and place to another."

"But the essential attributes of greatness are universal, Monsieur le Président, and so, first and foremost, let me congratulate you on your splendid speech. The United States supports the historic transition to the new system of governance that you have embarked upon."

"Ah," said the President, his annoyance fading into uncertainty.

"But we have concerns, nevertheless." Darlene willed her face stern, and in a voice befitting the Ambassador of the United States of America, she said, "About the matter of Joseph Rendjambé. The lack of progress in the investigation of his death is concerning."

This angered Bongo anew. "That matter is with our police."

"But, Monsieur le Président, in the matter of the investigation, there is one step you could take to strengthen bilateral ties. You will recall, in your capacity as Minister of the Interior, we extended an offer of assistance from the FBI crime laboratory, immediately after Monsieur Rendjambé was found dead. You could accept our offer to help, Monsieur le Président."

"We have already informed your government that the offer is under consideration. Meanwhile, our police investigators are doing all that can be done."

"Quite apart from the technical reasons for accepting the offer, Monsieur le Président, there are, may I say, political reasons. If you should accept the offer, it would help assuage certain lingering suspicions."

Bongo looked out the window toward the ocean to control himself. After a moment, he turned back to her, thunder on his brow. "What exactly are you implying?"

Darlene backpedaled from suggesting outright that the United States believed Bongo had ordered Rendjambé's death. "Monsieur le Président, please know that my government is very impressed with the great foresight and courage you have consistently displayed. Our offer stands, extended in a spirit of friendship and cooperation. We wish to assist during this momentous time as the Gabonese people go forward, under your wise leadership, in establishing a multiparty democracy. You are leading the way in Africa, and we are very pleased with the progress thus far, guided by your deep insight and your vast experience. We wish only to see the elections succeed in burnishing your reputation in the world. Think of your legacy!"

Bongo looked at her levelly. "As I said, the offer is under

consideration."

"Well then, Monsieur le Président, perhaps we could return to the reason why you asked to see me today? What exactly do you have in mind when you say you seek to strengthen bilateral ties?"

A smile began playing in the corners of Bongo's mouth. Darlene had delivered a shot that had knocked him back on his heels. The knowledge that he was dealing with a very capable woman reanimated him. "In the matter I wish to discuss," he began, "I know the United States will want assurances of our good faith. So let me proffer them now, Madame l'Ambassadrice. I hope you will so inform your government."

"Rest assured, Monsieur le Président, that I shall dutifully convey your assurances of good faith."

"Your government should be aware, as is the government of France, that whereas we are a small nation, and not strong, we are nevertheless prepared to defend our rights."

"Of course, that is natural and as it should be. May I know; is there a particular issue that will require your government to defend its rights?"

"I want you to know that we are prepared, Madame l'Ambassadrice, to disclose the results of the official review of the oil concessions we conducted almost two years ago. You are, of course, aware we met with the executives of your top petroleum companies as part of the review. The report is over there on my desk."

"You said you plan to disclose the findings?"

"I am prepared to release the report. But I am holding onto it for now, pending a response from the government of France to certain questions we have put to them. If we do not receive a satisfactory response soon, then we will consider releasing the report, revealing the full details of the terms of the oil concessions to the entire world. Let me say that certain other nations, including the Powers that are friendly to the plight of the small, would not be shocked by what is in there. I am confident that international opinion would understand if we were to seek recourse."

"I see." Darlene made no other comment. If Bongo was reviving the offer he had made to hand over the French oil concessions to American companies, the offer he had made twice before, in veiled terms both times, during two previous spats with Paris, she had orders not to encourage him. She was to do nothing to upset France, whose promised contribution of troops to the invasion being planned to liberate Kuwait was essential. Alternatively, any veiled threat Bongo might make about turning to Moscow or Beijing carried little weight under current circumstances.

"We are simply seeking better terms, Madame l'Ambassadrice, and I want you to know that those terms could be of interest to the American oil industry."

So, that was it indeed. "That is your message, Monsieur le Président?"

"Quite so. For some time relations with our former colonizer have been – strained. I know that you are aware of this, through our mutual friend."

Had he just referred to Philippe Berrier? Darlene had been expecting he might.

"He often spoke highly of you, that you are a woman of true character and discretion. Are you aware that he has been recalled?"

"Recalled?" Darlene was surprised, then instantly sorry to learn Philippe had gone. Her face must have showed it, because Bongo smiled knowingly.

"As of yesterday. The French have yet made no official announcement. I thought that perhaps Monsieur Berrier might have telephoned you. I know he often shared information with you."

"That is the nature of diplomacy, Monsieur le Président, as you are well aware. Embassies share information. In fact, on several occasions he brought me messages he said were directly from you. I often wondered why you did not deliver them to me in person."

"Perhaps I should have," said Bongo. "I'm sure you are wondering why he was recalled. You must have your suspicions. You are aware of our, shall I say preferences in the matter of French politics. You know that Monsieur Berrier was not supportive of the Socialists' avowed intentions to end certain longstanding agreements made by President de Gaulle. That is why I insisted he be named Ambassador. In the naming of ambassadors, I have rather unusual prerogatives with Paris, as I imagine you know."

Bongo smiled mildly, waiting to see her response, but Darlene remained silent, keeping her face a polite and attentive mask.

"I know that you are aware of the role that the son of President Mitterrand is playing in our political transition. A most unhelpful role, I wish to make clear."

In his eyes searching hers, Darlene thought she could see a glint of desperation. The strongman long accustomed to near absolute power was confronted by world events that were crowding him in a direction he did not wish to go. He wanted Darlene to feel they were conniving together.

"I am trying to find a way to articulate to you, Madame l'Ambassadrice, that we are in a position to offer something that could greatly benefit very important interests in the United States, Texans who are friends of President Bush, as a matter of fact. But as I have said, we cannot make any move in your direction without prior assurances from your side."

"As to this offer that could greatly benefit very important interests in the United States," said Darlene, "the friends of President Bush you referred to, I assume you mean Texas oil companies. You certainly understand, Monsieur le Président, that I am not empowered to enter into any agreements. I would have to consult my government."

Bongo nodded slightly.

"Then I shall convey your message to my government. All I can promise is that I will return with a response, as soon as I have one. That is all I can say for now."

"Then I will wait for you," said President Bongo.

There was not time in the short car ride back to the Embassy for Darlene to debrief her team, and she would not have done so in the hearing of the chauffeur, in any case. The Marine inside the blast-resistant cage in the chancery buzzed them through, and she led the way upstairs and down the hushed hallway. They passed the dark-paneled conference room, but she didn't direct them inside. She led them instead to the end of the hall, to a metal door with a keypad beside it. Tom tapped in a number, and there was a click. With some effort, Tom pulled on the door. It made a sucking sound as it opened, and he swung it wide. He reached inside and snapped on overhead fluorescent lights, and stepped aside for the

Ambassador to enter first.

Entering last, Harry realized this was the Bubble, the Embassy's secure room. He had heard rumors of its existence, but he didn't have a secret clearance and wasn't supposed to know of it, much less go inside. The walls curved, like the interior of the hull of a boat. The four of them took seats at a blond wooden table, their faces pale in the bright overhead light. Harry became aware of a faint rushing sound from machinery, presumably blocking electronic surveillance. The rushing sound and the curved walls of the closed space made it seem to Harry they were inside a moving submarine.

In the room where they were able to speak freely, the Ambassador asked what had transpired in the conference room at the Palace.

"The Minister of Foreign Affairs talked the most," said Tom, consulting his notes. "He made a speech about the importance Gabon attaches to improving relations with the United States. There wasn't much of substance to what he said. About fifty Gabonese students are currently studying petroleum engineering at various graduate programs in the States. The Government of Gabon pays their full tuition. The Minister stressed that fact, mentioning specifically students attending the University of Texas, Texas A&M, and Texas Tech."

"That fits," said Darlene. "Bongo's trying to interpret American politics according to a logic he understands. He's thinking in what he assumes are American tribal terms. Pamela?"

"The Minister of Culture and Sports has never impressed me much," said the USIS director. "He asked whether we would be able to expand our International Visitors program. He said, all selected in the past have returned very impressed by what they experienced. He mentioned Charles Ndong specifically, the lecturer in African social systems at Omar Bongo University, the one we sent on a tour of American colleges."

"Well, what do you know," said Darlene. "Isn't that the man who passed us that amazingly detailed profile of major opposition figures? So it seems, in fact, he was being steered by Bongo's people, as I suspected."

"One could conclude that's the case," said Pamela. "And maybe now they're even telling us as much. Maybe they're even telling us we owe them one."

"I'll have to think about that," said Darlene. "Harry?"

Harry didn't understand what was happening. He cleared his throat nervously. "The Minister of Rural Development," he began, glancing at his sparse notes, "said basically they really like the Peace Corps. He said the big push to build schools on the Batéké Plateau responds to one of President Bongo's top priorities. He said that with the elections coming up, the government expects volunteers will respect their obligation to stay out of the campaigning."

"Tom, what did you say to that?"

"I told them you issued written instructions to all the volunteers, reminding them of their obligation."

Darlene nodded. "Good."

"Can you share with us, Ambassador?" Tom asked, with his look of thoughtful concern, "what President Bongo said to you?"

Harry felt uneasy that he was allowed to hear any of this. The Ambassador noticed and said. "You're not to tell anyone what's being said in here, Harry. You may not tell anyone that you were even in this room, or that this room exists. Do you understand?"

"Yes," replied Harry. "Yes, Ambassador Jones."

"We'll have to write a cable, Tom, about what the President said. Nothing unexpected. He's making the same move in our direction that he made two times previously. He did the same thing both times Mitterrand won election. He made the same pitch to Ambassador McNamara nine years ago. He told me he'd welcome it if we supplanted the French in Gabon. He hinted of oil concessions on generous terms if we did. He specifically mentioned the friends of President Bush, the Texas oil men."

"Texas oil men?" Tom's brow furrowed deeper above his wire-rimmed glasses. "Ambassador, you're right," he said, "that fits."

21. Show Us

Franceville

"I have done all that I can," Dr. Muengo confessed when Charlie returned from the plateau with Justine's brother Jonas and her mother, Mama Angélique. The three joined Dr. Muengo at Justine's bedside in the crowded Akièni hospital ward on a hot afternoon. "I have given her an injection to ease her suffering, a mild sedative to make her sleep. I have injected her with antibiotics, trying to figure out the cause of her abdominal pain. I am very concerned. Justine is my most capable nurse."

The French-trained physician looked tired, overworked and underpaid, but glad to be out of his native Zaire, where the government appeared to be on the verge of collapse. Charlie was just as tired. He had slept little during the week since leaving Mayumba. He had spent long hours behind the wheel, but concern for Justine kept him alert. He knew he was running on adrenaline.

"Her case doesn't appear to be gynecological. If she had something simple like the stomach flu, or food poisoning, I would expect improvement. But it has been a week since the symptoms began, and she is not improving."

Dr. Muengo waited again for Jonas to translate to Mama Angélique. He noticed Charlie studying him, and when their eyes met, Charlie looked down at Justine. Dr. Muengo's gaze followed to the nurse who had once been his lover, and now was in love with Charlie. Her face was drawn, and she slept uneasily, beads of sweat on her brow.

"There are no symptoms of a urinary tract infection. Originally, I thought perhaps gallstones, or kidney stones, but these too would have passed by now. Every day she says the pain gets worse. Even though there is no swelling of the thyroid, the growing mass in her abdomen and the weight that she's losing suggest this might actually be pancreatic cancer."

Cancer! Charlie was shocked at the word. His over-worked mind raced at once in a thousand directions, touching on all contingencies. I will take her to America for treatment, he decided in a flash, and in the same instant wondered, where will I get the money?

"I suggest that you take her to Franceville," said Dr. Muengo, "or better still, to Libreville. She needs to see a specialist."

Jonas translated for Mama Angélique, dressed in widows' black, and as the schoolteacher spoke, the thin face of Justine's mother grew even grimmer. She replied to Jonas in Téké.

"We must go to Franceville," Jonas said to Charlie, snapping him back, "and we must bring the twins with us."

Charlie hesitated. "Can we move Justine?"

"Yes," said Dr. Muengo, "the sedative I've given her will enable you to move her without too much discomfort."

"We have to go, Charlie," said Jonas. Charlie had never seen him more serious. "We have to go to Franceville, right now!"

"Please call me Yves," said Dr. Monteux, a Frenchman not much older than Charlie. The two of them had met at Natalia's.

Charlie ignored Dr. Monteux. "What are you going to do?" he demanded, expecting Yves to be a doctor first, and a damned good one.

"I have gone over the work done in Akièni. Dr. Muengo is very competent, I must say. I double-checked everything, and he did exactly what I would have done."

Unnoticed by the others, Justine began to stir, awaking surprised to find herself in Franceville General Hospital. Charlie, her mother and brothers listened intently to the young doctor. She recalled meeting him at Natalia's dinner party, Yves, the Frenchman with gray eyes. Jonas translated for her mother. She smiled to see her mother, Jonas and the twins, but frowned knowing the twins were not in school. Quickly, she realized that Dr. Monteux had taken over her case. "Can I have some water?" she asked.

Everyone looked at Justine. Her mother sat on the bed and helped her daughter drink from a plastic bottle. Justine smiled when her mother took her hand, but lacked strength to speak, worn down from pain, woozy from the drug. She had trouble following what Dr. Monteux was saying to Jonas and Charlie.

"There is no inflammation of the bowels showing in the x-rays. The x-rays reveal no mass associated with the pancreas. I've drained the fluid from the swelling in her abdomen, and taken blood, and I've sent the samples to our lab for testing. We should have the results tomorrow."

The next morning, Charlie returned to the hospital with Jonas and the twins from his new house in the Cité de la Caisse. Justine's mother had spent the night in the hospital, sleeping on a mat on the floor beside her daughter's bed.

Four beds crowded the uncomfortably hot room, all of them occupied by female patients watched over by relatives. Charlie managed to wangle two chairs from the nurse's station for himself and Jonas. The twins and Mama Angélique sat on the edge of Justine's bed when Yves entered wearing a white lab coat, a stethoscope around his neck, carrying a clipboard.

"Good news," he said. "The blood work came back normal, and there is nothing unusual in the fluid sample. But this leaves us with no indication about the cause of her condition. The pain is consistent with ulcerative colitis, but in that case, she would have blood in her stools, and diarrhea. Instead, she is constipated. I can't say what is causing the swelling. And if the swelling is just some sort of mysterious fluid retention, then what is causing the pain?"

Nurses drained the fluid from Justine's abdomen in the afternoon, but that night, the swelling returned. It was the same the following day. As the sun set on the second evening, Charlie bewailed his beautiful girl wasting away. Her appetite was gone. Justine couldn't sleep without medication, and she was no longer able to move her bowels. A look of fear had crept into her eyes, her beautiful almond-shaped eyes, receding into her head.

"Isn't there something more you can do?" Charlie pleaded with Yves.

Dr. Monteux's senior colleague, Dr. Dumas, the co-director of the hospital, took charge of the case. Tall and angular, a severe-looking man, he seemed faintly to disapprove of Charlie's relationship with an African woman. Charlie understood that his involvement as the white boyfriend complicated the case, but he reasoned that the French in Gabon dealt with such situations all the time. He could endure the senior doctor's judgmental air, as long as they found the cause of Justine's suffering. But they weren't able to find a cause.

"For a more accurate diagnosis," Dr. Dumas concluded, standing by Justine's bed with her file in his hand, Yves and a Gabonese doctor beside him, "we should perform a laparoscopy, but I'm afraid we do not have the equipment here."

Charlie felt like punching the wall. Nearly two weeks had passed since Justine first doubled up with anguish in Mayumba. Charlie had an idea. He bent to give Justine a quick kiss, and told her he would be back.

Hector heard Twisted Sister before he saw it, the roar of a diesel engine screaming up and down, shifting between second and third gear along the rutted road through Quarter Sable. The rattling, banging truck rounded a stand of trees at high speed before bouncing into the chantier. Charlie braked to a sliding halt.

Hector jumped down from the scaffold where he was laying block and hurried over to Charlie. He knew Charlie had come about Justine. "How's she doing?"

"Not good," said Charlie. His eyes looked haunted. Word had spread in Franceville and among the Peace Corps volunteers in the Haut-Ogooué that Charlie's girlfriend was in the hospital, maybe dying.

Hector yelled to his foreman, "Gilbert!"

"Monsieur?" responded a worker in a tattered blue jumpsuit.

"Clean my tools for me! I'm going with Monsieur Charlie. There's an emergency!"

Dr. Dumas directed the nurses to administer Justine an enema the night before, and again the morning of the procedure. Franceville General Hospital had never sent a patient to CIRMF before, but CIRMF had the most modern medical equipment in the province, including a laparoscope. At Hector's intervention, Natalia had told her colleagues at CIRMF about Justine's case, smoothing the way for her transfer to the research facility.

Before leaving Franceville General in an ambulance, Dr. Dumas injected Justine with something to make her sleep. At CIRMF, attendants wheeled her into an examination room. The head veterinarian, an Italian woman, would oversee the use of the laparoscope. Natalia insisted that she and Charlie be allowed to observe the procedure. They stood side-by-side, their backs to the wall on the far side of the air-conditioned operating room.

Sedated, Justine lay covered by a green sheet on an operating table that previously had only been used for gorillas and chimpanzees. Dr. Monteux and three Gabonese doctors observed as Dr. Dumas tipped Justine's head back, inserted a thin black tube into her mouth, and fed it down into her stomach. The doctors watched a small monitor. Charlie shivered to watch the tube going in, thinking, that is impossibly far inside her. Natalia took Charlie's hand.

Dr. Dumas withdrew the tube, cleaned it and the doctors discussed their observations among themselves, making notes. Then Dr. Dumas moved around the table and gently inserted the tube into Justine's vagina. The doctors and the veterinarian watched on the monitor, the doctors taking notes, discussing what they saw. Natalia squeezed Charlie's hand. He was thankful she was with him. He was thankful for everything everyone was doing. He blinked in desperate gratitude.

Dr. Dumas withdrew the tube a second time, cleaned it, turned Justine onto her side and inserted the tube into her anus, feeding it further and further into her than seemed possible. All five doctors and the veterinarian studied the little screen.

When the procedure was finished, the veterinarian went to the door and called for an attendant to wheel Justine back to an outer room where her mother and brothers waited. Dr. Dumas, the CIRMF veterinarian, Dr. Monteux and his Gabonese colleagues looked at Charlie, then at Natalia, still holding his hand.

"No signs of cancer," Dr. Dumas announced. "Nothing in her esophagus or stomach, nothing in her lower bowel. There are signs of slight trauma to the basal layer of the uterus, typical of a dilation and curettage, which is performed after a miscarriage, which I understand she suffered on two occasions."

"So she's okay?" asked Charlie, his voice a stranger's croak in his own ears.

Dr. Dumas betrayed slight sympathy. "Monsieur, we have no idea what is causing the pain and the swelling. I recommend she see a specialist in Libreville, for additional tests." He looked at the senior Gabonese doctor to speak.

"Ou bien," said the senior doctor, tall for a Gabonese, his hair sprinkled with gray, "peut-être il faut suivre le traitement indigène."

Natalia seized Charlie's hand in both hers and pulled on it, and spoke to him urgently in English. "Look at me, Charlie, and listen. Do you understand what that means?" She searched his eyes with real concern. Charlie nodded, glum and fearful about what the Gabonese doctor had just said. "Charlie, listen, you must be very careful here. Justine's life might be at stake, and you mustn't deviate from medical treatment. They are saying you should try indigenous treatments, but there might not be any margin for error!"

"Fawk," said Timo, limping out onto Charlie's porch with a bottle of beer. Justine rested in Charlie's bedroom with her mother. Charlie had recounted what the Gabonese doctor said at CIRMF, about seeking indigenous treatment, and Natalia's view of the idea. He had seen ati practiced in the village of Okouya, and knew what indigenous treatment amounted to. He had little faith in its efficacy.

"Fawk," Timo said again, twisting the palm of his hand against the mouth of the bottle, like someone pushing on the butt end of a screwdriver, a habit he had acquired as the construction program's roaming transport driver out of fear of being poisoned. Timo slept in multiple villages in a region where witchcraft was widely practiced, and took every precaution to protect himself. He carried a machete in his truck and slipped it under the pillow of every bed that he slept in. He never drank out of a glass, and always insisted on seeing his beer opened in front of him. Before drinking from any bottle, he used the palm of his hand to polish the mouth clean. Timo sat down with a thump beside Hector on the bench of planks scavenged from a school worksite, and glared as he took a swig of beer.

The twins Mbou Blaise and Mpiga Gérard sat on a planter that sprouted young shoots, wide-eyed and listening to the two Africans, the truck driver named Timo they didn't know and their brother

338

Jonas, and three Americans of different colors, Charlie the white man, Hector brown like a métis, and the one named Dabrian as black as a Gabonese.

Jonas leaned against the wall with his arms folded, waiting silently. He had given up trying to make Charlie see there were no other options. Dabrian, who had arrived in Franceville earlier in the day, sat on the bench with Hector and Timo. The dream had come to Dabrian again before dawn. The dream raft had become a sailing ship, ornately carved and painted. He was the captain, but there was no crew. They had perished somehow. Dabrian held a long tiller, pushing and pulling to port and starboard, steering the ship through foaming rapids. He knew very well what lay ahead, but there was no way to make shore. All he could do was hang on and steer as the ship crashed on through whitewater waves. Then suddenly the ship slipped into calm waters. There was a sail now, helping push the boat toward shore. Someone was on a beach waving to him, an old woman he recognized, naked above the waist, wearing necklaces and painted all red and white.

Charlie couldn't grasp what Jonas was trying to get through to him. "Why would somebody do that to Justine?"

"Why it was done doesn't matter, Charlie." Jonas pushed away from the wall. "Think what the doctors have told you. They have done everything they can, and she is not getting better. We have to accept that someone has put a curse on her."

"Jonas, you have a gun. Let me use it. I'll find out who's responsible. I'll make it look like a hunting accident!"

Hector chuckled humorlessly. "I know some gangbangers in L.A. who could do the job."

Jonas shook his head. "Even if you found who put the curse on her, Charlie, you can't just go and kill him. That would be murder."

"Someone's trying to kill Justine! What do you call that? Isn't that murder?"

Timo raised mournful eyes. "Dese fawkin' people!" he screeched. "De one who get de nex' thing, dey kill him out tout de suite! Dey want dat dey all stay in de same fawkin' hole. You know, my brudder, dat's why we must leave dem like we find dem!"

"We must find out who did this," said Jonas. "And then we must undo what he has done."

"How?" cried Charlie.

"We have to hire an ngaa-bwa to cast a counter spell."

"Oui!" said Timo.

"What good will that do?"

"It will save Justine."

"How?"

"By turning the unkébé back on whoever put the spell on her in the first place."

"What do you mean, turn it back?"

Timo looked sternly into Charlie's eyes. "It will kill the man."

At that, Charlie's vision turned dark, and he focused off to distant hills. Slimmer than when he went through *stage* just a year earlier, still a very big young man, he clenched his fists atop his thighs, his unshaved jaw set. Hector watched Charlie. Dabrian sensed what was going to happen, but had not yet said a word. Timo took another swallow of beer, while Jonas waited patiently for Charlie to speak, although he really didn't have a say in the family's decision. They were going to fight witchcraft with witchcraft.

Finally, Charlie asked, "Do you have someone in mind?"

Dabrian spoke for the first time. "She's waiting for us," he said.

Amaya Mokini

Early the next morning, Hector roared up Charlie's driveway driving Twisted Sister, a light wooden frame covered with plastic mesh assembled in the pickup bed. Justine would ride in comfort on a foam rubber mattress. The mesh would allow the air to flow, keeping her cool and diffusing direct sunlight so she wouldn't burn.

Charlie carried Justine to the truck. For days, she had been too weak to walk, too light, too frail. Cradled in his arms on this morning, however, she was alert. "I'm sorry," she said, her voice as dry as dust. "I knew growing old would be bad. I just didn't know it would happen this soon."

Charlie did his best to laugh for his beautiful fighter. Her mother had braided her hair, a hopeful act that touched Charlie. He set Justine gently on the tailgate, climbed up, lifted her again and carried her on his knees onto the makeshift bed. Mama Angélique, still in mourning, still wearing widow's weeds, crawled in alongside, put a pillow beneath her daughter's head and covered her with a bright blue print pagne.

Jonas reached under the mesh past Charlie and squeezed Justine's hand. "You'll be all right," he said to his sister. "You'll be all right."

The twin brothers climbed in last, and Dabrian shut the tailgate. "Everything will be all right," he said to the boys. "We're going to save Justine, bien sûr."

Timo and Hector waved grimly as Dabrian drove Twisted Sister away. Jonas rode in the cab, to give directions.

As they pulled out of the Cité de la Caisse, Justine asked Charlie to feel her swollen abdomen. When he put his hand on the ghastly bulge, it yielded like a water balloon. It horrified him to feel.

"Does it hurt when I press on it?" he asked.

"No. The pain moves around, like an animal inside me. Sometimes it's in my lower back. Other times it's in front, down low or higher up toward my chest. Some days it's a pain so sharp that it makes me curl up in a ball. Other days it throbs and makes me sick to my stomach."

The prescription painkillers helped, but Justine didn't like how they put her to sleep. She only took them when she couldn't stand the pain. When they crossed the river, leaving the city of Franceville behind, she took a tablet, because the truck's vibrations were making the pain worse, and soon she was blessedly asleep. Dabrian drove slowly, not wanting to jostle Justine, and because the mesh could not withstand the beating of the wind at high speed. He passed through his village, Ondili. When he came to the junction of the Talking Tree, the massive iroko tree whose spirit protected the surrounding villages, the tree that spoke to a road-building crew and stopped them from cutting it down, Dabrian continued east toward the plateau.

Justine slept all the way to Lékoni, two hours, and was still asleep when they turned north out of Lékoni across rolling sand hills, the grass sparkling green, the early afternoon sky bright blue. Hector had thought to load a tarp in case of rain, but on that day, rainy season showers fell everywhere save on them. Twisted Sister made slow progress on the rough track. After a time, Justine awoke and asked for water. She talked drowsily with Charlie in French, then for a while with her mother in Téké before falling asleep again.

Twisted Sister crawled past a succession of Peace Corps villages, each with evidence of work on a new school underway. Volunteers and their workers waved and wondered about the strange-looking frame in the back of the Peace Corps truck that didn't stop, as passing Peace Corps trucks almost always did.

At Jonas's direction, Dabrian turned east on a faint track toward the Congo. In the bed of the truck beside Justine, facing backward, Charlie noted the turn. Blaise and Gérard wore an identical look of juvenile ferocity. Mama Angélique kept close watch over her daughter. Jonas, riding in the cab, guided Dabrian to their destination. Charlie wouldn't have known what to do without the others here with him. He would have been losing his mind.

Twisted Sister climbed a high ridge onto the watershed separating Gabon from Congo, and there in the near distance was a low conical mountain. "That is Amaya Mokini," said Jonas, "our sacred ancestral site. Look down there by the stream at the foot of the mountain. That is the village where we are going."

Dabrian descended into the valley. "All the huts are built with thatch," he exclaimed as they neared the village. The huts reminded him of schoolbook illustrations of Iroquois longhouses. "There are no metal roofs," he said.

"Yes, they are built in the traditional way," said Jonas. "This is a pure place. All who live in this village are untainted. There are no metal roofs, no plywood doors, not one nail in any of the houses. Nothing in this place has come from the white man."

Entering the isolated community, a dozen houses woven from fronds of raffia palms, Dabrian thought to himself, This is where I'm supposed to be, here in this village, at this time. Before he could bring Twisted Sister to a full halt, a group of scrawny, knobby-kneed, barefoot children surrounded the truck, grinning and yammering at the curiosity of visitors. The children were visibly less well-nourished than the children in Ondili, Dabrian's village. A thin-limbed, pot-bellied boy toddled over, naked, holding an older girl's hand. A handful of men and women wrapped in pounded raffia cloth approached the truck. Dabrian got out, a black man with physical features no one recognized.

Charlie provoked gasps when he stood, a giant white man. Justine crawled to the tailgate on her hands and knees, and he lifted her tenderly, his face brave for her, masking the anguish he felt. She wanted to walk, and he supported her, going slowly behind the others to a hut set apart a little distance off.

A small, old woman sat on a stool outside her house in a dull-colored raffia cloth sheath, a second raffia cloth around her shoulders as a shawl, a woven raffia hat, and multiple necklaces adorned with red feathers, bird claws and white cowry shells.

Dabrian had last seen the old woman in the dream, waving him ashore. He had met her in Okouya, the ngaa-bwa who unleashed his atura afou, the old woman who ruled this last reserve.

She acknowledged Dabrian with a nod to say she had known they were coming. Dabrian saw it in her shrewd and wrinkled face.

She turned her gaze on Charlie, and studied him with hooded eyes. She began to speak.

Jonas translated. "She says she knows you, Charlie. She was in Okouya while you were sick. She says there is a hole in you, burned there by terrible things done to you as a child. You have tried to plug the hole by caring for no one. Now you have learned to care for another, and the hole is closing. You are becoming fully human. She says you must breathe easy now, for you have come to a place where people are healed."

Charlie sobbed from the sudden rush of relief. Tears whelmed in his eyes and he wiped them away, embarrassed that bystanders had seen.

The ngaa-bwa led them into her hut. It had no windows and no interior rooms. It took a while for Charlie's eyes to adjust to the gloom. Justine lay down wearily on a mat beside a small fire. Soot caked the underside of the low curving thatch roof. Charlie knelt beside Justine and touched her hip, her shoulder, and winced to feel her bones. "I love you," he whispered. Justine opened her dark eyes and smiled.

Charlie and Dabrian sat side-by-side on a small, short bench, their knees under their chins. Jonas and the twins sat on stools. Mama Angélique sat on the mat beside Justine, stroking her daughter's forehead. Scorched stones ringed the fire. Against one wall, shelves fashioned from saplings held the healer's wares, antlered animal skulls, clumps of feathers and strange wooden things, leather sachets and rows of blackened clay pots.

The ngaa-bwa squatted and spoke to Mama Angélique. Jonas translated. "She has asked to hear Justine's problem."

Mama Angélique spoke at length, describing her daughter's symptoms and the futile medical tests of the doctors.

When she finished, the ngaa-bwa produced a shard of mica and gazed into it for some time, before placing her small strong hand on the thin pagne covering Justine's swollen belly. She closed her eyes, and after a few moments began to moan, stiffening as a shudder ran through her.

Suddenly, the ngaa-bwa flung open the pagne to reveal, just beneath Justine's skin, a swelling on her abdomen writhing like a creature alive. Charlie turned to Dabrian in horror-struck rage for the ngaa-bwa to get rid of the thing.

The old woman put her ear on the hideous undulant swelling. She calmly listened for a time before mercifully closing the pagne. Then she rose to her feet, rooted through the shelves for two leather sachets and a soot-covered pot, which she filled with cloudy liquid from a gourd. She squatted on her heels by the fire, and balanced the pot on a rock while the liquid heated. With intense concentration, like a puzzler sorting complex pieces, she pointed at Justine's belly and spoke.

"What's she saying?" Charlie demanded.

"There is a scorpion in her womb," said Jonas.

Charlie reacted like he'd been slapped. "What?"

"She's been cursed. Someone has sent a scorpion into her. It has been stinging her, and the poison from many, many stings is causing the swelling and pain."

Dabrian saw Charlie's muscles bulge with a need to lash out, to punish someone. A scorpion, he thought. Of course. He understood. He remembered the moment his atura afou first stirred, and became manifest, when the ngaa-bwa placed his hands on the forehead of a woman in a shroud, and scorpions came swarming out of the winding sheet.

"She wants us to know her name," said Jonas. "She is called

344

Eloguemonono Alouo. She is skilled in the old ways, and she will help us. She says someone in Okouya did this, someone very evil. She asks us to remember that she was called to Okouya. No one asked her to come. She was called. She says she was unable to eradicate all the evil she found. There was too much, and it was very strong. The person who did this has very strong unkébé. She is going to give Justine some medicine now. When next Justine urinates, the poison will be expelled, and the swelling will go down."

"She'll be cured?" Charlie asked, wanting intensely for Justine's ordeal to end.

Jonas repeated Charlie's question. The old woman answered. Jonas translated. "She says Justine won't be cured until the scorpion is driven out of her womb. Someone who wants to kill her sent it to creep inside her. The scorpion has built a nest. It will not be easy to flush it out. We must begin by learning the name of the sorcerer."

Dabrian looked around. Charlie, his face clenched in fury, seemed horrified, enraged and helpless to do anything. Justine's mother appeared resolute, her thin face etched from a lifetime of hardship. At last, someone had explained to her what was wrong with Justine. Finally, they could make a plan.

Charlie watched every move the ngaa-bwa made. He wasn't sure he actually believed there was a scorpion inside Justine stinging her, but someone was making her suffer and he wanted to know who that was. He wanted violent revenge.

When the pot began to boil, the ngaa-bwa sprinkled in a pinch of dried leaves from one of the leather sachets and a pinch of red powder from the other. She peered into the steam rising from the pot, concentrating, saying nothing. After a few minutes, she took the pot off the flames, her short fingers insensitive to the heat, and set it in the sand. She breathed on it until the steam had dissipated, then gazed into the potion and described the layout of Okouya, drawing an L-shape in the sand. She put her finger over the spot in the village where the sorcerer lived.

Jonas translated. "She says a man who always wears a blue hat has been making unkébé in secret for many months. A big man, a politician, hired him to kill Justine."

"I want him killed!" Charlie bellowed, in a voice Dabrian had never heard him use. Both of them knew who it was, the man in the blue hat, the man-bat Dabrian had seen approaching Justine smiling, with mischief up his sleeves.

Eloguemonono Alouo resumed talking, and Dabrian closed his eyes, listening to the old woman's voice. An image materialized, waves of faint colors, and Dabrian saw the man-bat in Okouya wearing an incongruous blue yachting hat, and saw something fly into the man-bat's mouth.

He opened his eyes and saw the ngaa-bwa speaking directly to Charlie. Jonas translated. "The unkébé requires a soul to eat, Charlie. Your secret enemies chose Justine because she is your girlfriend, and she is a stranger to Okouya."

"But why kill her? Why not kill me?" Charlie's eyes narrowed, his jaw clenched tight. Incredulous, confused and enraged, he wanted to tear the whole world apart.

"Killing Justine will accomplish two things. First, it will enhance the politician's power, which is their main purpose. Second, it will exact revenge against you for something you did."

Charlie pounded his fists like sledgehammers on his knees. "How can this be my fault?"

Mama Angélique wailed at what the ngaa-bwa said next, and Jonas translated.

"The spirits of two grandmothers have been protecting Justine, but they are not strong enough to resist for much longer."

"What are we going to do?" Charlie wailed. He wanted action. "Ask her, Jonas. Ask her!"

And Jonas rattled off the question.

Okouya

From her doorway, Sharon watched a Land Cruiser with a strange contraption in the back approach from the east. As it drew closer, she saw it was a Peace Corps truck, a black volunteer driving. She couldn't remember his name until he pulled alongside her Land Cruiser and got out: Dabrian.

Jonas got out of the passenger's side. She recognized the village schoolteacher, who'd been absent for two weeks. Twin brothers hopped out of the back followed first by a woman dressed in black,

346

then another much older woman wearing nothing above the waist but a tangle of necklaces.

"Hello, Sharon," said Dabrian. "How're you doing?" He took her gently by the arm to draw her away from the door of her house, hoping to compel her to listen. "Let me explain."

"Let go of my arm!" Sharon barked. "What's going on here?"

Charlie, calm, composed and resolute now that they had a plan, carried Justine in his arms, leading the others into the house where, until recently, he had lived.

"Hey!" Sharon yelled. "What are you doing, Charlie?"

Dabrian gripped her arm again. "Sharon."

She glared at him, her eyes blazing. "Get your hands off me, now! Get those people out of my house!"

"We need your help," said Dabrian.

Charlie came back outside. "I'm sorry, Sharon. There was no way to tell you ahead of time we were coming."

"What the fuck is this, Charlie? What makes you think you can just waltz into my house with your girlfriend? What, is she, sick? And who are those other people? Who's that half-naked old woman? She's gross!"

"I know this seems strange," said Charlie. The ngaa-bwa had gone over the ruse with him carefully to make sure he controlled his emotions.

"Strange!" Sharon howled. "Strange!"

"Sharon," said Dabrian, "listen. We're here to reverse an evil spell."

"What the fuck are you talking about?"

"A spell has been put on Justine."

"Aw, Christ on a crutch, are you shitting me? Charlie, you come here bringing people, you just walk right into my house, and Dabrian, you tell me you're here for some kind of voodoo bullshit! I'm supposed to just say, oh, sure, go ahead, that's fine?"

Affable Obongi Louis, formerly Charlie's landlord – now Sharon's – appeared, smiling, his blue beret tipped at a rakish angle. Louis shook Charlie's hand. A gentle old man named Ankambi wearing a snaggletooth smile and a filthy old sport coat that smelled of wood smoke followed. Leaning on a well-worn wooden staff,

Ankambi shook Charlie's hand too. The only old man in the village who wore shorts, he had very sturdy legs for an old timer. When Charlie lived here, Ankambi became convinced that he owed his continued good health to a tumbler of cold water from the refrigerator that Charlie poured for him every day. "Mpa mi andja," he said.

Charlie smiled contritely at Sharon. "I'm sorry. He says he wants some cold water. Can I get him a glass?"

Sharon gave up. "Whatever," she said.

Against her better judgment, Sharon relented, and let Charlie and his weird entourage spend the night in her house, but she didn't like it. When she came out of her bedroom the next morning, already in a foul mood, and found Charlie down on all fours by her refrigerator, she almost lost it. "What the hell are you doing now!"

"Shhh, the wick needs trimming," Charlie whispered, "that's why your fridge isn't getting cold." He pulled the kerosene pan out and set it on the concrete floor. A rag and packet of razor blades lay atop the pan, right where he'd left them. "I should have taken more time to show you how to do this."

"I've got to go to work!"

"Shhh. Justine's asleep."

Sharon didn't care if she was speaking too loud. "Look. I'm really sorry your girlfriend is sick, but this is my house, and I want to get into my refrigerator."

Tormented by his helplessness, Charlie had not slept well in what had once been his spare bedroom. He drowsed through the night, cuddling Justine, praying to God, or whoever out there might save her. Justine's mother and the ngaa-bwa had slept on the salon floor on mats. Their early morning stirring roused him. Unable to get back to sleep, he came out to fiddle quietly with his old refrigerator, doing everything he could to keep his emotions in check. With nothing to do but hope and pray for Justine to get well, he needed something to take his mind off the situation. He felt culpable for Justine's suffering because he had unwittingly angered people when he decided which men to hire for his work crew, as Édouard had told him before leaving Okouya for good. Charlie needed something to do, or he would explode.

"Let me just show you this," Charlie whispered. He blew out the guttering flame.

Sharon hated to admit that her frigo wasn't working as well as it had when she inherited it from Charlie. It wasn't making ice at all. She knelt grudgingly, knowing it was in her own interest to learn how to maintain the kerosene refrigerator.

Charlie unscrewed the hot burner and lifted it clear from the kerosene pan using the rag. "The key is a blue flame. Yours was yellow," whispered Charlie. "Now, to get a blue flame you need a clean wick and chimney." He pulled the collar from the burner and pointed to the crust of carbon on the wick. "Start with the wick. You have to trim it about twice a month." Charlie unwrapped a new razor blade. "One of the second year volunteers taught me this after I swore in. Now I'm teaching you. Slice away the crust. Make sure the edge is square and straight. Cut it again, so you get rid of any fuzz. There, that's good."

"That's it?"

"No. Now the chimney." Charlie got to his feet and took the long wire brush clipped to the back of the refrigerator and handed it to Sharon.

"Use it like a ramrod. Jam it right down in and knock all the soot out the bottom. You need to keep the chimney clean, so it'll draw."

Sharon clipped the brush back in place.

"Now we'll put it back together. Kneel down next to me. Now, use the rag to wipe the little window on the collar there clean. Careful, don't to crack it. Set the collar back on the burner; like that, right, and now screw the burner back in the pan. Yep. Now, light the wick."

Sharon softened as she struck a match. Charlie was trying to help her. "I appreciate this," she said, "I'm sorry I got pissed off, but Jesus, you know, you got to admit, this is awful strange."

"No problem," said Charlie, not wanting to think of that. "You've got to lift the pan so its wheels align with the track. You need a tight seal between the burner and the chimney. Slide the pan all the way in." With their heads almost touching, they looked under the frigo together. "Jiggle the pan," Charlie coached. "Feel the collar fit tight up into the base of the chimney? You'll hear a click."

There was a soft little pop and abruptly a neat, blue flame burned in the window. "That's it," Charlie grinned. "You'll have ice in two hours."

"Well," said Sharon. She looked at Charlie, his handsome face close to hers, and she relented as they got to their feet. "Thanks. This is a bizarre thing you're doing, you know."

Charlie didn't reply.

Sharon turned her face toward the sound of people talking as they approached her house. She sighed and gave up on the idea of any breakfast, and walked outside just as Dabrian, the twins and Jonas with the ngaa-bwa and Mama Angélique came to the door. Sharon's truck started up, and roared off to the school chantier.

The old ngaa-bwa Eloguemonono Alouo entered issuing orders. Jonas was to resume teaching the children. Justine was to remain cloistered in the spare bedroom with her mother. It was good Mbou Blaise and Mpiga Gérard had come along, bringing with them the power of twins. They would need to stay by their sister's side, along with Dabrian and the power of his atura afou. As for Charlie, the otangani was not to go into the village at all. He could receive visitors, if any came to greet him, but he was to stay in the house and control himself.

With that, the ngaa-bwa walked back out into the village and began to greet everyone she found at home. The old women especially were excited to see she had returned. Eloguemonono Alouo spent some time visiting each household, strolling up one side of the village and then down the other, eyed by scowling men who didn't like seeing she had returned.

Okorogo René sat in a sling chair beneath the thatched roof of an open-air hut, waiting for the ngaa-bwa to come to him. His plan had been succeeding, until just now. The grand council of elders had named him the new nkani-ntsie, but now the old ngaa-bwa was back. She had arrived the previous afternoon with the otangani and the kakouma woman, who had not yet died. This did not bode well. He watched suspiciously. The ngaa-bwa approached, as a woman should, with her eyes averted in deference to the land chief of the westernmost Louzou.

With her eyes down, Eloguemonono Alouo asked permission to enter the shade of his hut. He said yes, and she stepped inside.

"Greetings, Nkani-Ntsie."

"Greetings, old woman."

"Are you well, Nkani-Ntsie?"

"I am well."

"And the people, they are fine?"

"The people are fine.'

"And the fields, everyone has finished planting?"

"Yes, the fields are planted."

"That is good, Nkani-Ntsie, very good," said the ngaa-bwa Eloguemonono Alouo. "I am here with a request."

"What is it?"

"I have been asked to help people in this village."

"Who?"

"There are many. I don't ask their names."

Okorogo examined her for a moment. "If you have come to help," he said, "then you will be treated accordingly."

"Mvelewe, Nkani-Ntsie," said the ngaa-bwa, thanking him, bowing and backing away, betraying no sign that she had come here to kill him.

Charlie received visitors throughout the day, villagers who welcomed him back warmly, as though he'd been gone for years. That evening, his former workers came to say hello, carrying their own sling chairs to sit outside, to spare Sharon the annoyance of having more visitors in her house. Édouard, of course, had moved away as soon as he received his official work certificate, and Charlie was sorry he wouldn't see him.

Eloumba Jean-Paul, the village scrivener, furniture maker, carpenter and magasinier, brought a bottle of palm wine. He was a shy man. Small talk did not come easily. Charlie went inside where Sharon was cooking herself dinner and asked if she would like to join them. Sharon didn't drink. She made a face at Charlie taking all the glasses she had inherited from him. Atcholo Jean-Luc, the master mason who had directed the plastering of the teachers' houses, sent a boy to Oyamba Jean's bar to bring beer. Jean's brother Oyamba Benjamin came with the village's most skilled hunter, Ndebi Marc, brave enough to speak out against Charlie at the palaver. Marc had found the bones of the dead twin. In a sense, he had restored Oyamba Hilaire's eyesight. Oloumba Bruno came, the proud man with many children who had shown the most interest in finishing concrete. Makokomba Alphonse, the former ringleader of the teenage boys, was the last to arrive. He had visibly matured. He was pleased to tell Charlie he had taken a wife, and she was already expecting a baby.

Dabrian sat with the men but said little. They were curious about him, a young man the same color as they, but clearly different, a noir américain. "Do black Americans eat the same food we eat?" asked Oyali Albert, the rod buster who had been with Charlie the night his laundryman attacked the old man Lengori with a machete.

"Some foods are the same, or similar," said Dabrian. "Collard greens, yams, okra."

Albert turned his attention back to Charlie, and Dabrian closed his eyes in the cool evening air, and listened to the sounds of the voices. Another image drifted into view, the colors sharper this time, people sitting in a circle, a white rooster, a cloud of fireflies.

Jean-Luc asked Charlie, "I hear you came with Justine. Where is she?"

"She is not well," said Charlie. "She is resting inside."

Hearing this, the workers wished her a speedy recovery. They assured Charlie he could count on them to help, and Charlie felt more gratitude to his former workers than he had words to express.

In the days that followed, the ngaa-bwa began to practice ati, her healing arts, which is how she set her trap. She heard complaints about coughs and sore throats and headaches and backaches and sleeplessness. She prescribed appropriate combinations of roots and herbs. She explained how to concoct potions and poultices, which sort of sacrifice would appease which unhappy ancestor. On the fourth night in Okouya, she walked up and down the village to announce a big ati, protective medicine to ease all suffering in the village. She called on everyone to participate. No one, not even Okorogo, could refuse making medicine to protect the entire village. People would have asked why.

The following night, the grandmothers lit a great bonfire of wood they had spent the days stacking across from Sharon's house. Sharon refused to have anything to do with the proceedings. She shut herself up in her house as the sun went down and people gathered around the blazing fire. The ngaa-bwa wore a headdress made of the spotted hides of civet cats, their tails dangling like dreadlocks. She had daubed white clay on her face, red clay on her arms and legs. Many strands of white cowry shells, red feathers and black claws dangled from her neck. Leather strips with small bells circled her wrists and ankles. In a sheath on a belt around her waist, she carried a knife with a worn bone handle.

The men arrived with folded sling chairs and following the ngaa-bwa's instructions sat on the west side of the fire. The women, many with little children on their backs, unrolled reed mats and sat in the sand to the east, opposite the men.

Once most of the village had gathered, Charlie helped Justine out of the house, trailed by the twins and her mother. She walked painfully, leaning on Charlie's arm, her head covered by a pagne so no one could see her face. Charlie helped Justine lie down on a reed mat the old healer had positioned to the south of the circle between the women to the right and the men to the left. The ngaa-bwa carefully covered her with pagnes so that not even the top of her head was visible. Mama Angélique sat on a mat to one side, her legs straight out, back erect. The twins sat on mats to the other side. Flanked by Dabrian and Jonas, Charlie sat in a sling chair next to Justine. Among the men on his left, Charlie's former workers looked at him with sympathy and encouragement.

Soon, Okorogo arrived with his confederates. Oyamba Hilaire owed his eyesight to Okorogo and could not side against him; nor could Lenkongi Francis, the man known to have the biggest bangala in the village. Assélé Laurent, the mason Charlie had refused to hire, made no secret of his allegiance. He hated Charlie. Okorogo's suspicions were clear, and he and his men sat on the northern side of the circle, as far away from Charlie as possible. Dabrian watched Okorogo as he chatted, projecting an air of authority. He sensed something powerful Okorogo concealed on his person, something the man-bat would wield as a weapon.

Okorogo turned his attention to the ngaa-bwa squatting next to a mat near the fire. Eloguemonono Alouo opened a raffia sack and carefully arranged the contents on the mat: small pouches, several lumps of chalk-like material, a shard of mica, a hatchet, a rattle, ordinary items she handled casually. They exuded potency and inspired awe in the assembly. Her face, painted white and framed by civet cat tails, radiated great intensity, like hot iron radiates heat. Her narrowed eyes caught everything. She stood and watched as the last people arrived. The gathering grew hushed, and the chatter of voices died down, until only the crackling of the blaze and the tiny voices of cranky infants could be heard.

A milky white fog descended on the village, as the blue orb of a full moon rose behind the women. The mist evaporated around the fire, until it seemed a great glass dome sheltered the gathering. In the white murk beyond, the village huts looked to Charlie like black ruins, submerged in a lake.

In the silence the ngaa-bwa padded around the circle, the bells on her wrists and ankles jingling. She had commanded no drums or rattles, no instruments of any kind. She began to clap, and the grandmothers clapped, as she instructed, then the mothers, then the young men, and finally the grandfathers, each group in a different rhythm. The pattering of the hands became the sound of rain.

The ngaa-bwa led the women in a high-throated hum, and showed the men how to blend in a deeper bass rumbling. In the sound of the crackling fire, the cadenced clapping and chanting was at once enchanting and eerie, from centuries past, from a time before the white man came, before missionaries, firearms, manufactured goods and trading cloth.

When she was satisfied at the continuous clapping and humming, the ngaa-bwa went to her things, took up her rattle and hatchet and passed along the half circle of men. She brandished the hatchet, its hand-forged black blade shaped like the beak of an eagle. She circled around to the women, shaking the rattle, bur-r-r-r. After completing the circuit, from west to east, she turned and completed the circuit in the other direction, then she went to her sack and exchanged the rattle and hatchet for a hand-forged bell, which she struck with a smooth peeled stick, and began to dance, hitting the bell, making a hollow donk! donk! donk-donk!

The humming and clapping continued to flow, different

strands interweaving, twisting and entwining, like sea grass swaying in warm currents. The women's high humming whined like mosquitoes, the men droned like bees. In concert, the sound pulsed with energy. The ngaa-bwa began an invocation, a raucous chant, calling forth from out of the moonlit fog something Dabrian was able to see in the mist, the ripple of an unfelt breeze: faces talking to him, telling him trust your vision, before fading back into smoke and fog.

With a swift downward slash of her muscular arms, the ngaa-bwa silenced the humming and clapping. Villagers whispered furtively as she went back to her mat and bent over the raffia bag. Her necklaces swung forward and she fished something out, concealing it in her hand, and then she straightened and went to the fire. She stood there for a moment, before popping it into her mouth. She bit into it, and spat forcefully into the fire, causing a purple flame briefly to appear. Then she swung around, civet cat tails, breasts, necklaces whirling out, and she sang:

> "Otchièmi Tché! Tché! Tché!
> Otchièmi Tché! Tché! Tché!
> Wayaga mi mouana! Tché!
> Onyini mi ndjomi! Tché!
> Mewa kara youlou.
> Misomi mandjomi! Tché!"

The men and women began to clap again and sang along with the ngaa-bwa as she sidled around the fire.

Jonas translated for Charlie: "Little bird, when you take my child you must give me your house. When I come from the sky, I must enter your house."

The ngaa-bwa paced before the women, the grandmothers, the mothers with sleeping infants on their backs, shaking her rattle, bur-r-r-r, bur-r-r-r, and at the men, the fathers and the grandfathers, bur-r-r-r, bur-r-r-r. Then, glaring scornfully, she unsheathed the knife and held it up for all to see, stuck out her tongue, and began slicing it with the razor sharp edge. People gasped, but she did not bleed. She sawed the corners of her open mouth so hard the flesh of her cheeks wobbled, but the knife made no wound.

355

The ngaa-bwa returned the rattle to her cache of materials and drew an inch-thick stick out of the fire. Holding it up, with one swipe of the knife, she cut the stick neatly in two. The people gasped to see the keenness of the ancient blade, sharp enough to cut wood but not her flesh. Glaring fearsomely around the circle, the ngaa-bwa challenged anyone to doubt her power.

"Otchièmi Tché! Tché! Tché! Otchièmi Tché! Tché Tché!" chanted the villagers as the ngaa-bwa sheathed the knife and took up the mica shard, moving around the half circle of men until she came to one of the grandfathers.

Dabrian leaned close to Charlie. "Who is that?"

"Ngawaraga Bernard. He's only Christian in the village."

The ngaa-bwa gazed into the mica; then she gazed intently into Bernard's eyes. Unflinching, the old man stared bravely back.

"Otchièmi Tché! Tché! Tché! Otchièmi Tché! Tché! Tché!"

The ngaa-bwa raised her right hand slowly. Slowly, Bernard raised his to meet hers. Dabrian thought for a moment they would clasp hands, but the ngaa-bwa stopped short of allowing their fingertips to touch, and a small spark leaped from her fingertips to Bernard's.

"Did you see that!" cried Charlie.

"Yes," said Dabrian.

The ngaa-bwa leaned forward and spoke into Bernard's ear, and their fingertips touched. Then she moved to another old man, Ankambi, who for months every day drank a glass of cold water from Charlie's frigo, and she made a spark leap to his fingertips and spoke into his ear. When she finished with Ankambi, she moved to Obarigi, the most ancient man in the village, and continued around the western side of the circle, choosing several grandfathers for the sacrament, stepping past others as if they weren't there.

Dabrian studied Okorogo René, the man-bat, as he watched the ngaa-bwa pass him by, and one by one pass his confederates. Whatever Okorogo had hidden on his person, Dabrian knew it was in easy reach.

Suddenly and without warning, Justine sat up. Instantly Okorogo's face twisted horribly and he shot Justine the Evil Eye. She fell back as if struck by an invisible bolt and Mama Angélique flipped the pagne back over her daughter's face.

Dabrian felt Charlie's shock and righteous fury. He grabbed Charlie's thick bicep with both hands in time to stop him from bolting out of his chair to wrench off Okorogo's foul head. Charlie raged. He pointed and called on God to damn Okorogo straight into Hell. Dabrian leaned close, breathing the wrath out of Charlie and into himself.

Charlie's eyes flashed with fury. "Did you see what he did to Justine?"

"Wait," said Dabrian. "It's not time. Let the ngaa-bwa finish."

Charlie slumped back in his sling chair and glanced down at Justine's recumbent form. Everyone had seen Okorogo shoot Justine with the Evil Eye. Unnerved, their chanting and clapping had faltered.

The ngaa-bwa broke into an excited jabber, taking up her rattle again, and it rolled as she flourished it, stalking around the fire, white face, red limbs, white necklaces, reanimating the semi-circle of grandmothers. People looked around at their neighbors. Expressions of comprehension raced around the circle as the villagers gained new resolve, understanding that the ngaa-bwa was locked in mortal combat with a wicked man just revealed.

Okorogo and his accomplices could do nothing about the people taking courage from others, emboldened to join the ngaa-bwa in her fight. A grandmother stood up and denounced Okorogo, the soul eater, for the deaths of two babies within a day of each other. The bereaved mothers rose together and pointed accusing fingers at him. Shouting arose from men. They accused Okorogo of sickened goats, blighted crops as the chanting and clapping resumed, growing louder and louder, the people urging the ngaa-bwa to vanquish the evil man.

Okorogo's allies glowered at the ngaa-bwa fearfully and looked to Okorogo to defeat what was coming at them.

"Otchièmi Tché! Tché! Tché! Otchièmi Tché! Tché! Tché!" cried the people, and the ngaa-bwa took up her rattle and hatchet again, and began jumping and spinning, her necklaces flying, her withered breasts flapping, stomping her feet, bells jingling, the bur-r-r-r, bur-r-r-r-r of her rattle. Droplets of sweat flew off her, carved rivulets through the white clay smeared on her face as she began to complete the spell.

A great calm suddenly bloomed in Charlie, an acceptance of what was coming. He laid his head back in the sling chair and closed his eyes, but then like a spasm he felt his culpability. Justine was suffering, due to him. His heedlessness was the cause of this battle raging around him, of goodness and evil, of God and the Devil. The life of the woman he loved hung in the balance. He squeezed his eyes shut not to know this, to believe Justine would survive the attack, and a deep, smoky fatigue overcame him. Listening to the patter of hands like rain in the trees, he fell asleep, and dreamed he was in a car on a highway in a snowstorm, trying to understand what Coach Dawber was saying.

"Charlie!" Dabrian shook him. The chanting and clapping had ceased. The fire had burned down. The moon lay low in the western sky and a chill gripped the air. Infants slept peacefully on their mothers' backs. Justine lay still, in front of Charlie, covered in pagnes. He sat up and rubbed his bare arms and reached down to touch her shoulder, asking Justine through his fingers for her forgiveness, to tell her she would recover, and they would be together, after all.

On the far end of the men's half circle, the man-bat Okorogo sat intently, his hands concealing his instrument of power. Mama Angélique sat bolt upright in front of Dabrian. Mbou Blaise and Mpiga Gérard crouched on either side of their sister, Justine's guardians at this critical moment. Dabrian could feel a hypersensitive awareness flowing between the twins, two young leopards coiled to spring.

The ngaa-bwa moved backwards from the dying embers, bent at the waist, holding her knife by the blade, scraping a line in the sand with the bone handle. In her other hand, she held a white rooster upside down by its legs, wings akimbo, trying to orient itself, beak open, eyes blinking. Dabrian recognized it; the white rooster had been shown to him, and he knew what it would soon reveal. The ngaa-bwa traced a second line across the first, scribing an asymmetrical X in the sand. When she was done, Eloguemonono Alouo stomped about, exhorting the people for one final time.

Jonas explained the four arms of the X to Charlie. "The arm

pointing at you is for a foreigner. The arm aimed at the grandmothers is for the ancestors. The third arm points at someone from a different village. And that one," he said, indicating the line pointing straight at Okorogo, "is for a sorcerer from this village."

The ngaa-bwa bent over and placed the white cock on the center of the X, then pressed the bird into the sand with her foot. With her free hand, she pulled the rooster's neck taut and placed the ancient blade flashing orange from the light of the coals against it. The people were silent.

Okorogo leaned forward in his chair, elbows on his knees, fists clenched, and the Nima Louembé with his purple smock and necklace of teeth whispered so only Dabrian could hear. "This is why you are here. Now feel what you have been given!"

"Hear me!" The ngaa-bwa called hoarsely to the ancestors. "Hear me! Use this cock to show us who has been bringing fear and misery into this village! Use it to show us who has been causing sickness and grief! Use it to show us who has been working in darkness to let evil loose in this village! Use it to show us who has been trying to kill the woman Justine! Show us, so that his works will turn back upon him! Show us who has brought harm, who has worked evil, who has troubled the spirits of the ancestors, who has caused filth to come forth! Show us now that we may see who he is!"

With a swift upward slash, the ngaa-bwa cut the head off the rooster and leaped out of its way. Blood jetted from the headless bird, and it ran straight into the man-bat Okorogo's shins.

Okorogo jerked his feet and kicked the rooster flittering into the glowing coals, but the dying cock emerged flinging sparks and careened in a half circle to topple and roll to a stop shuddering, right on the center of the X.

In silence, everyone watched the last feeble jets of blood spurt from its neck, the cock clenching and unclenching its claws.

Okorogo's face was a mask, his pant legs speckled with blood. Without warning, the man-bat popped his fists open and shook his fingers at the creature. Incredibly, the headless bird began beating its wings, flipping sand in the air, rolling like a tumbleweed impelled by supernatural force, once, twice, three times. Then it slumped flat for the final time directly atop the line pointing at Charlie.

Okorogo glared at Dabrian in triumph, and then at Charlie, and then at the ngaa-bwa, her head down, face hidden by the civet cat tails.

The people watched in a state of shock.

Then the twins cried out in one voice, "Viezé bizi!" What had been flickering inside them spilled over and flowed out. "Viezé bizi! Viezé bizi!"

Golden fireflies filled the air.

"Viezé bizi! Viezé bizi! Viezé bizi!"

Everyone looked in wonder at the thousands, millions of flickering fireflies. A chorus of men and women took up the chant, "Viezé bizi! Viezé bizi! Viezé bizi!"

Show us! Show us! Show us!

A final spasm seized the headless bird, and it lifted its red-drenched white neck from the sand.

"Viezé bizi! Viezé bizi! Viezé bizi!" the people cried.

The rooster began propelling itself with its wings, like oars, dragging its claws across the center of the X, crawling toward Okorogo, its bloody neck stretched forth, pointing at the man-bat like an accusing finger.

Okorogo's hands were empty, his power spent.

"Viezé Bizi! Viezé Bizi! Viezé Bizi!"

Then the rooster slumped flat and grew still, stone dead at last, squarely atop the arm of the X pointing at Okorogo in his chair.

At that moment, Dabrian saw a darkness rise up out of Justine. Like a swarm of bees, the darkness flew straight at the man-bat and into his open mouth. Okorogo gasped and snapped his mouth shut, but too late. A look of sudden horror and dread warped his face.

The fireflies instantly vanished. The ngaa-bwa moved swiftly to Justine, Charlie kneeling with his arms around her. A cock crowed, and then another. The fog had lifted and to the east, Dabrian saw the first streaks of dawn lighting the world.

22. A Snake Out of the Earth

Akièni

Lying in bed in her bungalow, watching Charlie asleep in a sling chair, Justine thought to herself that such long eyelashes as his are wasted on a man. His huge hands rested on his great thighs, thick fingers curled, his head inclined to one side. His lips were parted, the curve of them sensuous, slightly cruel, ready to kiss or bite. She noticed Charlie had missed a patch shaving under his chin. He'd been shaving faithfully every morning for all the months since she told him, "I like what you look like underneath."

She watched him dream, his brow furrowed, eyelids fluttering. The dream vexed him. Then it passed, and he was still again.

Perhaps he knows I am about to break his heart, thought Justine. It was the last thing she wanted to do, her heart full of woe, but she was obliged, because she loved him.

Life had done its best to beat Charlie down. He had told her of the horrible things done to him as a child. By rights, he ought to have grown up an unforgiving brute. But he stood on his feet a gentle and caring man, with every reason not to be. He was beautiful, and sometimes her breath caught in her throat to see him looking at her, a giant among her people. She had never known anyone who approached life with such simplicity of purpose, an uncomplicated intention to do whatever needed be done. There was nothing deceitful about him, and that was what made him such a damaging force. He'd crashed into Okouya like a rock from a slingshot, flung from far away.

For many days, the knowledge had been settling in her mind, and with it, the unbearable resolve to do the last thing on earth she wanted to do. She forced herself to understand that what the ngaa-bwa Eloguemonono Alouo told her was true. She had to do it. And the knowledge was tearing her in two.

"What happened was a warning," the ngaa-bwa said.

"How can that be so? The sorcerer Okorogo did this to me, and you turned the unkébé back on him."

"Yes, my child, and now there are scorpions in his belly, hundreds of them, stinging him, and he will die. But he is not the only one. Didn't you see? They are many."

"I know, but can't they leave us alone?"

"No, they will not leave you alone. Bo ndjalawe anyanga. They hate you now. They hate the two of you. Their hatred will follow you, wherever you go."

"What if we leave? What if we go away to America?"

"It doesn't matter. What they have let loose will follow you wherever you are in the world."

"But I love him."

"And that is precisely why you must tell him to go, my child."

"That is so hard. I would rather die."

"Do you mean that? Think of your brothers, the twins. Think of your mother. They need you."

"But I love him. Can't I be with him?"

"I'm telling you, my child, what I know to be true. If you love him you must tell him to go, or one of you will die."

Charlie opened his eyes and saw Justine was awake. She had been crying.

"What's wrong?"

She shook her head, and made a smile. She dried her eyes. She wasn't ready for this, but she had to do it, because she loved him.

"What's wrong?" He rose towering to his feet and came to her, and she felt the weight of him sitting on the edge of the bed, and his large hand was on her knee.

She shook her head.

"Tell me, what's the matter?"

Instead, she said, "Charlie, I love you."

He smiled, relaxed visibly, and bent to kiss her. "I love you too."

"Don't ever forget that, Charlie, okay?"

"Okay. I won't."

"You are always asking me to tell you stories about my

childhood. Now it's my turn, Charlie. I want you to tell me a story about yours."

Charlie closed his eyes. Her request forced his mind back where he didn't like to go, back across the painful tumult of his miserable foster home childhood. He opened his eyes, casting about for a story to tell. Then he thought of one.

"Do you remember," he said, "I told you I used to play American football? Where the players put on pads and helmets and hit each other as hard as they can?"

"Like boxing?"

"No, not like boxing. You'll see it some time. I was a pretty good player in high school, because I'm big. So I got a scholarship to the University of Minnesota. I played defensive end. I wasn't as good at that level. Our team wasn't very good, but one year, 1986, we went to play Michigan. They are always a very good team. They used to beat us every year. But in 1986, we were in their stadium. It holds a hundred and five thousand people. Can you imagine a crowd that big? Can you imagine a crowd that big yelling as loud as they can? The sound is so loud it makes the shirt on your body vibrate."

"Louder than a jet engine?"

"Loud like that, yes. That game, we played better than we ever played. We kept hitting them as hard as we could, and we kept taking the ball away from them. Three quarters through the game, we were ahead by one touchdown, and they drove the ball down to our one-yard line, fourth down. I remember the look on my teammates' faces in the huddle. We knew they were going to run, and we knew were going to stop them. Stop Michigan. They came to the line, and I got down in my stance."

Charlie rose from the bed and showed Justine what a four-point stance looked like. "In a short yardage situation, like a goal-line stand," he said from his crouch, "for the linemen, whoever gets lowest wins."

He straightened and returned to sit on the bed, enjoying the wide-eyed look on her face as she tried to imagine what he was describing. She'd come back, she'd healed. He could see it in her eyes, in her face, her beautiful face that had become so thin.

"They snapped the ball and ran it at us, to the side I played on. I beat my blocker. Their running back came right at me and leaped into the air. I got my arm out and hit him with my shoulder around the waist as hard as I could, and one of our linebackers hit him in the chest, and the ball flew out, and one of our defensive backs caught it in the air, and ran all the way to the other end. But the referee said Michigan scored."

"Hah!" said Justine. "That's how referees are. They always do that for the home team."

"Well, sometimes it seems that way. The score was tied, but there was still a lot of time. We played hard, they played hard, and at the end of the game, with the score still tied, and just a few minutes left, our offense began to move the ball down to their end of the field. They couldn't stop us, not on that day. With no time left on the clock, we kicked the game winning field goal and we shut those one hundred and five thousand people up."

Justine saw the pride in Charlie's eyes at the memory of the achievement, and she put her hand on his, hating what she was about to do.

"That is a good story," she said gently, beginning. "So my turn now. Are you ready to hear the rest of the story I started before?"

"Which story?"

"The story about my grandmother and the snake."

"Oh." Charlie's expression slipped. "That." He tried to stop her from telling it with a question. "Why were you crying?"

"Don't you want to hear the rest of the story?"

He licked his lips. He didn't want to hear it. "Okay," he said. "Tell it."

And so Justine began, from the beginning, telling of the day when as a child her grandmother and her aunt took her and her brother Jonas along with them fishing, to help them dam up the small stream and bail out the water.

"You know the method I'm talking about?"

Charlie nodded. He had seen the women of Okouya fishing this way.

"We built a dam using the sand at the bottom of the stream, and as the water backed up, we bailed it out. As we bailed, we caught the fish we trapped. As we bailed, we uncovered a hole in the bank. My grandmother thought there would be fish in that hole,

364

so she stuck in her hand, and she felt something big that moved. She grabbed it and pulled on it but it was strong and she knew at once what it was. 'There's a python in here,' she cried, 'and I've got its tail!'"

Charlie gritted his teeth. He'd already heard this part.

"My aunt went and reached in with her, and they both got a grip on it. Do you know that a snake cannot back up?"

Charlie clenched his jaw and shook his head.

"So together they began pulling on the tail of that snake, my grandmother and my aunt, these two little women pulling on a very strong snake that was fighting to go forward. My aunt called to me, 'Take the machete and cut a vine and bring it! Quickly! A long one!' And I ran to do as she said."

Justine wanted to sit, so Charlie helped her up and plumped the pillow behind her.

"They pulled and pulled and the snake fought them." Justine pantomimed pulling on something big and round, thrashing violently back and forth. "When they'd pulled enough of its tail out of the hole, my aunt took a knife and she stuck it…" Justine stabbed with her fingers. "…straight through the snake's tail. My aunt yelled, 'Bring the vine here and poke the end through this hole!' So I ran to her and tried, but the snake was moving about, and the hole was small, so my aunt took the end of the vine from me and poked it through the snake's tail herself."

Charlie's mouth was upside down.

"She said, 'Pull it!' and I pulled until half of the vine was through. Then she sent Jonas and me to wrap the two ends of the vine around a tree and to pull on it in different directions, and while we did that, my grandmother and my aunt pulled on the snake, and together, we started pulling it out of the earth. It was three meters long, five meters long."

With her hands, she showed Charlie the girth of the snake, and with her arms she showed its power, how it flipped, and writhed.

"My grandmother hurried to Jonas and me, wrapped the ends of the vine round and round the tree and tied the ends fast. Then she ran back to my aunt. When they were ready, they gave one last pull and the python came all the way out."

Now Justine mimicked the head of the serpent, its mouth

gaping wide, lashing this way and that.

"We watched until we were sure it couldn't tear its tail loose, or snap the vine. Then my grandmother took the machete from me, and she sent my aunt to distract the python." Justine imitated her aunt, waving her arms. "When the snake lunged at my aunt, my grandmother rushed in and chopped off its head."

Justine made a chop with the side of her hand and fell back in bed.

Charlie drew a deep, shaky breath. After a while, he said, "I see where you get your courage."

"Did the story distress you?" Her smile faded. "Do you know why I told you this story?"

"No."

"Because we must kill the snake, you and I, and it will be hard."

He frowned to know what she meant, but she closed her eyes, her head on the pillow. Talking still fatigued her, and he thought she was dozing off.

Then she opened her eyes and said, "I'm sorry for what has happened, Charlie."

The unkébé, he thought, but it seemed she didn't mean that at all.

She felt for his hand. "It has been for a reason."

"What has?"

"Now is the hard part."

"What do you mean?" They were through the worst.

All she could do was say it. "I can't be with you anymore, Charlie."

When he comprehended, it hit him like a shot to the chest.

"This is what we've been shown. I don't want to tell you this. It is so hard for me, but I have to be brave." Tears rolled down her cheeks. "Don't you always tell me how brave I am? The ngaa-bwa saw it." And lest her will dissolve at the sight of his utter desolation, Justine hurried through what she had to say.

"She told me how it must be. We're from two different worlds, Charlie, and we cannot be together, or one of us will die. What Okorogo started will follow us, if we are together. You have to leave me. I would give my right arm to have it otherwise, because I

366

love you, I want to be with you. That is why I'm telling you this. You must go." Justine began to sob.

Charlie's head whirled. He felt sick. He swallowed bile. It was happening again, with Justine! The first person he had ever truly opened his heart to.

She wiped the streaming tears from her cheeks with both her hands.

She meant it. He could see she truly meant it. He should have known. It would always be this way, for him.

"And if you love me, you must listen, Charlie." Her voice was choked. She had trouble getting out the words. "We cannot be together." The tears streamed from her eyes, her beautiful up-tilted eyes, red and whelming with tears. She hated the terrible hardness of his face. She did not want to be yet one more to hurt him, but this was as it had to be, because she loved him, and she squeezed his hand, but he did not respond, and she was tired, and there was no more strength.

23. Getting Away With Murder

Okouya

The three Oyamba brothers were the only customers in Okouya's lone bar. Jean, the owner, fished three beers from a pail of cloudy water. One by one, he popped the caps, and they rattled on the plywood counter. Benjamin, the youngest brother, was his most regular customer. Hilaire, on the other stool, was the oldest. Benjamin pulled greedily from his third bottle that morning, while Jean and Hilaire sipped from their second.

"I'm telling you, it's true!" Benjamin insisted, wiping his mouth with the back of his hand.

"How do you know?" asked Hilaire, who had spent a year blind, mute and partially paralyzed, before Okorogo cured him.

"Do you think I'm lying?" said Benjamin. "I wasn't the only person Édouard told, before he moved away. He was afraid of Okorogo."

"Don't say his name out loud." Hilaire glanced nervously over his shoulder, out the open door.

"Why? Are you afraid he can hear you?" Benjamin laughed to see their oldest brother frightened by the spirit world. "Okorogo is dead!"

"You think you are fearless," grumbled Hilaire, "but you're only fearless because you're a souse."

"You're just angry because you lost out! Yes, he healed you, but you allied yourself with Okorogo because you thought you would benefit. Well you won't, because he's dead, and I'm telling you, Akoa Édouard refused to succeed his father as our nkani-ntsie because Okorogo was attacking his family with ndjobi, with those people over there." Benjamin jerked his head in the direction of the small crowd of mourners across the way, the last of the people sitting vigil for the dead sorcerer they had buried the day before.

369

Suffering from a horrendous swelling in his abdomen, Okorogo waited vainly for Milla's taxi to arrive and take him to the Congo in desperate search for a remedy. His screams from the agonizing stings of the multitude of scorpions crawling through his innards tore through the village, terrifying young and old alike, until he finally died.

"What our little brother is saying is true," said Jean, a respected member of the village council of elders. "Hilaire, admit it. We all know Okorogo was bringing back the hurtful practices, ndjobi, and the older methods as well, ongala, okani and ondjandja. He was bringing them all back. Admit it, my brother."

Hilaire sighed. "Yes, it is so," he said finally, and the three brothers took thoughtful swigs.

Speaking gently, wanting to restore harmony, Jean, the middle brother, said to Hilaire, "You should not have gone along with him."

"The man healed me. I owed him my support."

"You expected to profit!" declared Benjamin.

"I was not in favor of eating a soul!" Hilaire shouted, annoyed that neither of his brothers believed him. "You weren't there!" Their expressions remained dubious. Benjamin tipped up his bottle, and Hilaire shook his head. "There was nothing I could do to stop him, and anyway, the politician Badinga is to blame."

"You shouldn't have gone along with it," Benjamin insisted. "The kakouma woman did nothing to deserve what Okorogo did to her."

Hilaire protested. "Everyone wanted the good things the politician promised."

"Speak for yourself," said Jean. "I for one am glad Okorogo is dead and I don't care who hears me say it. I resisted when the grand council appointed him nkani-ntsie, after Chief Oyamba Paul died."

The three brothers fell silent at the memory of their homonym, the late land chief of the westernmost Louzou.

"I'm going to want another bottle," said Benjamin. "I think maybe I'm going to want another ten."

Akièni

Justine stared at the letter from the National Director of Human Resources, and looked at the signature, a flourish of squiggles and a blue ink stamp. She read the letter a second time. Her request for a transfer to the General Hospital in Franceville was officially approved.

All the pain came back as she held the letter, the pain in her belly, and the pain in her heart. Charlie was gone. He just stood up and walked out, without a word, without looking back. With a yawning and empty certitude, Justine knew she would never see him again, unless she did something about it. But what could she do? She had made a terrible mistake, and he was gone.

Her life was returning to what it had been, before an evil man with soaring ambitions put a curse on her. The twins were back in school. Her mother, Mama Angélique was taking care of the laundry, cleaning the house and cooking meals, helping her daughter regain all the weight she had lost, now that the scorpion had been flushed from her womb.

This morning her mother was at the market. People had been visiting in a steady stream, all the neighbors, the nurses and the staff at the hospital. Even Dr. Muengo had come by, after work, for a few days. He gave Justine daily injections of vitamins, until one day he reached out to stroke her forehead, and she brushed his hand away. He hadn't come back after that.

With a sudden sharp rap at her open front door, Justine's neighbor Commandant Lentchidja stepped inside, a burly man, his belly hanging over the belt of his khaki uniform, his black kepi cap shoved back on his bullet head. This wasn't a social call.

"Can I help you?" asked Justine, alone in the house.

"There's a problem," said the Commandant. A subaltern with a holstered pistol and handcuffs on his web belt followed the Commandant into Justine's salon.

"What sort of problem?"

"A man has died," said Commandant Lentchidja.

Reclined on the couch, Justine motioned for the Commandant to have a seat on a worn velour chair. The subaltern took the matching chair opposite him.

"Who died?" asked Justine.

"The new Louzou land chief, Okorogo René," said the Commandant, his one wandering eye fixed somewhere over Justine's shoulder, the other burning into her. "You must know him, because the family has filed charges against you. They accuse you of bewitching him."

Before she could gather her thoughts and react, Justine heard the sharp crack of plastic sandals on the veranda, stamping off mud. A second later, Mama Angélique appeared in the doorway, sinewy arms and work-hardened hands, dressed all in black. She slipped off her sandals and came inside, her purchases in a basket on her back, like she was returning from the fields. Concerned to have seen two gendarmes entering the house, she set the basket on the floor. "What is this?" she demanded to know.

"Greetings, Mama," said Commandant Lentchidja, as Mama Angélique sat on the couch by her daughter.

"Greetings. Why are you here?"

"There is a problem."

"What is this problem?"

"Okorogo René has died," said Justine.

"Really!" Mama Angélique was pleased.

Justine explained. "Okorogo's family has accused me of bewitching him."

"At this point, Mama," said Commandant Lentchidja quickly, "we are just collecting facts."

Mama Angélique rose and took a step toward him, jabbing her finger at him like a weapon. "That wicked man made an unkébé intended to murder my daughter, to benefit himself and a politician! Everyone knows. Ask anyone. We did what anyone would do. We cured my innocent daughter by turning the unkébé back on its maker. If it has killed him, well then, so be it. His death is justified."

The widow's vicious outburst startled the two gendarmes. With her lips pursed, her thin hard face remorseless, Mama Angélique returned to her daughter's side. She took Justine's hand defiantly to show a mother's love had prevailed.

The Commandant's tongue poked out between his lips. "Perhaps, Mama," he said, "we can take down your statement here. Prepare to take notes," he said to the subaltern, who removed a notebook from his shirt pocket. "Are you admitting then, Mama, that you and your daughter took part in a ritual to reverse a suspected unkébé worked on your daughter?"

"My daughter was dying and helpless. We took her to the etangani doctors in Franceville. They did all their tests and found nothing. They told us to resort to indigenous treatments."

"How did you identify Okorogo René as the man who worked the unkébé on your daughter?"

"Through the ngaa-bwa, Eloguemonono Alouo."

The subaltern's eyes widened at the mention of the legendary witch from Amaya Mokini.

"She detected a scorpion in my daughter's womb, and divined that Okorogo René was the ngaa-mpiaru who sent it there."

"And what did you do, once you knew?"

"We confronted Okorogo René in Okouya, and we reversed the unkébé."

"The ngaa-bwa Eloguemonono Alouo and you, alone?"

"My sons were there, and two Americans. They drove us."

"Which Americans?"

"The black one, and the white one who was in love with my daughter."

"What is the name of the white one in love with your daughter?"

"Charlie Sinclair," said Justine, and saying Charlie's name pierced her heart.

"We are not trying to hide what we did," said Mama Angélique. "All the villagers in Okouya participated."

"Where is this Charlie Sinclair now?"

"He has gone home to America," replied Justine, wiping a tear from the corner of her eye.

The Commandant considered this for a moment, frowning.

"Pardon, mon Commandant," said the subaltern, "but perhaps we have the name we need."

Libreville

The CIA Africa Division Chief wore a pale gray suit, the shoulders dappled by rain. Walter Cummings lifted one of Darlene's paired Mbigou soapstone heads from a bookshelf. He ran his thumb along the female's striated plaits, feeling the slipperiness of the stone, then set it back beside the male on a green and yellow Ghanaian kente cloth runner.

A case officer assigned to Libreville for barely two months, Julie Burton watched her superior move unhurriedly to look at the blazing colors of an oil painting, framed in red mahogany.

"It's called, *Taxis at Makolo Market*," said Darlene.

Two days earlier, a cable arrived informing Ambassador Jones that the Directorate of Operations in Langley had tacked a stop in Gabon onto the Africa Division Chief's trip to Cameroon. As soon as she read the cable, Darlene called Julie into her office. "Why didn't you inform me?"

Julie was as surprised as Darlene. "Nobody told me he was coming, Ambassador. This is the first I've heard of it."

"What's he want?"

"Honestly, I don't know."

Cummings bore a rank equivalent to a three star general. Twice, he'd been decorated with the coveted Intelligence Star. He stepped past a gleaming rubber plant and took a moment to examine a pastel drawing of little girls winnowing rice, before crossing the Ambassador's office to a low table where a three ring binder marked Classified lay next to a basket of glass beads. He moved a throw pillow aside on the sofa and sat. The women flanked him in armchairs just as a gust of wind threw rain lashing against the windows.

Political officer Hughes waited at the Chancery entrance for the guards in yellow slickers and black rubber boots to process the white Land Cruiser at the main gate, its wipers whipping back and forth. The gate opened, the SUV pulled into the lot and parked. The doors swung wide and two umbrellas popped open over Harry Bowman and Stu Easton who hurried through the downpour. Tom showed them where to put their dripping umbrellas and walked them to the blast proof glass cage. Harry and Stu flashed their badges for the uniformed Marine, who buzzed them through. Upstairs in a hushed hallway they passed a dark-paneled conference room on the way to a metal door at the end. The political officer tapped a number on a keypad, a lock clicked, and with some effort, he pulled against a sucking sound to swing the door open for the Peace Corps director and his APCD. Harry let Stu step through first, and then, for the second time in four months, Harry entered the Bubble, the Embassy secure room where he was not permitted entry.

The Regional Security Officer, Ray Sims, scowled at the sight of Harry. "What're you doing, bringing him in here?" he demanded of Tom. At the foot of the blond table under fluorescent lights sat the DCM, Jerry Andrews.

"It's okay," Tom said, taking a seat next to Ray. "The Ambassador wants him here."

"The whole Peace Corps brain trust," said Jerry. Three weeks from departing post to retire, a carefree short-timer now, Jerry was trying to joke with Ray, but Ray Sims had no sense of humor. He continued glaring balefully at Harry for being in the Bubble against all regulations.

Half expecting he might be told to leave, Harry gingerly took a seat. As Stu removed a sheaf of handouts from his briefcase, and set the stack on the table with two pens, Harry opened his spiral notebook and wrote, "Emergency Action Committee."

The door clicked open and Pamela walked in. Harry sat up straighter at the sight of her thick blonde hair and green eyes set off by the lilac jacket she wore. The USIS director, single, good looking, and cracking smart sat in the empty chair next to Harry. He smiled at her, trying hard not to think of the reception, a year before, when he first met Pamela, and where she managed to make it quite plain to Harry that any advances from him would not be welcome, somehow without saying a word.

Wearing reading glasses, head bowed, Cummings leafed rapidly through the classified cables. Darlene watched him, his face soft and worn as an old moccasin, the recessed overhead lights reflecting through his thinning black hair. The Navy had taught her to trust in the chain of command, but her parents had raised her to be wary. Perseverance, preparation and guardedness had been essential to her advancement along a career path dominated by white men. Hard-won experience had taught Darlene that surprises always were ugly.

From the bio Langley had cabled him in Yaoundé, along with his revised travel orders, Cummings knew Ambassador Jones was a political appointee, not career Foreign Service. Her office décor told him as much. There was no American eagle statuette, no paintings of warships at sea, no photographs of her shaking hands with important people, no framed awards. The African artwork and traditional crafts reminded Cummings of an up market gift shop, hardly typical of a former naval officer. Scanning the most recent classified cables, looking at the recipients on the routing slugs, skimming the first and final paragraphs of each, Cummings could see Ambassador Jones was reporting through the normal channels to A/S/AFR, the Assistant Secretary of State for African Affairs. But in several of the cables, she'd copied the NSC, keeping the White House directly informed.

She's political all right, thought Cummings, as he closed the black binder. He picked up the basket of glass beads and studied them for a few moments before glancing first at Julie Burton, a covert case officer, then at Ambassador Jones. "Tell me why I'm here," he said, his keen blueberry eyes peering over the half glasses on the tip of his nose.

Taken aback to think the intelligence chief didn't know why he'd been rerouted to Libreville, Darlene asked, "What have you been told, Mr. Cummings?"

"Assume I've been told nothing," he said, and slipped his glasses inside his jacket.

"Then I assume that you don't know the Gabonese government sent us a dip note threatening to close the Peace Corps program," said Darlene. "They allege that volunteers have meddled in the election campaign. We're putting together a contingency plan to evacuate the volunteers, if it comes to that, which is what we'll be meeting about shortly to discuss. Obviously, you have no way of knowing a second dip note was just delivered by presidential courier. One of our volunteers is wanted by the gendarmes for questioning in connection with the death of a man."

Walter Cummings waited a few seconds, to see if there was more. "Is that all?" he said. "They had me fly down here because of your Peace Corps volunteers?"

The sudden irritation was unexpected. "My instructions are to provide you with a full briefing of the situation, Mr. Cummings," said Darlene, "so if you'll permit, I'll back up and put our current situation in context." She sat perfectly erect, composed, hands folded in her lap. "Unrest among the university students began last year, followed by threats of a general strike from the labor unions. In the past, President Bongo would have acted quickly and decisively, thrown some people in jail and perhaps sent in the army to crack heads. But this time, because the global geopolitical situation is changing so rapidly, he had to find a different response."

Mary, the Ambassador's secretary, entered the office carrying a tray of cups and saucers. Cummings had asked for tea. Darlene would have guessed a senior intelligence officer preferred black coffee.

Blowing thoughtfully, Cummings sipped and reflected on the changes he'd lived through in his career. To see a white Foreign Service secretary serving coffee to a black woman ambassador, careful to close the door behind her when she left, that was change. He was curious to observe how Darlene would handle this briefing. It revealed a lot about a person. He found her attractive, watching the shapes her mouth made as she talked, speaking without notes, an articulate woman, and completely self-possessed.

"In the past," Darlene was saying, "when the Gaullists were in power in France, Bongo's number one priority, protecting privileged relations with the métropôle, made sense for all the right reasons. France is a permanent member of the Security Council in the event Bongo should ever need the U.N., and France maintains a standing guarantee of military intervention to protect Bongo in the event of a coup attempt. That guarantee was the strongest of the bonds that the White Sorcerer forged." Darlene cocked her head to make certain Cummings caught her reference to Jacques Foccart. "That promise kept the leaders of France's former African colonies in line, and aligned with France."

A smile creased Cummings' face to recall the career of Charles de Gaulle's onetime puppet master in Africa, the man in the shadows, as Foccart had widely been known.

The man's smile did not reach his eyes, Darlene observed. She was as alert as a falcon, while he sat as still as stones. "You'll recall," she resumed, "Bongo tried to block the rise of the French Socialists by contributing funds to opposition political campaigns on the right. He had to have known François Mitterrand would learn about those campaign contributions, and would retaliate if he won, which he did. Bongo had to have been worried what Mitterrand would do with the Deuxième Régiment Étranger de Parachutistes."

"The Foreign Legion contingent Foccart stationed here," said Cummings.

"Yes, based at the airport," said Darlene with a nod at having just gauged the depth of Cummings' knowledge of Francophone African affairs. "Both times, when Mitterrand won election, Bongo tried to make a move in our direction, away from the French Socialist government. After Mitterrand's reelection in 1988, two years ago, Bongo made a point of congratulating President Bush on his own election the following November, the first African leader to do so. That same month, Bongo's Minister of Education formally requested Peace Corps to triple the size of the school construction program. Bongo wanted to blanket the Batéké heartland with schools, and I'll come back to that in a minute. Peace Corps agreed only after the White House pushed for it, to reciprocate. Peace Corps recruited two supplemental groups of construction volunteers and trained them out of the normal cycle. The first group swore in a year ago in December, which as it happened was the month Ceausescu was executed in Romania. The video on the news unnerved Bongo completely. Perhaps you noticed the cable we wrote, Mr. Cummings, when you were looking through the class file just now? A few months ago, Bongo called me to the Palace and made the same pitch he made to my predecessor, Ambassador McNamara, nine years ago."

Cummings smirked. "Which was what? More Peace Corps?"

Darlene smiled at the sarcasm. Maybe there was no agenda behind the intelligence officer's visit, nothing to fear. Maybe he was here to help. "Bongo talked in veiled terms, telling me, as I understood it, if the United States were to supplant the French in Gabon, U.S. oil companies might enjoy generous terms."

"What was behind the request?"

"I can only conjecture. Bongo's nervous about all the changes going on in the world, certainly. Ceausescu's death made him think of what can happen to a dictator who won't yield to popular demand. And then there's the irritation of Mitterrand's son, Jean-Jacques."

"Ah, yes, Papa M'a Dit." Cummings shook his head. "Daddy Told Me. That fat bastard might have been given Foccart's place, but he can't fill those shoes."

"Be that as it may, as I'm sure you know, Jean-Jacques's been trying to get for the Socialist Party all the goodies the Gaullists used to get. He's been pressuring Bongo for better terms. Bongo finally retaliated against Jean-Jacque's strong-arm tactics by ordering a full-scale government review of France's oil concessions. Bongo invited a dozen top Texas oil executives to Libreville, cowboy hats and all, all very splashy and heavily televised, all intended to rattle France's cage."

"I saw the reports," said Walter Cummings. "This happened before the Berlin Wall came down."

"Correct, which produced an immediate reaction here. University students demanded elections. The labor unions threatened a general strike. Right about the time that Gorbachev made a similar move in the Soviet Union, Bongo convened the Central Committee of his party and they formed a Special Commission for Democracy. Faster than anyone expected, Bongo accepted the commission's report, and announced there would be elections. Et voilà, Papa M'a Dit had a new angle to try, a different approach to furthering French Socialist Party interests, and presumably his own. He began funding one of the new opposition parties."

Cummings made an affirming grunt. "Papa lui a dit."

"Did he? Did President Mitterrand tell his son what to do? Perhaps Jean-Jacques has been operating on his own initiative. In any event, now that the campaigning is in full swing, with Election Day less than two months off, all those Peace Corps schools being built on the Batéké Plateau are paying off for Bongo in ways he could not possibly have foreseen."

"Jobs for the boys, buying their votes, good old fashioned patronage politics."

"In politics it's good to be lucky, but as things have turned out, Bongo couldn't have picked a worse time to try again to delink from France and move closer to the United States. He made his move a week before Saddam Hussein invaded Kuwait. Bongo's not lucky all the time. Secretary Baker has told all chiefs of mission worldwide that French cooperation on Resolution 660 is essential. We're to do nothing to upset the French. We need the French to contribute troops to the coalition. We're not messing in France's sphere of interest down here."

"So, no encouragement from you."

"Correct. I did not encourage Bongo to strip the French of their oil concessions and hand them to us, and I won't, unless, of course," said Darlene with a mischievous smile, "I receive instructions to the contrary."

Cummings snorted. "The coalition notwithstanding, the offer's got to be a temptation in Washington. I suppose the oil industry would love to have it both ways, get Kuwait back *and* get their mitts into Gabon's oil reserves."

"I should think so. In any event, Mitterrand's socialist principles haven't proven to be all that sturdy. Not when it comes to promoting democracy in Africa. The speech he gave in La Baule shows that. Bongo has been crowded into a corner by world events. His decision to hold multiparty elections has been driven by factors beyond his control, and multiparty elections in Gabon happen to be a very big worry to some very big interests up there in France."

"Elf has no truer friend than Omar Bongo."

"And the oil interests in Paris, they throw more weight than the Socialist Party. They like Bongo just where he is. The Foccart network is providing Bongo with expert advice. The entire electoral framework is designed for rigging. We had an assessment done. We know the details. I embargoed the report."

"It's no surprise for me to hear you say the French oil interests, in collusion with the Foccart network, are working against the French Socialist government."

"Or perhaps, working against the French Socialist Party," Darlene added. "Or maybe, working against Daddy Told Me, operating on his own hook."

Cummings took a moment to consider the murky possibilities. "This brings us up to date?"

"To the point where things started getting dirty."

"You're referring to the Rendjambé assassination."

"Yes. At first, the official cause of death was a drug overdose. Folks didn't buy it. There were riots in two major cities. The French consulate was torched in Port Gentil. Here in Libreville, protestors set fire to the hotel where Joseph Rendjambé's body was found."

"I assume you have people in the field. What are they hearing?"

"Mr. Cummings, this is a small post. Most of my officers are junior. Frankly, they haven't been able to gain access to Bongo's inner circle. That's why we asked to have a case officer assigned here."

Cummings looked at Julie Burton, her expression watchful. She was his, the spook, an undercover case officer declared as a diplomat, dressed the part in a black chalk-stripe pants suit with a collarless white blouse. It was unheard of to send a CIA case officer on TDY to a country with no chief of station in place, but extraordinary times necessitated extraordinary measures, and these were extraordinary times.

"How are you managing?" Cummings asked Julie.

Dark circles beneath her eyes revealed that Julie Burton wasn't getting adequate sleep. She spent her weekdays filling out her cover as the Embassy economics officer, writing cable digests of the mundane documents she collected, the roundtables and seminars she attended, the meetings she had with business people, opinion leaders, and government officials. Her real work began at night and on weekends, when she became one of the friendlier fixtures on the diplomatic circuit, chatting up influential Gabonese nationals.

"I'm fine, sir."

Cummings knew Julie Burton's résumé without having to see it. Recruited out of graduate school, proficient in at least one foreign language, trained at Camp Peary, the Farm as everyone called it, she knew how to drive fast, how to smash a car through a roadblock. Julie was trained in hand-to-hand combat. She could handle a variety of firearms. She knew how to spot people following her, and how to shake a tail. She had been through stressful situational role-playing that winnowed out weak recruits. Julie had learned to lie using any of the dozens of plausible ruses to gain access to secret information. She knew when to judge the moment was ripe, when to begin dropping hints to local contacts that she might not be who she had said she was, that there could be more to their bond than just friendship, that the information the new friend possessed was important enough for the United States to pay for it.

"So tell me," Cummings asked Julie, "how did Rendjambé die?"

Julie glanced at Darlene, who nodded. "All we know is he was poisoned after meeting Ambassador Jones."

"I invited the most viable opposition presidential candidates to the Embassy," Darlene explained. "Joseph Rendjambé was the most capable of them all. He asked what we could do to help. Nothing unusual in that. They all asked us to help them win. But a week later, Rendjambé was dead."

Cummings looked again at Julie. "Who was behind it?"

"It wasn't amateurs, sir," Julie replied. Her perfect diction came from the best private schools. "Without a leader, Rendjambé's party is foundering. We presume that was the intended consequence."

"Where will his supporters go?"

"There's talk they'll cast spoiled ballots in protest. If they don't do that, and if they bother to vote at all, their votes will probably go to the older of the two other major opposition parties, the Bûcherons, simply because of name recognition. They've been around longer."

Cummings laughed, genuinely amused at another in the infinite surprises of African politics. "The Lumberjacks? I'm afraid to ask what the other party is called."

"The PND, sir. The National Democratic Party. They're new, led by Antoine Badinga, a Gabonese businessman supposedly, but actually a gangster who got his start working for Sarkis Soghanalian."

Cummings began kneading the knuckles of his left hand. The Agency used Soghanalian often. Cummings himself had employed Soghanalian on more than one occasion. He was unaware of any connection to Badinga. "I'll have that checked out," he said. "What else?"

"Badinga used the contacts he made through Soghanalian to branch out on his own, brokering arms deals around the continent, guns for diamonds mainly. He made a small fortune, which is what brought him to the attention of Jean-Jacques Mitterrand."

Cummings shook his head. "Daddy Told Me. He's forever

popping up in the company of scoundrels. So how many political parties have formed?"

"Thirty-seven total," said Darlene. "It's purposeful. Bongo wants to splinter the opposition into as many parties as possible. The requirements for forming a political party are relatively easy to meet. Once certified, each party is given the equivalent of one hundred thousand dollars from state funds."

"That's a pretty big incentive to form a political party," Julie added. "And it's hard to say how much money Bongo is diverting from government coffers into his own campaign."

"What's Badinga like?" Cummings asked Julie. "Have you met him?"

"Yes sir. Shaved head, no neck. He talks fast and exudes a crude kind of charm. In front of a crowd, he's an effective speaker. I'm told he has appalling table manners."

"The classic African Big Man," said Cummings. "There must be some kind of factory churning them out. What sort of electoral system have they established?"

"Single member districts for the National Assembly, plurality voting for both the legislative and presidential elections, which will take place on the same day. No absolute majority means no second round. Whoever gets the most votes wins, even if it's less than fifty percent."

Cummings turned to Darlene. "You don't think the opposition has any chance of winning the Presidency, do you, Ambassador? How about a slim majority in the National Assembly?"

"That's more likely. If all the little parties win a seat or two each, the opposition might end up with more Deputies than the ruling party. In that case, the National Assembly won't be a legislature, it will be a mob, and Bongo won't have any trouble buying the support of the smaller parties to build a majority coalition. We believe that's the outcome he's planning for."

"But first he has to win reelection. Does Badinga or anyone else stand a chance?"

"Badinga's a Batéké from the Louzou clan, the former First Lady's people. They grew discontented after Bongo threw a fit following the humiliating divorce and dismissed every Louzou clan member from the government. Now Bongo is scrambling to win them back. He's sent truckloads of rice and cattle to be distributed. There are all those jobs building the Peace Corps schools. On the other side, thanks to Jean-Jacques Mitterrand, Badinga has a substantial campaign chest. He has more money than any other candidate, by far. He's picking up support in the cities by spending big on urban youth, sponsoring free concerts, soccer tournaments, giving away caps and tee shirts. The other major candidate, Mba Abbesole, comes from the largest tribe in Gabon, the Fang. Being a former priest, he's probably got the Catholic vote." Darlene turned to the young case officer. "Julie, what do you think? Could Bongo actually lose?"

"Well, considering that all the minor parties will peel off their little fractions of voters, Mba Abbesole will likely win the Catholic vote nationwide and the Fang vote up north. Badinga's bound to cut into Bongo's Batéké base in the east and will probably win among urban youth. The combined effect might be enough for either Badinga or Abbesole to outpoll Bongo."

"If, Mr. Cummings, and it's a huge if," stressed Darlene, "if the vote count is clean. But it won't be clean. Gabon's electoral system is designed for rigging."

"This analysis is compelling, Ambassador."

"Your case officer deserves a lot of the credit. How would you sum it up, Julie?"

"Thank you, Ambassador. Sir, the way we see it, the son of the President of France is putting Antoine Badinga in play right where it threatens Bongo the most, in the cities and in half his tribal base. It doesn't matter that Badinga won't win. What matters is leverage for when the elections are over, when it's time to kiss and make up, and talk about those oil concessions again."

"I get that part. But what's Bongo doing besides handing out rice and cows? He's not the sort to be sitting still."

"No sir," said Julie, "he's not sitting still. He's buying off everyone who matters. He's held separate talks with the main opposition candidates, cutting deals, working out who gets what after the election, so that he retains as much power as he can. Rendjambé refused to deal, and we think that's why he was assassinated."

"What sources have you developed?"

Julie grinned. "The senior aide to the President's chief of staff has developed a taste for small batch bourbon, sir, and he seems to believe I might actually be falling in love with him."

Cummings made a small smile, and turned to Darlene. "Is it safe to assume your FSNs can't be relied on, Ambassador?"

"Some of them probably report both ways, but it's hard to know which ones. So we don't place a lot of confidence in any of them. Before Julie got here, our two best sources were the French ambassador and the French advisor to the secret police."

"Huh!" said Cummings, surprised. "Who's their ambassador?"

"Philippe Berrier. He's been recalled. He was a Gaullist, accredited when Jacques Chirac served as prime minister in the cohabitation government. He made no secret of the fact he disliked the Socialists, which is probably the reason Paris yanked him. Naturally, he despised Mitterrand's son." Darlene shrugged. "Françafrique," she said.

Cummings shifted his weight, looked at his wristwatch and asked, "What time did you say we're meeting?"

The heavy metal door clicked open with a whoosh of air and the Ambassador walked in. They all stood when Darlene entered the Bubble followed by an older man. Behind him came Julie Burton. All business, Ambassador Jones told everyone to sit and took her place at the head of the table. Everyone knew Julie Burton, the new econ officer, or so they thought. The staff looked curiously at the older man.

"We have a visitor from Washington," said Darlene. "Let me introduce Walter Cummings, the Africa Division Chief of the CIA."

The surprise around the table was audible.

Cummings smiled. "I'm declared. That's why the Ambassador can tell you. The Gabonese government knows who I am."

"Ambassador," said Ray Sims, "we have someone in here without a security clearance." As an agent of the Diplomatic Security Service, the RSO was delegated certain authorities that even an ambassador couldn't contravene, but Darlene Jones had done so by having Harry Bowman brought into the Bubble.

"I know," said Darlene, annoyed that the RSO had challenged her authority in front of Walter Cummings. "I want Harry here.

385

There are bound to be questions about the logistics of evacuating the volunteers, if it comes to that. Harry will know best how to get them out of there. We wouldn't want to leave anyone behind, would we, Ray?"

Everyone looked at Harry. He blushed above his beard. His unprofessional appearance bothered Darlene, his embroidered African shirt, his sandals and beard. He hadn't expected to be called to this meeting. Tom Hughes, whose opinion she valued, had told her that Harry ran day-to-day operations at the Peace Corps. Tom and Harry played tennis together. Tom and Harry were her smart white boys.

"Good," she said. "Then let's start with the evacuation plan. Stu, can you brief us, please?"

Stu Eaton passed the handouts around. "On the first two pages is a list of sixty-seven volunteers to be evacuated if the government of Gabon orders us to," he said. "You can see about a third are in the Haut-Ogooué. The rest are pretty evenly distributed in the other eight provinces. Sixty-two are at their posts. Five are here in Libreville, the four volunteer leaders plus one receiving medical treatment. The logistical challenge is how do we get them all into Libreville? The last page, the spreadsheet, is our cost estimate and budget. We've tried to plan for every contingency, right down to tripling-up volunteers in hotel rooms while we book them on flights out of the country."

Stu gave everyone a moment to study the distribution of volunteers and the budget figures. "The plan and the budget are Harry's work," he said, "and Harry will explain how we'll bring the volunteers in."

"If we have to evacuate," Harry began, and abruptly his voice clogged up. He cleared his throat, nervous at all the eyes on him, especially the steely blue eyes of the tough-looking man from the CIA. "The volunteers will have to come in on bush taxis, except the ones in the Haut-Ogooué and the Ogooué-Lolo, where the school construction volunteers have pickup trucks. They can drive in with as many volunteers as they can carry. I'm still figuring out the details. The first big challenge is how to get word to the volunteers. Normally, in emergencies we send messages to volunteers through the gendarmerie short-wave radio system. That's probably how we'd have to do it."

"And that brings us to the main question," said Ambassador Jones, "What's the likelihood that President Bongo is in fact going to kick the Peace Corps out again?"

Bongo had done it once before, twenty-three years earlier, just a few months after taking office after the death of Léon Mba in 1967, to show the French where his loyalties lay.

Darlene flipped open a manila folder. "Last week I was summoned to the Foreign Ministry and handed a diplomatic note." She tapped the page before her. "This is a first-person note, a diplomatic correspondence of the highest importance, signed by the Minister of Foreign Affairs, the President's son." Darlene looked around the table, her eyes stopping at Walter Cummings. "If what this dip note alleges is true, if Peace Corps volunteers have indeed been participating in the election campaign, then we have a clear breach of the framework agreement, and a contravention of my explicit written instructions to every volunteer to stay well away from the candidates and from the campaigning."

"Ambassador," said Cummings, "in the event Bongo lets the Peace Corps remain, what will you do if the allegation is found to be true?"

Darlene replied with finality. "If I find out a volunteer has in fact been involved in the election campaigning, I'll terminate that volunteer, and so inform the government of Gabon."

Stu Eaton nodded his head.

Darlene turned to the next sheet of paper in her manila folder. "This morning a presidential courier delivered a second dip note, another first-person note. This makes two bombshells they've dropped on us now. This second dip note is signed by the Minister of the Interior, meaning this comes directly from Omar Bongo."

"He holds that portfolio, I gather?" said Cummings. "He's the Minister of the Interior?"

"Yes, and Minister of Defense, the ministries that control both the armed forces and the police. Bongo trusts no man with control of the government's weaponry. It's a fairly common arrangement among African dictators, as you know. They learn from each other how to avoid being overthrown. In this second dip note, as Minister of the Interior, Bongo is transmitting an official request."

"Is this about the Peace Corps too?" asked the DCM mildly, feigning ignorance, stroking his gray beard, as if he didn't already know.

Darlene ignored Jerry's brass and lifted a third piece of paper from her manila folder. "This is from the Commander of the National Gendarmerie. It seems one of our Peace Corps volunteers is wanted for questioning in connection with the death of a village man, apparently a newly named Batéké land chief of the Louzou clan. The volunteer's name is," Darlene consulted the page, "Charles Sinclair." She looked at Stu. "Director Eaton, where is this volunteer?"

Stu was prepared for the question. Darlene had phoned him as soon as she received the dip note, catching him just before he left for this meeting. "Charlie Sinclair early terminated two weeks ago," said Stu. "It was his choice. He'd grown disillusioned. It happens to some volunteers. They decide to quit. There's nothing we can do except send them home. Obviously, we had no idea he was wanted for questioning in someone's death." Stu looked to Harry.

"This will sound weird," said Harry, "but since Charlie left, we've heard that it had something to do with his Gabonese girlfriend, and witchcraft."

The Bubble buzzed at the word.

"Jesus, Stu," said the DCM. "First you got volunteers mixed up in politics. Now you got a volunteer, wanted by the law, who was mixed up with witchdoctors too?"

"What happened to Charlie's girlfriend isn't all that unusual," said Harry. "She got sick and went to the hospital. In Gabon, when doctors can't figure out what someone has, they often send the person back to the village, to try traditional remedies. Maybe I could go out to Charlie's old village and try to find out what happened."

"This isn't a good time, Ambassador," the RSO interjected, "to have a Peace Corps administrator go upcountry nosing around."

"Ray," said Darlene, "do you have a better suggestion? We need to know how the man died, don't we, so we know how to respond."

"I'll go see Gilles."

"Ray's referring to the French advisor to the secret police, Mr. Cummings. He's been a reliable contact." Addressing the group again, Darlene said, "Here's what we're going to do. Stu, I want you to call in all the volunteers from the Franceville area, just that area, and only the ones who might know what Charlie Sinclair was up to. We'll want to talk to each of them. Harry, you'll do that through the gendarmerie radio, right?"

"Yes, ma'am."

"Tom, I want you to draft our responses to both dip notes. In the first one, to the Minister of Foreign Affairs, acknowledge receipt, and say we understand and share the government's concern about alleged volunteer involvement in the campaigning. Acknowledge we recognize this would be a breach of the framework agreement, if true. We are very eager to have the charge substantiated. Use that term charge, to show them we understand both the gravity and the fact that it isn't proven. We therefore would greatly appreciate whatever information they can provide."

"Got it," said Tom, making notes.

"Next, for our reply to the Minister of the Interior, regarding the matter the gendarmes are interested in; address it to both the Minister of the Interior and President of the Republic. Say that the volunteer in question has terminated his service and left the country. Jerry, there's no extradition treaty with Gabon, correct?"

"No," said the DCM.

"Double check that, Jerry, to be sure. Tom, tell the Minister of the Interior, Omar Bongo, we're bringing in all volunteers who might know something about the matter; the volunteers who might shed some light on whatever happened out there. Make it clear that we will not permit the police to interrogate any of them. I don't want any phone calls from angry parents, no letters from Congressmen. We'll handle any questioning to be done. But to guide our inquiry, we need whatever details the government can provide. And make it crystal clear that we are not, repeat not evacuating the volunteers."

"Are we sure, Ambassador?" Tom asked, as he finished making his notes, "that we don't want to let the police question them, the volunteers we bring to Libreville?" He looked up. "Maybe we should, to show them we're cooperating."

"Ambassador, what if," drawled the DCM before Darlene could respond, "somebody killed that chief in the village, and what if our

389

guy did it?" Andrews, deadpan as always, dry as a stick, but no one laughed.

"Why then, Jerry," said Darlene with a glint in her eye, "in that case, it would appear, wouldn't it, that a Peace Corps volunteer named Charlie Sinclair has gotten away with murder."

24. A Way Back

Libreville

Hector and Dabrian turned away the moment Rebecca began to cry. Embarrassed for her sake, they looked out over the sea. Waves rolled in from the west as the sun sank between towering clouds. Shouting young men dribbled a soccer ball bouncing unevenly through sand churned by their feet

"What do you suppose Charlie's doing right now?" Hector asked, his voice raised to be heard over the fuzzy blare of soukous music pouring from the beach bar's blown speakers. The fluorescent lights suddenly flicked on, casting a blue light.

"What have they got going on in Minnesota?" asked Dabrian. He tried again to get the waitress's attention. "Dance polka? I can't see Charlie dancing polka."

"I can't see Charlie dancing at all," said Hector.

"What month is this? November? Probably freezing his ass off by now."

"They say living in the tropics thins your blood," said Rebecca.

Dabrian and Hector turned to look at her, wiping tears from her cheeks with the palms of her hands. She managed a smile. Her nose was red, and she put her glasses back on.

"I don't suppose that's true," she said. "Blood doesn't get thin, does it?"

"No, I don't suppose it does," said Hector.

Dabrian held up three fingers to the waitress. "After this round, we should head into town and get something to eat."

"Any place special you want to go, Rebecca?" asked Hector.

"Oh, suddenly you're so considerate? I get to choose, because it's my last supper. Is that why?"

"Last supper in Libreville," said Dabrian.

"Something like that," said Hector. Whatever animosity there had been between the two of them, it was over as far as he was concerned. He didn't want to part ways with Rebecca on bad terms.

"How about the fish place over in Glass?" Dabrian suggested.

Rebecca shrugged. "You know, I don't care if I got early terminated. It's a good story, actually. What I did was a good thing. I'm leaving with no regrets."

"Right," said Dabrian, drawing out the word.

Rebecca hooked her long hair back behind her ears. "I have my pick of three grad schools. I have my dissertation topic all ready to go. I'm sure glad I thought to bring all my notebooks with me. When the gendarmes came to Otou with the message, I guessed this might happen."

"It sucks they won't even let you go back and pack your things,' said Hector.

"Sharon says she'll take care of it for me."

"It still sucks."

"If you see him, will you make sure Philbert knows what happened to me? He'll wonder."

"Sure," said Dabrian, recalling Rebecca's brawny boyfriend. She hadn't hooked up with him for his brains.

The soccer players dispersed in the dark, filing past. Two of them went to the bar, the sun slipping into the sea as the fading light of day streaked the western sky.

"Give me a cigarette," said a broad-shouldered young soccer player, sweaty and sprinkled with sand.

"No one here smokes," said Dabrian.

"Then give me a beer."

"Buzz off," said Hector.

"What's your name?" the young man asked Rebecca, brazen, a knowing look.

"I said beat it," warned Hector, "or I'll kick your ass."

"If I had the chance," said Rebecca, as the soccer player left, "I'd tell the Ambassador I wanted to try to change things. The opposition parties have no resources. They asked the United States government for help, but they refused. If I had the chance, I'd tell the Ambassador she's a hypocrite. I read her book. She didn't stand up for her principles. I'd really tell her off."

"I bet you would too," said Hector.

Rebecca smiled to find herself endeared to dark little Hector Alvarado, at the very last moment, on the day before she would return to the United States. "I gave you a hard time, didn't I?"

"Yes you did, Rebecca. I know what it's like to be on the receiving end."

Rebecca laughed as their beers came, and they refilled their glasses.

"If I had the chance," she said, "I'd tell the Ambassador, in my own small way, I was trying to change history. I wrote the speech. I advised Georges, the candidate, to start carrying a broom, you know, one of those whisk brooms the women use? I told him it would be a symbol for the women voters. I was proud of that speech. He'd start by asking if the people received rice from the ruling party, and when they said yes, he'd say, and did they receive a cow from the ruling party, and when they said yes, then Georges would deliver it. That rice and that cow were yours in the first place, he'd say, paid for with money stolen from you, totally breaking the taboo, and then he'd start denouncing Bongo's corruption, saying his party was a new broom, and a new broom always sweeps clean. Then he'd yell out, waving the broom back and forth, 'Eat the cow! Vote for me!'"

"I wish I could have seen that," said Hector.

"The people loved it, hearing the truth, but it scared them too. I guess I won't know how the voting goes."

"Eat the cow, vote for me," said Dabrian. "I'd vote for him."

"I don't imagine he really has a chance, but would you guys write to me, and tell me how Georges did, even if he doesn't win?"

"Sure," said Dabrian.

"I'll write to you, Rebecca," said Hector. "I'm not that good at writing letters, but I'll write to you."

Rebecca's face crumpled to think Hector, with whom she had quarreled so bitterly, wanted to make peace, and would actually write to her, and she struggled for a moment to keep from crying again. She heaved a sigh, and gulped beer. "I'll miss you guys," she said, trying hard to keep her voice from quavering.

"We'll miss you too," said Dabrian, touching her hand.

Akièni

Natalia had never taken her boxy little Peugeot 405 out of Franceville, except for trips on the paved highway west to Moanda. She needed glasses to drive and sat bolt upright, heading north with both hands on the wheel, the driver's seat slid all the way forward. Hector had talked her into taking her car, instead of his Land Cruiser. "The road to Akièni is in good shape," he insisted. "Your car will make it just fine. It'll be an adventure."

The autumnal rainy season had been over for weeks, and bone-dry laterite dust hung pink in the air, whipped up by southbound vehicles and an unseen truck ahead that Natalia did not manage to overtake. Her Peugeot had air conditioning, so the windows were up, and the air in the car was breathable.

"We're almost there," said Hector when they approached the bridge over the Lékoni River. He braced the shiny pot of ajiaco on the floor between his shins, to keep it from overturning, his feet bare but for a thin pair of red flip-flops. "Akièni's at the top of this hill."

Natalia downshifted and accelerated up the steep embankment.

"Justine lives near the hospital," said Hector, as they entered the town, passing the gendarmerie on their left and the Catholic mission on their right. "Take the left just past the post office."

"There isn't much here to see, is there?" said Natalia, making the turn.

"No, there isn't much to see in Akièni. That's the hospital ahead. Justine lives in one of those government bungalows. We'll have to ask, but I don't know her last name. Let me ask this kid."

The boy in faded blue shorts, barefoot, with knobby knees, stepped back fearfully as the car with two foreigners braked to a halt alongside him, the window going down.

"Eh, petit, viens!" said Hector. "C'est où la maison de l'infirmière Justine, qui a deux frères jumeaux?"

"The nurse with twin brothers?" said the boy, visibly relieved that was all this was about. He pointed to the house.

Natalia parked in front. Hector carried the pot up to the front porch. Through the open front door they saw Justine resting in her salon, her eyes closed, bare feet elevated on the arm of the faded velour couch. "Koh, koh, koh," said Pablo.

Justine opened her eyes and recognized them at once. "Natalia! Hector!" she cried, swinging her feet to the floor with a smile that lit up her face. She rose with some difficulty, adjusting her pagne. "Entrez, entrez!"

Mama Angélique came out of the kitchen dressed all in black wearing a severe expression on her face to shake hands with the visitors. She took the pot from Hector, and spoke to Justine in Téké.

"My mother asks if she should heat this for lunch."

"We're fine," said Natalia, but Hector rubbed his hands together and nodded with a grin.

"I could use something to eat."

At Justine's bidding, her mother returned to the kitchen. "Please, sit down," she said, gesturing toward the worn matching wine-colored armchairs. She eased herself onto the couch and asked, "What brings you to Akièni?"

"Hector wanted to see how the school that he started is coming out," replied Natalia, "and of course we wanted to see you. I made a pot of ajiaco. I remember how much you liked it."

"You are very kind. Where are you staying? Or are you going back to Franceville tonight?"

"We're spending the night in Obia," said Hector. "That was the first *stage* site I ran. We saw the school driving by, but we wanted to come here first. One of the former stagiaires is finishing it. Do you remember Ronnie Clavelle?"

Justine frowned, trying hard to recall. "I've met so many Americans."

"He has a big beard and a glass eye."

"Oh yes. The mechanic."

"That's right. Ronnie helped Charlie fix up Twisted Sister."

A fleeting wince crossed Justine's face. "Twisted Sister," she said, and forced a laugh.

Natalia recognized Justine's pang of heartbreak at Hector's mention of Charlie's name, and changed the subject. "Do you know, this will be my first night staying in a Gabonese village?"

"You will find it very quiet at night," said Justine. At a clatter of crockery, she turned to see her mother setting the table. "Do you have any news of Charlie?" she asked in a cautious tone.

Natalia could see how hard Justine was struggling to keep her feelings under control. Thin and weak, her face almost gaunt, this was not the strong, bright and vivacious personality Natalia remembered.

"Oh yeah," said Hector, "that's the other reason we came by." He slipped a folded piece of paper from his shirt pocket and gave it to Justine. "This is Charlie's address in the United States. He said to give it to anybody who might want to write."

Justine took the paper but did not unfold it. "Thank you," she said.

Natalia saw the tremor in Justine's hand as she set Charlie's address on the side table. The weight Justine had lost brought out her high cheekbones, and made her wide-set eyes seem larger. Natalia was struck again by Justine's beauty, and she reached over to touch her arm. "We were all surprised that he left so suddenly."

Hector shook his head. "I drove him to the airport. One day he's here, the next day, like that, poof, he's gone."

Justine looked at the floor. "He had a good reason to go."

"What was the reason? He wouldn't tell me why he was leaving. It had something to do with what happened to you, didn't it, Justine?"

"Hector." Natalia gave him a sharp look to stop. His lack of discernment could be so irritating.

"That's what everyone is saying."

"Be quiet, Hector! You look much better, Justine," said Natalia, "but you've lost a lot of weight. How do you feel?"

"Better," said Justine. "I'm gaining weight. Having my mother here helps. I'm eating well again. Soon I'll be able to go back to work." She didn't mention the letter approving her transfer to Franceville. She intended now to retract her request.

Heedlessly Hector kept on. "Charlie's not the only one who's gone. Rebecca's gone too. Did you hear about that, Justine? The Ambassador terminated her."

"What? Terminated?"

Hector snapped his fingers. "Like that. Gone. Fini. Sent home for getting involved in the election campaign. Did you know about that?"

"No, I didn't."

"Yeah, one day, out of the blue, a couple weeks after Charlie left, the gendarmes came out to all the sites with a message saying we were called in to Libreville. The Embassy wanted to question us. The Regional Security Officer, a retired cop, he tape-recorded what each one of us said, like we were suspects. Did you ever meet Harry Bowman? He was there too. We couldn't all fit in the Peace Corps guesthouse, so they put some of us up in a hotel. The air conditioning was nice, but you couldn't afford to eat in the restaurant on the per diem we had. We went to the beach during the day and we went out at night, and we compared notes about what the RSO asked us. It was like an interrogation."

"They were asking about Rebecca?"

"It ended up being about Rebecca, once somebody mentioned her name. No one admitted to giving her up, but once the RSO had her name, we all confirmed that we heard the rumors, about her chauffeuring one of the candidates around in her truck. A few people said they actually saw what she was doing. That was it. Rebecca was on the next flight out. Gone. They didn't even let her go back to her village to pack her stuff. Somebody had to do that for her."

"I'm sorry for Rebecca," said Justine.

"She should have known better."

Natalia agreed. "What she did wasn't very smart."

"Well, Hector, at least while you were there, you could go to the beach," joked Justine, and images of her magical trip to Mayumba with Charlie came swirling into her head, the elephants and whales, the hippopotamuses going into the ocean, and the Forest of Bees. Hector didn't know of the road trip, and all the things she and Charlie had seen. No one knew. It would always be her secret with Charlie, who was gone.

"They didn't send us back right away," said Hector. "Everyone was called back for a second time. The RSO had more questions. It turns out Charlie is wanted by the police."

Instantly Justine pictured Commandant Lentchidja and the subaltern with a holstered pistol coming into her house, the day they questioned her. "What do they want him for?" she asked, although she knew.

"Somebody died, a land chief in Charlie's old village. The Embassy wanted to know about the death. We all figure that's probably what the police want him for. Tell me, Justine, was the land chief really a witchdoctor? Sharon McGuire, the woman with the short hair who replaced Charlie? She said Charlie showed up with his sick girlfriend, which was you, and Dabrian, and an old half-naked woman painted all red and white. She said the old woman was a witchdoctor too. Sharon said they had a ceremony, and soon after that, the land chief died. Dabrian said it was just a healing ceremony, but was that what killed the man?"

Justine couldn't answer, blinking, her mouth turned down.

"Is there any truth to what they're saying? Was Charlie involved in killing the land chief?"

"Stop, Hector," said Natalie.

"No," said Justine. "It's all right. Charlie didn't kill anyone."

"They really zeroed in on Dabrian, because he drove, and was there. Sharon said she stayed in her house. You might not remember very well, but I was in Franceville when all of you left. You were really sick. You were going to find a traditional healer. I told them what Charlie told me when he showed up at Natalia's house, his bags packed, trying to act real calm. I could tell something was eating him, something bad had happened to him. He said he needed to go. He said he was going to early-terminate. Just like that. I tried to talk him out of it, but he'd already bought a plane ticket to Libreville. He gave me the keys to the house and his truck, and at the airport, he gave me his address and said goodbye. He never even looked back."

Justine sobbed, and choked it back.

"Hector, stop!"

Natalia moved to the couch and took Justine's hand, surprisingly cold on such a warm and humid afternoon. Tears leaked from Justine's eyes, and she wiped them away.

"Can't you see you're upsetting her?"

Justine shook her head. "It's all right." She undid her pagne, dried her eyes, then tucked the printed cloth again under her arm. She picked up Charlie's address, unfolded the paper, studied his handwriting for a second, and put it back on the table. She cleared her throat. "Rebecca was terminated, you said."

"Yeah," said Hector, "she finally admitted to what she did." He grew animated again. "The last thing she said on her last night with us, was she was leaving with only one regret. She said she was sorry that she wasn't going to be here for the election."

Franceville

On Election Day, Hector awoke before the birds, as he always did. He slipped out of bed gently so as not to awaken Natalia. On a Sunday, she would not want to be awakened for a couple more hours. Bare-chested, barefoot, wearing only a pair of gym shorts, Hector tiptoed into the kitchen to make coffee. While it brewed, he checked in the refrigerator to make sure there were eggs. He was accustomed now to the brown eggs from the large-scale poultry farm they had opened down in Boumango. As the fragrance of the brewing coffee filled the room, he looked at Natalia's calendar on the refrigerator door. December 8, 1990. He wondered if he should go buy fresh baguettes. Would any of the boulangeries be open on Election Day? He guessed not.

When the coffee was ready, Hector filled a mug, opened the sliding glass door to Natalia's back patio, and went out into the cool predawn. He sat on a wrought iron chair, his coffee mug on a glass table. The first light of day was visible through the trees above the roof of the neighbor's bungalow. A mosquito whined near his ear. Hector contemplated the bird of paradise flowers in Natalia's garden, orange petals like the heads of crested cranes looking about. Far away, a rooster crowed. Birds began stirring, twittering. He recognized the cooing of a red-eyed dove. A grey-headed sparrow alit on the patio bricks, eyed Hector, and flittered away when he lifted his mug. He could see the bougainvillea covering the neighbor's carport, white and lavender bracts as thin as tissue paper shivering in an unfelt breeze. He breathed into his coffee. Steam rose into his eyes. Hector thought, this is going to be a lovely day.

Mama Marianne opened the Shade of the Mango Trees Bar on Election Day morning in breach of a ministerial decree prohibiting the sale of alcohol while the polls were open. But Mama Marianne always opened at eight o'clock, even on Sundays. Chef de quartier, friendly with the Mayor of Franceville, whose white Peugeot was sometimes seen parked out back of her bar on evenings when Mama Marianne was nowhere to be found, ministerial decrees were of no concern to her.

All the Haut-Ogooué volunteers had been ordered to report to the provincial capital as a precaution, in case the voting turned violent. This decision had emerged over the course of several phone conversations between Skip Lomax, the new volunteer leader in Libreville, the former sign painter who had replaced the departed Jim Bonaventure, and Ronnie Clavelle, who had recently stepped up as regional logistics coordinator, after Charlie early-terminated.

Both Peace Corps houses in the Cité de la Caisse were jammed to capacity Saturday night, and by 8:30 Sunday morning, Peace Corps trucks began arriving at Mama Marianne's bar. Toad, Nate and Dabrian, three of the most senior construction volunteers brought metal chairs out under the spreading mango tree, carrying frost-rimed green beer bottles ice cold after spending the night in Marianne's deep freezer. Only five of the group of eight who trained at Boundji remained in Gabon, and Hector was holed-up with Natalia at CIRMF.

"Yah!" Timo hollered, grabbing onto Ronnie's hand in glee as two more Peace Corps pickups arrived, the circle of chairs under the ancient mango tree growing. Timo loved seeing all his brothers gather in one place, the display of Land Cruisers parked bumper to bumper, each with a full tank of gas in case they had to make a run for it, although where they would run to wasn't clear. Three English teachers, two young women and a young man from the small cities of Moanda, Okandja and Lékoni were listening as Timo ranted to Ronnie. "Dese fawkin' people! You can never know what dey got in dere minds! Dat's why we mus' all stay togedder now, so we can be ready for de nex' t'ing! Yah!"

"I say, if the shit hits the fan, we head for the Congo," said Cleon Renfrew in his battered straw cowboy hat.

"Oh that's a bright idea, Cleon," sneered Freddie Jackson, a TEFL teacher from Okandja. "Don't you know the Congo's a Communist country? They got Cuban-trained militiamen with Kalashnikovs in every village, just waiting for the imperialists to invade. What do you think they'd do if a pack of Americans rolled up in a bunch of pickup trucks?"

"Open up with their AK-47s," said Toad. "D-d-d-d-d!" he said, pointing the mouth of his empty bottle, "d-d-d-d-d!" swinging the bottle from side to side, mowing everyone down.

Timo couldn't sit still. He'd planned a feast for later. A squadron of young girls dragooned from Mama Marianne's quartier were slow-cooking bush meat he'd procured in villages on his way into Franceville. Laughing raucously just as the wire-haired anarchist from California pulled in, Ricky Brenner, the last construction volunteer to arrive, Timo let go of the bearded logistics coordinator's hand and went to Kevin Pfeiffer, plodding like a plowman out of Marianne's tin-roofed bar clutching six green bottlenecks between his fingers. Timo grabbed two and gave one to Sharon McGuire, Charlie's replacement in Okouya, her hair still short and mannish.

The only woman in the construction program since Rebecca was sent home, Sharon had taken up drinking. "T'ank you, my brudder," she said, before turning back to Lisa McAdams, the TEFL volunteer wearing a faded black tee shirt emblazoned with I LOVE THE JUNGLE in peeling red letters. Two construction volunteers, Cleon, and Jason Richards, with blond dreadlocks down to his shoulder, his acne nearly cleared up, listened to Sharon recount how hard it is to kill a pangolin. "I kept whacking and whacking and whacking the thing with a machete," she said. "Those fuckers just won't die."

"That's disgusting," said Lisa. On the back of her tee shirt was KURTZ.

Dabrian watched them indulgently, savoring the biting cold beer, the young Americans gathering like a noisy tribe under an ancient mango tree. He was calm and acutely aware of his atura afou, his power, like a panther crouched at his feet.

Akièni

Standing in line to vote in the morning cool, the sun in her eyes, warming her face, Justine couldn't stop thinking about Charlie. She'd seen him in a dream last night, and the euphoria still lingered, along with the heartache of waking up to realize it wasn't true.

Eating breakfast, she imagined how wonderful it would be to see Charlie walk in through the door. That he was gone stung her like grief. She should never have listened to the ngaa-bwa, should not have believed that she and Charlie could not be together. But it was too late, and she tried her best not to think about it anymore, but she missed Charlie with an ache in her bones. She imagined him standing here with her in the line, as she explained what was happening in her country, looking up at him, seeing him smiling, handsome and strong.

She had mailed a letter to the address Hector gave her. She confessed her error in telling Charlie to leave, and wrote to him, will you come back to me?

The line, already long, and growing longer every minute, snaked around an avocado tree. The whole of Akièni it seemed was turning out to vote, now that voting would actually matter, now that there was more than just one party.

Justine wasn't sure who to vote for. She'd never voted before, because it never seemed worth the bother. What did it matter, she asked herself, voting to renew Bongo's mandate for another term, or voting to validate the nominee for their constituency, proposed by the ruling party to sit uselessly in the rubber stamp National Assembly?

The Louzou clan felt little love for President Bongo after the purge following his divorce from the First Lady, after Bongo summarily dismissed all Louzous from their government posts. The stream of money sent back to the villages dried up. Cash awards from the First Lady's dance group competitions stopped coming, as did trips to Libreville for the lucky few who caught the First Lady's ear with a catchy praise song, or her eye with a flattering school essay or a moving personal letter. Resentment began to grow. For the first time people began to speak out openly against Bongo. Many of Justine's friends and neighbors were saying without fear that the election provided an opportunity for retribution. One of their own was running for President, a Louzou named Antoine Badinga.

A gendarme with an AK-47 patrolled the lengthening line as voters inched toward two tables manned by four poll workers. Justine recognized an elderly lady who sold nkoumou at the market presenting her national identity card. The first poll worker located the old woman's name on a list and ticked it off. The next poll worker handed her two ballots. She proceeded to the second table where a muscular young man showed her how to mark the ballots. Justine wondered if that was correct for him to do. The nkoumou seller folded her ballots, and she continued to two wooden boxes where a fourth poll worker showed her which ballot to drop into which box.

"Is that all there is to voting?" Justine asked the man standing behind her. He didn't understand the sense of her question. She took another step forward as the line advanced, certain only that she was going to vote against Antoine Badinga, the man whose people had tried to kill her.

Libreville

It was dark outside when Ambassador Jones pulled out the blue wire behind the decoder box, and her television changed to the snowy Gabonese state channel. They were broadcasting a music video on Election Night. Why in the world aren't they showing returns? Darlene wondered irritably. She plugged the satellite decoder back in and the picture changed to CNN replaying a six month old video clip of Saddam Hussein ruffling the hair of a little European boy. Darlene returned to her couch and sat near the telephone on the side table, her walkie-talkie, notepad and a cup of tea on the coffee table before her, while Bernard Shaw reported that Saddam Hussein, in an effort to stave off the impending invasion, had decided to release all the foreign hostages he'd been holding. After a break came a story on the legislative elections in newly reunified Germany. A correspondent in Bonn described the landslide victory of Helmut Kohl's coalition that won sixty percent of the seats in the Bundestag. In stark contrast to Gabon's music video, CNN showed a graph of the election results and a live shot of Kohl loyalists cheering. When the story changed to Ted Turner and Jane Fonda announcing their engagement, footage showing the happy couple in a number of locales, Darlene thought of her husband Calvin, and wondered what he was doing right then. Suddenly tired and homesick, she switched the television off.

Darlene and her small team had done what they could with their inadequate budget to observe voting in Gabon's three largest cities. She personally had spent Election Day visiting polling stations in Libreville, while members of her team observed the process in Port Gentil and Oyem. The turnout appeared high, due in part to novelty and curiosity, as close to orderly as anything in Gabon ever was. All day long, she'd jotted down thoughts for the reporting cable she would write in the morning. She began rereading her notes.

The walkie-talkie squawked, Tom, code name Madison, calling in from the Ministry of the Interior. Darlene pushed the mike button. "This is Brooklyn. Go ahead, Madison."

"There's no change," said Tom. "They're still not letting any diplomatic observers inside the return center, and they just sent out word that the collating process will go on for at least another day. There's not much point to hanging around here, over."

"I guess not, Madison. You might as well go home. It's been a long day for everyone, over."

A long day and a flawed election, but a step in the right direction, thought Darlene, as she sipped her cold tea. She recited aloud the phrase she would use in her cable: Democracy is never fully achieved; it's always in a state of becoming.

She liked the phrase. Then, loneliness washed over her. She leaned back and wondered if she should call Calvin. Is he at the restaurant? Or home watching football? Or somewhere else? Darlene pulled out an album of summer photos taken before she returned to Gabon from annual leave. She found Calvin's most recent letter inside, various phone numbers scribbled on it, a page and a half in her husband's crabbed hand, hard to read as much for his poor penmanship and truncated writing as for the subject matter.

"United Telecom is acquiring U.S. Sprint. Signaling System 7 is exciting. It's changing everything, network management and call completion. Digital signals transmitted through fiber optic cables, drop a pin on a table and it's heard a thousand miles away! They're showing it on a TV ad. Stock prices in my portfolio are pushing through the roof! Miss you already. Calvin."

Darlene turned to the pictures. An attendant had taken a photo of her with her father and her sister Eunice at the nursing home in Brooklyn. Her father looked so frail, a husk of the hard-working man from her childhood. He'd been married for fifty-four years to their mother when she died, and he didn't know how to live without her. Increasingly confused, he was becoming a burden to Eunice. The last time she and her sister talked on the phone, Darlene heard the resentment in her voice. "While you're out there changing the world, Darlene, I'm struck here taking care of Dad. It's not fair."

In another picture, Calvin and Uncle Web stood in front of the restaurant and club on Frenchmen Street. She looked at the painted brick cottage with the slate roof. The only interior photo they'd taken showed just the fireplace. There she was in the lush backyard, in shorts, wearing sunglasses. There was Calvin Junior, who would be nine in February. There was her husband at the grill wearing an apron that read: Real Men Don't Use Recipes. Calvin had her take his picture posed behind the wheel of his white and burgundy Lincoln, the door open, pretending to be talking on the car phone. She could hear him saying, "Darlene, you don't need to work anymore."

She wanted to ask him, "What will I do when I get bored of doing nothing, Calvin?" and she closed the album and picked up the receiver and began to dial.

Saint Paul

The *St. Paul Pioneer Press* gave the story only an inch. Omar Bongo had won the first multiparty election in Gabon since independence. Four inches of snow fell that day, and six inches fell two days after Christmas, when Charlie received a letter from Gabon, a pale blue aerogram inside a stamped envelope addressed by Mrs. Dawber.

Mrs. Dawber had answered the phone when Charlie called from the airport. She was surprised to hear he was back in America, and glad that nothing was wrong. Or at least, Charlie led her and Coach to believe there was nothing wrong. He was back from yet another thing in his life he didn't want to tell anyone about, ever. Instead, he told the Dawbers he'd learned French, which he could speak pretty

405

well.

"The plateau was really beautiful," he told them. "I have pictures. The people there are friendly." As he said that, he thought of the man who sent a scorpion into the body of the woman he had wanted to love. "Peace Corps just wasn't for me," he said.

Coach scowled. He didn't like to hear that. He didn't approve of quitting. He bawled Charlie out like he used to at practice. "Winners never quit, and quitters never win, Charlie! You have to pull up your socks and get on with it, decide what you want to do with your life. You're a grown man now, Charlie."

"You seem subdued," said Mrs. Dawber in an attempt to smooth things over. "Is anything the matter? Coach is right, you know. You do need to get on with your life."

Charlie didn't need to be told he wasn't welcome to live at their home anymore. It was awkward, staying with them for the week it took him to sort things out, buy a used pickup truck, rent an apartment and furnish it from Goodwill. He found a menial job in a warehouse, in the receiving department. Until he decided what to do next, the warehouse job would do. It paid the monthly rent. His fleabag apartment didn't require a lease. There was nothing holding him in Minnesota. He could leave at the drop of a hat.

Charlie opened the pale blue aerogram from Hector. Strewn with spelling errors, the spiky handwriting yanked Charlie right back to Africa.

"I'm taking it easy, finishing the stage school in Quartier Sable. Have you heard Bongo almost threw Peace Corps out of the country? You won't believe it, but it was because of Rebecca. She got involved in the campaigning." Three times Hector had tried to spell the word, and even the third attempt was wrong. "They called all the volunteers in from the Haut-Ogooué to Libreville and asked everyone about Rebecca; and about you too, Charlie, because the gendarmes want you for questioning about a man who died in Okouya. What's that about anyway? I asked Justine and she really didn't give me an answer. The ambassador ET'ed Rebecca and the director of all of Peace Corps, Paul D. Coverdell himself, had to fly to Gabon. They say he personally apologized to Bongo. Must have worked. Bongo hasn't kicked us out. Me and Natalia went to Akiéni to see Justine. She's better now. I gave her your address. Maybe she'll write. Ronnie stepped up and took the Franceville job. We aren't sure how we're going to get the school built in Souba. Nate Jenkins is finishing Otou. Natalia's fine and says hi. Everyone hopes you're doing okay, Charlie. You should write when you have a chance, and tell us what you're up to. That's it for me. Take care, Hector."

A cold snap came on the fourth day of the New Year, 1991, a Friday. When Charlie got back from the warehouse that evening, there was a single letter in his brass mailbox, addressed to him in Mrs. Dawber's handwriting. He ripped open the envelope and found another pale blue aerogram from Gabon, this one from Justine. His hands trembled as he tore it open.

"Cher Charlie, How are you? I am feeling better every day. Whenever I see one of the American trucks in Akièni, I think of you. I see them in town almost every day, so I think of you all the time. Hector and Natalia came to visit. He gave me your address. This is how I can write to you. I was sad you left, without even saying goodbye. You didn't even argue. I made a mistake when I told you to go. I understand that now. The twins are doing well at school, and they say hello. Jonas says hello too.

"Charlie, Okorogo René is dead. The ngaa-bwa's medicine worked. Commandant Lentchidja came around asking questions, but you were gone. I wish it could have been different for us. What will you do now that I tell you I have changed my mind? Will you come back to me? I hope you will write to tell me you will return. Maybe you won't. Maybe you have found another girl. I know how you are. I know I will never find another man like you. I miss you so much." She signed the letter in English, "I love you, Charlie. Goodbye. Justine."

Charlie walked outside on that clear and bitter cold evening and got in the old Ford F-150 he'd bought. He drove west as the red sky turned black. He had made enemies in Okouya without knowing it; enemies who encouraged an evil man to choose Justine for the unkébé that almost killed her, and made her tell him to go. He had left Gabon hardening his heart, trying to relegate Justine to the string of people who had sent him away. He knew how to pack and go. He'd been doing it all his life. But she had written him a letter.

Charlie drove until it was the dead of night, and the road had shrunk down to two lanes. He followed headlights deep into the countryside. All the while, through the windshield, he could see Justine's up-tilted black eyes, eyes that pinned him in place like a dart. That beautiful girl had torn his world wide open, sliding across the seat of his Land Cruiser to show him the rain forest, sitting under the stars beside him in the back of Twisted Sister where he told her what he had never told any girl before, ever. She was the only person he had ever opened his heart to like that, and she betrayed him, told him to go. What now?

Near midnight, he came to a deserted roadside rest area and pulled over by a snow-covered picnic table. He got out into the biting cold of a still and moonless night and looked up, and for the first time since he had left Gabon, Charlie saw the hard white light of the stars.

"What is it, Justine?" he asked her, bouncing across the wobbly vine bridge. "All the stories you told me." There was a letter in his pocket and he wanted to know, was she really asking him to come back to her. Staring up into the black heavens, his breath boiling about his face, Charlie shouted, "What do you want me to do?"

A shooting star whipped across the sky just then, fast and silent, a flicker coming in from the void. In that instant, Justine stood next to him, her arm around his waist, and Charlie knew, smiling up at the stars, he would figure a way back.

Acknowledgements

One Degree South was nearly fifteen years in gestation.

Knowledgeable persons will spot the various anachronisms and liberties I have taken with Gabonese history and geography, but I hope they will agree the story is rooted in essential truths.

I owe a great debt of gratitude to a number of people who took the time to read this story in various stages. Cara Hesse gave me an early hard rap and a needed lesson in depicting women. Harlan Hale inspired me to think I might actually have a story to tell, and gave me the title. Sarah Leddy rejuvenated my flagging confidence in the dead of winter and helped more fully develop central characters.

Both Terah DeJong and Darcy Meier provided needed encouragement at points when I was faltering. Both taught me the necessity of putting in the hard work of clearing away brush. In validating the sections on the role of France in Africa, Sebastien Pennes gave me a tremendous boost when he pronounced the story a good read. My editor, Tom Driscoll, has been a wonderful teacher in the crafting of long form fiction and making the mystery of the omniscient narrator less enigmatic.

Finally, I owe a great debt of gratitude to the Batéké people of southeastern Gabon, and particularly to the residents of the village of Okouya who welcomed me among them and took good care of me while I helped them build a school.

About the Author

Stephen L. Snook is a specialist in international development who has spent over 25 years living and working in Africa. In addition to Gabon, where he served as a Peace Corps volunteer, he has worked in (or visited) Botswana, the Central African Republic, the Democratic Republic of Congo (formerly Zaire), Ghana, Guinea, Kenya, Liberia, Mozambique, Rwanda, Senegal, Somalia, South Africa, Tanzania, Zambia and Zimbabwe. Steve has a doctorate in political science from the University of Florida. He is married, the father of three daughters, and currently lives in Vermont. This is his first novel.

Made in the USA
Charleston, SC
04 February 2015

3832751 0R00237